HIS GRACE, THE DUKE

ALSO BY EMILY RATH

JACKSONVILLE RAYS SERIES

SPICY HOCKEY ROMANCE

That One Night (#.0.5)

Pucking Around (#1)

Pucking Ever After: Vol I (#1.5)

Pucking Wild (#2)

Pucking Ever After: Vol. 2 (#2.5)

Pucking Sweet (#3)

Pucking Ever After: Vol. 3 (#3.5)

Pucking Strong (#4)

SECOND SONS SERIES

SPICY 'WHY CHOOSE' REGENCY ROMANCE

Beautiful Things (#1)

His Grace, The Duke (#2)

Alcott Hall (#3)

STANDALONES

CONTEMPORARY MM OMEGAVERSE

Whiskey & Sin

THE TUONELA DUET

North is the Night

HIS GRACE, THE DUKE

EMILY RATH

KENSINGTON
PUBLISHING CORP.

kensingtonbooks.com

Content notice: *His Grace, the Duke* contains descriptive sex scenes involving a polycule (MMMF); impact play; light bondage and sensory deprivation; sleep deprivation; mild bloody violence; brief/vague discussion of past childhood trauma; pregnancy and childbirth (epilogue only).

KENSINGTON BOOKS are published by:

Kensington Publishing Corp.
900 Third Avenue
New York, NY 10022

kensingtonbooks.com

All Kensington titles, imprints, and distributed lines are available at special quantity discounts for bulk purchases for sales promotions, premiums, fundraising, educational, or institutional use.

Special book excerpts or customized printings can also be created to fit specific needs. For details, write or phone the office of the Kensington sales manager: Kensington Publishing Corp., 900 Third Avenue, New York, NY 10022, attn: Sales Department; phone 1-800-221-2647.

The K with book logo Reg US Pat. & TM Off.

ISBN 978-1-4967-5613-8 (trade paperback)

First Kensington trade paperback printing: November 2025

10 9 8 7 6 5 4 3 2 1

Printed in China

Electronic edition: ISBN 978-1-4967-5616-9

Interior design by Kelsy Thompson
Interior art by Lucy Rose
Author photograph by Jennifer Catherine Photography

The authorized representative in the EU for product safety and compliance
is eucomply OU, Parnu mnt 139b-14, Apt 123
Tallinn, Berlin 11317, hello@eucompliancepartner.com

To Jacqueline Durran, costume designer on Pride & Prejudice *(2005). You gifted us with the outfit in Matthew Macfadyen's "walks through a field at dawn" moment . . . and my life has never been the same.*

AUTHOR'S NOTE

HELLO, BEAUTIFUL READERS! Sorry about that little cliffy in book one. It couldn't be helped. There's just too much story to tell! Be forewarned, *His Grace, The Duke* is book two in the Second Sons series. If you haven't already read *Beautiful Things,* STOP HERE (spoilers below).

If you've read *Beautiful Things*, then you know where we are:

- The duke is engaged to Piety Nash.
- Burke is reluctantly ~sort of~ engaged to Olivia Rutledge.
- Renley has some major explaining to do.
- And Rosalie and James are currently on a midnight carriage ride to London.

Keep in mind this is a polyamorous romance, so our heroine has multiple suitors, and she won't be picking just one in the end. Prepare yourself for a much spicier book as each relationship naturally grows. And yes, I'm talking about relationships between the guys too. If you've followed me on TikTok, you'll know what I mean when I say this story earns an Emily-approved emotional 5 sword-cross ranking. You're welcome. :)

Grab your smelling salts and get ready to clutch your pearls. Let's give Rosalie and her gentlemen a happily ever after worth swooning for.

XO,

THE LORDS AND LADIES AT ALCOTT HALL

In the British social hierarchy, the order of rank is as follows:

- King/Queen
- Duke/Duchess
- Marquess/Marchioness
- Earl/Countess
- Viscount/Viscountess
- Baron/Baroness
- Baronet/Lady
- Knight/Lady

Names and titles can be confusing, but I tried to keep it as true to the time period as possible. The following are characters with titles, presented in order of rank (high to low):

The Corbins (Dukes):

- George Corbin, The Duke of Norland
- Harriet Wakefield Corbin, The Dowager Duchess of Norland, George's mother
- Lord James Corbin, The Viscount Finchley, George's younger brother

The Rutledges (Marquesses):

- Constance Rutledge, The Marchioness of Deal
- Lady Olivia Rutledge, daughter

The Swindons (Earls):

- Mary Swindon, The Countess of Waverley
- Lady Elizabeth Swindon, eldest daughter
- Lady Mariah Swindon, youngest daughter

The Blaires (Viscounts):

- Diana Blaire, The Viscountess of Raleigh
- Lady Madeline Blaire, daughter

The Oswalds (Knights):

- Sir Andrew Oswald, esq.
- Lady Anne Oswald, wife of Sir Andrew
- Miss Blanche Oswald, daughter

1

James

THE CARRIAGE SWAYED gently as a team of four horses pulled it steadily onward. It was dangerous to travel at night, but light from the full moon and a sea of stars guided the way. Dawn was soon approaching. The colors were already shifting; the indigo was not quite so depthless. Soon a spray of pinks and purples would break over the horizon.

James hoped to be in London well before sunrise. He wanted to beat the morning traffic and avoid any early-rising busybodies who might recognize his coach arriving at Corbin House. Tucked under his arm, Rosalie shifted in her sleep. He stifled a smile.

When they first started their journey north, it hadn't escaped his notice how she kept herself as far from him as possible. Wedged in the corner of the coach, she did her utmost to not even look in his direction. Who was it that she didn't trust? James . . . or herself? He wasn't sure. All he knew was that if he clenched his jaw any tighter, he might break his teeth.

But if Rosalie resolutely had nothing to say, then neither

did he. The only indulgence he allowed himself was to glance over every so often and trace the feminine arc of her neck with his eyes, illuminated by that bright moon.

She finally fell asleep, and he breathed a sigh of relief. At least when she was asleep, he could look at her without restraint. She still wore his evening coat over her ball gown, his mother's necklace around her throat. His mind flashed with images of their stolen moment in the library. It made him almost feral when he brushed his fingers over that damn necklace, feeling how her soft skin warmed the pearls. He imagined her wearing other Corbin family jewels and nothing else . . . stretched out naked on his bed, reaching for him, wanting him—

Christ.

She was right not to trust him. He couldn't get her out of his head.

But in sleep, our true desires surface. A jolt in the road had her jerking away from the window. That's when she leaned towards James, her head falling on his shoulder. She let out a contented sigh as she curled into him, her left arm drifting until her gloved hand settled on his thigh. She hadn't noticed when he shifted slightly, wrapping his arm around her.

That was two hours ago. Two hours of holding her in his arms. It was all he could do not to move. Her hair was falling out of its elegant style. One curl fluttered in her face, swaying with the movement of the carriage. He wanted to tuck it behind her ear, but he was afraid to wake her and watch her recoil. Part of her *must* trust him. Part of her felt safe in his arms. She could admit it in sleep. Could she ever admit it when she was awake?

"Whoa . . . *whoa*," the coachman called.

The clatter of the horses' shod hooves told James they were now on cobblestones. One more change over and they would be in Town.

Rosalie pressed into him as she sat up, blinking as she looked around. Bright, golden torchlight flickered outside the windows to either side as they entered a carriage yard. The coachman was already calling orders to a pair of grooms to change out the tired team. Realizing where she was, she shifted away. "Sorry," she murmured. "I fell asleep." She wrapped her arms tightly around herself, suppressing a shiver. James frowned. She'd be warm again if she would just stay in his arms. To anyone else, he would have said as much, but she was too stubborn. If James said anything, he was sure she'd opt to ride atop the carriage like a piece of luggage.

She peered out the window, blinking in the harsh torchlight. "Have we arrived?"

"Not quite. This will be the last change over. We'll be in Town in another hour."

"Did you sleep at all?"

"No."

She stifled a yawn, pressing herself back into the corner, arms crossed tight inside his evening coat. That would have to be his first stop this morning. James had an entire wardrobe waiting for him at Corbin House, but Rosalie had only the clothes on her back. Hardly appropriate attire. In fact, it was downright scandalous. But it was also their easiest problem to fix.

James was a bloody fool. He never acted impetuously, and this was why. He would be arriving in Town with the sunrise, his family's unwed ward on his arm, both of them still dressed for the ball from which they fled like thieves in the night.

"We need a plan," he said, breaking their strained silence.

Rosalie glanced over at him. "A plan?"

"Yes. We need an excuse to have just taken off like we did."

She was quiet for a moment. "What did you have in mind?"

He shrugged. "I've been mulling it almost since we left but I can't think of any good reason why we'd leave like we did that doesn't link us romantically . . . What if we say your aunt was taken ill? Would she play along?"

Rosalie worried her lip. "And I just happened to receive news of it late at night while dancing at a ball? And you rushed to bring me to her side?"

She didn't need to say what they both knew. It was a hopelessly weak excuse.

"I thought perhaps an engagement party," she said, peering out the window again.

James frowned. "What?"

"Our excuse," she replied, watching the footmen scurry in the yard. "We rushed to London to throw together a surprise engagement party for His Grace and Piety. The sooner we set the date, the easier our quick exit can be forgiven." She turned back to face him, golden light from the torches illuminating her beautiful face. "It's not exactly foolproof, but—"

"No, it's brilliant," he muttered. It was a lie that worked on so many levels too. "I'll write a note to George as soon as we get to Corbin House and have him bring everyone to Town. Next Friday, we'll throw a party to celebrate the engagement. Naturally, I needed your assistance in the planning. You clearly have a good eye for it."

She smiled faintly. "Your mother is the planner. I just did as she bade me."

Both their smiles fell at mention of his mother, for was she not the reason they both felt the need to flee so recklessly in the night? His mother who was threatening to steal their happiness by shackling Burke in marriage to Oliva Rutledge, a woman who hated the very idea of him. James would lose his best friend and watch him suffer in a marriage doomed to fail. Rosalie would lose her . . . what were they now? Friends? Lovers? Burke admitted to sharing carnal relations with her in the music room. James had been trying very hard not to picture it. Did Rosalie know he knew?

His own memories of last night sat like a stone in his chest. God, he'd said such hateful things. The moment the words were spoken, he regretted them. It was a reflex, born out of misplaced anger. The look of pain on her face still haunted him. He had to say something. He had to apologize or at the very least explain.

"Rosalie . . ."

She turned to face him. "Yes?"

He sighed. "About last night in the library . . ." She went utterly still.

"I was angry and upset," he explained. "I said things I didn't mean. I'd appreciate it if we could . . . can we put it behind us? Can we forget it ever happened?"

Something flickered in her eyes. It came and went so fast, he couldn't read it. "What part exactly didn't you mean, my lord? The part where you called me low-born and loose? Or the part where you claimed all my air with your tongue in my mouth?"

Shit.

He shifted awkwardly on the bench seat. "I suppose . . . both."

She turned away to face the window. "Fine. Consider it forgotten."

Those four words launched like arrows shot from a bow.

He rubbed at his chest, sure he might feel one of the shafts. "We're ready out here, m'lord," the coachman called.

James tore his eyes away from Rosalie. "Drive on," he called back. In moments, the carriage was rattling off as the new team pulled them ever closer to their destination.

After a few minutes of silence, James felt Rosalie's eyes on him. He turned slowly to face her. She looked so tired, so vulnerable. He wanted to wrap her in his arms again.

"Don't for one moment think that I can't see through this ruse," she said, her voice simmering with frustration.

He opened his mouth to apologize again, but no words came out.

She scoffed. "James Corbin, Viscount Finchley . . . you forget that we stood in that library as equals. I got inside those thick walls of yours at last. I know you're doing the noble thing here, pushing me away. I know you and admire you . . . and I kissed you back."

James had suddenly forgotten how to breathe.

She leaned a little closer and her intoxicating spiced floral scent enveloped him. He'd been caught in her perfumed snare for hours. "I know duty means everything to you. So, we'll not mention it again, but only if you tell me the truth here and now . . . will you dream of it?"

"Christ, Rosalie. Don't ask me for what I cannot give."

Her gaze softened. "You can't give me the truth?"

"Not this truth," he muttered. "Not when it will do neither of us any good to hear it."

"The truth is all we have, you and I," she replied. "From the moment we met, you've given me your truths, no matter how cruel. Without truth between us, there is nothing."

She sounded so forlorn. He just wanted to make her happy again. He wanted to see her smile. *He* wanted to be the reason she was smiling.

"Here is my truth," she went on. "You've filled my dreams since the first night I met you. Even when you showed me nothing but open animosity, I dreamed of you. I dream of a gentler touch from your hands, gentler words from those lips that kiss me so well."

Her eyes trailed down his face, settling on his parted lips. He knew she possessed more than one sketch of them drawn with her own hand.

Bloody fucking hell.

This woman was going to be the death of him. It took everything he had to turn away, looking resolutely out the window, rather than take her in his arms again. He wasn't the sort for intimate reveals. No woman had ever held his interest long enough to be worthy of his heartfelt vulnerability. But she was right: She'd gotten inside his walls last night.

He sighed, letting himself break just enough to slide his hand across the velvet of the bench seat, seeking out her gloved hand. She was waiting for him, her fingers lacing with his. He pressed his forehead to the cool glass of the window and closed his eyes.

"James," she whispered. "Do you ever dream of me?"

This carriage was to be his confessional. He would say the words aloud, her touch would absolve him, and then they would begin the essential business of forgetting. They would both forget, for nothing had changed.

Duty over love. Family.

Title.

"James . . ."

The words were on his lips. She deserved to know. He *wanted* her to know . . . but that would be cruel to them both. He gave her hand a squeeze and dropped it back to the seat. "To dream implies sleep," he muttered, his eyes locked on the outline of the looming city, framed in softest lavender by the rising sun. "And that is a luxury I cannot afford."

2

Rosalie

"WE'RE HERE." THE gentleness of James' voice clashed with the stiffness of his resolve. It had been almost an hour since their last conversation, and he was still looking out the carriage window.

Rosalie watched with a heavy heart as his Corbin mask slipped firmly into place. His shoulders squared, his beautiful green eyes hardened, and that imperious chin lifted. James, the man who kissed her with a passion verging on obsession, was firmly locked away. In his place sat Lord James, Viscount Finchley.

Heavens, but it was an impressive transformation. This was the man she met on her first night at Alcott Hall. The lord who challenged her and sneered and treated her like an inconvenience. Her weary Atlas, carrying all the world's troubles on his shoulders.

The carriage rattled into the courtyard of Corbin House and Rosalie peered out the window, taking in the handsome grey stone walls that stretched three stories high. It was still quite early. Morning light tinged the stone a hazy blue.

"Let me do the talking," James said, voice low.

She shrugged out of his evening coat and tried to hand it back to him.

"Keep it."

"I can't," she replied. "You know how it will look."

He huffed. "It will look like a gentleman offered a lady a coat to keep her warm. Anyone who says otherwise will answer to me."

"James—"

"Keep the damn coat," he growled, leaning into her space until his face was mere inches from hers.

Her breath caught in her throat.

His gaze softened slightly, those green eyes rooting her to the spot, as he raised a hand and brushed his thumb over her parted lips. "I can't wear it if it smells like you," he whispered, his voice pained. "I cannot think. Rosalie . . . I can't breathe."

For the briefest of moments, he touched his forehead to hers. Did he know? Did he see the way she was holding her face in the crook of her elbow all night, using his scent to calm her to sleep? The coat smelled so wonderfully of him—wool and leather oil and faint notes of spiced cologne. But now it smelled like her too, so it was tainted.

No, not tainted. Tempting. *Too* tempting.

"Just put it back on," he said, dropping his hand away from her. "And leave the talking to me."

He scooted away just as the carriage door swung open. He stepped out in his waistcoat and shirtsleeves, taking all Rosalie's air with him. She shrugged herself back into the coat, grateful for its warmth.

"Good heavens," came a high, female voice. "We didn't know to expect you, my lord. Gracious, you must be exhausted.

What were you thinking, driving through the night? Dangerous—downright *reckless*—oh, I do hope nothing serious has happened at the great house." By the way the woman fretted, equal parts servile and maternal, Rosalie felt sure she must be the housekeeper.

"Good morning, Mrs. Robbins," James replied. "I know this is highly irregular, but I bring good tidings. His Grace is newly engaged."

"Well—that is—" The lady blustered, and Rosalie could well imagine why. "That is simply wonderful news, my lord! May we know who is to be the new duchess?"

"Miss Piety Nash," James replied. "I arrive express from Alcott where it was just announced. I'm on strict orders to prepare an engagement party. His Grace wants no expense spared," he added. "George was explicit that it be held in a fortnight. I came ahead of the rest of the group with Miss Harrow, for there is much to plan and I require a feminine eye."

Rosalie smirked. It was masterfully done—shifting the blame of their expedition onto the duke. George Corbin was surely eccentric enough that his staff would easily believe he sent his brother to London in the dead of night to plan a party for him.

"Miss—who, sir?"

Until that moment, James had been standing in front of the carriage door, blocking Rosalie in. He stepped aside now and held out a hand for her. She took it, letting him help her down the step.

"Gracious," cried Mrs. Robbins. She was a short and stout lady with a ruffed collar at her neck and frizzy blonde hair tucked under a mobcap. She glanced from Rosalie to James. "Good morning, miss. Welcome to Corbin House."

"Good morning," Rosalie replied, giving the woman a smile.

James still held onto her hand, leading her forward. The footmen bustled around behind, shutting the carriage door and flipping up the step.

"Mrs. Robbins, may I present Miss Rosalie Harrow," James said, his tone almost bored. "She is my mother's ward. She was indispensable in arranging the Michaelmas ball. When I told her of my mission to plan a society soiree in less than a fortnight, she was only too happy to lend a hand."

Rosalie watched Mrs. Robbins take in her disheveled hair, her ball gown and jewels, James' coat. "Well, let's get you both inside, then. A spot of tea and breakfast—"

"Nothing for me," James replied. "But please show Miss Harrow up to the Burgundy Room." He turned to Rosalie. "I have business this morning. We can meet this afternoon to go over the schedule of events. Does that suit you?"

Rosalie knew what he was doing. He needed to confer a sense of authority to her. He wanted the staff to see her as more than a guest. "Yes, of course, my lord," she replied.

He gave a curt nod. "Excellent." With that, he turned and walked off, leaving her in the company of Mrs. Robbins and the two footmen.

"Well then, John, Tanner, you heard Lord James. Bring the lady's luggage to the Burgundy Room," said Mrs. Robbins with a snap of her fingers.

The young footmen exchanged a confused look. "But she has no luggage."

Corbin House was just as beautiful as Alcott Hall, though on a vastly different scale. The halls were narrower, the ceilings unpainted, and the architecture and furniture stylings all had a more modern feel. Rosalie followed dutifully behind Mrs. Robbins up to the second floor. With no luggage to tote, the footmen had quickly disappeared.

"You must have had a terrible journey," Mrs. Robbins said, keys jangling at her hip. "If we had known to expect the family, we would have opened the house."

"Please don't make yourself uneasy on our account," Rosalie replied, trotting to keep up. "It was beastly of us to arrive like this, but His Grace says 'jump' and it falls to us to say 'how high?'"

Mrs. Robbins turned left at the stairs, taking Rosalie down a long hall. "Larders empty, half the staff on leave. If I had even a day's warning . . ."

Rosalie let the woman fret aloud as they made another turn at the end of the hall. Mrs. Robbins opened the first door on the right and disappeared into a dark bedroom. She immediately went over to the window and opened the curtain a crack, just enough to let a little light pool inside. Then she moved over to the mantel and pulled a servant's cord. Rosalie was sure a bell was ringing somewhere in the depths of the house.

"You're welcome to take a rest, dear," said Mrs. Robbins, turning down the coverlet on the bed. "You look dead on your feet. There's a wash basin in the corner. Fanny will bring you some hot water. And there's a proper washroom in the hall."

A knock at the door had both women turning. "Come in, Fanny," Mrs. Robbins called.

A pretty, red-haired maid with copious freckles stepped

into the room. She had a sleepy look on her face that disappeared as she took in Rosalie standing by the bed.

"Fanny, this is Miss Harrow. Please see she has everything she needs. Miss Harrow, should you require anything, please let any of the staff know."

"Thank you, Mrs. Robbins," Rosalie replied, offering the woman a grateful smile.

The maid glanced around the room confused. "But . . . why is she in here?"

Mrs. Robbins tsked. "Lord James expressly requested this room. We'll bring in some flowers and I'll have the girls dust it up a bit, and it will be right as rain." She moved towards the door, keys still jangling at her hip. "And it sounds like we'll soon have a houseful, so we'll need every room we can get."

The housekeeper ducked out, leaving Rosalie alone with young Fanny.

The maid was still surveying Rosalie from her tousled hair to her satin slippered feet. "How can I help, miss?"

"Umm, perhaps some hot water," Rosalie replied. She desperately needed a wash, especially after the events of last night.

Oh, heavens. She was all but naked under her gown. She'd quite forgotten that Burke ruined her chemise. When Fanny helped her undress, she'd find Rosalie in nothing but her stockings and stays!

"And *umm* . . ." Rosalie would surely die of mortification. "Could—could you perhaps . . . find me a spare chemise?"

The maid paused at the door. She turned slightly, her face unreadable. "Yes, miss. Right away."

3

Rosalie

ROSALIE WOKE WITH a wince, raising a hand to massage the painful crick in her neck. It was disorienting at first, sitting up to see dark shapes out of place all around. The events of the previous night quickly came screaming back to her, reminding her of where she was and why.

She sat in the middle of the four-poster bed, her borrowed chemise slipping off her shoulders. The house was quiet as a tomb, save for the soft *tick tick tick* of the clock on her mantel. The curtain was still open only a strip, wide enough to glow on the clock's face.

Ten o'clock.

She gasped. She'd only meant to close her eyes for a moment. Instead, she'd slept for three hours! She slipped off the bed and dragged open the curtains. Bright sunlight flooded the room. It was slightly larger than her room at Alcott. The walls were a wine red with a gold pattern to the paper. The furniture was all dark wood, while the mantel and fireplace were black marble. She had the distinct impression this was meant to be a masculine space. The art was not florals, but landscapes, and there was little else that might cater to feminine needs.

A dark wood door framed either side of the bed. Rosalie opened the one closer to the window and found a shallow, shelved closet stacked with linens. The door to the other side was locked. She rattled the handle, looking around for a key. Perhaps it connected to a water closet or a washroom.

Passing a mirror, she frowned at her reflection. Her fashionably styled hair was in shambles all around her face, loose curls hanging down, even while the rest of the pile teetered lopsided on her head. She had dark circles under her eyes, and the imprint from the lace on the edge of the pillowcase was creased into her cheek.

Working fast, she tugged all the pins out of her hair until it all hung in a thick mess of dark curls down her back. She did her best to catch all the pearls woven into her braids, but a telltale *plink plink* told her at least a couple slipped through her fingers. Once the mess was down, she fixed it back up in some semblance of a style.

Before she could dress, there came a sharp knock at the door.

"Yes?" she called.

"It's Fanny, miss. You're needed downstairs. Mrs. Robbins says it's urgent."

To Rosalie's utter shock—AND annoyance—the urgent business downstairs had nothing to do with any kind of party planning. No, the truth was far more irritating. In her rush to appear, Rosalie wore only her chemise and slippers, with James' evening coat wrapped around her like a pelisse. She stepped into the sunny morning room to find the most fashionable woman she'd ever seen smiling at her.

"You must be Miss 'arrow?" The lady fluttered across the room like a fairy. She was dressed in canary yellow silk that fit her like a glove, showing off her ample assets. Her dark locks were done up in curls and she wore a sparkling feathered headpiece.

Rosalie tugged the lapels of James' coat tighter over her chest. "I am."

"Mon Dieu, your beauty was not understated," the woman cooed. "I am Madame Lambert, modiste extraordinaire." She posed with a flourish, one hand arched in the air like a dancer. "But you may call me Paulette," she added, dropping her hand back to her side. Those dark eyes took in Rosalie from tousled head to slippered foot. "I see I 'ave not come a minute too late." Her smile quirked, the red paint on her lips stretching wide. "You're missing a dress, ma chérie."

She fought her blush. "Yes . . . umm . . ."

Before she could finish her sentence, the modiste turned to direct the movement of three house maids who came bustling in with an alarming display of boxes balanced between them. Two footmen followed behind with yet more boxes.

"Set ze big ones just 'ere," the modiste said, pointing to the table.

The footmen did as they were asked, excusing themselves immediately, shutting the door as they left.

The modiste crossed the room. "Well then, let's get you into ze first gown—"

"Wait!" Rosalie looked from the modiste to the maids to the towering pile of boxes. "There's been a misunderstanding. I have clothes. I really don't need—"

"Don't be silly, ma chérie," the modiste said with an airy laugh. "Rule number one: If a lord wants to buy you a new wardrobe, you let him."

The maids giggled and the modiste had the audacity to flash them a knowing wink. They were surely going to get the wrong idea about her and James now.

"I 'ave everything he asked for," the modiste said, opening the top box to pull out a devastating ball gown encrusted with shimmering beads.

All three maids gasped. One put a hand over her mouth to contain a squeal of excitement.

Rosalie's mouth fell open in surprise. "He can't possibly think this is suitable for a day dress," she cried.

"Of course not," the modiste replied. "This is for ze opera. Ze other boxes 'ave morning dresses and walking dresses and a habit for riding." She gestured to each with a wave of her hand.

Rosalie sighed. "I already have a riding habit."

Yes, the one James bought her not two weeks ago. She hadn't even had the chance to wear it yet.

"Well, now you shall 'ave two," the modiste replied, handing off the ball gown to the waiting maid. "Don't worry, ma chérie," she added, stepping forward to pat Rosalie's hand. "Ze viscount took care of everything. You shall be more beautiful than any woman in ze *ton*."

Rosalie's frown deepened. "And what else did 'ze viscount' order, pray?"

The modiste pulled a list out of her dress pocket with a

flourish, smiling as she read it aloud. "Five morning dresses, two promenade dresses, two pelisses, three spencers, five evening gowns, two ball gowns, assorted gloves for day and night, two bonnets, slippers, leather half boots, riding boots, and assorted undergarments and ribbons for hair and the like." She glanced up from her list, adding, "Oh . . . and I may 'ave included one or two items not on your lord's list, but he will be pleased all ze same . . . and he will not notice the added expense." She winked, and Rosalie wanted to die.

"I most certainly don't need all of that," she cried. "And he is not *my* lord," she added indignantly, one eye glancing to the grinning maids. She held out her hand. "Give me that list, and I'll shorten it. Really, all I need is something suitable for this morning so I can go to my aunt's house and get my *own* things."

"Nonsense," the modiste replied, giving the list a protective pat in her pocket. "Ze viscount already paid me. I am simply 'ere to check sizes."

"Wait . . . this is all mine?" Rosalie's heart was racing. This was too much. Such an extravagant gesture would surely have the whole *ton* in uproar. She glanced again at the gorgeous champagne beaded gown and the tower of boxes covering the table and chaise. "I thought you just brought samples for me to try."

"Your viscount said it was urgent, and I see he must be correct," replied the modiste, still eyeing Rosalie's shambles of an outfit. "Now, I am quite a busy woman, and I 'ave other stops today. So please, if you are finished pretending you don't want to see what I 'ave in zeez boxes, then take off your lord's coat, and we will begin with ze ball gown. I call it *La Victoire*."

Rosalie felt dizzy. Was this his great business? James

bought her more clothes in one morning than what she currently owned altogether. And if the ball gown was any indication, he'd spared no expense. She frowned again. She'd already warned James once that she didn't like extravagant gifts. He thought he could have his way by ordering all this, then sneak out of the house. But he couldn't stay away forever. He'd come back, and then she'd have her say.

"Fine." She shrugged out of his coat and tossed it aside. "Let's get this over with."

An hour later, Rosalie was growing tired of playing doll. Just as she feared, the gowns were all the highest quality. She'd never owned a dress half so fine as the first morning dress she tried on—a pretty peach satin with corded burgundy and gold piping. The ball gown made her feel like a queen . . . and it was one of *two* that now inexplicably belonged to her.

"Just look at zis one, ma chérie," Paulette cooed, holding up a beautiful forest green walking gown. "It's a new design from Paris." She turned it around and Rosalie's heart skipped a beat.

The dress had a low "V" cut to the bodice, and the inner lining of the skirt was pink with a printed pattern of flowering vines and little blue birds. Rosalie loved it. Paulette helped her step into it and slip it up over her hips. The sleeves ended in points over the backs of her hands, and there were little strings that could be tied at the wrists.

"It fits you so well," said Paulette, fastening it up the back. "And your viscount was clearly right."

Rosalie's hands stilled their inspection of the patterned skirt. "Right?"

"Green is ze perfect color for you," Paulette murmured in her ear.

"He never said that," she said with a distracted laugh.

Paulette came around the front, giving the bodice little tugs as she checked the fit. "Did he not?" She paused, both hands on Rosalie's shoulders. "Then why can't you stop blushing thinking of ze green in his eyes?"

Rosalie's mouth opened, but no words came out.

"You should wear it today to thank him for his generosity," Paulette said with a knowing smile.

"I am not with him in that way," Rosalie whispered, one eye darting over to the watchful maids. "I am a ward of his family, of his mother. The dowager duchess assured me I would be fitted for new dresses. He is only doing as his mother bids him." She said this loud enough for the maids to hear.

Perhaps if Rosalie said the truth often enough, she might begin to accept it too.

Paulette just smiled. "Of course, ma chérie." A door slammed somewhere down the hall.

"Ahh, maybe zat is ze lord now," Paulette said, dropping to her knees to check the hem. "We shall test ze viscount's indifference to your beauty."

Behind her, a maid stifled a nervous giggle.

Rosalie rolled her eyes. There was clearly no convincing the modiste. At the same time, her heart began to beat a little faster, knowing she would see James again so soon. She was annoyed about the dresses, but so much had been left unsaid between them. That last moment in the carriage, his thumb grazing over her lips . . .

Rosalie was distracted by shouting and another slamming door. Someone was in a heated argument. Why was James badgering his servants? She was instantly on edge wondering what must have put him in such a foul mood. Footsteps echoed through the closed door. He was coming on swift feet.

"She is with the modiste," came the shrill voice of Mrs. Robbins. "I simply cannot let you barge in. She may be indecent—"

"Like I bloody give a damn!" Rosalie's heart stopped as she gasped. That wasn't James' voice.

Paulette stilled too, her hands on Rosalie's hem. She glanced up, first at Rosalie, then over her shoulder towards the door. The maids twittered a rush of whispered words, eyes wide, as the morning room door snapped open.

Burke stood in the frame, eyes thundering as they locked on Rosalie.

4

Rosalie

Rosalie took a deep breath through parted lips, letting her eyes trace over Burke. He stepped fully into the room, his stormy gaze sweeping once around, taking in the teetering piles of dress boxes and loose tissue paper. His magnetic pull charged the air between them as he gave her a look torn between wanting to strangle her or kiss her breathless. Was it possible the others could miss this heat between them?

Mrs. Robbins shuffled in behind him, huffing in indignation. "Really, Mr. Burke, this is most inappropriate. Come away this instant."

Burke's eyes locked on Rosalie. "I need to talk to you," he said, his deep voice raising gooseflesh down her arms.

The modiste glanced from Rosalie to Burke. "Well, ze plot thickens," she murmured just loud enough for Rosalie to hear. "Bonjour, Monsieur Burke."

Burke's eye flicked to her. "Paulette," he said with a tight nod.

Paulette gave him one of her knowing smiles, and jealousy churned in Rosalie's stomach. Why was Burke on first-name terms with a London modiste?

Rosalie put a false smile on her face. "You have not heard, Paulette. Monsieur Burke is newly engaged."

Mrs. Robbins and the maids all squealed with excitement. "I am pleased for you," said Paulette, still glancing curiously between them. "Who is the lucky woman?"

"Lady Olivia Rutledge, daughter of the Marquess of Deal," Rosalie replied. She knew she was being childish, but her heart was too battered for her to act sensibly.

Burke said nothing, but a muscle twitched in his jaw.

"Oh, my heavens," Mrs. Robbins gasped. "A marquess' daughter for our dear Burke? And His Grace settled too! A happy Christmas has come early to Corbin House."

The maids fell into fits of girlish giggles. "We need to talk," Burke repeated. "Now."

Mrs. Robbins bobbed on the balls of her feet, clearly at a loss for how to handle the situation. The maids watched in confusion, smiles falling.

"We're nearly finished here," Rosalie said, brushing her hands down the fabric of the new dress. "Mrs. Robbins, perhaps you could show Mr. Burke to the library. I'll be along as soon as—"

"I'm not going anywhere," Burke growled, taking a step closer. "I'll do this with an audience if that's really what you want. Either make them go, or let them stay and hear every word I have to say."

Rosalie's heart thrummed in her chest as she glanced from the modiste to the housekeeper.

"Really, Mr. Burke, I'll not tolerate rudeness," said Mrs. Robbins, bringing herself to her full height. She still hardly reached the middle of his chest.

Burke turned on her with a glower. "Mrs. Robbins, I have not begun to be rude—"

"Enough," Rosalie called. She squared her shoulders at Burke, even as she spoke to the housekeeper. "Mrs. Robbins, please forgive Mr. Burke. He had a long journey, and he's clearly overtired." Burke opened his mouth to protest, but she cut him off with a raised hand. "If he wishes to speak to me again in this lifetime, he *will* go wait in the library. Perhaps you could be so good as to bring him a cup of coffee," she added. "It might help him recover his good humor."

Burke simmered with rage. Rosalie was sure, if she dared to touch him, his skin would crackle like a log on the fire.

"I think I 'ave everything I need," came Paulette's voice from her side. She gestured to Rosalie's dress. "Keep zis one. It fits you perfectly. Please tell your viscount I will 'ave ze rest altered and delivered tonight."

It was impossible to miss the way Burke flinched at the words "your" and "viscount." With a last growl, he turned and stalked out, shutting the door with a snap.

"Good gracious, whatever happened to put him in such a foul mood?" cried Mrs. Robbins. She turned to Rosalie. "Are you alright, dear?"

"I'm fine," Rosalie said softly.

Mrs. Robbins gave a curt nod. "Well, what a day. Clara, come help me with the coffee then, before he has another fit." She snapped her fingers at one of the maids and they both quickly left.

Rosalie blinked a few times, swallowing her tears. She glanced over her shoulder to see the other two maids were busy putting the clothes back in their boxes. "Was that really necessary?" she muttered at the modiste.

Paulette just smiled again. "You handled him well. I never thought I'd see ze day our Burke bowed to the will of a woman."

“You know him.” The words were out before she could stop them. “Mr. Burke . . . you . . . you’re acquainted?”

“Oui, I ‘ave known him most of his life,” Paulette replied. “His maman is my close friend . . . and he is like a son to me,” she added, giving Rosalie’s arm a gentle pat.

Rosalie heaved a sigh of relief, tears stinging her eyes again. Heavens, what was wrong with her? She couldn’t remember the last time she cried so much in a single day.

Paulette cupped her cheek. “Whatever happened between you, he is here. And if he is here, he is yours.”

The modiste’s soft-spoken words were enough to crack Rosalie into pieces. She raised her hands, pressing her palms over her eyes as she took a few shuddering breaths. After a few moments, she calmed, lowering her hands from her face.

Paulette stroked her back. “Better?” Rosalie nodded.

“Bon. Now, leave zis mess with me.” She gave Rosalie’s cheek another pat. “Go to him, before he drowns himself in his coffee for want of you.”

5

Rosalie

WITH THE HELP of a footman, Rosalie was directed to the library. She slipped inside, closing the door softly behind her. It was nothing like the library at Alcott Hall. This was a long, narrow space with dark paneled shelves. A few wide windows took up one wall, letting autumn sunlight pool across the carpets. A seating area framed an ornately carved marble fireplace, which crackled with a cozy fire.

Burke sat on the long red sofa facing the door, waiting for her. He launched to his feet as soon as the door clicked shut.

She leaned back against the wood. Her chest rose and fell with each deep breath, watching him cross the room towards her. "Never do that again," she declared. "You embarrassed me in front of Mrs. Robbins. In front of—"

She didn't get the rest of her admonishment out before Burke had her in his arms, his mouth covering hers, silencing her words with a passionate kiss. His hands cupped her face before sliding into her hair, digging into her messy curls as he tipped her head back. She was lost for a moment in the feel of him, the strength of his arms, the rich taste of coffee on his tongue, bitter and warm.

He pressed her into the door with his hips and broke their kiss, his lips seeking purchase lower on her jaw, her neck, the exposed "V" of her breasts. The door rattled as their weight shifted, and the fog of lust around Rosalie cleared.

"Wait," she gasped, pushing against him. "Burke, wait—*stop*—" She broke free of him, slipping under his arm.

He turned on his heel to follow.

It was a mistake to come to him like this. She couldn't think clearly when he was looking at her. She needed space. Heavens, she needed a chaperone. Nothing else could guarantee she behaved, not when her emotions felt so inflamed by his mere presence. No man had ever made her feel so *wild.* It scared her as much as it excited her. She didn't like feeling so out of control.

She spun around when she reached the bookshelves, and he was right there, boxing her in. She flung out both hands, pressing against his chest. "We are not doing this. We need to talk—"

"Then talk," he growled, his hands holding tight to her shoulders as he dropped his face to her neck, eagerly breathing in her scent.

She bit back a whimper. Her body was a traitor, melting for him as she felt the stubble of his jaw against her skin. She shivered with want, hands fisting his coat lapels. "Burke, I'm so angry at you. I'm angry at—*everything*—"

His hands lowered back to her hips as he gave her another desperate, claiming kiss.

She jerked free with a gasp. "No! You're a beast and I could scream." She shoved against him. "I'm furious and hurt and-and desperate for you. I can't—I hardly even know myself!"

His hands tightened on her hips. "Show me," he rasped in her ear. "I want all your rage, your passion." His hands slid up her hips, over her breasts. "Unleash it on me. Show me how I make you feel. Christ, I *need* it."

Something inside her snapped, and she was fighting him for dominance in another bruising kiss. "You make me crazy," she hissed. "Why did you agree to this? I watched you dance with Olivia. You couldn't warn me?" She tried to jerk away. "She's your fiancée! Oh *god*—you're a devil sent to ruin me—"

"And you're the siren who's bewitched me!" He held both her wrists with one large hand, raising his other to her mouth and brushing her lips with his thumb. She blinked back tears at the look of hurt in his eyes.

"You've upended my entire life, ripped out my heart, laid bare my fucking soul. I can't escape this pull—can't escape *you*." He gripped her jaw tight, raising her chin to meet his stormy eyes. "You can run, and I will follow. I will always follow because we belong together. You know it too. So, stop bloody fighting it."

He spun her around, his own anger overpowering hers as he pressed her against the shelves. She stifled a moan as his hot mouth sucked on the nape of her neck. Meanwhile, his hands worked feverishly to raise the front of her dress.

"Burke, someone could come in. They'll see—"

"Let them see," he panted. "Let them hear us. I hope they're right outside the goddamn door. I want them to hear you cry out my name." His left hand snaked around, cupping her sex, opening her with his fingers. At the first touch, they both groaned, aching with that perfect moment of connection.

She pushed her hips against his hand, desperate for more friction. "Oh *god*—"

His breath was hot in her ear as his right hand came between her legs from behind, two fingers sinking deep inside her.

She gasped, knees almost buckling. This was an entirely new sensation. Both his strong hands pleasured her at once. She bit back a cry as his wet mouth pressed kisses to her neck.

"You're going to come for me. Now. Hard and fast. Beg me for it."

"Burke," she whimpered.

"Not good enough." He nearly lifted her off her toes with the force of his fingers burying themselves inside her. "You make me desperate, Rosalie. I'm mad for you. You're *mine*."

Rosalie sighed with longing, opening her legs wider.

"You think I had a choice? They forced me to hurt you with that display in the ballroom. I couldn't warn you—couldn't get to you in time."

Rosalie was ready to tip over the edge. She pressed her forehead into the curve of her arm, eyes shut tight as she rode both his hands. "Burke, please—"

"You're so beautiful when you beg. But I'm not ready to end your suffering. I've been dying a slow death for hours, desperate to be near you, to hold you in my arms." He teased her with tongue and teeth on that soft spot behind her ear. "I searched for you the moment the waltz ended, and what did I find?"

"Burke—"

"You and James *missing*. Gone like a puff of smoke. No word. No note. You ripped the air from my chest. You left me on my knees, aching for you."

His fingers circled back up to her sensitive bud. She sighed as he found it, giving it the lightest touch that made her toes curl.

"Then I had to come here and find you being measured for your fucking trousseau. I could kill him for it," he growled. "You're mad? I'm livid. I see only red. I see only *you*. God, you own me. I can't breathe. Can't think—"

His words were barely registering. Rosalie was too lost in the pleasure he gave her. She needed this release like she needed air. "Burke, please," she whimpered. "Finish me—"

Burke pinched her bud and she shattered. It wasn't the slow, cresting waves of euphoria she rode with him last night. This was a desperate kind of release that clawed its way out of her. It was like breaking the surface after nearly drowning in deep water.

She sagged against the bookshelves, legs shaking. Her breath was ragged as he pulled his hands away, leaving her empty and wanting more. The skirts of her new dress fluttered down around her legs as he stepped back. She turned to face him, still leaning against the shelves. "I'm sorry we took off like that. It was selfish. But it wasn't about you."

His eyes shot up and he scowled at her.

"Well, it wasn't *entirely* about you," she admitted. "From my first night at Alcott, everything changed, and I just . . . I needed perspective and I couldn't get it there. I was lost in the dark. I couldn't see my own hand before my eyes. And James—"

"Was more than willing to offer you a new perspective. Yes, I'm aware."

Clearly, he was still angry. It was settling in his shoulders and swirling in his eyes. She gasped as some of his words finally registered. "Wait . . . what did you say about a trousseau?"

He glowered and turned away.

She put a hand on his shoulder. "Look at me." His shoulder

stiffened. "Oh, Burke . . . do you think I mean to marry James? Is that the new perspective you think I seek?" She put a hand on each of his shoulders. "Burke, look at me." She waited until she had his eyes before saying, "I am not engaged to James. I told you last night what happened between us. He doesn't want me in that way. If you don't trust him at his word, trust me at mine: I am not now, nor will I *ever* be engaged to James Corbin."

"I thought you ran off with him to elope," he admitted. "Everyone did. We all—everyone said it. They were so sure. It was the only thing that made sense." He dragged both hands through his black hair, looking anywhere but at her.

She reached for him again and he stiffened. "You're shaking," she whispered. "Oh, Burke . . ." She wrapped her arms around him.

He stiffened for a moment, but then he was clinging to her. He dropped his head to her shoulder, breathing her in as he pressed his face to the curve of her neck. "I thought you were eloping with him," he said again. "Oh god, I thought—"

He thought he'd lost her. He thought she'd heard the news of his engagement last night and rushed off to London to marry his best friend to spite him. No doubt vicious gossips like Elizabeth and Blanche spun him up, painting a sordid picture of what must have happened between Rosalie and James—hours alone in a carriage, this house to themselves, then Burke arriving to find her being fitted for a new wardrobe that did indeed rival a trousseau.

She kissed his forehead. "I would never do that to you," she murmured against his brow. "I would never hurt you in such a way. I am not half so spiteful that I would consider trapping myself in marriage as a suitable punishment for you being forced into a fake engagement."

His head lifted off her shoulder. "It's never going to happen."

She smiled sadly. "You may not have a choice. You would marry her to protect James—"

"No," he growled, forcing her to look at him. "It will never happen. Do you hear me? I will *never* marry her."

"You cannot lose your position because of me. I will not shoulder that burden." Her eyes closed as she fought back tears. "Oh god, I should go," she whispered. "I told James I would go. I have done nothing but disrupt all your lives. I will keep hurting you if I stay—"

"No." His hands were impossibly gentle as they cupped her face. "Leave, and I will follow. Have I not proved that already?"

The words broke her heart, even as they shored it up again. "Burke, stop letting me in," she whispered. "I'm no good at this. Needing someone and being needed. I'll hurt you, and I couldn't bear it. Please, just push me away. Save yourself—"

"Never," he replied. "What did you say to me last night?"

His smile made her melt. The grey in his eyes was a storm she wanted to get lost in. "We said many things—"

"You are my siren," he murmured. "I hear only your call. This thing with Lady Olivia will get sorted one way or another. I really don't care. I only care about this." He kissed her again, his lips soft and seeking. "I care about you. About *us*. I make you this vow: I will marry you, or no one."

6

Burke

ROSALIE'S SURPRISED LITTLE gasp sent Burke's heart racing faster. He meant every word. He would marry this woman today if she'd let him. This very hour. From the moment they met all those weeks ago, he couldn't be near her and not want to look at her . . . to touch, to worship, to *claim.*

She consumed him. Or he ached to be consumed. Either way, it didn't matter.

She blushed, trying to lean away. She was nervous. Retreating. Building her walls. He saw the way her heart fluttered. He felt it rising and falling between them as he pressed in slightly.

"Heavens," she said on a breath. "So now you want to marry me?"

He raised a hand and let his fingers trail along her jaw, down the line of her neck. He didn't bother to hide his smile as he felt her lean into his touch. This little siren was always hungry for more. "Would you ever let me?"

She sighed, closing her eyes tight, before she whispered, "No."

It shouldn't have hurt him to hear her say it aloud . . . but it did. The twinge was most definitely there. And she knew it too.

She leaned in. "Burke, I love you. But—"

"But no cages," he replied, placing two fingers over her parted lips to quiet her. "I know. I respect your choices, I do. I just . . . please don't explain it again. I don't think I can bear to hear you deny me twice in the same breath."

"But do you believe me?" she pressed. "You believe I have no intention to marry your friends either? I like my life. I like making my own decisions, being my own mistress—"

"I know," he repeated, more firmly this time. She quieted with a nod.

Looking at her made his heart ache. The long hours he'd just spent thinking she'd left him for James were a torture. He'd been a madman. A man possessed with a single purpose: getting to Rosalie. Following Rosalie. Holding Rosalie again.

Was it possible to still miss a person when they were right before you? When you actually had your hands on them, feeling their warmth against your skin?

"You are so beautiful," he murmured. "I want to feel you everywhere. Every moment, I want you. I want your skin against mine. Married . . . unmarried . . . I just want to be yours."

She closed her eyes again, shaking her head with a soft whimper. "Burke, this is madness. How can this be real?"

He cupped her cheek with a gentle hand. "You know you feel it too. You've felt it from the beginning."

"I don't even know your name," she whispered, opening her eyes. "You won't tell me."

He grinned. "And if I tell you, you'll marry me? Is that your condition? I accept—"

"There should be no conditions between us," she replied with exasperation. "You should *want* to tell me. You should want me to know everything about you. No secrets. No hiding. I couldn't bear it."

His smile widened. There was no great mystery to his name. Indeed, if she was really interested, she could have asked any of a dozen people at Alcott to reveal the secret. Hell, even Blanche Oswald knew it. But he was willing to play along. Let this be his great sacrifice for his unpardonable behavior in the morning room.

"Fine," he said with a fake sigh. "If it means that much to you, I suppose I can tell you my name. But I must warn you, it's terrible."

She leaned in, eyes alight with new interest. "Tell me."

"There's only one person living who actually uses it," he hedged. "Not even my brother calls me by my Christian name. Not Tom. Not James—"

"Just tell me," she cried, slapping his chest.

He laughed, snatching her hand and planting a kiss on her palm before she could pull away. "It's Horatio."

She blinked, her lips slightly parted. "Horatio? As in . . ."

"As in 'There are more things in Heaven and Earth, Horatio, than are dreamt of in your philosophy.'"

She smiled softly, her dark eyes sparkling with delight. "*Hamlet*, right?"

"Aye, my mother is a whore, but a well-read one," he replied, giving her hand another kiss. "*Hamlet* was always her favorite."

"So you are Mr. Horatio Burke," she murmured in the sweetest voice. Raising a hand, she cupped his cheek. "And now you are *my* Horatio."

The sound of his name on her lips made his cock twitch.

Which was deeply confusing, as the only person he allowed to use it was his sweet maman. Perhaps it was her claims of ownership that had him aching. Or perhaps it was merely Rosalie's touch that excited him. Her presence. That spiced floral scent that filled his senses. She was still using his massage oil. She had to be nearly out of it by now. Was she rationing? Did she think of him as she dabbed it on her delicate wrists?

"Stop looking at me like that," she whispered.

"Like what?" he replied, knowing damn well what she meant.

"Like . . ."

He leaned in, ghosting his lips over hers, teasing them with the tip of his tongue. "Like what, sweet siren?"

"I want you too," she whispered. "I want all of you. The parts you show the world, and the parts you hide away. I want Horatio and Burke. Can you ever let me have both? Even without the piece of paper binding us one to the other . . . can you learn to *trust* me with both?"

"I'm untrusting by nature," he admitted, cupping her cheek again.

She covered his hand with her own, turning her face to kiss his palm. "We can both try. That's all either of us can ask of the other. Patience and the will to try . . . the will to trust. I said I love you, and I meant it. I loved you as Burke, and I mean to love you as Horatio too. Will you show him to me?"

He groaned, pulling away from her. "Christ, enough. Say more, and I'll show him to you right here on the library floor." He glanced over his shoulder towards the door. "I can't imagine we'll be alone much longer. Tom was only going around the corner. If not him, a nosy maid is sure to come in with a tray at any moment."

Rosalie blinked. "Renley? He came with you?"

"Of course." He stepped away from her, checking the time on the mantel clock. "I'm surprised he's not back already." He sank onto the sofa, stretching out his long legs. "Marianne said you met last night. Did you like her?"

At the lady's name, Rosalie flinched. That was proof enough for Burke to confirm his suspicions. He smirked.

"Did she—she journeyed north with you?" she murmured, her cheeks blooming pink.

"Yes, well we were rather impatient to follow after you," he mused, taking a sip of his coffee. He watched her with open curiosity. What thoughts now spun through his sweet siren's mind? "She offered Tom and I use of her carriage. Did you like her?" he repeated. "I sensed from Tom that perhaps the two of you didn't get on . . ."

Rosalie sank onto the sofa opposite him and busied her hands with pouring herself a cup of coffee. "Yes, we met," she replied, her voice clipped. "She told me their happy news."

Burke raised a brow. "Happy news?"

She nodded, both hands holding tight to her cup as she raised it to her lips. "Their engagement. Marianne told me herself."

Burke's heart stopped. Fear mingled with rage and confusion. It wasn't true. It couldn't be true. He rattled his cup onto the saucer, smacking them both down on the side table. "What the hell are you talking about?"

"Renley and Marianne," she replied. "They're engaged."

7

Tom

"TOM—WAIT—"

Tom shrugged out of Marianne's reach, his feet moving him swiftly towards the front door. "I have to go."

From the moment he stepped foot in Marianne's townhouse, it felt like he'd become trapped in some strange dream. She'd been so anxious that he stay, offering him tea, then luncheon. The table was already set for two, and those pale blue eyes were open wide, pleading with him for his continued company. He figured it was the least he could do to repay her kindness for bringing them to London in the dead of night.

It was clear Marianne had something on her mind. After his third refusal of a second cup of tea, she finally admitted the truth: She'd lied to Rosalie at the ball and told her they were engaged.

All the pieces of the previous night clicked together with a violence, nearly making him dizzy. That haunted look Rose gave him. The way she recoiled and ran. The tears in her eyes. Without even realizing it, Tom had given her as much of a reason to flee as Burke, leaving them both scrambling to chase after her.

"I don't understand why you're so upset," Marianne cried, following him down the hall, one hand clinging to his uniform.

Tom growled and spun around, jerking his arm free of her touch. "Are you really so obtuse? You told Miss Harrow we're engaged. We are *not* engaged!"

Marianne stepped back as if his words were a physical blow. "Why are you being so hateful?" she whispered, raising one hand to press over her heart. "This isn't like you, Tom."

Tom dragged a hand through his unruly curls. "Christ, Mari. You're telling people I proposed to you. I *never* proposed to you."

A small smile flashed on her lips. "Well, that's not entirely accurate."

"Fine, but I have not proposed to you in many, *many* years." He leaned his face down towards hers. "And if you'll remember, the one and only time I ever *did* propose, you said no."

"Ask me again."

The words shot through the air, knocking Tom breathless. A strained moment stretched between them as they stared into each other's eyes.

He took a shaky breath. "Mari—"

"I mean it, Tom. Ask me." Her hands fluttered out to grip his arms, stopping him from turning away. "I know you feel what there is between us. I know you want me too. I wrote to you, and you came. You said such beautiful things, Tom. I knew then that you must still love me!"

He groaned. This was an unmitigated disaster. Nothing she said was untrue, exactly. He *had* traveled to London expressly to visit her. But she'd completely misunderstood his purpose. He apologized for his resentment and wished her well.

Nothing in his tone or manner should have encouraged her to think he wanted anything more than a clean break at long last.

"Marianne, that wasn't—"

"I know you have a softness for the girl," she went on. "She's sweet and innocent. A rose as lovely as her name."

He grimaced, surprised by how much he disliked the sound of Rose's name uttered from Marianne's lips.

"But she is a passing fancy," Marianne pressed, raising a hand to cup his face. "You will soon forget her. For what you and I have is so much more. We have a connection, Tom. Your spirit is bound with mine. It has been for these eight long years. Was I wrong to end Miss Harrow's suffering? Was I wrong to tell her what we both know to be true?"

He pulled her hand off his face. "And what is that?"

Her eyes glistened with tears. "That our love is for the ages. Whether now, or in a year from now, the fact will remain: We are meant to be together." She leaned up on her toes, inching closer. "Tell me you can deny it, Tom. Tell me you can deny *us*."

Her free hand tightened on his arm as she gazed longingly into his eyes. Eight years had done nothing to lessen her beauty. Her icy blue eyes, her porcelain smooth face framed by dark curls, those perfect apple cheeks blooming pink. She was beautiful . . . but it no longer caused Tom's pulse to race. The intensity in her eyes no longer made him weak. The curve of her lips no longer called him to claim her. The feel of her in his arms no longer set him on fire.

She was beautiful, yes . . . a beautiful stranger.

In truth, the feel of her wrapped around him now was making him squirm. His gut clenched as he imagined Rosalie walking through the door, seeing Marianne so close. He stepped away.

"You're determined to hurt me," she said, voice trembling. "I see it in your eyes. I feel your resentment. You still blame me for Thackeray. You want me to prove my devotion by denial. I'll do it—"

"No, Mari." He felt suddenly so tired, so emotionally drained. "God, I'm so sorry. I'm sorry for everything. I've always been so tongue-tied around you, such a fool. I don't know how to just say what I mean and assure you that I mean what I say . . ."

"Love makes us do crazy things," she replied.

He closed his eyes and shook his head, taking a deep breath. "No." He opened them, jaw set. This had to end. He had to make her understand. "Immaturity makes us do crazy things. Ignorance and jealousy, they make us crazy. For those have been the driving factors that have kept me tied to you all these years. Not love . . . not really."

"You're being cruel again," she whimpered, wiping at her eyes.

"Mari, look at me."

Her wet lashes fluttered up as she met his gaze.

He took a deep breath, trying to find the right words that would leave her in no doubt of his intentions. "I loved you once," he admitted. "I loved you and would have married you *then*. But eight years have now passed."

A soft sob escaped her as she tried to turn away, but he grabbed her shoulder. These words had to be spoken for *both* of them.

"I've traveled around the world and around again," he went on. "I've seen and done so much in the last eight years. I'm not the same immature lad of sixteen, chasing after your skirts, desperate for a smile or a look. I'm not the jealous man of eighteen who wanted to kill Thackeray when he won you fair and square—"

"Oh, but Tom, I wanted you then too. I wanted you to come save me. I never loved Thackeray. How could I as long as you walked the earth?"

How desperate had he once been to hear these words from her lips? Now they rang hollow. Giving her the gentlest smile he could muster, he let the hammer fall. "I am not the man for you, Mari. I can never be that man. I could never make you happy in the way you deserve—"

"But what of *your* happiness?" she cried. "You want to rank up, yes? You want to be captain? I can fund it for you, Tom. Together, we can make any life we want. I have Thackeray's money. I have this house. We could be free—"

"I *am* free," he countered.

The moment the words were spoken, a weight lifted off his chest and he took an unrestricted breath, his mouth curving into a relieved smile. He was already free. Free of Marianne's pull, free of doubt, free of indecision. He leveled his gaze at her, shoulders set.

Marianne shrank away from him, reaching blindly behind her until she felt the back of a chair. She sank down, tears falling.

"Oh, Mari . . . I'm more sorry than I can say," he offered, feeling the words wholly inadequate for the depth of his emotion.

He *was* sorry, and not just for her benefit. He was sorry for himself too. For the wasted years. For his anger, his long-suffering jealousy. What a fool he'd been. What an insufferable arse. In this moment, standing in Marianne Young's entry hall, Tom resolved himself to being the master of his own happiness.

He dropped to one knee at her side. "You will recover from this in time."

She gave a little sniff, not looking at him.

"Besides, why should you bother with getting remarried?" he added, determined to see her smile again. "You're in a position so many women would envy." He pulled a handkerchief out of his pocket, offering it to her.

She took it with a shaky hand.

"You are mistress of your own house, with control of your accounts. You are well-loved in society, with friends aplenty and a busy social calendar. What need have you to bring a man into your life who would only upend your comfort?"

She dabbed at her eyes. "You wish me to remain alone forever?"

"No, of course not," he said quickly, rising back to his feet. "But don't marry to please a man. Don't marry someone like me, a wastrel of a second son who you would have to support financially."

"You're not a wastrel, Tom," she said through her sniffling.

He gave her a crooked grin. "You haven't known me for a long time, Mari. For all you know, I am King of the Wastrels on three continents."

This earned him a little hiccupping laugh as she dabbed at her eyes again.

"If it is truly your wish to marry again, find a good man," he went on. "A man who will not be intimidated by your independence. A gentleman who is independent himself and not in need of a wife he can use as his personal bank. Marry a man who is mad about you and you about him. Someone who makes your heart race and your passions flare white-hot, even as your soul settles, rested in comfort entwined with theirs. If you find that in another person, marry them without delay. Until you find that . . . well . . . be your own mistress. Live your life on your terms. I wish you well, Marianne. I always will."

He turned to leave at last, grabbing his hat off the side table.

"And what of you?" she called, rising to her feet, his handkerchief still clutched in her hand.

He glanced over his shoulder as he donned his hat, slicking his curls back behind his ears. "What of me?"

Her watery eyes were wide, her cheeks blotchy and her nose red from crying. She looked at him with such open longing. It made his heart twist in his chest. He hated hurting her, but he couldn't make his heart beat for her again. Never again.

"Have you found that person?" she whispered. "The one who fans the flames of your heart and eases the quiet of your soul?"

His mouth went dry as his mind suddenly flashed with visions of his future—his deepest desires, all his unspoken cravings. What might it take to make those dreams a reality?

Clearing his throat, he gave a soft laugh. "That was my advice for you. I imagine my own path will look quite different."

With a nod, he took his leave.

As he closed her front door, he heaved a sigh of relief. Standing in the shadow of her house, he resolved to leave Marianne and everything she represented resolutely behind him. Striding off down the street, he didn't look back.

8

Burke

BURKE AND ROSALIE waited another quarter of an hour in the library, expecting Tom to arrive.

When he didn't, Rosalie asked if she could call a coach to go to her aunt's house.

"Would you like to come with me?" she asked, her voice quietly hopeful as she kept her attention on her cup of coffee.

Something inside Burke's chest clenched tight. "You want *me* to meet your aunt?"

"Of course," she replied, taking a sip.

"Not James or Tom? You want it to be me?"

She set her cup aside with a huff. "Did you expect to stay in the shadows?" Crossing her arms, she leaned forward, dark eyes narrowed. "You don't get to pick and choose which parts of my life you claim. If you're in my life, you are *in* my life, Horatio Burke."

God, he loved this woman. Heaven help him, he was mad for her. He smirked. "Agreed. And I heartily look forward to claiming all parts of you . . . day and night."

She ignored him, which made his smile broaden.

"It's unlikely my aunt will even be home at this hour," she explained. "But I think she would like to meet the people with whom I now share a house and a life."

"And a bed," he added with a grin. He couldn't help himself. He loved making her blush. His effort was rewarded with a flash of pink in her cheeks that faded into the dark curls framing her face.

"We shall not be shocking her with scandalous falsehoods," she replied, rising to her feet. "I have never shared a bed with any member of this household—family or staff or even canine . . . though, during my first week at Alcott, one of the hunting dogs slipped into my room and hid under the bed. He made a valiant effort to join me, but was rebuffed."

"I consider myself rather cleverer than a hound and harder to bully," he replied. "Let your maid try and drag me out by my scruff, and we'll see who has the stronger mettle."

"Two things, sir," she said, collecting his cup with hers and placing it on the tray. "First, I have no maid, so I will be doing my own dragging."

He chuckled, reaching for her, but she stepped away, her brows still lowered in mock seriousness.

"Second, if the moment ever arises when you *are* in my bed with my hands on your scruff, you will beg me to bully you. Now, are you coming with me or not, because you can't wear that."

He barked a laugh, glancing down at his evening ensemble. He'd long since loosened the knot of his cravat and unbuttoned his waistcoat. She was right: He didn't want his first impression with her only living relative to be marred by the fact that he was wearing day-old dress clothes.

"Give me ten minutes to change," he said, rising to his feet. "I'll meet you in the entry hall."

9

Tom

TOM RETURNED TO Corbin House to find it bustling. Two carts were parked in the courtyard with footman hurriedly unloading crates. The staff had no warning to expect the family's arrival, and Mrs. Robbins was clearly overcompensating. She'd ordered enough food to feed an army.

Entering through a side door, Tom was nearly bowled over by a delivery boy.

"Easy there, lad," Tom grunted, stumbling out of the way.

"Sorry, sir!" the boy called, not slowing his steps.

Two more servants swept past him, cleaning buckets on their arms. Down the long hallway, the housekeeper emerged, a maid trailing behind her.

"Ah—Mrs. Robbins!" Tom called. "Where is Miss Harrow?"

The housekeeper's smile was warm and inviting. "Bless my eyes, is that you, Mr. Renley? My, how handsome you look in your officer's uniform."

"Yes. I—"

"Renley!"

Tom turned to see James striding towards them. "When did you arrive? Is Burke with you?"

"I just got in," Tom replied, looking around at all the scurrying servants. "Where are they?"

James gave a look to Mrs. Robbins, dismissing her. She bobbed a quick curtsy and took off. "They're not here," he replied, voice low. "I arrived home to find Mrs. Robbins in a state."

"A state?" Tom didn't like the sound of that.

"Aye, apparently Burke barged into the morning room while Rosalie was being fitted for gowns and demanded to see her alone. Then they up and left."

Tom's gut twisted. He was too late. "Where did they go? Are they—they're coming back, right?"

"The footman said they were going to Cheapside," James replied.

That gave Tom some relief. "Her aunt lives in Cheapside. They must have gone to visit her."

"Where have you been?" James demanded.

Tom tugged off his hat and tucked it under his arm. "I was seeing Marianne home, and—"

A side door burst open and a trio of men staggered through balancing a heavy rolled carpet between them.

"'Scuse us, m'lord," the front man muttered as they passed.

James sighed. "Come to my study. If we talk here, we'll likely be run over." He led the way down the hall to his study. Tom glanced around as he entered. The dark blue walls were lined with cases of leather-bound books. The curtains were tied back, letting a shaft of late afternoon sun slant over the large desk. James sat behind it, reaching for a decanter and two glasses. He poured a measure of port into each glass and slid one across the desk at Tom. "Go ahead and say it."

Tom sat, snatching up the offered glass. "You shouldn't have taken off like that. Do you have any idea the storm you've left in your wake?"

"How bad is it?" James muttered, eyes focused on his glass.

"I believe the word 'pincers' were used . . ."

James grimaced. "And Miss Harrow?"

"General sentiment was that you must have kidnapped her. The Swindon sisters thought it appropriate to act it out last night to everyone's general amusement."

"Bloody perfect," James muttered.

"The focus is on you at the moment . . . not her."

"Thank God for that." James drained his glass. "The story is that we are planning a surprise engagement party for George and Miss Nash. We'll celebrate here with a large party on Friday. The whole *ton* is to be invited."

"Ah . . . that explains the chaos," Tom said, taking another sip of his port. "James, why did you do it?"

James sighed. "I don't know. It seemed like a good idea at the time."

"And now?"

"Now?" He refilled his glass. "Now I am so goddamn tired I can barely see straight. And there is still Burke to deal with."

"I take it you haven't seen him yet?"

"No. They were gone by the time I returned." He glanced up, meeting Tom's eye. "How mad is he?"

Tom let out a slow breath. "On a scale from one to ten, I'd say a solid eight."

"Damn . . . is that an eight like when I broke the ladder

to the treehouse? Or an eight like when I promised him that new horse and kept it for myself?"

"He's out for blood, J," Tom admitted.

"I guess I deserve it."

He sounded so dejected that Tom felt his own resentment fizzling away. His thoughts turned to Rosalie. "Is she alright?"

James nodded. "She will be." He glanced up. "But I'm glad I caught you. We need to talk . . ."

Tom stiffened. "Is it my turn for an admonishment?"

"No admonishments," James replied calmly. "I'm not your father or your confessor that you need a lesson in morals from me. But I *do* feel obligated to ask about your intentions. Do you mean to compete with Burke to win her?"

"Win her?" Tom couldn't help but laugh. "This is not a race, James, and she is not a trophy. Besides, she doesn't want to get married."

"What lady of sense does not eventually succumb to marriage?"

"Succumb? That's quite a romantic word for it."

James took another sip from his glass. "You know what I mean."

"No, I'm not sure that I do." Tom leaned forward, elbows on the desk. "Are you to imply we shouldn't trust her at her word?"

"Trust a young lady who thinks of marriage as nothing but a cage? Hardly," he replied with a dry laugh. "Marriage is a sound opportunity for advancement. It is social security. It can be an advantageous partnership. Surely, all these are merits in its favor."

"Yes . . . to you. But James, you are a viscount. In your social circle, marriage is a convenient means of solidifying titles and estates. Of course you would see it as a useful business transaction. But Rosalie doesn't."

"You buy her nonsense, then, of marriage being a cage? I thought all you Renleys were meant to be romantics."

"It is not nonsensical to a woman who has never seen anything but a bad marriage to assume that marriage has no redeemable qualities," Tom replied. "I doubt very much that a rousing speech from you will change her mind . . . especially if you're going to use words like 'succumb' in its defense."

It was James' turn to shift awkwardly, looking pointedly down at his glass.

Tom narrowed his eyes. "Oh, hell . . . you've already tried, haven't you?" He leaned farther over the desk. "You gave her a James speech, didn't you?"

James' eyes flashed in indignation. "A James speech?"

"Aye, a declarative speech by James Corbin, whereby the listener feels wholly incapable of allowing any opinion to rest in the mind except the one James puts there. A James speech. You gave her one." It wasn't a question. Tom already knew the answer. "Well, how did it go?"

James was quiet for a long moment. "She yelled at me, if you must know," he muttered.

Tom laughed deep, crossing his arms over his chest.

"So where do you fall, then?" James challenged. "No doubt you harbor romantic notions about marriage as a blessed union?"

He was quiet for a minute, considering all that had happened in the last days and weeks. "You know . . . I really thought I could do this," he admitted. "I thought I could set my feelings aside and marry out of obligation. And I thought I would find peace with it because it was the right thing to do . . ."

"And now?"

"Now?" He sighed, stretching out his legs under the desk. "Now, I believe that to marry without love would break me. I cannot live in such a way—to have someone so close, so intimately woven into my life, and not feel a deep and abiding love for them . . . it won't do. I am resolved to find more than a wife."

"What the hell does that mean? What is *more* than a wife?" James stiffened. "Oh . . . please don't tell me you're taking a page out of George's book and seeking *two* women—"

"No," Tom said, raising a hand with a laugh. "I don't—God, I don't even . . . you know what I really want?" James raised a brow as he brought his glass to his lips. "I want a tree."

James snorted. "You've lost me completely."

Tom laughed again. "I think I've lost myself, but I've only just had the idea." He mused for a moment. "Have you ever wandered through the forest and seen two trees growing together?"

"Of course," James replied.

"Well, that's what I want. I want to find someone who can grow with me, sharing in strength and purpose. I want roots buried deep. I want to be so entangled in another person that I don't know where they end and I begin. I want—" He paused, taking in the look on James' face. "I'm not making any sense, am I?"

"It makes sense," James replied. "But it also sounds bloody exhausting . . . all that twisting and bending and supporting of limbs."

Both men laughed.

"I imagine that if I ever find the right person, it will feel as easy as breathing," Tom replied.

James eyed him. "And is Miss Harrow your tree?"

Tom groaned, snatching up his glass. "Christ, you're relentless."

"Answer the question."

Another quiet moment stretched between them.

"She might be," Tom admitted. "I've never felt this way about a woman, J. She is . . . she's like a song I can't get out of my head. But I can't make her want the same things as me. And I'll not try to change her. If she is meant to be in my life, she will have to be the one to make that choice."

James' frown softened. "So you don't intend to pursue her, then?"

Tom gave another exaggerated sigh. "You know, if lording ever loses its charms, you'd make an excellent hound. Always on the hunt—"

"Renley . . ."

"I have no intention of walking away," he replied.

"You're as bad as Burke," James muttered. "He thinks he can have her without any question of marriage and no one will bat an eye. It's madness."

Tom just shrugged. "She's her own person. Yes, she's a lady. And yes, she's a ward of this house, but she has every right to make her own choices. If she wants Burke on terms that are acceptable to him, who are we to stand in their way?"

"They'll ruin each other, and you're content to just sit back and watch?"

Tom huffed a laugh. "James, I'm going to tell you something my father used to love to say: 'You can lead a horse to water, you can even make it drink . . . but you can't lead a stubborn man anywhere.'"

James rolled his eyes again. "And I suppose I am the stubborn man?"

Tom got to his feet. "You are all the stubborn man," he replied. "You, Burke, *and* Rosalie. You are perhaps three of the most stubborn people I've ever met. And I will tell you this now, and pray you heed me: If they think they're being managed, they will both dig their heels in and fight you every step of the way."

James' mouth tightened into a firm line. "You think I intend to meddle?"

Tom gave him a knowing look. "I love you, James. A better man surely does not exist. But I think you quite literally cannot help yourself. Not when it comes to Burke. He has always been your greatest weakness; the only knife worth twisting." He drained his glass, setting it down with a clink.

"I *can* control myself, you know," James challenged.

"I'm not the one you need to convince, J. Best say those words again in a mirror."

James scowled.

"If you care for them, which I know you do, you'll leave them to manage their own affair," he finished with a smile. At the sound of James' frustrated groan, he snatched up his hat and slipped out of the room.

10

Rosalie

ROSALIE AND BURKE returned to Corbin House with the setting sun.

"Welcome back, miss," said a tall footman, taking the small traveling case she offered him.

"Have they already rung the gong?" Burke asked, handing over his great coat to the other footman.

"Yes, sir. Lord James and the lieutenant are in the drawing room. Dinner is about to be served."

The heels of Burke's boots clicked sharply on the marble floor as he swept across the entry hall.

"Oh, Burke, we're so late," Rosalie cried, sticking close to his side as he led the way through the quiet house. She hadn't meant for them to be out so late, but traffic from Cheapside to Mayfair had been terrible.

"We can have dinner delayed if you'd like to change," the taller footman said, almost jogging at Burke's side.

"Not necessary," Burke replied. "We'll go straight in."

Rosalie's heart fluttered with each step she took, knowing

she was about to see James and Renley again. She didn't feel prepared to survive a dinner with all three men together.

There was no time to attempt an escape before Burke was shoving his way through the door.

"Mr. Burke and Miss Harrow," called the footman. His wig tipped askew as he lunged forward to catch the closing door before it hit Rosalie.

Inside the spacious drawing room, James and Renley scrambled to their feet. They sat at the far end of the room on a pair of sofas. Unlike Burke and Rosalie, they were both dressed for dinner—tailored black coats and trim pants with neutral waistcoats, starched collars, and crisp white cravats.

James had his auburn curls brushed and tucked behind his ears. His fierce green eyes locked on her in an instant. "Finally," he called in welcome, setting down his glass of wine. His smile fell as he glanced from Rosalie to Burke . . . Burke, who was barreling towards him.

"Oh shit," Renley muttered, slapping his drink down and reaching out for Burke's arm as he passed. "Burke—don't—"

Burke shoved past him.

"Burke, *no*," Rosalie cried, running after him.

"You know I'm sorry," James offered, making no attempt to move away or even raise his hands.

In a fit of speed she didn't know she possessed, Rosalie raced around the sofa and flung herself in front of James just in time. She stretched her arms wide, using her body as a human shield between the two men. "Burke, that is enough—"

"Get out of my way," he growled, hands reaching out as if he meant to physically move her aside.

"James is not to blame for what happened," she cried.

James put a hand on her shoulder. "It's okay . . . step aside."

"No!" She pressed into him, arms still wide.

Renley placed a hand on Burke's shoulder. "Come on, it's not worth it."

"Rosalie, move," Burke said again. "Someone is getting punished for this—"

"Then punish *me*!"

James' hand went stiff on her shoulder. Across from her, Burke and Renley looked at her with wide eyes. A tense moment stretched between them all as her words hung in the air.

Burke's eyes narrowed. "What did you just say?"

She lowered her hands but kept her chest puffed out and her chin raised in defiance. "You heard me. James is off limits," she declared. "If you are so determined to seek justice for what we did, then punish *me*."

Behind Burke, Renley groaned, keeping a firm hold on his friend's shoulder.

"Consider me in your debt. You can choose—"

"Deal," Burke said, even before she'd finished the offer.

She blinked. "Deal? But—"

"I accept," he repeated, those stormy eyes luring her in.

She frowned. "Given your penchant for tricks, I can only imagine what awaits. Will you make me perform a duet again before the entire house party? Make me recite poetry? No embarrassment should be off limits—"

Burke let out a vicious laugh.

"Burke," James warned.

Burke ignored him, inching closer. "You say 'punish me' in that siren's tone, and you truly expect me to make your punishment *public*?" He stepped toward her, lowering his mouth to her ear. "There is no world in which I would waste this chance on another piano duet."

A shiver coursed through her.

"Burke, that's enough," James muttered, his grip on her loosening slightly. In that moment, she realized she was still pressed against him. She tried to shift away, but he held her still.

"She started it," Burke replied.

"I don't need her fighting my battles," James countered. "If you need to thrash me to get a little of your own back, then do it."

"Oh, for heaven's sake," Rosalie huffed. "We have much more important matters to discuss tonight. For starters—"

"I am not engaged!" Renley barked.

Rosalie blinked, swallowing the rest of her sentence. They all turned to look at Renley.

"I'm sorry," he said quickly. "I know this wasn't about me yet, but I was dying holding it in and, well, it's not true."

"What?" James said at the same time Burke muttered, "Oh, thank Christ."

Rosalie took a breath. "But Marianne said—"

"She lied," Renley pressed. "She was confused about how we left things last week. And I think perhaps she was jealous when she saw us dancing together—"

"Of course, she was jealous," Burke said with a scowl. "She meant to put Rosalie in her place. I hope you shredded her to ribbons. Is that what took you so long today?"

"Wait, what the hell did I miss now?" James growled, looking between the three of them.

Rosalie felt dizzy. Renley had yet to look away. Those

depthless blue eyes were locked on her, his expression open and pleading. He wasn't engaged. Marianne lied.

"Are we finished now?" Burke pressed, angling himself towards Renley. "Can we finally put Marianne behind us for good?"

Renley nodded. "It's finished. I told her in no uncertain terms that we're done."

Beside her, Rosalie felt James stiffen. "But she told Rosalie you were engaged last night? She actually spun such a lie?"

Renley nodded, his gaze back on Rosalie. "And I'm so sorry. God, you have no idea—if I'd known last night—"

"It doesn't matter," she murmured. This was all too much to handle. She needed food. She needed sleep. She needed one blessed moment to collect her thoughts without one of these men trying to tip her world off its axis with new proclamations.

"It *does* matter," Renley said, taking her hand in both of his. "Rosalie, I—"

"Excuse me, my lord."

Rosalie stiffened, as did all three men. They turned as one to see a footman standing in front of the open drawing room doors. If she hadn't been blushing before, she certainly was now.

"What is it?" barked James.

"Dinner is ready."

Before she quite realized how it had happened, Rosalie was sitting at one end of the impressively long table in the Corbin House dining room. It was decked in full splendor—silver candlesticks and servers, crystal glasses, artfully designed floral arrangements. Everything sparkled.

Across from her sat Burke and Renley, awkwardly glancing up every few moments, trying to catch her eye. James sat at the head of the table. Behind each of their chairs stood a footman, ready to serve each course. The meal was orchestrated by the ancient butler, who guarded the corner of the room like a gargoyle.

They all sipped their first course of pumpkin soup. It was delicious, but Rosalie couldn't get over the discomfort of feeling the presence of the footmen looming around the table.

"Well, this is awkward," Renley muttered, breaking the uncomfortable silence.

Burke and James both paused with their spoons half-raised.

"I know why *I* was feeling anxious," Renley went on. "But what do the two of you have to be so uptight about?"

Burke scowled as James set his spoon down with a clink, reaching for his wine.

"Did something else happen that I don't know about?" Renley glanced across the table at Rosalie, determined to get answers.

She shifted uncomfortably on her chair. She was a terrible liar at the best of times. If he looked at her now, surely what he'd see was her mortification. Not that she regretted anything that happened, but she *did* hate feeling like she was keeping something from him—from any of them—even unintentionally.

And what Renley didn't know about last night could easily fill a novel. Starting with the fact that James had kissed her in the library. Passionately. Aggressively. Like a man starving for much more than pumpkin soup. And that was before she'd argued with Burke in the music room, an argument that ended with him on his knees, pressing her against the piano, his mouth between her legs.

Her heartbeat echoed in her ears as she remembered the aching fullness, of riding his cock on the sofa . . . the floor. She glanced up and met Burke's gaze. The fire blazing in his eyes told her he was thinking about the same thing. She looked pointedly away and he chuckled. She set her spoon aside, reaching for her wine.

Renley missed nothing of the exchange. "Oh hell . . . something *did* happen. What did I miss?"

Burke cleared his throat, adjusting his napkin in his lap. "We have company."

"Rosalie is not company," Renley replied.

"He means the staff, Renley," James clarified in that annoyed tone.

Around the table, the footmen tried not to shift, as if they weren't listening intently to every word uttered.

"Wilson," James called.

The butler stepped forward. "Yes, my lord?"

"Have the footmen serve the courses and leave. We shall dine *en famille* tonight, and every night until my brother and mother join us."

The butler stiffened. "My lord, the presentation of each dish is—"

"We don't care about presentation," he countered. "A mince tart is a mince tart whether it is served on a silver tray or a napkin."

"Of course, my lord."

In minutes, the table's end was laden with an odd

assortment of trays and plates stacked with each course. There was a tray of cod fillets drizzled with cream sauce, fresh salad, roasted chicken and potatoes, lamb chops with a mash of asparagus and peas, a selection of wedged cheeses, dried fruit, and a two-tiered tray of assorted petits fours. The footmen did their best to fit it all within arms' reach.

"And the wine, my lord?" said Wilson.

"Leave the bottles on the table," James replied. "We'll serve ourselves."

"Very good, sir."

Rosalie watched the footmen file out of the dining room through a side door. The butler was the last to leave, giving everything a final appraising look before he closed the door with a soft snap. That sound let out all the stifling tension in the room. Burke loosened the tie of his cravat. James' shoulders fell as he sank back into his chair, glass of wine in hand.

Renley was the only one to help himself to more food. He speared the chicken with his fork, piling a few shaved slices onto his plate. "So . . . what happened last night?"

James' face was a mask of cool, calm. Rosalie was completely unprepared when he held her gaze and said, "Well, for starters, Burke and Rosalie fucked on the piano."

11

Rosalie

RENLEY'S EYES BLEW wide as he glanced from Rosalie to Burke. "You did *what*?"

"They were together last night in the music room. All over the music room, in fact," James replied.

Rosalie shut her eyes tight, unable to meet Renley's piercing gaze.

"That's enough, James," Burke growled.

"This happened last night? Where the hell was I?" said Renley.

Burke leaned forward, elbows on the table. "I think it's only fair to start at the beginning. We wouldn't want to leave anything out . . . like James accosting Rosalie in the library."

"What?" Renley bellowed.

Perhaps, if she tried hard enough, Rosalie could self-combust in her chair. That would surely get her out of this situation . . .

"Is that what you told him?" James murmured.

"Of course, she told me," Burke replied. "We have no secrets."

Rosalie met James' eyes and saw the pain there, the confusion.

He raised a brow in quiet indignation. "I accosted you?"

She let out a breath. "I never said that. I said you kissed me—I—*we* kissed."

"So . . . you kissed?" Renley interjected, looking between them. "Is that all? Just a kiss?"

James was the first to look away, eyes back on his uneaten plate of food. "Just a kiss," he muttered. "It didn't mean anything. I was angry about George. She caught me at the wrong time."

Rosalie's heart sank. *Just a kiss?* She still felt the weight of his hips pressing her into the bookcase. She was clinging to it by the end, as he was clinging to her. Oh, yes, just a kiss. A kiss she'd kiss every night of her dreaming. Meanwhile, James wouldn't look at her. He wanted it forgotten, for she was wholly unsuitable. A more imperfect match for the Right Honorable Viscount Finchley there could never be than Rosalie Harrow with her empty pockets, loose morals, and total lack of social standing.

James looked past an indignant Renley, eyes only for Burke. "I didn't mean for it to happen, and it won't happen again."

"I won't hold you to that," Burke replied, making Rosalie's breath catch in her throat. "I just need to know," he added. He leaned towards James, grey eyes locked on his dearest friend. "Don't hide things from me, James. And don't run from me ever again. Or the next time I catch you, I'll cut off your goddamn legs. Just try and run then."

The corner of James' mouth quirked into a smile. "Fine."

"How touching," Renley replied with an eye roll, reaching

past Burke for the tray of petits fours. "Can we go back to you and Rosalie in the music room?"

"No, we cannot!" Rosalie cried. "There is only one issue that matters right now, and that is Burke's engagement to Oliva Rutledge. They cannot possibly be expected to go through with it. We need a plan." At this, she looked to James, who was still pointedly avoiding her gaze.

"Can't they just . . . *not* get married?" Renley said with a shrug. "George's nuptials will overshadow all else, and Burke and Lady Gorgon can go their separate ways."

The look of hope in Burke's eyes made Rosalie grimace. "If only it could be that simple," she murmured.

Renley frowned. "I don't understand the problem—"

"The problem is that my mother has decreed that if Burke does *not* marry Olivia Rutledge, then she will disown him . . . and me if I help him," James explained.

"Holy hell," Renley muttered. "This happened last night?"

James nodded. "Not to mention the fact that if Lady Olivia tries to wriggle free, my mother is prepared to ruin her."

"Our challenges, as I see them, are two," Rosalie announced. "First, we must get the duchess to change her mind. She must be made to see that this marriage is not in the best interest of either party. She must agree to let them part."

"Hell will freeze over before she changes her mind," James muttered, reaching for a bottle of wine.

Rosalie wasn't ready to reveal the ace up her sleeve: She knew a salacious secret about the duchess. If the duchess refused to see reason, Rosalie was not above threatening her. She was willing to do anything to protect Burke . . . and by extension James. But all peaceful means of reason and request must be exhausted first.

"What is the second challenge?" Burke pressed.

"Umm . . . well, we must convince Olivia not to marry you, obviously," she replied.

Renley and Burke both snorted.

"Done," said Burke.

"She hates him," Renley added.

"Well, she hates everyone. I'm not special—"

"It's not that simple," said James, still slouched in his chair. He glanced to Rosalie and she nodded, sure he understood her.

"Why?"

She turned to Burke and Renley. "What I say now does not leave the four of us. It was confided in me by Olivia in a moment of sincere vulnerability. If you bring it up with her, she will know I've told you, and she will hate me for it."

Burke nodded, followed quickly by Renley. "I think we should all agree that whatever is spoken between the four of us is sacred," Renley replied. "No secrets, eh?"

Rosalie and Burke shared a look before they both nodded.

James sat like a statue, his tired eyes focused on the flickering candles.

Renley glanced his way. "James? Are you in this?"

James turned slowly to face him. "Do I have a choice?"

"We all have a choice," Burke replied, his voice firm. "But think carefully. If you mean to agree out of obligation to me, or out of some misplaced idea of protecting us, then just go. You stay because you want to stay."

James set his glass aside. "I'm staying."

He didn't look at Rosalie as he said the words, but she felt some small fluttering of relief. Whatever else he thought of her in terms of her unsuitability, he would help her help Burke. It was enough. It *had* to be enough.

She took a deep breath. "Olivia is not in the position to be turning down eligible suitors," she explained. "She is almost twenty-seven, and this will be her third engagement. She's tired, angry, and scared. So scared, in fact, that she threw herself at the duke during the house party, offering him sex in hopes he would propose . . . but she lost her nerve. "The duke kicked her out. James and I found her in the hall . . ."

"God damn him," Renley growled, clenching his fist around his wine glass. "So, what do we do?" He glanced around at each of them.

James rubbed his temple with a tired hand. Burke just sat there with a face like he'd swallowed a lemon.

"There is only one thing we *can* do," Rosalie said. "We must get Olivia to jilt Burke."

James let out a dry chuckle. "Christ . . . you think you're going to find someone better for her, don't you?"

She lifted her chin. "Exactly. The only way to break apart Burke and Olivia, with minimal reputational damage, is to secure for her a better match. If Burke jilts Olivia, she will be ruined. And that we cannot allow. But the only way a lady jilts a man and gets away with it is if she marries up . . ."

Burke dragged a hand through his dark hair.

"I've never played matchmaker," Renley admitted. "It's quite possible my involvement will make things worse, seeing as I can never manage to say the right thing when it counts, but you have my help all the same. What must we do?"

Rosalie smiled. "To begin, the three of you will write me a list of eligible bachelors. Then, we'll contrive reasons to bring them in contact with Olivia. The whole Alcott house party will come to Town, yes?" she asked, looking to James.

James nodded. "I don't see how they'll avoid it. George will drum up enough enthusiasm. We'll have a full house in a day or two."

"Good. Until Burke is down that aisle, we still have time," she replied.

James pushed back from the table and stood. "Where are you going?" Rosalie said, eyes wide.

He snatched up his plate of half-eaten food. "Back to my study. There is much to do, and no time to do it. It appears I'll be working through the night."

She stood too. "Let me help you—"

"No." The word was harsh, almost a bark.

Rosalie flinched. "You can share the load with us," she replied. "Let me help with the engagement party, at least. It was my idea—"

"Tomorrow," he replied. "Get some rest. I'm sure we'll scheme better in the morning. And eat some of this. Don't let it go to waste."

He didn't wait for the others to try and stop him. Holding his plate of food in one hand and a bottle of wine in the other, he shouldered his way out of the dining room.

12

Rosalie

"I'VE LOST MY appetite," Burke muttered, sitting back in his chair and pushing his plate away. He reached for the wine instead. "Rose, are you alright?"

Rosalie glanced across the table at Renley. His concern was genuine as he took in her every expression, trying to determine how he might help. Was she alright? Since arriving at Alcott, all her carefully laid plans had unraveled. Was it any wonder she felt so wild and unconfined when no part of her life was going according to plan? She'd been freefalling for weeks, like a bird tumbling through the sky, caught on a sharp wind. One gust might blow her left, even while she beat helplessly with her wings to fly right.

Renley must have sensed her turmoil. "Tell us what you need, Rose. Are you hungry?"

Burke was watching her too, those stormy eyes settling back to a soft grey now that the excitement was over.

She let out a slow exhale, looking around at the splendor of the feast growing cold on all the plates. The idea of putting cold mutton with a pea mash in her mouth made her want to gag. "I . . . um . . . no," she replied. "I think I will retire. A bath and some sleep will set me right."

"Shall I show you to your room?" offered Burke.

"I know the way." She glanced from Renley to Burke. She was sure Renley was desperate to say more, but she felt too fragile to handle more emotionality tonight. "I know how you all like to gossip about me. You have my permission to ask Burke anything."

"I wasn't going to gossip," Renley replied. "I just want to know you're alright. I want . . . last night with Marianne—"

She raised a hand. "Please, don't. I believe you that it was not as she said, that you made her no promises. I just . . . I need a little time. Let me sleep on it?"

Renley was all man: broad and strong, with that sharply chiseled jaw. But in this moment, he looked almost boyish with his tousled curls and wide blue eyes, all full of hope and fear. He was anxious for her acceptance, anxious to say everything now and have it out in the open. She fought the urge to run her hand through those curls. She longed for the comfort of his arms around her, like they were in the storage room, her cheek pressed against the anchor tattooed on his chest.

That was never in the plan either. These men were *never* in her plan. Now look at her, longing for them both. Renley was her safe harbor and Burke was her storm. Home and freedom. Peace and passion.

Not in the plan . . . but plans change.

And thank God for that.

She moved around the table, the satin of her dress whispering across the polished wooden floor. Renley was closer, so it was him she went to first, her arms wrapping around his waist as she pressed herself against him, her face buried in his cravat. His arms were around her in an instant as he sighed into her embrace. She breathed in his intoxicating scent of sea and salt and sun. How could a person smell like bottled sunshine, even in the dead of night?

He kissed the top of her head, resting his face there and breathing her in. He wasn't quite so tall as Burke, but he was broader, thicker at the waist and more muscled. He tipped her chin up. "Did I ruin this before I even had the chance to try for it?" he murmured, searching her eyes.

Smiling, she pulled him down to her, meeting her lips with his, tasting the sweet notes of red wine on his mouth. His hands moved to her face as he angled her exactly how he wanted her, teasing with his tongue until she opened for him. They kissed soft and slow, reassuring each other that the comfort and friendship they both felt still thrummed strongly between them.

She broke the kiss, smoothing down his cravat with her hands. "We'll talk more tomorrow. Good night, Renley."

He tucked a loose strand of her hair behind her ear. "Good night, Rose."

She turned away to find Burke waiting for her. His arms wrapped tightly around her shoulders as he peppered her forehead and temple with soft kisses. "I love you," he murmured, his breath warm against her ear. "You are safe here. Safe with me—with *us*."

She turned her face into the hand that cupped her cheek, kissing his palm. She raised her own hand to hold his there, letting his warmth soak into her skin. "Good night."

He kissed her lips once, twice, letting her go. "Good night, love."

Rosalie found her way upstairs through the dark house back to her room. She opened the door and let out a little gasp. The maids had certainly been busy. The sheets were turned down, the curtains closed, and a cozy fire crackled in the hearth. Not to mention the new feminine touches everywhere—bouquets of fresh flowers large and small sat on each surface, lace doilies dotted the side and end tables, and there was now a stocked dressing table with glass bottles of perfume and hair powder in the corner, blocking access to the shelved linen closet.

Paulette had also followed through with her promise. Stylish dress and hat boxes sat stacked in the opposite corner. Rosalie went to the armoire and pulled open both doors. It was full of all her new clothes. She recognized most of them as things she'd tried on earlier, but there were a few new selections too.

She pulled open each drawer, noting the carefully folded petticoats and chemises, new stockings and garters, stays—both half and full, and a pile of colored, silky underthings that Rosalie was positive James had not ordered. She shut that drawer with a snap, stifling a giggle as she imagined him standing at the counter in Paulette's shop asking to see samples.

She fished a chemise out of the top drawer and moved over to the mantel, tugging the servant's cord. She only had to wait a few minutes before Fanny arrived. Rosalie was pleased to discover a sleek, modern bathing chamber was situated directly across the hall from her room. Soaking in the deep, copper tub did wonders for her aching muscles. She gave her hair a thorough wash with a fancy French tonic that smelled strongly of rose oil.

Within the hour, Fanny had Rosalie sitting at the dressing table back in her room. She meticulously brushed and set Rosalie's hair. The dark curls around her face were wound up tight with bits of pink ribbon.

Fanny soon left, and Rosalie sank onto the bed, sighing with relief to be stretched out on the soft surface. She slipped her legs under the coverlet. She'd barely let herself settle when her doorknob rattled. She looked up, expecting it to be Fanny.

Of course, it wasn't.

13

Rosalie

BURKE STOOD BAREFOOT in the doorway, grey eyes narrowed as he scanned the room. His shirt was untucked, hanging loose on his broad frame. "I saw the light . . . what are you doing in here?"

Rosalie sighed. "Ask yourself, sir. Do you never knock on a lady's door? It's a terrible habit, and I mean to break you of it."

"You haven't seemed to mind in the past," he replied, still looking around.

"I have minded every time," she cried. "Burke, why are you in here?"

"Why are *you* in here?"

"Well, I'm not shoeing horses, am I?" She gestured to her position on the bed with an irritated wave of her hand. "I'm trying to sleep, or at least I *was* until you barged in."

He moved over nearer to the fireplace, inspecting the stack of dress boxes. "Who put you in here?"

An unsettling feeling sank into her chest. "Why? What's wrong with this room?" She crawled out of the bed, her fatigue forgotten. "Oh, I *knew* there was something. Is it haunted?" Why that was her first thought, she had no idea. She clearly read too many gothic novels. Either way, panic leeched up her spine. "I swear, if James put me in here as some kind of cruel joke—"

Burke turned sharply. "James put you in here?"

Rosalie wrapped her arms around her middle. "Burke, please just tell me what's going on."

The corner of his mouth tipped into a smile. Turning on his heel, he swept from the room, closing the door softly behind him.

Rosalie stood next to her bed, mouth open in surprise. "What—*Burke*," she hissed, rushing over towards the door. "You cannot just leave like that!"

As she settled her hand on the knob, there came a rattling behind her. She shrieked and spun around, pressing herself against the door.

Scritch . . . scratch.

The soft sounds came from the opposite door. The door clicked open and swung inward to reveal Burke yet again. He was backlit by a warm fire glowing in the connecting room.

"Burke, what—"

He leaned against the frame. "This is my room," he said, gesturing with a nod to the other room.

"What?" She paced around the end of her bed. "James put us in adjoining rooms?"

Burke took two steps back, letting her see into his much larger room. Touches of Burke were everywhere. Art to his tastes decked the walls—hunting scenes and landscapes in warm greens, golds, and browns. Messy stacks of books were piled on the table. His coat was flung over a chair and his boots sat flopped by the door.

"Oh, that *devil*," she hissed. "This is so inappropriate. Why would James do this?"

"Easy," Burke said with a laugh. "Ladies are usually roomed in the east wing, true enough. But I'm sure James spun an appropriate tale to Mrs. Robbins about needing all the rooms for the coming guests."

"He has put us in adjoining rooms! Is he trying to start a scandal?"

He just shrugged. "I'm not sure anyone in the house knows these rooms functionally adjoin anymore. George always kept the key well-hidden when he lived in here. For the longest time an armoire even sat before this door," he added, glancing around. "If we're discreet, no one need know we have a key," he finished with a wink.

She rushed back into her room. "I need to pack. I need to move. I—"

Burke just stood in the doorway chuckling. "Do you plan to drag all of this through the house tonight?"

She spun around to glare at him. "You could help me."

His gaze heated as his eyes roved slowly down her body. "You are so beautiful when you're angry."

She wrapped her arms around herself, knowing it did little to hide her shape in the paper-thin chemise. "Don't flirt with me. Why would James do this?"

He sighed. "It's just a peace offering. He's been conflicted about you . . . to say the least. I think he'd made up his mind at Alcott to try and keep us apart. Clearly, he's reconsidered. This is his way of blessing our union."

Rosalie felt a twisting in her gut. This was more than just a peace offering. James meant to wash his hands of her once and for all. Now that he'd placed her in Burke's arms, he could walk away. Treacherous feelings of sinking self-worth were mirrored by rising anger.

She chose anger.

"How *dare* he," she snarled. "What a high-handed, despicable thing to do! He does not own us, Burke. He doesn't get to keep doing this—making decisions for the rest of us and just assume we'll go along."

Burke watched her intently, arms crossed as he leaned against the doorframe. "What do you intend to do about it, little siren?"

"I mean to have words with him. The clothes, the rooms, dismissing our help tonight—that man will learn he's not an island, or so help me . . ." She didn't even know how to finish the threat, so she just let it hang, chest heaving as she took a shaky breath.

Burke took a step closer. "Can I watch?"

She blinked. "Watch what?"

His stormy eyes danced with interest. "I want to watch you excoriate James."

"And why would you want that?"

"To see you both together, tempers flared . . . voices raised. It is sure to become my new favorite pastime."

Warmth pooled inside her. "You would enjoy watching us argue?"

He closed the space between them and reached for her hand, placing it over his stiffening cock. Her breath caught as desire burned though her. He leaned in and brushed his lips along her jaw, pulling her flush against him.

"I would see the two of you undone," he whispered. "I would see you dominate him in all the ways I know you can. I want him on his knees, bending to your will. I want you to *own* him." He ran his lips along the shell of her ear, making her shiver. "Own us both. Show us your power until we bend only to you. Worship only you . . . need only you . . ."

She stroked him, lost to the visions his words conjured in her mind.

"I want you to remember the sound you just made," he murmured, using one hand to tug on the front tie of her chemise. "Make it again with my cock in your mouth."

She bloomed, feeling that strange siren's magic coursing through her. Only Burke could wake it in her. She felt powerful, beautiful, controlled. She opened her eyes, taking in the look of longing on his handsome face. Her smile widened. He was done for. She would have this man. She would make him beg. She dropped her hand away and stepped back. "Take off your clothes," she whispered. "And get on my bed."

With a devilish grin, Burke stepped past her into her room, tugging his shirt off as he went. He dropped it to the floor. The mix of candle and firelight danced across the planes of his muscled back and shoulders. He stopped by the side of the bed, undoing the fastenings of his pants. He slipped them down over his hips, exposing his backside to her as they pooled at his ankles.

Rosalie could barely breathe. Burke was naked in her room, beside her bed, waiting for her. He turned slowly to face her, hard cock on display. He stroked it lazily with one hand. "Where do you want me?"

Leaving her lonely perch by the door, she crossed over to him, pushing him down onto the edge of the bed. Their lips collided in a fevered kiss as she climbed atop him. Burke pulled her tight to him until she felt his hardness. She scrambled for the hem of her chemise, tugging it up over her head and tossing it away. Their naked bodies pressed together. She shivered as her sensitive nipples grazed his chest.

"I want you." Burke's breath was hot against her open mouth as he kissed her. "I ache for you—need you—"

"You have me," she panted, touching every part of him she could reach. "I'm yours."

He dropped his mouth to her breast, teasing her nipple with his tongue. She arched into him, feeling the slide of his cock between her legs. Eager for more, she pressed down with her hips. At the feel of her wetness, he gave a sharp moan, instinctively pushing her hips away to give himself relief.

"Too much," he groaned, lifting his mouth from her breast. "I've been dying for you."

She scrambled off his lap. "Lie down."

Without hesitation, he slid fully onto the bed. He scooted back on his elbows, his stomach muscles flexing as he pulled himself towards the head of the bed.

She crawled onto the bed and straddled him again, her hips spread around his thighs. She quickly wrapped her hand around his length, stroking him from root to tip. He sank back against the pillows.

"What did you say to me this morning?" she whispered, stroking him slow. "'You're going to come for me. You're going to *beg* me for it.'"

He threw an arm over his face as he took deep breaths. "Christ, I'm already so close."

She rose on her knees, scooting back until she could take him in her mouth. She swiped her tongue over his tip, tasting his tart, salty release. His cock twitched against her lips. She slid both hands up his thighs, gripping tight to his hips as she sank down on him, stroking and teasing him with her tongue.

"Fucking hell," he panted. His fingers wove into her mess of curls, and he fisted them tight. A sharp pain in her scalp sent a jolt of need straight to her aching core. She couldn't contain her cry as she took him deeper, feeling him hit the back of her throat.

He gripped her by the shoulders and pulled her off. "*Ungh*—stop—"

Feeling bold, she let her body slide along the naked length of him. He wrapped his arms around her, holding her tight as she braced herself on her elbows. She kissed down one side of his jaw, then the other, latching onto his neck, sucking and teasing with her teeth.

"You're a goddamn siren." His rough hands roamed from her backside up her sides to her shoulders. "I feel you everywhere. Feel your wet heat drawing me in. You want me, don't you? Want me inside you."

"Are you trying to make *me* beg?" She trailed kisses down his chest as her hand snaked between them, wrapping around his cock again.

He was still trying to take charge, even as his body coiled tight, fighting the urge to release. "God—*yes*." He cupped her face with both hands, kissing her as if he were trying to pull her very essence into himself. They broke apart, panting.

With her mouth still against his, she whispered, "Let go, Burke. This is for you. My Horatio. My Burke."

"I don't deserve you. Don't deserve this . . ."

Heat radiated over her skin at the very idea. "You are *mine*," she challenged. "I say what you deserve. I decide what happens next. You want to hear me moan your name?"

"Yes," he sighed on a deep exhale.

She gripped his chin, tipping it up until he held her gaze. "Then give me what I want."

She slid back down his body, sinking her mouth onto him.

She hollowed her cheeks, taking him deep. Holding tight to his hips, she worked him with mouth and tongue until he was crying out, lifting his hips and spilling down her throat. She swallowed everything he gave her, rewarding him with sounds that made him twitch in her mouth.

Moments later, she sat up, balancing on her knees over his pinned legs. Burke lay naked and panting, arms limp at his sides, body slicked with sweat. He looked so beautiful. She wanted to sketch him like this—his parted lips, the tip of his chin angled down, the sweep of black hair over his forehead, the fluttering of his dark lashes.

Contentment sank into her chest, spreading down her limbs, curling its way around her very bones. She was in love with this man. Completely. Irrevocably. It scared her as much as it soothed her. Each time they gave each other pleasure, she felt a new tie binding herself to him. Each new thing she learned about him tightened the knots.

She climbed off him, crawling up his side until she could curl into him, one arm draped over his naked chest. He shifted slightly, eyes still closed, and pressed a kiss to her forehead. "I love you," he murmured, half lost to sleep already.

She closed her eyes as her breathing fell into rhythm with his. She was right on the edge of sleep when a rattling sound jerked her awake.

"*Burke*," she hissed, trying to cover her nakedness.

He was wide awake in an instant, rolling over as the door opened.

"Only me," said Renley, slipping into the room.

"Christ, Tom." Burke flopped back on the bed, breathing hard.

Rosalie blushed furiously, pulling the coverlet up over her

breasts. What was it with these men and not knocking on doors?

Renley glanced around the room. He was dressed similar to Burke—black pants and a loose white shirt. The deep "V" of his shirt revealed the swirls of ink on his chest. "So . . . James really must be contrite," he mused.

"It would appear so," Burke muttered. His arm curled around her waist as he tucked into her, not caring that Renley was there.

He may have no questions, but Rosalie did. "Renley, what are you doing?"

"If you're going to make this work, might I offer two words of caution?" he replied, still leaning against the door. "First, always make sure you're alone. If you're not, do try and keep it down. I've been lying across the hall listening to the symphony of your shared moans."

"Oh no," Rosalie whined with mortification, rolling her face into the pillows. He was right—she'd completely lost hold of her senses. Nothing mattered in the moment but Burke—pleasing him, watching him come apart.

"Second, never forget to lock the door." To prove his point, Renley turned the latch, locking all three of them in the room together. He swept through into Burke's adjoining room and Rosalie could only imagine he was doing the same to that door.

He came back with a pillow tucked under his arm, taking no notice of the very naked Burke stretched at Rosalie's side. He paused only to blow out the candles flickering on the bedside table. Circling around the end of the bed, he came to Rosalie's other side and did the same thing to those candles. The only light left in the room came from the dying fire.

Renley tossed the pillow down next to Rosalie and tugged off his shirt. She fought to contain her runaway heart as she took in his beautifully sculpted chest, those broad shoulders and strong arms. The firelight flickered, making the tattoos on his chest dance as he flexed and moved.

He shed his pants next, dropping them to the floor. Burke's legs were long and lean, adding to his height. In contrast, Renley's thighs were thick muscle, dusted with soft golden hair. She tried not to focus on his half-hard cock at eye level. She thrilled at the thought of that impressive length filling her. Swallowing her nerves, she scooted back against the curve of Burke's hip.

Renley flipped back the coverlet and sank down onto the mattress, sliding his legs in before flopping his head down on his pilfered pillow. Burke tucked his face into the nape of Rosalie's neck until she could feel his warm breath fanning gently between her bare shoulders.

Renley's presence filled the bed. He was inches from her, completely naked, and making no attempts to touch her. He seemed content to just fall asleep.

"Renley . . ."

"Is this alright?" he whispered. "I'm so tired. And I know you want more time," he added. "I won't ask you for anything. I just need to be where you are."

Her heart split open at the words. With a slow exhale, she let her doubts melt away. If he wanted Marianne, he would be with Marianne now. Renley wanted *her*. So much so that he couldn't stay away, even after hearing her with his friend.

She reached for him in the dark, running her hand through his soft curls, as she melted against his lips, drinking in that taste of bottled sunshine. Burke's arm stayed looped around her waist as Renley inched closer, his hardness brushing against her thigh as their mouths opened to each other.

His kisses made her drunk. She could live off the kisses of these men forever. Who needed air or food? Trivial compared to the ambrosia of Renley's taste on her tongue. She sighed as she felt his calloused hand cup her breast. His fingers tweaked her nipple, sending a jolt of want shivering over her skin. But then he dropped his hand away, breaking their kiss too.

"Good night, Rose," he murmured, sliding back an inch to give her space.

In moments, she felt the breathing of both men even out. This time last night, she was running from them, certain neither would ever choose her. They wouldn't possibly put her first. Now they were naked in her bed, folded in her arms.

I need to be where you are.

She repeated the words like a prayer.

I need to be where you are.

As content as she felt knowing Burke and Renley were here, she couldn't shake the feeling that something was missing.

Not something. *Someone.* James.

She sighed, heart heavy. James Corbin, the man who couldn't let himself be loved. The man who perhaps needed love the most. Was he still awake somewhere in the depths of the house? Undoubtedly. Was he all alone in his study, pouring over accounts, making lists, thinking of her too . . .

Curled between his two closest friends, Rosalie resolved herself to breaking through his tough outer walls. She had more than enough love to give, and Burke and Renley seemed willing to share. Would James ever believe she could love them all? Could he let himself love her in return?

14

Rosalie

ROSALIE WOKE ALONE in her bed. She was disoriented for a moment, her hands reaching out to feel the sheets to either side of her. Cool, crisp . . . empty. She blinked her eyes open, her mind full of memories of the previous night. She'd fallen asleep in Burke's arms, turning in the night to be held by Renley.

She sat up, the sheet sliding off her bare shoulder. Her nipples pebbled in the cold air. The curtains were still drawn over the windows. The fire was out too, accounting for the sharp chill. She could just make out the face of the mantel clock.

Half past eight.

She slipped off the bed and tugged open the closest curtain, looking around the room. All evidence of Burke and Renley was gone. She tugged on her chemise, rubbing her arms to warm the chilled fabric.

Had she dreamt it all?

No, they were definitely here. They must have slipped out with the dawn. It was for her benefit. An unmarried lady's reputation was worth more than gold. And given Rosalie's low social standing, it was quite literally her only currency.

She should appreciate the gesture . . . but she didn't. For now she stood cold and alone, her old nemesis self-doubt creeping in. To have them slink away made what they did together feel wrong. She couldn't bear the idea of waking every morning to find them disappeared like puffs of smoke.

She moved back over to the bed and paused, a small smile quirking her lips. Not all proof of their presence had been removed. Three pillows still lined the top of the bed. She pressed a cool pillow to her face, stifling a smile. Salt and sunshine on a summer day. *Renley*. She snatched up the other one and her lungs were filled with a spiced currant scent. *Burke*.

She set the pillow down, smile falling. They had been here, but this is all she could expect. Stolen moments. Secret looks. Hidden kisses. Longing touches in the quiet of night. It was enough. It had to be enough. She was too afraid to dare want more.

Dressed in one of her new gowns—a pretty cream thing with a blue pinstripe—Rosalie went in search of breakfast. She paused in the doorway of the morning room, eyes wide. All three men were present. James and Renley sat side by side at the table near the window, with Burke standing between them. Soft morning sunlight filtered in around them as Burke leaned over, one hand splayed on the table's top. They were discussing something, gesturing to the papers spread between them.

"Miss Harrow, my lord," called the footman. All three men snapped to attention.

"Good morning," she murmured, feeling the rush of warmth flood her cheeks.

"Morning," they each repeated.

Feeling their eyes on her was heady. She needed something fortifying. She followed the intoxicating smell of fresh coffee over to the buffet table.

Burke left the others by the window, meeting her in the corner. He looked at ease, dressed casually in breeches and boots with a simple red waistcoat and brown morning coat. Perhaps he'd already been for a ride in the park.

"Good morning," he said again, helping himself to more coffee. "How did you sleep?"

"Exceptionally well," she murmured, adding a cube of sugar to her coffee. Heavens, why couldn't she look at him? She was being ridiculous. Nonsensical. Childish. Three words Rosalie loathed to associate with herself.

He leaned in, brushing his shoulder against hers as he reached for the sugar too. "Everything alright?"

"Of course," she replied, tasting the lie on her tongue.

He sighed, setting his cup down and placing a hand at her elbow. "Better to just come out with it, love. You've clearly got a bee in your bonnet."

She sniffed, replacing the cream jug on the silver tray. "I am not wearing a bonnet, sir."

"Rosalie, why can't you look at me?"

She glanced up. Burke's stormy grey eyes watched her intently. "It's nothing," she started to say. "It's silly. I feel silly even thinking it."

He just waited, raising one dark brow in question.

She let out a slow breath, giving her coffee a stir with a slender silver spoon. "It's just that I woke and you were gone. Which, of course, is fine. It's . . . you obviously couldn't stay . . ."

He was quiet for a moment, lips pursed. "I see . . . and now you question everything."

He had the nerve to chuckle, and she felt a shiver of annoyance shoot down her spine. "Do not laugh at me. I—"

Whatever she was about to say was silenced by his lips on hers. His hand cupped the back of her neck, holding her still as he kissed her once, twice, three times. Each kiss a little deeper, a little more inviting. She tasted the coffee on the tip of his tongue as he flicked it against her lips.

She gasped, shrugging away. "What are you doing?" She glanced wildly around the room, thankful to see the footman had stepped out.

"Tom, come here," Burke called over his shoulder.

Her breath caught. "Burke, don't—"

He cupped her face with his hand, silencing her with a stern look. "I will not hide from them," he said. "Between the four of us, there are no secrets. You are mine, yes?"

Her heart fluttered. "Yes," she whispered.

"And I am yours," he replied, kissing her brow before turning back to his coffee.

Renley appeared behind them. He looked well-rested too, outfitted in fawn breeches and riding boots with a blue waistcoat and handsome, stone-grey coat. "You bellowed?" he said at Burke, giving Rosalie a warm smile. "Good morning, Rose."

"She woke to find us gone," Burke replied, testing the sweetness of his coffee. "She thinks we mean to pretend it never happened. That we now only exist in the dark of the night, like strange creatures of moonlight . . . or a pair of bats."

Renley's blue eyes narrowed as he directed all his attention at Rosalie. "Is that true?"

"No. I didn't. It wasn't like that," she replied lamely. It was exactly like that.

"We left early this morning to set ourselves to work on the task you assigned us," Renley explained.

"Blame no one but yourself that your morning did not involve four eager hands and two starving mouths," Burke added. As he spoke, he trailed his hand up her arm and over her shoulder until his fingertips brushed the bare skin of her collarbone.

Rosalie batted his hand away. "That is quite enough." Both men laughed.

"Tonight, if you're very good, your moonlight men may appear bringing gifts to honor their goddess," Burke murmured, brushing his lips along her temple.

"I said enough," she replied, giving him a little shove.

Renley just laughed, leaning in to kiss her temple on the other side.

"If you're all quite finished, I'd like to get this settled," James called from across the room.

Rosalie gasped. How had she forgotten he was still in the room? These men made her lose her senses completely. The closer they got to her, the less control she had over herself. She felt hot and bothered, her cheeks burning. If they wanted her, they could have her. Anywhere. Everywhere. She ached for them.

It scared her. In her experience, men were not to be trusted. What made these men so different? She'd never felt such a desire to be protected and cherished. And she refused to feel ashamed about it in front of James. He knew what could be his if he but reached out his hand to her. She refused to beg. So he would watch her wear the clothes he bought for her and kiss his friends, and if he didn't like it, that was too bad.

She followed the men over to the opposite side of the room with her cup of coffee in hand. "What were you all doing when I came in?" she said, taking the seat Renley offered her.

"Reconciling," replied James, shuffling a few of the papers on the table.

Rosalie paused with her cup halfway to her lips, eyes darting from James to the other two.

"Not with each other," Burke snorted. "We made out lists of eligible bachelors." He reached around James for the piece of paper on the table. "We've agreed on twelve names," he said, handing it over to her.

She set her coffee aside and accepted the list, letting her eye scan the page written in James' narrow, slanted scrawl.

"Don't get too excited," said James, groaning as he stood and stretched. "I'd say the bottom three should be scratched, but Burke insists they stay."

"Who are we to determine if they should make the cut?" Burke countered. "Just because *you* wouldn't marry them, James, doesn't mean the gorgon won't find them suitable. They're more suitable than me," he finished with a shrug.

"Everyone is more suitable than you," sniped James, sinking down onto the closest sofa, one arm flung over his tired eyes. "And I wouldn't marry any man on that list."

"Oh, I don't know," Burke mused. "You covet Lord Halliston's barley holdings. Don't tell me you couldn't be lured down the aisle for a cut of those yields."

"I doubt he'd accept my proposal," James muttered. "Not many would accept you as a permanent house guest. Always under foot. You're worse than a corgi."

Renley snorted, joining James on the sofa.

"Please, can we dispense with calling Olivia a gorgon?" Rosalie interjected, eyes still on the list. She pursed her lips, hitting the end. "Renley . . . I'm seeing no military men here. Where is your list?"

"I don't have a list," he replied, stretching out next to James. "She's made it quite clear what she thinks of men in uniform. I doubt any of my bachelor friends will fit the bill."

"Hmm . . . you might have a point." Rosalie knew all too well what he meant, having heard Olivia thoroughly trounce him at dinner on their first night at Alcott. "Tell me about these other names then. Are they all unmarried lords between twenty-five and forty?"

"I don't have their exact ages, but I'd guess yes," James replied.

"Some of these names are familiar to me," she admitted. "Lord Henry Morrow . . . he's a second son as well, yes? Isn't his father an earl?"

"Aye, and so is Lord Tarley," Burke replied. "He's a bit of a prig. James wants his name off the list, but his father is the Earl of Southeby. He's of age, he's unmarried, so he stays on the list. Leave it to the gorg—Olivia to decide if she wants him."

She nodded. "We need to see who on this list is in Town, and then do our best to get the others here as soon as possible."

"Already on it," Burke replied.

"We'll make the rounds to the clubs this evening and see who we can find," James explained, getting up off the sofa.

She nodded again. "When will the group arrive from Alcott, my lord?"

"Tomorrow," he replied. "I just got word from George this

morning. He's ecstatic about his surprise party." By his tone, one would think the word "party" actually implied a particularly bad case of smallpox.

Tomorrow. Her heart thumped dully. That gave her only today to enjoy this time alone with them.

"What can I do to help with planning?" she asked, taking a sip of her coffee.

"Christ, do it all," James replied.

She nodded. "I'll see to it at once, my lord. I'm sure when your mother arrives, she'll take the rest of the arrangements in hand."

His shoulders stiffened at mention of his mother. He turned away, moving towards the door. "I'm out the rest of the morning," he called over his shoulder. "You're all on your own for luncheon." He left without looking back.

15

Rosalie

ROSALIE PASSED THE rest of the morning flitting between the company of Mrs. Robbins and Burke and Renley. The men broke their fast with her before taking her on a quick tour of the downstairs rooms of Corbin House. After the tour, the trio split to attend to various errands—Burke to the gunsmith, Renley to his officer's club, and Rosalie to a working luncheon with Mrs. Robbins in the parlor. It was simple fare—sliced cold ham and salad, tomato soup, and spiced apple tea.

The housekeeper proved herself more than equal to the task of planning a society soiree. Rosalie sat back, thoroughly impressed, as Mrs. Robbins walked her through a range of details from floral designs, to guest lists, to ordering carved ices. The woman had accomplished all this in less than a day! "Of course, I will leave it to the family to settle on an overall style for the evening," rushed Mrs. Robbins, shuffling a few stationery samples out of a messy folder.

"Lord James has asked me to tackle the particulars," Rosalie replied, spreading some salted butter on a slice of toast. "If we leave it to him, it may have all the pomp of this luncheon."

"Too true," the housekeeper said with a snort. "Dinner and dancing, perhaps? That's always sure to please. Or a night of performances? We could bring in a troupe from the London ballet, or the opera—*oh*—the circus!"

Next to Mrs. Robbins, a maid feverishly took notes, nodding along.

"Hmm . . ." Rosalie was thinking fast. This event must serve the dual purpose of satisfying the duke's desire for spectacle and providing enough space for mingling and conversation. For they needed the freedom to nudge Olivia in the direction of the eligible bachelors. "What if we dispensed with a formal dinner?" She glanced from Mrs. Robbins to the maid. "I doubt His Grace would much enjoy being stuck in a chair through both dinner *and* a performance. He'd rather mingle with his guests."

"Oh yes, our master has always been a social butterfly," Mrs. Robbins said with a laugh.

"Perhaps we could have a sort of informal reception," Rosalie offered. "To encourage a more celebratory atmosphere. No seated dinner. No endless rounds of courses and everyone stiffly waiting to turn."

"Oh, what fun," cooed the maid.

Mrs. Robbins leaned closer, giving her tea a stir. "And for the menu?"

Rosalie closed her eyes, picturing the night in her mind like a painting. "I'm imagining footmen in the family livery weaving through the crowd, bright candlelight, trays of canapés and delicate French pastries."

"Yes, fresh oysters," said Mrs. Robbins, nodding at the maid to take note. "Scotch woodcock and pâté, caviar, quail's egg quiche. And for the sweet course?"

Rosalie smiled. "An assortment of marzipan, sweet jellies and petit fours, flavored ices. I'm sure the pastry chef will know how to dazzle us. If the staff here is anything like that at Alcott, we will all be left in wonder at their culinary artistry."

Mrs. Robbins was not the type to let compliments penetrate, not when she was focused on her task. She read over the maid's shoulder, making sure it was all jotted down. "Mm . . . good, good. And for entertainment?"

Rosalie's smile widened picturing James rubbing shoulders with jugglers and fire-eaters all evening. "I think I quite like your idea of performers. But let them mingle in the crowd and entertain," she added. "Nothing formal. But we should have a set of dances to close out the night."

"Excellent," said Mrs. Robbins, rattling her tea aside and rising from the table. "Come with me, Miss Harrow, and I shall have you appraise our choice of linens."

The day carried on with Rosalie following in Mrs. Robbins' wake. In the span of a few hours, she'd been taken on a full tour of the house, met the chef, and coordinated with the butler on selecting a set of rooms that would be opened for the party. All the while, the house buzzed with staff feverishly working to make the house ready for the impending arrival of the rest of the house party.

At half past five, Rosalie finally escaped Mrs. Robbins and went in search of her bonnet and pelisse. She was determined to walk the gardens before the gong was rung for dinner. She made her way to the main stairs in the front hall. One hand on the rail, she raised her foot.

"Arrrgh!"

Rosalie shrieked and darted out of the way as a footman balancing a massive vase of flowers tripped mid-step. He tumbled down the stairs, and she watched the vase land on the steps, shattering into a thousand pieces.

CRASH.

The shards splintered everywhere, skittering down to slide across the marble floor. The poor footman grunted, a garden of fresh-cut flowers covering him and the steps.

"Are you alright?" Rosalie cried, rushing forward. She had to climb a few steps to meet him. She dropped to her knees.

The footman sat up, wig askew, his livery soaked by the spilled water. "M'fine."

She took him by the elbow, trying to help him up.

As soon as he put weight on his ankle, he yelped like a dog and dropped back to the stairs, pulling Rosalie down with him.

"What in heaven's name?" called Mrs. Robbins, emerging from around the corner. "*Oh*—gracious me—"

Two more footmen materialized, taking stock of the damage with wide eyes. They quickly rushed forward to help.

"What happened?" Mrs. Robbins shrieked.

"He tripped," Rosalie replied, hand still on his arm.

"Gracious," Mrs. Robbins said, flustered. "You leave this to us, dear. You'll be needing to get upstairs, yes? Just around the corner. Past the picture of the hounds is a servant stairwell."

"I can help—"

"Nonsense," the housekeeper cried, shooing Rosalie away. The stairs were soon swarmed with the butler, two more footmen, and two maids all ready to tackle the mess. Heaving a sigh, Rosalie slipped away from all the commotion. She found the door to the servant's stair easily enough. She didn't make it two steps up the narrow stair before a slam from above told her someone else was in the stairwell. Heavy boots came spiraling down in a rush.

"Hello there," she called, just as the occupant came round the corner. She gasped and stepped back along the wall, coming face to face with James.

His face was set in a scowl. "What is it with you and stairwells?"

16

James

JAMES HALTED ON the step as he took in the sudden appearance of Rosalie. Her dark eyes were wide, her mouth opened in surprise. She instinctively leaned away from him, one hand rising to her chest.

"Heavens," she breathed. "Why must you always pop out at me like that?"

"They are *my* stairs. Why do you always seem to haunt them? I begin to suspect you must lie in wait for me."

"I do no such thing, my lord."

His irritation flared. He'd been annoyed since that morning, watching Burke kiss her bold as brass in the morning room. No. That wasn't entirely true. Witnessing that kiss was nothing compared to the jealousy that churned in James last night, knowing they were upstairs together.

Burke found him this morning looking far too calm. Too satisfied. It left James in no doubt about what happened. Then Renley had to enter the room, glancing covertly at Burke like they shared a lover's secret. Neither man said anything, but James knew.

It confused him as much as it made him curious. How could they stand to share her? How could they bear to see another man touch her, kiss her, make her moan?

And now you're thinking of her moaning.

He blinked, focusing back on her. She was looking at him with those eyes that drowned him, those parted lips . . .

Goddamn it. Focus, James.

"Why are you in here?" he snapped. "We have proper stairs for guests, you know."

She bristled at his rudeness. He didn't blame her. "A footman fell on the stairs and injured himself," she explained. "Mrs. Robbins directed me this way."

"What happened?"

"He was rushing with a vase of flowers and tripped," she replied. "I tried to help, but apparently I was just in the way."

"Damn," he muttered. Now that she said it, he could hear the faint sounds of a commotion. "Is he badly hurt?"

"Just a sprain. Mrs. Robbins has it well in hand."

He frowned. "I'm sure. I'll go see to it all the same."

"Yes, of course. Excuse me, my lord."

As she attempted to step past him, James shot his hand out, pressing it against the stone wall. "Stop."

They each traced the length of his arm with their eyes. The arm that now blocked her path. Why was his heart suddenly racing?

"My lord?" she whispered.

"Stop," he growled, feeling the storm front building in his chest. "Stop that."

She looked up at him, those beautiful brown eyes full of confusion. "Stop what, my lord?"

"That," he snapped. "Why are you calling me that? You've been doing it since—it's driving me mad."

Her complexion heated as her eyes narrowed. "What am I supposed to call you? Are you not a viscount?"

"Yes, but—"

"And was it not you, my lord, who demanded just yesterday that I forget any notion of a growing acquaintance between us?"

Christ, why did she make everything so difficult? "That's not what I meant—"

She huffed. "James Corbin, Viscount Finchley, a lord who demands every piece on his chessboard play according to his rigid rules. *You* are the one who wants me relegated to my proper square. Only now I gather you don't actually know which square that ought to be, so let me enlighten you."

She took a step closer, trying to even the ground between them. He had to hold his breath to avoid choking on her intoxicating perfume.

"I am neither your wife nor your intended," she said, eyes blazing. "You have made it clear that I am not a suitable social acquaintance. That leaves but two options: Either I am a business associate, or I am a servant. To my knowledge, we have no pending business. Thus, I am resolved to assume you mean to treat me like a member of staff. *That* is my square, sir. I, in turn, shall treat you like my employer." She raised herself up to her full height. "Now, if you'll excuse me, my lord, I've taken up quite enough of your time. I will be on my way."

Her words hit him like the spray from a double-barreled shotgun. As he assessed the damage, she ducked under his arm, determined to flee. Recovering quickly, he spun on his heel and snatched her arm as she passed.

"Unhand me," she hissed.

"Don't walk away from me." He knew exactly what to say to rattle her cage. He lowered his lips to her ear and rasped, "I have not dismissed you yet."

She sucked in a breath, righteous anger flashing across her face. "You're being a brute!"

He smirked, still holding tight to her arm. "If you're going to be difficult, two can play your game."

"*I'm* being difficult?"

"Yes! You are one of the most difficult, obstinate, infuriating women I've ever met. You swan through life with all the grace of a hurricane, leaving devastation in your wake—"

She scoffed, her cheeks blazing pink. "Comparing me to a swan? Heavens, that is quite the denouncement coming from you—"

"Don't make jokes," he snapped. "I can't stand them."

"You *love* jokes," she countered. "You live for them. You and Burke exchange ten a day. You just don't like being the target, *my lord*."

"God*damn* it." He boxed her in with both hands, pressing them against the cool stone wall. He lowered his face inches from hers, that spicy floral scent making him weak. "I will rage if you call me that again," he said, voice hoarse.

They stood like that for a moment, foreheads almost touching, mouths inches apart, breathing the same air. He watched the rapid rise and fall of her chest, knowing his was doing the very same. This close, he could trace with his eyes the gentle curves of the tops of her breasts as they disappeared into her dress. He tried to look away. He *had* to look away. This was impossible. Intolerable.

Don't do this.

His breathing became ragged as he felt himself pulled to her, leaning closer.

Do not break.

She tipped her chip up. Was she daring him to kiss her?

Or simply refusing to back down? Or both?

Let her go.

He groaned, his elbows going slack, dropping an inch closer.

He was going to break.

She sucked in a sharp breath, shifting away. "What else can I call you?" she asked, not meeting his gaze. "What are we to each other but master and servant? I will not raise the suspicion of this house by being overly familiar with you. That will serve neither you nor I."

"A compromise, then," he muttered.

She huffed a little laugh. "What possible compromise can there be?"

He pointed down the stairs at the closed door. "Out there, I will be the viscount and you will be Miss Harrow. I will swallow my irritation when you dismiss me with each cold utterance of 'my lord' . . . but you must stop looking at me like that."

She blinked, lips parting again. He hated when her mouth did that. Damn, he loved it . . . and he hated it. "Like what?" she whispered.

He raised a hand, ghosting his fingers over her lips. "Like I mean something to you."

Her breath left her in a rush. He felt the warmth of it against his fingers. "James—"

"Outside this stairwell, we shall play our roles."

She still held his gaze, those dark eyes searching his. "And in here?"

A long moment stretched between them. Neither of them moved. Neither of them breathed. Then James broke. He dropped his forehead to hers, letting himself shift his hands to her shoulders. She didn't stiffen under his touch, thank God. She let him sink into her, keeping her chin tipped up so their foreheads could stay pressed together.

Her lips were so close he could kiss her. He could *claim* her. Taste her like he did in the library. Nothing sweeter. Such a forbidden fruit.

But that's not what he needed from her now. Surprising himself, he pulled her from the wall, wrapping his arms around her shoulders, tucking her head under his chin. She didn't hesitate, bringing her arms around his waist. He couldn't remember the last time he held someone or let himself be held.

"I can't sleep," he murmured into her hair. She stilled but didn't pull away.

"It's been going on for months," he added. "I'm . . . I think it could drive me quite mad if I don't . . . if I can't fix it."

"Have you seen a doctor?" she asked, her voice muffled by his cravat.

He nodded. "Three."

"And?"

He relaxed his hold on her. "They've all prescribed various tonics and curatives. But each one makes me groggier than the last. It's not so much a sleep they induce, but a sleep-like death. They leave me miserable. I'm done with them."

She broke their embrace, shifting away. He let his hands fall to his sides, even though he wasn't ready to let her go. She surprised him when she raised her hands to his shoulders. Slowly, she kneaded the muscles there, her grip gentle but firm. It was muted through the layers of his bulky coat and waistcoat, but it still felt good. He groaned, eyes closing.

"Atlas holds up the sky as a punishment," she murmured. "It is not a noble act, James. It is a torture. Why do you choose to bear so much alone?"

He opened his eyes to meet her worried gaze. "There is no one else," he said with a shrug.

Her hands stilled, then dropped away. "You're wrong. If you would but open your eyes, you'd see that you are surrounded by people who think the world of you, people who would help you if you'd only let them."

He gave her a weak smile, feeling his walls rebuilding now that he lacked her touch. "I don't know how to let others help me. It's not in my nature."

She returned his smile. "I know. We are very similar in that respect. I too struggle to let others in. 'Infuriating,' I think you called me."

"I'm sorry. It's not you—"

"Don't apologize," she said with a laugh. "I *am* infuriating. And distant and judgmental, selfish. And I'm not a very good Christian most days . . . or a very good lady. I am neither chaste nor demure. Come to think of it, I might just be your nightmare."

Her smile was intoxicating.

"Well, you'll have to be my *waking* nightmare, for I never sleep," he added, making them both grin.

"I'm sorry," she muttered. "I doubt very much that I'm helping . . ."

James breathed a deep sigh. "No—it—I feel better," he replied, surprised to actually mean the words.

Her smile brightened her face. "Good."

Before either of them could say another word, the gong rang out. She jumped, head spinning towards the sound. Then she looked at him, already resigned to what was coming next.

"Miss Harrow," he said with a nod. He left her there, feeling her eyes as she watched him walk away.

17

Rosalie

SOMEHOW, ROSALIE FOUND her way back to her room and managed to change for dinner. She was lost in the moment of her encounter with James, replaying their conversation in her mind. Each time she thought she understood who he was and what he wanted from her, he changed his behavior. It was maddening.

At first, she had been certain she was merely a nuisance. As the weeks at Alcott wore on, she distracted him by nature of being hopelessly unsuitable. By the night of the ball, it became clear his interest was not entirely chaste. She still felt the heat of his kisses on her lips. But the carriage ride to London confirmed her suspicions: James had no interest in romance. For him, this was purely physical—he wanted her scent, her touch. No emotions. No friendship. He asked her to respect his boundaries, and she knew it was the right course of action for them both.

But heavens if she didn't dream about it . . .

Just last night, she'd fallen asleep between Burke and Renley, dreaming of a world where she might have James too.

A world where he could love her and let himself be loved. She wanted to imagine a man like James Corbin could want her. That she could be enough. But in the harsh light of morning, those dreams were gone, faded away with the dew. James remained cold and distant, wholly uninterested. Who was he to be upset that she did as he asked and remained distant in return?

But then they had to meet on the stairs. Here was a different James entirely. A vulnerable James. A James with worries and cares he was willing to confide. He was leaning on her. Literally.

The man is infuriating!

Well, Rosalie would not be standing around waiting for him to decide whether he wanted her. She had entirely too much on her plate to fathom wasting another moment on sussing out James Corbin and his mercurial personality. She was going to live her life on her terms, and if he chose to be part of it, he must be the one to bend to her.

She shimmied herself into one of the new evening gowns—a dusky pink design with a pleated skirt and lace accents at the bust and sleeves. Just one more way James was determined to drive her mad: dressing her like his own little doll. She should throw all the clothes in the lake!

But that would leave her with nothing suitable to wear . . . Sighing, she fastened the dress in the front and added the three-strand pearl necklace. It was a bit formal, but wearing nothing looked just as strange. She wore the diamond clasp to the back, which helped to lessen the grandeur of the look ever so slightly. With a nod to her reflection in the mirror and a calming breath, she went in search of the gentlemen causing her such trouble.

Rosalie didn't make it past the entry hall before she found them all together. Burke and James were both dressed in sleek black coattails, crisp white waistcoats and cravats, and sharply tailored pants. Their shoes were polished to shine and Burke looked like he may even have a bit of pomade slicking back his hair.

Renley stood to the side, saying something low to Burke as the butler handed off an evening coat, top hat, and gloves to James. A footman quickly did the same for Burke.

"Good evening, Miss Harrow," called the butler in that gravelly voice.

She paused on the stairs, one hand on the rail, as three sets of eyes turned towards her. "I forgot you would be out this evening," she said in greeting. It was true. In the rush and bustle of the day, it had completely slipped her mind that they were making the rounds at the gentlemen's clubs tonight.

"We were just heading out," said Burke, stepping over quickly and offering a hand. She took it with a smile, letting him escort her down the last few steps that were now completely clear of the broken vase. He led her over to the others.

She glanced at Renley, who was still dressed in his riding attire from the morning. "Are you not joining them?"

He shrugged. "I'm not a member at White's or Brooks'. I leave the politics to these two."

"I'm only a member because *he* forced them to let me in," Burke added, shooting James a glare.

"The coffee at White's is superb," James replied, donning his hat.

Burke laughed. "True enough. You know I will consent to

nearly anything for a good cup of coffee . . . including a tortuous night spent drinking and smoking with men I despise. Dandies, the lot of them."

"Surely the aristocracy are not all bad," James muttered.

"I've long made an exception for you, but even you have your moments," Burke replied, donning his own hat.

James narrowed his eyes. "Good to know you tolerate me . . . since I pay all your bills and shelter you and clothe you and feed you and—"

"Enough." Burke elbowed him. "You've made your point. Lead on, oh magnanimous one."

James turned to the butler. "We will probably be out late."

"Very good, my lord," replied Wilson.

Burke nudged Rosalie. "Don't get into any trouble while we're away, eh? A sensible dinner, a quiet night spent reading by the fire, and in bed by nine o'clock."

She laughed softly. "Are you listing my itinerary, or what you'd rather be doing, sir?"

He smirked. "Both." He turned to Renley. "Keep her entertained 'til we get back?"

Renley glanced down at her, his mouth splitting into a grin. "We shall recite from Fordyce's sermons, cozy by the fire."

Burke looked around, noting the position of the butler at James' side and the pair of footmen by the doors. He stepped a little closer to Rosalie, lowering his voice. "I'm not kissing you farewell because the footmen have loose lips . . . but know that I want to . . . and I fully intend to make up for it later."

She inched away from him, giving him her best siren's smile. "Only if I let you."

A muscle in his jaw twitched as his grey eyes narrowed. "Temptress," he muttered.

"Go now, sir. Get yourself unengaged as quickly as possible."

"Christ, I'd quite forgotten the whole purpose of this charade. Now I'm even more miserable." He turned away, shrugging on his overcoat. "Come on, James. Let's get this bloody over with."

The footmen and butler followed James and Burke outside, leaving Rosalie standing alone with Renley.

"You need not bother changing for dinner if it is just we two," she said. "We could ask for trays in the library."

He turned to her with a smile. "I have a better idea. What if we dispense with dinner altogether? You run up and get changed, and we'll take to the park for a sunset ride."

Rosalie pursed her lips. "That is the opposite of Burke's itinerary."

Leaning in, Renley grinned like an imp as he murmured, "And you desperately want to say 'yes.'"

She bit her lip, fighting her smile. "Of course, I do. Give me ten minutes?"

Renley's laugh followed her up the stairs.

18

Burke

BURKE FOLLOWED BEHIND James into White's, nodding to the man who took their hats and coats. James had been downright surly in the coach, muttering under his breath and looking distractedly out the window. If they weren't in such dire straits, Burke might suggest they pack their bags tonight and take off for the continent. It wouldn't be the first time he used a trip to Greece to clear James of a bad mood.

But their collective straits had perhaps never been more dire. Between needing to guarantee George *did* get married . . . and maneuvering it so Burke assuredly did *not* get married, James and Burke had their hands full. There would be no sailing off for Greece until this was all sorted.

Burke had no doubt it *would* get sorted. And when it did, they would *all* sail away. Rosalie and Tom too. Burke had no doubts about them either. He knew exactly where he wanted Rosalie, which was between them all.

He stretched out his long legs to keep up with James as they climbed the main stairs, heading for the upper suites.

"This is ridiculous," James muttered for the fifth time.

"This will never work." He paused his steps, turning on his heel to stare daggers at Burke. "Why are we letting her talk us into this? Utter madness."

Burke laughed, glancing over James' shoulder towards the set of double doors that led into the cards room. He could hear the low rumble of conversation. He stepped forward and adjusted the knot of James' cravat. "Firstly, I shall tell you what you are constantly telling me . . ." He grabbed James by the shoulders and held his gaze. "Don't be defeatist."

James rolled his eyes, slapping Burke's hands away.

"And secondly," Burke added with a grin, "You know as well as I that the goddess that has fallen from the heavens into our lives could talk us into doing anything if it earned us so much as a look or a smile. Anything, James." He leaned in, eyes flashing. "*Anything*."

"Don't." James gave him a shove.

Burke just laughed. "Go on, then, tell me what happened."

James' eyes darted down as he attempted to turn away. "I don't know what you mean."

Burke snatched him by the shoulder. "I mean you and Rosalie. Something happened today. I know when you've had words with her because you get all . . . fidgety."

James jerked free, giving his waistcoat a sharp tug. "I don't fidget."

Burke swallowed a laugh as he pointed at James' hands still on his waistcoat. "You quite literally *just* fidgeted. With your waistcoat. You do that thing . . . the James thing." He mimicked James adjusting his waistcoat and lapels.

James dropped his hands to his sides, balling them into fists. "I am not fidgeting!"

"Whenever she gets under your skin—"

"She is *not*—" He paused as Burke failed to conceal a snort. James took a slow breath, looking murderously at Burke before continuing at a quieter volume. "She is not under my skin."

"Fine," Burke replied. "Keep your secrets. I'll just ask her about it later. I'm sure her version of events will show you in a positive light—"

"Goddamn it, nothing happened, alright? We spoke in the stairwell earlier. It was—we didn't—it was fine. I was on my best behavior."

Burke raised a suspicious brow.

"Fine, I was mostly behaved," he muttered under his breath. "We have an agreement now. It's fine."

"Yes, clearly it must be fine," Burke mused. "After all, you said the word 'fine' three times in the same breath."

James cast him an annoyed look. "Don't be a pest."

"Fine." Burke raised his hands in mock surrender. "You say it is fine, and so it is. You're fine, I'm fine . . . it's all *fine.*" He paused, waiting for James to look his way. "What is it with the two of you and stairwells?"

James just shrugged, his lowered brows back to brooding. A very small part of Burke was jealous. Though he didn't quite understand in which direction the jealousy tended. Was he jealous of James and his time alone with Rosalie? Was he jealous that Rosalie could so easily unravel James? Or was he simply despondent at being left out while they shared another heated moment?

It was a new and wholly unexpected sensation to be so excited by the thought of Rosalie and James together. Burke was certainly no saint. He'd indulged a few times in a playful ménage but never with another man. Certainly, never with

James. Now he was sharing Rosalie with Tom and sleeping in the same bed. He found his mind full of thoughts of his friends with Rosalie in all sorts of scenarios that would have even a London madam blushing.

As much as Burke might want to make his dreams a reality, he had to tread lightly. He didn't want to scare any of them off. He gave James a disapproving look. "James Corbin, a lady's honor is at stake. Shall I post monitors on all the stairs?"

"Please don't," James replied, and too quickly. "I want to avoid any of the staff witnessing our arguments," he added, avoiding Burke's eye. He took another slow breath, squaring his shoulders. "The woman is infuriating. I honestly don't know what you see in her."

Burke just smiled. Oh, what a terrible liar James made. They were both mad about her, and with good reason. Rosalie was a beautiful, clever siren that made Burke weak in all the best ways. She was every dream he never knew he'd had, and hell was going to freeze over before he let her slip away. No amount of posturing from James was going to frighten her off or make Burke change his mind.

With each passing day, Burke began to understand that she wanted the same thing as he did: to see James happy. The moment James finally broke down and admitted his ultimate happiness could be found in her, Burke would celebrate with champagne and the ringing of bells. For now, he had to play along with their ludicrous plan of distancing from each other.

"Chin up, my lord," he said, slapping James on the back. "Remove her from the equation if she irritates you so. Besides, you're not doing this for Rosalie. You're doing it for me." At James' silence, Burke narrowed his eyes, annoyance churning once more in his gut. "You are doing it for *me*, yes?"

"Yes—"

Burke leaned in, lowering his voice to a threatening growl. "Because whatever else may be happening with Rosalie, I was here first, James. *Me*."

Frustration flashed in James eyes. "You don't think I know that?"

A muscle ticked in Burke's jaw. "I don't take kindly to being usurped. She is still owed a punishment for even trying it. And I mean to collect."

James blinked twice before letting out a gruff laugh. "Oh, I see. You're not mad that she up and left you behind the other night. You're mad that she left with *me*. She took your favorite toy and that upset you."

Burke grit his teeth. "Laugh if you want, magnanimous one, but you're both mine."

James' smile fell.

Good. Burke wanted him on edge. Resentment flowed both ways. He gave his friend a level look. "She doesn't get to threaten what you and I have. Just as I'll be damned before I let you get between her and I in any way other than carnal."

Was James blushing? He swallowed, looking suddenly unsure of himself. "Burke—"

"I see you, James," he pressed. "You can hide nothing from me."

"Don't I know it," he muttered.

Burke smirked, satisfied to hear his friend admit the truth. "And know this as well: I'm playing by your rules for now, letting you manage this on your own. God knows if I use a heavier hand, I'll only get bit for my trouble. But I'll not stand by and watch you pace each other in circles forever."

James' frown deepened. "Now who's the meddling one?"

Eyes flashing with devilish intent, Burke leaned in, his face inches from James. "I learned from the *master*."

The word settled between them with all the subtlety of a cannon blast. James sucked in a sharp breath, green eyes blowing wide. "Burke, I—"

"Close your mouth, James. You look like a fish," Burke said with a laugh. He gestured over James' shoulder towards the doors. "Now, shoulders back. Smooth, confident smile. You are Viscount Finchley, brother to the Duke of Norland.

"You command every room you enter. White's is no exception. Let's strut in there and bag ourselves a new beau for my gorgon bride."

James turned away, giving his waistcoat another sharp tug. Burke couldn't help but smile. He stepped forward, opening the door to the cards room. A chorus of greetings met their ears, mixed with the thick scent of cigar smoke.

"Finchley!"

"Good to see you, man!"

"Lord Finchley, come join us for the next round!"

Taking a deep breath, Burke followed James into the smoky room, preparing himself for a long night of political diatribes and pompous posturing. But James was right: At least the coffee here was divine.

19

Tom

"HE DIDN'T," ROSALIE cried, tears in her eyes as she choked on her laughter.

"Aye, he did," Tom replied, reining his mount to a walk. "Three days underway and he made us turn around for a bloody parrot. We arrive back in port, and there the damn thing was, perched on the shoulder of the dockmaster."

She laughed again, tipping her head back. "And was your captain relieved?"

"He paid the man a gold sovereign for his trouble, and we took right back to sea, parrot safely aboard."

"He must have been quite the animal," she mused.

"He was disgusting," Tom replied with a grimace. "Loud and mean, it only liked the captain. The damn thing bit me twice." He held up his gloved finger, sure he still had a scar on the tip.

They both laughed, giving their horses pats as the animals huffed. The weather was glorious, the heath was in its full autumnal glory, and Rosalie proved to have a more than adequate seat on a horse. For the past hour, they'd been racing over hills and through the weaving glen trails. In between bouts of galloping, they slowed to a walk and Tom shared stories from his travels.

Rosalie was curious but not pushy in her questions, letting Tom lead the conversation. He appreciated this, and it made him more willing to share. People were often enamored with the idea of navy life, but they weren't always tactful in the way they asked questions. Some sailors may like to talk about tense skirmishes or storms at sea—anything to excite their audience—but Tom had always preferred to keep those memories private.

What lady seated next to him at dinner really wanted to hear the truths held in his soul? Shall he admit to his fear in the moment of battle, the way his hands shook, the way he was sick after? Shall he detail the sounds etched in his memory—the boom echoing across the water, the blood-curdling screams of a man cleaved by cannon blast?

No, that was not polite conversation. And yet the ignorant few had the audacity to believe themselves entitled to his worst memories for the sake of a thrilling story hour.

"Renley, are you well?"

He blinked, turning his gaze on Rosalie. Her fashionable pink riding habit brought out the rosy color in her cheeks. A jaunty hat sat perched on her head, with a little veil that swept down over one eye. He cleared his throat. "Well and recovered," he replied, gathering his reins. "Shall we race beyond to the next hill?"

She glanced over her shoulder with a pained look. "It is getting darker now, and I believe a storm is coming in . . ."

Tom had noticed too. Heavy clouds were rolling in fast. It would certainly rain tonight. He should turn them around and get her safely back to the house before the heavens opened. But he wasn't ready to go back. He wasn't ready for this moment with her to end. Whenever they found themselves alone, it was like Tom could suddenly breathe easier.

He'd noticed it from that first morning at Alcott Hall when they met at the top of the stairs. He'd come upon her inspecting a vase of flowers. He could close his eyes and see her standing there. She turned with surprise, those brows arched high and her dark eyes wide. Her lips parted as she took him in, her eye tracing him from head to toe . . . then he exhaled.

That's what Rosalie Harrow was for him: a breath of fresh air.

As soon as the words were thought, he felt a tightening in his chest.

Goddamn it . . . James was right.

Tom was as bad as Burke. Worse. Two hopeless romantics pining after the same woman . . . a woman who defied convention. A woman who'd made it clear she wanted no ties to bind her. But this attraction he felt wasn't going away. There was no moving past it or ignoring it. In fact, each moment spent in her presence only sank the feeling deeper into his very bones.

Holding her last night, their naked skin pressed together. God, it was heavenly. He couldn't remember a night of better sleep. He wasn't jealous hearing her with Burke . . . well, maybe a little.

Fine, perhaps more than a little.

Okay, he was miserable. Aching all over. His cock had been so hard. It was torture to lie there and do nothing, hearing her soft moans through the closed door. His body had moved on its own, pulling him from his bed, drawing him across the hall into her arms. He hadn't been sure how his intrusion would be received, but he simply couldn't stay away. Then she'd kissed him with such warmth of feeling. She trusted him, wanted him, found comfort in his arms.

And he wanted more. Christ, he *needed* it. That moment in the storage room was seared in his memory. He wanted another taste of her; he wanted all of her. And he wanted to see that look on her face—the calm adoration that told him without words that she breathed easier in his arms too.

He looked away from her, fumbling again with his reins. Anything to keep himself from saying or doing something they'd both regret. For, as much as he felt ready to declare himself, she'd been clear from the beginning.

Be my friend, she said. *Be my friend . . . or nothing.*

He grimaced. The word "friend" tasted like bile in his mouth. When he thought of her soft kisses, the sweep of her hands over his bare shoulders, the taste of her on his tongue . . .

Friends, indeed.

It was his own fault. All his nonsense with Marianne clouded the air between them. Rosalie may be attracted to him, but she didn't trust him. She wasn't ready to believe him when he said Marianne meant nothing. And could Tom blame her? What had he done to convince her otherwise? Most of their private conversations over the last month had centered on her offering him advice about Marianne.

He had to right this ship. He had to find a way to convince Rosalie that Marianne was in the past. Even more important, he had to explain his changing goals for the future. She still thought he was committed to the ludicrous idea of marrying solely to advance his career. Tom wanted to make captain, but he wanted to do it on his terms. There would be no marriages of convenience.

"Shall we turn back?" Rosalie called, already turning her mount around.

Tom took a deep breath, trying to find the words to begin. "Rose, I—"

"Race you towards the tree line," she called with a laugh, urging her little chestnut mare into a canter.

Thunder rumbled softly in the distance as the storm clouds rolled in. Tom's mount danced in place, eager to join the race. Tom squeezed with his heels and the horse took off, tearing over the grass on pounding hooves, chasing after that blur of laughing pink.

They didn't make it two hundred yards before the heavens opened. Rosalie let out a soft squeal as the first drops fell. In moments, they were both wet, urging their mounts towards the head of a forest trail that wove along the edge of the heath. The back gardens of Corbin House were still a good fifteen minutes away. Tom kicked himself for having let them ride out so far.

"I'm soaked through," she cried, slowing her mount to a trot as they neared the trees.

"I'm so sorry, Rose," he called over the rain, his mount coming level with hers.

She turned with a wide grin on her face. It lit her up from the inside, making his own chest feel warm. She was soaking wet, but she was happy. She was laughing and free. He would probably earn a mouthful from Mrs. Robbins when they returned, but he didn't care. It was worth it to see this smile.

A crack of lightning split the sky and Rosalie's horse shied. She settled the little mare with a few soothing words. "It's really coming down," she called over her shoulder, a hint of anxiety in her tone.

"Swing left!" Tom knew this heath well and knew where they might find shelter.

Coming to a fork in the path, Rosalie urged her horse left. The path was wide enough that there was little coverage from the trees overhead to soften the rain. It pounded down on Tom's head and shoulders, water dripping off his hat brim. In front of him, Rosalie's bright pink skirts were now almost purple with the combination of the dampness.

They rode a few more minutes down the path until Tom spied his quarry. "Let's take cover and wait for the worst of this to pass," he called, reining his horse even with hers to point out the small Grecian temple tucked into the trees. It was a simple thing, hardly more than a garden ornament, but it was large enough to fit them both.

She nodded, angling her mount towards it.

He swung out of his saddle first, boots squelching in the wet grass as he looped his reins in his arms and stomped over to Rosalie, offering up both hands. "Hop down."

She unhooked her leg from the sidesaddle and dropped down at his side.

"Give me your reins and run for cover," he said with a laugh, taking hold of the chestnut mare.

Rosalie didn't wait to be told twice before spinning on her heel and running for safety as another fork of lightning sparked in the sky.

20

Rosalie

ROSALIE'S BREATH CAME in sharp pants as she jogged up the three stone steps, slipping on the wet stone. She wrapped a bracing arm around a column to steady herself. Her heavy skirts dragged behind her as she stepped fully under the shelter.

She took a quick look around her new sanctuary. It was a monopteros with eight slender columns and a domed ceiling. She took two steps forward, inspecting the central statue posed on a plinth. It was some kind of maiden or goddess with her arms outstretched, her body contorted in an odd dancing pose. It was neither sophisticated nor handsomely carved.

Rosalie laughed aloud. She had a sudden image of some young gentleman with more inspiration than talent feverishly sculpting alone in a studio, ruining the proportions of the maiden's limbs with a heavy-handed chisel.

"Bloody hell, it's raining like anything," came Renley's deep voice.

She tore her gaze from the statue, watching him dash up

the stairs. Like her, he slid at the top, his eyes going wide as he threw out both arms to balance himself. She stifled a giggle as he met her gaze and let out his own laugh.

Moving past her, he took off his hat and popped it on the stone nymph's upturned hand. Then he peeled off his wet leather gloves and dragged both hands through his dripping curls. "I'm so sorry about all this," he said.

"It's not your fault," she replied, still feeling breathless. "This will soon pass. Then we'll head home before Mrs. Robbins sends out a search party."

She turned away, pulling the few pins out of her hair that secured her hat. She hung it over the stone maiden's other hand. Renley watched her every move. She smiled, patting her damp curls with a self-conscious hand. "You keep catching me in the rain, sir."

His gaze heated, those beautiful blue eyes darkening, and she realized it was the wrong thing to say. For now, they were standing mere feet apart, thinking about the *last* time they were left unchaperoned in a thunderstorm.

He closed the space between them, and Rosalie felt suddenly nervous. She fought the urge to laugh again. It was ludicrous. Hadn't she slept naked in his arms last night?

"Rose," he said on a sigh, his face lowering towards hers.

She sucked in a breath and leaned away, breaking their trance. "What happened with Marianne?" As soon as the words were out of her mouth, she wanted them unsaid. She vowed to herself she'd not ask. His life was his own.

But Renley looked almost relieved. "Nothing," he said, taking a step closer. "Nothing happened, I swear to you. I escorted her home. She told me what she said to you, and we argued. We are most assuredly *not* engaged."

Rosalie wrapped her arms around herself, feeling the chill of her wet clothes sinking into her skin. "Why would she tell me such a lie? What did she hope to gain?"

Renley leaned against the column to match her stance, with his arms crossed over his broad chest. "I think she saw us dancing at the ball. In fact, I know she did. I believe it made her jealous."

Rosalie blinked. "But you danced with many ladies at the ball. Elizabeth and Blanche, even Madeline twice. Did she tell all your dance partners of her prior claim?"

"No," he muttered. "Just you."

"Why only me?"

He shrugged, one eye watching the storm as a fork of lightning twisted across the darkening sky. "Because she knows you're different from the others."

"Different?" Her mind suddenly filled with images of the other young ladies—the grace of their dancing, the practiced flutter of their fans, the superior cut and color of their gowns. Rosalie's dress for the occasion had at least been new, but it was not the same kind of dramatic, beaded affair worn by Lady Olivia, or even Blanche.

"What did I do wrong?" she whispered. "What gave me away as being so different?"

He blinked, pulling his eye from watching the storm. "What? No." He pushed off from the column with his booted foot, crossing over to her. "You're not different. You're . . . God, you're perfect. I should have said it was *I* who was different." He raised both hands to cup her face. "Whatever this is, this feeling of being moored to you . . . apparently, I'm not hiding it very well."

His thumbs brushed along her jaw, and she fought the

urge to close her eyes. Her heart thundered in her chest to match the storm. "Renley—"

"Marianne has known me a long time," he went on. "No doubt she saw how I looked at you all night."

"And how were you looking at me?"

His mouth quirked into a smile as he brushed a calloused thumb over her parted lips. "The same as I am now . . . like you're the only one I see."

Her breath caught in her throat. "You flatter me, sir."

"No," he replied. "I'm no good at flattery. I speak only the truth. You captivate me, Rose. You have from the first night you stumbled into Alcott, half-dipped in mud with your hair all wild like a forest fairy." He smiled, tucking a damp curl behind her ear. "You have that same look now, you know—cheeks flushed, eyes fierce. The spirit in you calls out to me. I can't look away. I never want to look away from you."

Blinking back tears, Rosalie raised both her hands and covered his, giving them a gentle squeeze. "Renley, please—"

"You keep doing that," he said with a frown.

"Doing what?"

"Calling me 'Renley' instead of my name. It's a shield you like to use. You're keeping me at arm's length—"

"Oh, what is it with you men and your names?" She tugged herself free and paced away three steps. She couldn't breathe if she stayed standing so close. "You know, it does not signify. Plenty of married couples go their whole lives referring to each other only by their titles."

"It signifies with you," he replied, reading her like an open book.

She crossed her arms over her chest. "Why must you all press for such intimacy?"

He raised a brow. "Who else is pressing?"

"I didn't ask for *any* of this," she cried, ignoring his question. "Three weeks ago, I arrived at Alcott expecting to meet a woman who was once my mother's friend. That is *all*. And now I find myself so out of balance." She couldn't think of another way to explain it. "I'm so afraid I'll make a mistake. I know what you want, and I cannot give it to you. I can't—I don't know how to be what any of you want—"

He crossed the three feet separating them in a stride, his hands reaching for her face as he pulled her in close and kissed her deep. His tongue flicked lightly against her bottom lip as he pulled away. "You're fighting me," he said on a breath. "Fighting what you feel for me. I know you've been burned before. You've been hurt. God—" He groaned, his hands tightening as he leaned in, touching his forehead to hers. "Thinking of it, picturing it . . . you have no idea what it does to me. I would tear your demons limb from limb."

Hot tears pricked her eyes as she fought to contain her roiling emotions. "My ghosts are not your burden. I'm stronger than I look."

He met her gaze again. "Don't I know it. You protect your heart at all costs, as you should. You have it wrapped in bands of iron. Rosalie, you say you can't be what I want, and I say you're wrong."

She leaned her face into his hand. "We've talked about this and we—we want different things. Even setting Marianne aside—"

"And *is* she set aside?" He bent at the knees so he could look evenly in her eyes, his hands holding firm to her face. "Do you believe me when I say it's over? Do you believe she means nothing to me?"

"I want to," she admitted, her voice little more than a whisper.

"Then *do*," he pleaded. "You keep saying we must take you at your word, so take me at mine. I don't want Marianne Young. Just as I don't want to marry some society debutant with a reticule full of diamonds and a head full of bonnet ribbons."

"Then what do you want?"

"I want *you*."

Her heart stopped, breath in her throat. "Renley—"

His gaze softened, his thumb brushing her cheek. "You're a rare and wild thing, Rosalie Harrow. You let people think you're this little canary in a cage. I think sometimes you play the part so well, you even start to believe it. But I *see* you."

He lowered his hand, splaying it gently over her heart. She glanced down, watching as his hand rose and fell with each exhale. "You are not a frail, wounded bird," he whispered. "You are a phoenix, just waiting to burn bright. And I mean to be close enough to feel your every flame."

She struggled to keep the tears from falling. Why did he always know exactly what to say? "You would have me be free of all cages? You would accept me as I am?"

His smile fell as his eyes flashed with resolve. "The man who dares to change you will answer to me."

One moment they were standing inches apart. The next, she was in his arms, fighting him for dominance in a fierce kiss. She wrapped her arms around his shoulders, rising up on her toes to reach his perfect, soft lips. He groaned into the kiss, one arm around her waist while the other dug into her dark curls.

She opened herself to him, teasing him with tongue and teeth. The kisses sank deep. She felt the fire burning through her, chasing away the chill of the rain. He trailed kisses along her jaw to her ear. She fisted her hands in his damp curls. Renley sighed with pleasure as she gave a sharp tug, pulling his head back. Their gaze met as they both panted for breath.

The words on the tip of her tongue came spilling out. "I won't give up Burke."

A long moment of silence stretched between them, broken only by the pattering rain. "I would never ask it of you," he said at last. His breath was ragged as he added in almost a growl, "I want Burke right where he is."

He went to kiss her again, but she pulled back, heart in her throat. "Wait—what—can you mean it?" She narrowed her eyes, searching his face, one hand cupping his strong jaw. He held her gaze, his blue eyes blown black with desire.

He looked dangerous. Wholly unlike her laughing, kind friend. This was a man of deep passion. A man starving with need. "I say I want him where he is," he growled, nipping at her chin, his breath hot against her skin. "Between us, behind us, under us. I like to share, and I like to be shared."

Rosalie gasped, her body humming at the idea. "Renley—"

His voice lowered, a gravelly rasp in her ear. "I've wanted you from the moment I met you, Rose . . . but I've wanted Burke since I knew what it meant to want. He stays."

The finality in his tone had her whimpering with need. He plunged in for another heady kiss and they shuffled backwards, seeking something to brace against. As they moved, Rosalie snagged her heel on her sodden skirts and took a stumbling step.

"*Ouch.*" Her eyes shot open. The stone hand of the dancing nymph stabbed her between the shoulders. She arched her back, pressing into Renley to escape the sudden pain.

But Renley was off balance too. She shrieked, squirming away as his weight pressed her harder against the stony hand. Suddenly, the statue rocked, tipping off its plinth. It fell to the ground with an echoing crash.

They both took in a shaky breath, meeting each other's eye before they burst out laughing. Rosalie peered over the plinth, inspecting the damage. One arm of the statue was shattered into pieces and the body was cracked.

"Oh no—we broke it!"

Renley tipped his head to the side, eyes narrowed. "Hmm, is it just me, or does she look better this way?"

Rosalie slapped his chest with a laugh. "What are we going to do? Should we try to lift it back up?"

"Of course not," he replied, nudging the statue with his toe. "What kind of shoddy craftsman doesn't bolt it down? I say they wanted this to happen. We've done her a favor."

"You're impossible," she replied with another laugh.

He turned her to face him, his smile turning devilish. "I am merely enterprising. One goddess shall fall, so another may rise." He gripped her by the hips, lifting her onto the plinth and stepping between her legs.

He nuzzled her neck, kissing her once, twice, his teeth nibbling her ear. She hated herself for her next words. "Renley, the rain has eased."

His body went still, his face still buried in her neck. "A gentleman would stop, I suppose. A gentleman would see you safely home before they send out that search party."

She brushed her fingers through his damp curls. "Undoubtedly. But what would a sailor do?"

He lifted his head off her shoulder. "Do not tempt me to elaborate. It is not for a lady's ears."

His full meaning sent a shiver over her skin. But the low rumblings of thunder told her this was only a temporary hold on the storm. She sighed with resignation. "I think Renley the gentleman should take me home now."

He nodded, pulling away.

She halted him with a finger under his chin, placing a last soft kiss on his lips. "But know this, sir. I tremble with anticipation, eager to meet the sailor caged within."

21

Rosalie

THEY ARRIVED BACK AT Corbin House just as the heavens opened again. Dismounting in the stable yard, they found Mrs. Robbins clucking like a furious mother hen. She roundly reproached Renley for threatening a young lady's health, dragging Rosalie under the safety of her large umbrella with a strong arm. Renley acted appropriately contrite, standing in the rain to receive his admonishment.

With a final cluck, Mrs. Robbins took Rosalie under her wing and dragged her straight up the stairs, plopping her into a bath. Rosalie didn't complain. The steaming hot water felt divine. She soaked for almost an hour while Fanny helped her wash her hair again, using the same French hair oil that smelled thickly of roses.

In no time, she was wrapped in a dry chemise and her soft blue dressing robe. Her dark hair was braided, with the long plait draped over her shoulder. Mrs. Robbins perched her on the sofa in her bedroom before a roaring fire, a cup of hot chocolate clutched in her hands. She curled her legs under herself, letting the warmth of the fire heat her cheeks.

A tray sat on the table beside her with the remnants of an evening meal—thin-sliced beef on bread with a wedge of delicious cheese, leek soup with dill and a dollop of cream, and the crumbs of a ginger biscuit that she dipped into her cocoa.

She was nodding off when she heard low voices in the hall. The door to Burke's room opened and closed. She watched their shared door, imagining him on the other side with his valet. The soft voices continued until there was the sound of a closing door. A few minutes passed before she heard a soft knock.

"Enter," she called.

Burke stepped into the room wearing a patterned red silk robe over his bare chest. The swirl of his dark chest hair was visible in the plunging "V." He padded silently across the floor on bare feet. "You're still awake," he murmured, sinking onto the sofa and dropping his head into her lap.

She shifted slightly, setting her cup of cocoa aside. "And you are very late, sir."

He just grunted, reaching for her hand. He brought it to his lips, kissing her palm.

She dropped her other hand to his inky black hair, stroking it back with her fingers. "How did it go?"

"Awful," he muttered. "Morrow and Barbridge are off the list. We convinced Royce to come to the dinner on Friday."

She paused her hand. "Two off the list?"

He nodded, kissing her palm again. "Morrow is engaged to some French heiress. They're rushing a wedding by the end of this month. I think she might be in a family way already," he added, shifting to get comfortable.

It was a shame to lose such an eligible bachelor from the list, but Rosalie was glad to know. They had no time to waste. "And Barbridge?"

Burke wasn't listening. He turned her hand over with both of his as he kissed down her arm, pausing on the soft flesh of her inner wrist. He breathed against her skin before licking the pulse point. The feel of his warm tongue sent a jolt of fire through her body.

"Burke . . ." She tried to pull her hand away.

He held tighter, nipping the soft skin with his teeth until she hissed. She gripped his hair with her free hand and gave a little tug. He gentled, peppering soft kisses up her arm as he pulled her down over him. "Kiss me," he whispered. "End my agony."

She pursed her lips in a smile. "Are you in agony? You don't look it, I must say."

"I just survived five hours in a stuffy gentlemen's club," he whined. "I was forced to play hazard until James' pockets were empty. And I had to listen to not one, not two, but *seven* lords recount in excruciating detail the bountiful success of their harvests. Shall I tell you all of Lord Tarley's new milling machine?"

"Please spare me," she replied.

He wrapped his fist around her braid and pulled her down. "If I cannot be spared, neither can you. Now, kiss me like you mean it, or I shall recount every last syllable of his boring report."

She gave him a steely look. "First tell me what happened with Callum Barbridge."

He relaxed his hold on her. "His family wealth is utterly spent. The family must retrench. They've already vacated Glenrose Park. Poor Cal said if they can't turn it around, they'll likely lose the London house as well."

Retrenchment was common, unfortunately. Lords often lived outside their means, ruining their families and their estates at the gaming tables, or betting on risky speculations and losing it all. She might feel sorrier for Lord Barbridge if she knew the man . . . she certainly felt for poor Lady Barbridge.

"Are those the only three you met?"

"Yes, but James put out an alert at White's and Brooks' to send him word if and when others appear," he explained. "Between that and the invitations for the engagement party, we should wrangle several more eligible bachelors."

"Good," she murmured, giving his hair another stroke.

He glanced up at her, his grey eyes dancing with intensity in the firelight. "So, are you going to tell me about your evening ride with Tom through a perilous thunderstorm?"

She stilled. "Mrs. Robbins told you, then."

"Oh yes, she had much to say on the matter," he replied, shifting off her lap to sit up. He turned to face her, one arm slung across the back of the sofa, which opened the "V" in his robe even wider.

"Eyes up here, love," he said with a smirk, tipping her chin up with his finger.

She didn't bother blushing. The energy he radiated was unmistakable. She knew exactly what he wanted. She also knew what *she* wanted, what she'd been aching for since she'd first gotten a taste.

He brushed his fingers along her neck. "Did you have a nice time with Tom?" He was fishing, and they both knew it.

"Not as nice as it could have been," she replied, closing her eyes as his fingers trailed down, stopping just above the tie of her chemise.

He tugged her robe open so he could place a kiss on her exposed collarbone. Then he flicked her braid over her shoulder, repeating the kiss on the other side. "What happened?"

She arched into him, turning her face away to expose more of her neck. "We were interrupted."

His hand worked the knot of her robe as he kissed her chest. "Interrupted?"

"Yes," she breathed, raising both hands to rest on his shoulders. "A statue fell."

He tugged the robe off her shoulders, sliding a hand inside her chemise to cup her breast. "Falling statues," he murmured, kissing the swell of her breast. "Sounds dangerous."

Heavens, but this man knew exactly how to stoke her fires. She ran both hands through his hair, holding him to her as he lowered his mouth, teasing her nipple through the thin fabric of her chemise. "She was pushed—*ah*—"

He looked up at her with those hooded, stormy eyes. "And if no statues were pushed? What might have happened then?" He used both hands to loosen the chemise, giving it a gentle tug until it slid down her arms, exposing her breasts to the chill of the room.

She loved the way he looked at her, feeling his eyes on her. To be the object of his desire was intoxicating. She glanced down, following his heated gaze. Her skin glowed in the firelight as he took a breast in each of his hands, giving them a gentle squeeze. She arched into him, relishing the exquisite jolt that traveled from the tips of her nipples straight to her core.

"You didn't answer me, love," he murmured. "If no statues were pushed?"

"Burke . . ."

He glanced up, his thumbs still rubbing circles against her soft skin. He raised one of his dark brows in silent question.

"I want him."

The words settled between them. The fire crackled, casting golden light dancing across both their faces.

His jaw hardened slightly as his eyes narrowed. "Don't say it if you don't mean it."

"I want him," she repeated, trying to keep the trembling from her voice. "I'm aching with want of him. Burke, I need it. Need you both."

He released a slow exhale, dropping his hands away. "There is no going back from this. If I leave this room . . . if we do this . . ."

"I know," she whispered, brushing her fingers over his lips.

He leaned forward and claimed her mouth in a fierce kiss. Their tongues flicked together as they both moaned. She slipped her hands inside his robe to run her fingers over the bare skin of his chest and shoulders.

"Burke," she whined. "Please, I need him here with us—"

Burke pulled back, turning away from her. "I'm so goddamn hard." He dragged his hands through his hair. "I need a minute." He balanced his head in his hands, elbows on his knees, taking a shaky breath.

She put a hand on his shoulder, and he tensed, sucking in another breath. He was barely holding himself together. She let her hand drop away. After a minute he stood, drawing her up with him.

Burke's eyes flashed. "Do not break his heart," he muttered, leaving his unspoken threat hanging in the air.

She held his gaze, chin lifted in defiance. "Do not break mine."

With a nod, he turned and left through their joint doorway.

Sinking back to the sofa, one hand clutched over her chest, Rosalie could do nothing but wait.

22

Rosalie

BURKE'S DOOR RATTLED and Rosalie stiffened, glancing over her shoulder. From her spot on the sofa, she could see through into his room. Renley stepped inside first, followed quickly by Burke. Her breath caught when she noted that Renley was shirtless. He looked once around the room before spotting the open door. Then his eye settled on Rosalie. He glanced at Burke. "What are you—"

"I lied," Burke said, clapping him on the shoulder. "Go to her. She's waiting for you."

She'd come too far to doubt herself now. She stood, extending a hand to him, and said the only words that made sense. "Tom . . . please."

Calling him by name snapped his restraint. As he strode into her room, she tugged on her chemise, dropping it from her shoulders. It swished to the floor, leaving her naked. He was on her in a few strides, his mouth colliding with hers in a hungry kiss. She sighed into it, feeling the press of his bare chest against hers.

His hands were in her hair, on her shoulders, then grazing

down her sides as he bent her backwards with the force of his kiss. She gasped for breath as his rough hands slid over her backside. Renley lifted her clean off her feet, hooking her legs around his hips. She clung to him as he brought her over to the wall, pressing her against it. She licked and teased, matching his eagerness. She could taste the sweet notes of brandy on his tongue. He held tight to her bare thighs, grinding against her until she felt ready to come apart.

"I want you," she panted. "Make me yours, Tom."

"Never to wake," he said against her lips. "God, never—"

"Put her on the bed," came Burke's deep voice.

She gasped as Renley's hold on her tightened, then he was walking. He set her down on the edge of the four-poster, dropping to his knees between her legs.

"Lie back," he murmured.

She let herself sink backwards onto the soft mattress. "Give Burke your hands," he directed.

Burke took her wrists and stretched her arms up over her head, pinning them to the bed. His face loomed over hers. "Do you trust us, love?"

Her chest rose and fell with each breath as she held his gaze. Renley's hands were on her thighs, his breath warm between her legs. The sensation raised gooseflesh down her arms. "Yes."

Burke smiled, kissing her forehead. "We are going to cherish you, Rosalie. Give us your body, and we will make it our temple."

"It's yours," she said on a breath. "Take it—*ah*—"

Renley began to tease her. He sucked and played, driving her wild. Burke swallowed her cries with his mouth as Renley pressed two fingers inside her, then he devoured her, humming his pleasure at her every sound. But each time she started to clench around his fingers, he pulled out, leaving her panting and desperate for more.

Burke watched, keeping her hands pinned. "He's teasing you, love. He knows what you want. I think he expects you to beg for it."

She whined, feeling herself coiling tighter. "Please—"

"You are so beautiful like this," he murmured. "Look at how he pleases you."

Renley continued his caresses. She could feel the smile on his lips as he listened to Burke's words. With another teasing lick, she spiraled higher.

"He is on his knees," Burke went on. "Don't ask for his permission. Take control. My sweet siren bows to no one." With those words, he let her go.

On instinct she curled forward, digging her hands into Renley's hair. He groaned as she pressed forward with her hips, riding his face. His fingers dug into her thighs as he pulled her closer. Her pleasure escaped her in a low moan. Shaking like a leaf, she collapsed on the bed.

Renley sat back on his heels, wiping his mouth with a confident smile. Behind her, Burke shed his robe. He stood naked in the firelight, the lean muscles of his body tense. He stretched out on the bed, reaching for her. "Come here, little siren."

Her heart raced at the look of want in his stormy eyes. Still feeling boneless, she crawled up the bed and into his arms. He kissed her, his hardness pressing into her hip. She melted into him.

The bed dipped as Renley laid down behind her. He was naked now too, curling into her with a hand on her thigh. He brushed kisses over her shoulder.

Burke broke their kiss. "Face Tom, love."

She turned and he pulled her hips flush with his, his cock nestled tight against her. Renley wasted no time claiming her lips again. She could taste herself on his tongue. It made her ravenous.

"So beautiful," he murmured. Taking her hand in his, he put it flat on his chest. "Touch me, Rose."

Her hands did their best to memorize the shape and location of each of his tattoos. She traced the anchor with her fingers, the cross, the ship in full sail at his shoulder. He pressed in with his hips as her other hand wrapped around his cock. She smiled, feeling it pulse in her hand.

Burke scooted closer, his hand smoothing over the curve of her backside. "Rosalie . . . have you ever been taken here?"

Her breath caught as she broke her kiss with Renley. "No. Never."

Burke leaned closer. "Imagine it, love. You could have us both. Would you like that?"

She took a shaky breath. "Will it hurt?"

"Pressure more than pain," Renley murmured, kissing her lips, her chin. "And only at first. Then it's only pleasure."

Rosalie felt safe with them in a way no other man had ever made her feel safe. Slowly, she nodded. "I want you both," she breathed. "Tell me what to do."

Both men groaned with anticipation.

Burke's voice was like warm honey in her ear. "First, I want to watch you ride Tom's cock. Would you like that?"

Her heart raced at the look of desire mirrored in Renley's eyes. "Yes," she whispered.

"Then our sweet siren will cry out our names as we claim

you together," Burke said, knowing exactly what his words were doing to them. "Do you want that?"

"Yes," she repeated, eyes still on Renley. She was shaking with need. "Tom, I want you. Please, make love to me. I want to feel you everywhere. *Please—*"

"Enough." Rolling onto his back, he dragged her with him. "Come here, sweet goddess. Need to feel that perfect, sweet cunt." He helped position her over his hips. She was aching with the need to be filled. His cock jumped as she slid her hips forward, coating him in her wetness. "Let me feel you." He shifted his hips. "Need you—"

Burke's hand gripped Renley's shoulder. "Slow down, sailor. You're not riding our sweet siren bare."

Renley blinked, his haze of desire broken as Burke handed him a French letter. With a curt nod, Burke helped him shift her backwards off his hips. Rosalie let out a little frustrated cry. What was it about these men that she was so ready to abandon all reason? She'd chastise herself for it later. Now she just took a shaky breath, watching as Renley wrapped his cock with the letter.

"Don't come before I get inside her," Burke warned, his hands smoothing down the curve of her back.

Renley nodded, eyes only for Rosalie. He held her by the hips, helping her shift forward again.

"Take him slow," Burke murmured. "Nice and easy, love."

With one hand, she angled Renley's cock up, letting it settle at her entrance. He lifted his hips, and she felt the tip slide in.

"Look at me," Renley said, his voice raw.

She held his gaze as she sank down onto him, letting her

hips settle as she adjusted to his size. Renley's grip tightened on her hips as he flexed.

"How does he feel?" Burke asked, his hand still on her hip.

"So good," she replied on a breath, loving the way her body fit with his. Warmth spread from her chest and down her arms.

Burke leaned in, a heated glint in his eyes. "Claim him, love. Make him yours."

Rosalie pressed down with her hips and started to move. Renley's hands were everywhere at once—her hair, her shoulders, her breasts. He pulled her down to him, even as he arched up, seeking her mouth. Their kisses were open and eager.

"I wanted you from the first," she said between kisses. "One look in your eyes and I was lost."

His hand slipped between them. "Come for me." He rubbed circles on her sensitive bud. "Need to feel you come on my cock."

The ache was building. She sat back, reaching blindly for Burke. He shifted closer and wrapped her in his arms, kissing her breathless as Renley pleasured her. Renley shifted his hips and she gasped. Her core clenched tight as she cried out against Burke's lips. Release rolled through her until she was sagging in Burke's arms.

Renley lay beneath her, panting for breath. "So good. Burke, now," he muttered. "I can't—do it now—"

Her languid body folded over onto Renley's warm chest. His arms wrapped around her as he murmured incoherently in her ear. Burke shifted off the bed, but she was too disoriented to follow his movements. He came behind her on his knees, straddling Renley's legs. "Are you ready for me, love?"

She nodded.

Renley shifted beneath her. "Do you have—"

"Right here," Burke replied.

Renley grunted his approval. "Ease into it."

Rosalie's senses slowly came back to her. Her vision sharpened. She could feel the sweat on Renley's chest against her cheek. Renley was still inside her and Burke was behind her, one hand on her hip.

"We have oil to make it easier," Renley murmured. "He's going to start with his fingers."

She lifted up on shaky hands, looking over her shoulder in time to see Burke pour a liberal amount of oil into his hand. She was unable to control her gasp as she felt the first drip of oil.

"So beautiful. You take Tom so well, love. You're both perfect. I want you so badly." Then his fingers were on her, stroking over her entrance.

"Relax," Renley murmured. "Look at me, Rose. Look only at me."

She held his gaze as Burke's finger eased in. She bit her lip, letting her body settle into the new sensation.

Renley watched her. "How does it feel?"

"Strange," she replied on a sharp exhale. "I—*ah*—"

Burke was pressing in with two fingers now. "You're so tight, love. You were made for us. Look how well you take us both."

Her eyes shut tight as Renley kissed her. He lifted his hips, moving inside her. "I can feel him too," he said on a breath. "God, I want to feel you both."

"She's ready," Burke muttered, his hand on her hip while he pressed in with his fingers.

"Go slow," Renley replied. He looked at Rosalie. "Are you ready?"

She nodded.

"Use your words." He cupped her face to hold her gaze. "Tell us."

"Yes," she said on a breath. "I want you both. Burke, please. I want you inside me. Please, you're mine. My Horatio. My Burke—"

Burke gripped her face with his free hand and leaned over her back, skin against skin, and kissed her. His passion was barely contained. She felt the intensity of his need pulsing through him. It only made her own spiral higher. These men would be the death of her. She braced her forehead on Renley's chest as Burke put his hand on her hip and lined himself up.

"Nice and slow," Renley warned.

She gasped, feeling the tip of Burke's cock pressing against her entrance.

"Breathe, Rose," Renley murmured. "It's going to feel so good. You were made to be with us. Right here, just like this . . ."

She took a shaky breath, trying to keep herself still. The pressure was overwhelming. It made her tremble. Burke and Renley both groaned as he inched in.

Renley shifted beneath her. "God help me—*Burke*—"

She'd never felt so full in her life. Both men were murmuring, Burke's hands on her hips and Renley's on her thighs. She could feel them both—their hardness, their length. Burke slid in another inch, settling with a soft thrust. "You're ours. Do you feel this? Feel how we complete you?"

She whimpered, hands shaking as she tried to stay perfectly still. This was agony. It was ecstasy.

"Such a good girl." Renley brushed his lips against hers. "He's almost there."

With a slow exhale, Burke gripped her waist with both hands and pressed in until his hips settled behind her. They all let out a collective breath. He smoothed his hands over her hips. "That's it, love. How does it feel?"

"So full," she murmured, blinking away tears. Body full. Heart and soul full. How was she ever going to survive them?

"I'm dying," Renley said beneath her. "She's so tight. I can't—Burke, you have to move. God—*please*—move."

Burke's grip tightened on her hips. "Push in, Tom. Deep as you can."

Renley shifted beneath her, angling his hips forward. The fullness left a deep ache inside her. Was it even possible she could come again?

"Hold her still," Burke said, leaning over her to kiss her shoulder. She could feel his body tensing, the calm before the storm. Beneath her, Renley was hard as stone, his hips holding steady. "No one comes until I say," Burke growled in her ear.

Suddenly, he was moving. She cried out, pressing her face into Renley's tattooed chest as Burke drove into her. Beneath her, Renley's eyes were closed, his head tipped back. Burke's breath came out in sharp pants as he seated himself to the hilt over and over. She could do nothing as Burke sent them all careening towards the edge of a cliff. He curled his body over hers, his hand snaking between her legs to give her more pleasure. At the first touch of his fingers on her sensitive bud, she clenched tighter.

Renley felt it all. "Burke—"

"Not yet," Burke snapped. "Hold on."

Renley's grip on her hips tightened. She'd surely have

bruises in the morning. Each time these men touched her, they brought her to new heights of pleasure. Her aching core couldn't take much more. The tightness was almost unbearable. With each thrust, the sensation built. She was so close. Bliss was at her fingertips.

"Don't stop," she begged. "Please—"

Burke deepened his thrusts, pounding into her.

"Christ, I can feel you both," Renley panted, his voice pained. "Burke—I need you."

He reached blindly for his friend, grabbing Burke's forearm and pulling him forward. Rosalie was pressed between them, filled by them. She watched as Renley took Burke by the hair and jerked his face closer. Their lips met in a frenzied kiss—a clashing of teeth and tongues that made both men groan.

Watching them together, Rosalie shattered. With a cry, she felt her release course through her, shooting all the way down to her toes. She was breathless, shaking as it crested.

Renley broke his kiss with Burke, head falling back as his body stiffened. "Christ, save me."

Behind her, Burke started moving again, his breath coming out in pants as he increased his intensity. "That's it, love," he said between thrusts. "Do you want Tom to come inside you? He's aching for it. Look at him. Look at your power over him."

She moaned, letting herself look at Renley—his beautiful blue eyes, the sharp lines of his jaw, his halo of golden curls splayed slicked with sweat. He was so beautiful. He looked back at her with such raw, open need. His hands gripped tighter to her hips as he started moving in tandem with Burke.

"Tom," she murmured, pressing her lips to his. "Give yourself to me."

With a growl, he gripped tight to her hips and started thrusting up into her.

Feeling Burke and Renley moving together inside her was a new kind of paradise. She threw her head back, eyes closed tight, letting their passion spiral her higher and higher. Together, her men would make her fly. They would always give her exactly what she needed.

"We're going to come inside you, sweet siren," Burke said, his voice low in her ear. "Fill you. Own you. You belong to us."

"Yes. Oh God—"

Burke's hand snaked between her and Renley, his fingers working her bud until she was trembling. He curled over her, pressing her closer to Renley. "Come one more time. Let us feel it."

With two more thrusts, Renley lifted his hips, burying himself deep as he came. Burke followed right behind. At the same time, he pressed down with his thumb. Rosalie cried out a final release. It was all she could do to keep the splintering pieces of her soul together as they ruined her so beautifully, so completely. Coming down from the high, only one thought remained: She was irrevocably lost to them.

Rosalie was in a daze. She didn't know how or when it happened, but she was being carried in Renley's arms back towards the bed. She wore a fresh chemise, her body washed clean. He'd been so gentle as he tended to her, whispering soft words of affirmation. He kissed her forehead before setting her down on the bed.

Burke was waiting for them, his head propped up on one

arm. The intensity of his gaze had her feeling weak all over again. "Come here," he said, holding out his hand.

She shifted over, her whole body weak and shaky.

Burke wrapped her in his arms, weaving his legs in with hers. He kissed her forehead, her temple, her tender lips. "Do you know what you mean to me?" he whispered, bringing her hand to his lips and pressing kisses to each finger. "Do you have any earthly idea?"

She nuzzled into him, letting his words shelter her like a warm blanket. Movement behind her made her turn. Renley was still standing beside the bed. Her heart raced for a moment as she considered the thought that he might leave. She reached out her hand. "Please, don't go," she whispered. "Stay with me . . . with us."

Renley glanced over at Burke, a hopeful yet wary look in his eye. Whatever look Burke returned, it was enough to have Renley sinking onto the bed. Rosalie twisted in Burke's hold, reaching for Renley with both hands. He came to her, sliding close enough to touch her from hip to knee. She soaked in the features of his beautiful face and knew he was doing the same.

Behind her, Burke nuzzled her neck. "Tomorrow, everything changes," she murmured.

"Everything and nothing," Burke replied, kissing her shoulder.

"The house will be full of people who won't understand us, won't understand *this*," she added. "I won't see any of you ruined or compromised because of me."

"Leave our reputations to us," Burke muttered. "Yours is the only one that matters."

Renley inched closer to kiss her forehead. "You're safe with us, Rose."

The words should have been a balm; instead, they set her

on edge. She didn't know what was coming next. Tomorrow, the house would fill with gossips and social climbers. She'd have to contend day in and day out with a despondent duke, a domineering duchess, and a parade of preening ladies and their eagle-eyed mamas.

This peace wasn't meant to last. This joy, this feeling of utter contentment in their arms—it could never last. It was the most resounding lesson of her life. The first to learn, the deepest to scar. Nothing, especially love, lasted forever.

But she could give herself this moment. Nestled between her two beautiful men, cherished and protected, she would let herself feel everything in her heart. Tonight, she would dream of it, a beautiful dream of forever.

And in the morning, she would wake.

23

Rosalie

THE FOLLOWING MORNING, everyone was on high alert waiting for the arrival of the duke and the rest of the house party. Rosalie saw nothing of the gentlemen, as they were all out attending to various affairs. She spent the morning oscillating between trying to be helpful to the horde of harried servants and just trying to stay out of the way.

"When should we expect them?" she asked, helping Mrs. Robbins tend to a floral arrangement in the morning room.

"Oh, not 'til this evening. Just in time for dinner, if the roads are good. You won't be on your own much longer, dear. Perhaps you'd like to sketch this morning?"

Rosalie hissed and pulled her hand out of the flowers. Mrs. Robbins' words had distracted her and she had pricked her thumb on a thorn. She glanced down at the pad of her thumb, seeing a little spot of red. "Who told you I sketch?" she asked, giving her thumb a little suck to numb the pain.

"Lord James," Mrs. Robbins replied, her eyes focused on her work. "He had me set out some things for you and put them in the ladies' day room."

Rosalie stilled. James told the housekeeper of her hobbies? When? She ducked her face behind the flowers, hoping Mrs. Robbins wouldn't see her blush as her vision filled with memories of the previous night. His two best friends had shared her so passionately. She still felt them everywhere; her body ached with it. Those memories flashed with others—James pressing her against a bookcase, his lips on her throat, his voice in her ear—

"Miss Harrow, dear? Are you well?"

She blinked, glancing up at Mrs. Robbins, who was watching her with a curious eye. "I am perfectly well, Mrs. Robbins. Just a bit tired."

Mrs. Robbins pursed her lips. "Yes, well your ride last night must have been rough. You're looking a little stiff this morning."

Rosalie wanted to sink through the floor with mortification. She didn't miss the hint of accusation in Mrs. Robbins' tone. This woman was daring to challenge her about a reckless, unchaperoned ride with Renley through the rain. If she only knew the truth about the source of Rosalie's present discomfort, the poor woman would probably die of shock.

"I *am* sorry, Mrs. Robbins," she murmured, tugging loose a wilted carnation. "This position is new to me, and so are its many rules. I've never required a maid as a chaperone before. It was never expected of me." She turned, placing a gentle hand on the lady's wrist. "I will not risk the honor of this house by riding unchaperoned again."

Mrs. Robbins sniffed. "Well then," was her only reply.

Rosalie did her best to stay out of the way for the rest of the morning. By eleven o'clock, she was alone in the library on her hands and knees, pulling loose one of the large leather-bound books from a lower shelf. It claimed to be a ledger documenting all the artworks collected by the fifth duke during his grand tour. The book was wedged in tightly between several other thick volumes. She gave it a tug, pulling it free at last.

"You naughty little cabbage," a deep voice called from across the room.

She gasped. Rising up to her knees, her head swiveled to face the voice. Standing in the open doorway was the duke, looking as rakish as ever.

The more she got to know them, the more she saw the resemblance between George and James Corbin. James was taller and wider in the shoulder, his hair more auburn than brown, and with a bit more of a curl. And his eyes were a deep, forest green, while the duke had blue eyes a near perfect match to their mother.

Rosalie sucked in a breath and scrambled to her feet, dropping into a little curtsy. "Your Grace."

"Don't 'Your Grace' me, Cabbage," the duke said with a grin. "I'm on to your games now. You think I don't know this little engagement party was all your idea?"

Her heart pounded. Was she in trouble? "I—"

He held up a hand to stay her. His signet ring flashed in the sunlight. "Don't bother denying it. My brother is many things, but a surprise party planner is not one of them." He pointed a finger at her, giving it a wiggle. "No, this was all *your* little scheme."

She set the heavy book down. "Your Grace, I'm sorry if I offended you."

"Offended?" He let out a barking laugh. "Whyever would

I be offended that you're using me as your excuse to cover the tracks of your salacious midnight escape?"

"Heavens," she said on a breath. "Is that how it's being described?"

His smirk widened. "By some. By me, certainly." He came around the sofa. "It's quite brilliant, your idea. It obfuscates all manner of sin." He cast her a knowing look.

She did her best to look blankly back at him, even while her heart raced. She never knew how to act around this man. One minute he would be taciturn and sullen, making little conversation. The next he could be found bouncing on his heels, juggling candlesticks, and rutting into maids. He lived his life in the extremes—pleasure and pain, boredom and excitement.

He sank onto the sofa and crossed his legs, watching her intently. "I must admit, I never expected a pretty little cabbage like you to buy off a duke. It's quite scandalous."

She opened and shut her mouth twice, searching for the words to reply. "Your Grace, I assure you, there is nothing—"

"As I say," he went on, raising his hand again to silence her. "I do not care to know. All I care about is that I will get to see James dressed and polished and forced to fawn over me for a whole evening. His low spirits are sure to lift mine sky high."

Rosalie couldn't hide her own smile now. He was teasing her. Would he dare let himself be teased in return? She stepped around the opposite sofa and sat, flashing him a conspiratorial look. "There will be a fire-eater."

He leaned forward, eyes wide. "Tell me more."

She feigned indignation, crossing her arms. "I couldn't possibly, Your Grace. That would ruin the surprise."

He laughed, one arm stretched over the back of the sofa. "I am looking forward to it immensely."

She glanced over at the clock. "We were not expecting you to arrive so soon, sir."

He just shrugged. "Mama loathes taking the journey in one swoop. We started last night and were obliged to stop at an inn where I was force-fed a very questionable cut of mutton with salty potatoes." His face pinched with disgust.

Rosalie was quite sure the potatoes were reasonably seasoned; George Corbin was just used to having all his meals prepared by a French chef. "And who made the journey with you, sir?"

"Oh, we were a proper caravan, like Moses leading his people out of Egypt. Can't bloody escape them," he added under his breath.

"Will the Nashes be staying here?" She hadn't quite gotten a read on Piety Nash, or her twin sister Prudence . . . other than that they were ambitious social climbers. If Rosalie planned to make her life here with the Corbins, she'd need to establish a good working relationship with the soon-to-be lady of the house.

"Naturally, my intended will stay here," he replied dispassionately. "There is much to plan. And the marchioness and Burke's lovely intended are here." He ticked the people off on his fingers, oblivious to the way Rosalie stiffened. "Viscount Raleigh took his wife and daughter home, but they'll no doubt be joining in the festivities."

Rosalie's heart gave a sad little flutter. Of all the house guests at Alcott Hall, Madeline Blaire was the only other person she genuinely liked . . . outside of her gentlemen, of course.

"The Oswalds were all too happy to be invited," the duke went on, confirming her fears. Blanche Oswald was one of the silliest girls she'd ever met. "And Countess Waverley and her daughters couldn't take a hint. The countess even rode in our carriage. I blame you for that, as Mama must have a female travel companion. Is that not meant to be your job now?" He raised an accusing brow at her.

"I'm sorry, Your Grace," she murmured. "The events of that night were not . . . I regret causing any humiliation or frustration."

He got to his feet, and she did the same. He eyed her curiously. "You don't have to stand when I stand, you know."

"It feels odd to stay seated in your presence, sir," she admitted. She didn't like being told she was deficient in manners twice in one morning. Swallowing her frustration, she added, "If I do wrong, please continue to instruct me. I'll learn the rules eventually."

He lowered his brows, his mouth tipping up on one side. "Yes, but will you ever actually follow them? For those are two different talents, Cabbage."

She met his gaze, seeing the playfulness there. Why was he being so cordial to her? The last time they spoke in private, he demanded to know his mother's secrets. She didn't like worrying about having to unravel his motives. Surely there could be none, for she was nothing to him. He must be teasing because she was an easy target.

"Well, I must carry on," he said, breaking his gaze away from her. "Lots to do when you're a duke, eh? Never enough time in the day."

She dropped into a curtsy. "Your Grace."

He snorted a little laugh as he turned away. "Lesson number

two: You don't need to curtsy to me when we're alone," he called over his shoulder. "Oh—" He paused at the doorway and turned, that rakish smile back on his face. "I suppose I should have said this from the first, but my dear Mama is asking for you."

24

Tom

"YOU'VE BEEN QUIET this morning," Tom muttered, following along at Burke's side as they wove through the busy street.

They were on their way back to Corbin House from the auction lots. Burke always had an excellent eye for horses. He handled all the Corbin family's hunt, stud, and racing portfolios, earning a percentage of the profits. He seemed pleased with this morning's find.

Meanwhile, Tom was in turmoil. The events of last night troubled him. Well, one event. A line crossed. A liberty taken. He was terrified to speak his fears aloud and have them realized. But not to speak them was impossible. It's the reason he tagged along, hoping to get a moment with Burke alone.

"Can I assume you mean to suffocate me with this heavy silence?"

"There is nothing to say," Burke muttered.

They were moving down a narrow street of shops in the ironworks district. The clang of blacksmiths' hammers rent the crisp morning air. A stray dog darted in their path, chased after by a street urchin.

"I think there is," Tom countered. "And I think I know what it is, and if I'm right—"

"Christ, Tom. We're not talking about this now." To prove his point, Burke stretched out his long legs, weaving faster through the morning shoppers.

Desperation clawed at Tom as he elongated his stride to keep up. "Burke, *please*—"

Burke suddenly stopped and spun on his heel. Snatching Tom by the front of his open great coat, he dragged him into the narrow alley between a typesetter's shop and a key repair store.

Tom grunted as Burke shoved him up against the grimy brick wall, stained black with years of smoke. Burke kept a hand on his shoulder. The brim of his hat was pulled low, casting a shadow over his stormy grey eyes. "You want to do this here? Right here, Tom?"

"I'm sorry," Tom murmured. There were no other words to be said. He knew this had to be about their kiss last night. In the moment, Burke had accepted it. Hell, in the moment he'd kissed Tom back with enough passion to rip Tom's soul apart.

But Horatio Burke did not kiss men.

Ever.

Tom knew this. He just hoped that perhaps, with Rosalie between them, it might be different. Perhaps Burke could let himself share his passion. Clearly, Tom was wrong. "I'm sorry," he muttered again.

"Stop saying you're sorry," Burke snapped. "Why the hell are you sorry?"

"I . . ." Tom swallowed. "I know we touched at Alcott, but that was different. That was about her pleasure, not ours. And there was nothing wrong in it." He was stumbling all over his words. God, he could barely think straight. "But last night . . . the kiss. Burke, it doesn't have to happen again—"

"Stop talking," Burke growled. He lowered his face until his mouth was inches away, until they were sharing breath.

A slow ache pulsed in Tom's cock. He couldn't help it. What the hell was Burke doing? He closed his eyes and leaned away.

Burke cupped his jaw and jerked his chin up. "Look at me, Tom. Look me right in the goddamn eye. If we're having this conversation, let's bloody well have it."

Tom opened his eyes, feeling the strength of Burke's hands holding him in place.

Burke's eyes swirled with angry storms of darkest grey. "You think I didn't like it? Is that what this show of remorse is about? You wandering behind me all morning like a kicked dog?"

Tom bit his lip, fighting back the words. They'd never spoken so openly about this subject before. *Never*. Apparently now was the time, and this was the place. This dingy, rank alley that smelled heavily of smoke. "You don't like men," he whispered.

"Of course, I don't," Burke huffed. "I like women. I *fuck* women. I worship at their feet and drink from their perfect cunts. One woman in particular I now claim as my goddess. There will be no other women for me."

Tom closed his eyes again, nodding, heart quietly breaking. Burke wanted Rosalie. Only Rosalie. Tom could well understand, for he wanted her too. He just wanted . . . *more*.

"I said look at me," Burke growled, squeezing Tom's jaw tighter.

Tom opened his eyes.

Burke leaned in, his thumb brushing over Tom's parted

lips. "I don't like men. I don't fuck men . . . but *you* are not men."

Tom blinked, confused and wholly distracted by Burke's thumb on his mouth. "I don't understand—"

"You are Tom. *My* Tom. You are all fucking mine."

As the words rumbled from Burke's chest, Tom sagged against the brick wall, his breath escaping him in a sharp exhale.

"The two of us have been linked since we were twelve years old," Burke went on. "Do you remember the day?"

Of course, Tom remembered it. He still dreamed of it sometimes. It was the day Burke nearly drowned. They'd been fording the river one spring day. Neither was prepared for the strength of the current after a week of heavy rain. Burke was immediately swept under. It was the scariest moment of Tom's young life—diving in after him, reaching blindly for him in the swirling darkness, dragging him to the surface and pulling him to shore. "I remember," he murmured.

"We are part of each other. Always have been." A silence stretched between them, and Burke's eyes narrowed as his scowl deepened. "Goddamn it, say something."

What words could ever suffice? Instead, Tom grabbed Burke by the neck, crashing their lips together in a hungry kiss. Burke groaned, parting his lips to tease Tom with his tongue. Tom wanted to die. To feel Burke so close, to have him in his arms, his taste on his tongue. It was perfect. It was heaven.

It was over in seconds.

Burke jerked away. He staggered back, wiping at his mouth with his leather-gloved hand. "We can't—fucking Christ. We can't, Tom." He sank back against the opposite wall, eyes darting towards the busy street. No one noticed them here in the shadows. No one cared.

Tom flicked his tongue over his bottom lip, savoring the taste of Burke's kiss. His cock was achingly hard now. He needed to know if Burke was equally affected. But instead of heat in Burke's eyes, he saw only frustration, worry, guilt. Such a combination had shame twisting in Tom's gut. He pushed off the wall, inching closer. "Burke, it's okay. It doesn't have to happen again."

Burke pounded his fist into the brick twice, cursing under his breath.

"We can be with Rosalie, and not with each other. It's enough. I swear it's enough for me. I won't push you again. I'm sorry. Please, let us just be as before."

Slowly, Burke lowered his fist from the wall and turned. His expression was impossible to read in this darkness. "I just told you that you're mine, that you always have been, and your response is to say you want us to be as we were before? *Friends*?" He said the word like a curse.

"I just kissed you and you pushed me away saying 'we can't,'" Tom countered. "Burke, I will not lose you to this. I will swallow it. Bury it. Christ, I'll *burn* it out of me if I have to," he growled, one hand pressing over his heart. "I will never risk our friendship. I *can* control myself. I will—"

Burke cupped Tom's face with both his gloved hands. The leather was cool, foreign. Tom ached to feel the warmth of Burke's skin against his. He fought to keep his eyes open, too afraid to look at his friend and see more guilt and shame there.

"I am telling you that I don't want you to be my friend," Burke pressed. "You are more than a friend to me, Tom. You have been for a long time. I think it just took sharing you with Rosalie to fully understand the true scope of what I want."

"And what is it that you want?"

Burke laughed, lowering his hands to Tom's shoulders. "I want to kiss you again." He leaned in. "I want to taste you with my tongue until you're moaning my name."

"Burke," Tom whispered. This couldn't be real.

A devilish grin tipped Burke's lips. "I want my hands in your hair, my cock in your mouth, and I want to *own* you, Tom Renley. When I call a thing mine, I mean it."

Overcome, Tom dropped his forehead to Burke's shoulder. "I want you too," he murmured. "God, I've wanted you for so long."

Burke stiffened. "But nothing can happen between us without Rosalie's consent," he declared. "When I say we can't, that is what I mean. She doesn't know how we feel, what we want. And I will not have secrets between us."

Tom wanted to laugh. He wanted to shout. He wanted to take Burke in his two hands and claim him against this filthy alley wall. "She already knows."

It was Burke's turn to blink and pull back. "What?"

"At least, she knows what I want," he clarified. "I told her."

Burke's eyes narrowed. "And what do you want, then?"

Tom's smile widened. "Last night she called you Horatio. You let her use it as an endearment."

"So?"

"So, that's what I want too," Tom murmured, heart in his throat.

Burke huffed a laugh. "You're not calling me Horatio, Tom."

"You let her say it," he challenged.

"Yes, well, she lets me come inside her," Burke replied with a grin. "It's a more than even trade, I think."

More than even.

Tom stepped closer, heat flooding to his hardening cock.

"If you say I'm yours, you better be ready to claim me in all the ways that matter."

Burke went utterly still.

Tom raised a hand and brushed it lightly down the arm of Burke's coat. "Picture it . . . Horatio." He noted the way Burke hissed in a breath and inched closer, running the tip of his nose along Tom's jaw. "You could claim us both at once. I'd sink my cock into her, and you'd take me from behind. Each thrust of yours would bury me inside her. You could ruin her on my cock while you come inside me. Own us. Devastate us."

"Bloody fucking hell." Burke sank back against the wall.

"Tell me you don't want it," Tom teased, following him to the wall, pinning him down with a push of his hips. "Tell me your cock isn't hard right now. Tell me it's not weeping at the image of me on all fours, Rosalie beneath us both. Tell me, Burke. Lie to me."

With a feral growl, Burke's hand slipped between them, cupping Tom's painfully hard cock. Both men moaned as Tom pressed into his hand.

Panting, Tom shifted back a step. "My only condition is that when we're alone, I get to call you Horatio too."

Burke laughed, dropping his hand away. "Why do you suddenly give a damn about calling me Horatio?"

"Because I like sharing these secrets with you," he replied. "I like seeing you in a crowded room and knowing I've watched you take our girl. I like knowing what you say to her, how easily you get her to come. It makes me come faster too."

Burke groaned.

"These secrets are ours, Burke. Not yours. Not hers. *Ours*. Horatio is a secret you keep, and you gave it to her. I want it too."

"Fine," Burke muttered. "If it means that much to you, call me Horatio."

Tom smiled, leaning forward to kiss his jaw. "Oh, I will. But I intend to earn it first. People you come inside get to say it, yes? That's the rule?"

Burke held his gaze, his look hungry. Slowly, he nodded.

Peace settled in Tom's chest, knowing they understood each other. "Don't worry, we'll work up to it. But first we tell Rosalie our intentions. Until then, we keep our hands off each other, agreed?"

A playful smile tipped Burke's mouth. "Can you bear to wait?"

Tom adjusted his hat and coat with a matching grin. "Don't worry about me. I've lasted this long. The real question is . . . can you?"

25

James

JAMES HANDED OFF his great coat, top hat, and gloves to a footman, his eyes locked on the butler. "Where is she?"

"In your study, my lord," Wilson wheezed.

James ground his teeth, stalking off across the entry hall. Damn foolish to leave the house this morning! He wanted to be here when his mother arrived to head her off. But he hadn't expected them until later this evening. It didn't make any sense.

Of course. Bloody George lied about their travel plans.

Making a resolution to kick George in the shins when he next saw him, James made his way to the back of the house. A footman stood outside the open door of his study, jolting to attention as James approached.

"Is she in there?"

The footman nodded.

Taking a deep breath, James squared his shoulders and entered.

"Ah, there you are, my darling. How good of you to come greet me at last."

His mother's tone was icy, even if her words were cordial. She sat behind his desk, blonde hair piled in a stately column of curls, her face flawlessly powdered and rouged. Her armor was firmly in place, and this study was her chosen battlefield. She was ready to draw blood.

"Mother," he said with a curt nod, going straight to the drink cart. "Can I get you anything?" he called, rattling around as he poured three fingers of whiskey into a glass.

"No," she replied. "James, come sit. We have much to discuss."

With his liquid reinforcement in hand, James leaned against the cart. "I don't need to sit for this. Just say what's on your mind."

"Don't get flippant with me. I am furious with you. I raised you better than to pull such a scandalous stunt before the whole *ton*! I may be just an overbearing mother to you, but I am still mistress of this house. I am a duchess—"

"Only until George marries. Then it will be the lovely Miss Nash who claims that title."

She hissed like an angry cat. "That little tart will *never* replace me. I will be Duchess of Norland until I die—"

"Incorrect. The moment Father died, you became a dowager," he needled.

Her lips quivered like she was holding in a scream.

"But don't worry," he added. "Loss of rank is not completely devoid of perks. As a dowager duchess, you are granted the most comfortable chair at every social gathering. That must be seen as advantageous."

"I will not be made irrelevant!"

Before he could reply, she let out a few sobs. His darling mother loved crying for an audience. It usually worked on

George, but only because crying women made him so deeply uncomfortable. It embarrassed James to admit how many times it had worked on him in the past.

"I don't know what I've done to earn your spite, James. It cuts straight through my heart." She pressed a hand dramatically to her chest, jewels glittering on her wrist.

He just rolled his eyes. "Come now, Mother: You and I both know you don't have a heart—"

"If I am heartless, it is because the demands of this life ripped it from my chest! Who do you think ran all of this while your father still lived? You think he could manage it on his own? No," she answered, her tone full of scorn. "No, he was too busy with his bad investments and his risky speculations, his drinking and his gambling and his *whores*."

James blinked, wholly taken aback. "What are you—"

"Your beloved father was spending the estate's money faster than we could bring it in," she snapped. "*I* had to secure Alcott Hall. I made the tough choices, James. I kept us in these houses, in this title, in this comfort. You think you are the silent duke?" She scoffed, waving a dismissive hand. "Please, child, I invented the position. I work to secure a title I can never claim. A title both my sons now take completely for granted!"

"I take nothing for granted," he growled, slapping his glass down. "Since Father died, I have done everything to take care of the family as George has been derelict in his duty. We both have suffered. We both have put in work thanklessly for the betterment of a family that does not respect us. I didn't see you then, and I am sorry for it. But you are not seeing me now—"

"Oh, I see you," she replied with a glare. "I see a spoiled, ungrateful fool! You are selfish, James. Why can you not just do as I say? I need you to help me keep this all together, and you are determined to watch it fall apart!"

Her words found their marks, sinking deep into his chest, leaving him breathless. He could practically feel the strings tied to each barb. How soon before she began to tug on them? How soon before he was once again dancing to her tune? James was her own dutiful marionette.

He was exhausted. He couldn't live like this anymore. He took a deep breath and dragged a hand through his hair. "I thought I was doing the right thing by helping you force George down the aisle, but now I see how wrong I've been."

"You know as well as I that he must secure an heir. Otherwise, the weight will really fall on your shoulders," she challenged. "You think you feel the pressure now? Oh James, you sweet boy, it will break you. You're far too soft, too weak. You *need* me!"

More words hit their target. As much as he tried to shield himself, she knew what to say to burrow her way under his skin.

I'm not strong enough. Nothing I do will ever be enough. Too weak. Too caring. Too compromised—

He took a shaky breath and exhaled it. James wasn't soft. Did Burke not complain about all his hard edges near daily? Part of James wanted to let his guard down. God, he thought of the way Rosalie looked at him in the library, her dark eyes so full of interest . . . interest in *him*.

He remembered the feel of her soft lips on his, asking him without words to be let into his heart, into his life. But he couldn't do it. *This* was the reality of his life. How could he afford softness when he was constantly on the offensive, battling his domineering mother or compensating for his worthless brother? And when they were not trying his patience at every turn, he had a dukedom to run.

Hold it together. The center must always hold.

No, anything soft in James had been chipped away long ago. Burke might believe there was something left, but he was wrong. James was all hardness now. Walls and walls and walls of cold, hard stone.

He met and held his mother's cold gaze. "I've been your puppet, Mother. You've manipulated me. You threaten me and belittle me when every day I am fighting for this family. But you don't see me—"

"Of course, I see you—"

"You don't see me," he said louder. "You claim everything I do as your own—"

"I birthed you and I raised you," she cried, standing and stepping around the desk until her jasmine perfume filled his nose. "Whatever your successes, they are *mine*. You are my creature, James!"

Before another word could be spoken, George strolled into the room. "Look who I found," he called in a sing-song voice. "Oh dear . . . are we quarreling?" He glanced from one to the other. "Shall we come back later?"

"Of course not." Their mother waved her hand for him to enter.

James glanced away from the door, needing a moment to school his features, knowing exactly who trailed behind his brother.

His mother was ready with an admonishment. "Miss Harrow, why did you not come to me the moment I arrived?"

"I'm sorry, Your Grace, I didn't know," came Rosalie's soft

voice. It touched James like the stroke of a feather down his spine. He bit the inside of his cheek to keep from groaning, his face still turned away. He moved over to the sofa and sat down heavily.

George sank onto the sofa across from him, a little smile on his face. "Yes, I found her in the library . . . on her knees."

James glanced from George to Rosalie, a tightness coiling in his chest. Her cheeks now matched the soft pinkish purple of her gown.

"George, don't be crass," their mother snapped.

"How is it crass to say she was on her knees?" he replied with a chuckle.

"I was retrieving a book," Rosalie added. "I didn't hear any commotion in the house until His Grace found me."

She was working very hard not to look at James, for which he was grateful . . . and annoyed. They'd yet to speak alone since that moment on the stairs. He'd been avoiding her. If he was hurting her with his distance, he didn't care. It was better this way.

"Well?" his mother huffed. "Is someone going to start talking? I think I deserve an explanation."

"Hmm . . . I think we all do," George added, his tone mockingly somber.

James was going to add a punch to the ribs to the shin-kick George had already earned. "Miss Harrow, you can go. This is a family matter—"

"I will say when my ward is dismissed," his mother snapped.

"She had nothing to do with this. She was dragged into my plans against her will—"

"Are you saying you kidnapped her?" George asked. "A

midnight kidnapping from a duke's ball, a carriage escape to London—heavens, what an event. Your life is the stuff of novels, Cabbage."

"Don't call her that," James snapped.

His mother turned. "And what do you call her, James? Tell me plainly: Do you intend to marry her?"

Rosalie gasped as James sputtered. "What—*no*—"

"You ruin her in the eyes of good society, making her useless to me as a ward. What else is left other than you either marry her, or cast her out?"

He could see the look of horror on Rosalie's face. "Nothing happened between Miss Harrow and me," he declared. "Anyone who dares to impugn her honor will answer to me. I asked her to accompany me because I knew she would help to plan the party for George—"

"Don't you spit that lie at me again, James," his mother cried.

"It is no lie. The date is set, the invitations sent. On Friday, all of society will see I made no lie. She planned it all with Mrs. Robbins, leaving me free to do the other work that brought me to Town."

"Oh, yes? And what work might that be?" George said with a raised brow.

"You have never once questioned my business affairs," James countered, his eyes narrowed at his brother. "I do your job, and you're happy for me to do it. I will not answer you now, since I know your present curiosity is only rooted in seeing me discomfited in Miss Harrow's presence."

Their mother took a step closer. "And what is this nonsense I hear about you placing her in the bachelor's corridor? Have you no sense of propriety?"

James dragged both hands through his hair, not daring to look at either George or Rosalie. He didn't want them to ruin this ruse. "Bloody hell, Mother. How many times in how many ways must I say it? I do not care about Miss Harrow. I stuck her in the bachelor's wing with only Renley and Sir Andrew for company because I thought it is what *you* would wish." He pointed a stern finger at her. "Six rooms remain for the ladies and all six are necessary. Miss Harrow's comfort is certainly secondary to that of a marchioness, am I correct?"

He raised a brow, waiting for her response. When she just scowled, he added, "Put Miss Harrow wherever you like. Hell, give her my room. Put her with the servants, set up a cot in the conservatory by the pineapple plants. I do not care." He was careful to enunciate each word.

Next to him, Rosalie's stillness spoke louder than a scream. Damn, but he hated himself sometimes.

His mother spun around to face Rosalie. "Well, I want to know what compelled you to agree to my son's ludicrous schemes. Why did you not come to me directly? You have been my ward for less than a fortnight, and already you have distressed me and embarrassed me so greatly—"

"I am not your ward."

James had to blink twice, unsure if he had seen Rosalie's lips move. But there she was, chin raised, eyes glistening with tears, staring down his mother glare for glare.

His mother narrowed her eyes. "What did you say?"

Rosalie dared to take a step closer. "I said I am *not* your ward."

26

Rosalie

TEARS STUNG ROSALIE'S eyes, but she wasn't going to let them fall. She squared off against the duchess, her heart beating wildly in her chest. She heard the horrible things this woman shouted at James, at her own son. Rosalie knew bad parenting better than any person living. She could taste the cruelty and manipulation on her tongue. It had the bitter tang of iron. It sickened her.

From the moment she'd entered the room, she wanted nothing more than to fling herself in front of James, determined to stop any more blows from touching him. Even when he spoke harshly of her, she wanted to be his shield. He stood there now, eyes wide, watching her with an anxious look on his face.

The duchess called out in a loud voice, "Well, Miss Rose? Are you or are you not my ward? For if you are not, you will pack your bags and leave this very hour. I will not waste my time or my generosity on an ungrateful girl who does not understand the value of rank and respectability."

She turned her full attention to the duchess. "You speak of respect, and yet you have offered me *none.*"

The duchess gasped. "You impudent little—"

"You summoned me to Alcott under false pretenses," Rosalie pressed. "You knew what you wanted when you invited me. You waited until I was already here before you demanded I become your spy. You manipulated me, Your Grace. Playing on my emotions, using the memory of my dead mother as your way into my confidence."

"Lies," the duchess retorted. "I loved Elinor—"

"I am not here because of any warmth of feeling you harbor for me or my mother. I am here because you don't want to lose control!"

The words hung in the air between the four of them. Neither of her sons dared to move. They were too shocked by Rosalie's display. Rosalie was equally shocked.

The duchess broke first, blinking away angry tears. "You dare presume to know me?"

Rosalie inched closer, a soft smile on her lips. "I know only what you have *told* me."

The duchess simmered with fury and resentment . . . and a whisper of fear. Rosalie could see it as the faintest of glimmers in the lady's deep blue eyes.

James stepped forward, missing nothing. "What have you told her, Mother?"

The duchess ignored the accusing looks of her sons. She narrowed her eyes at Rosalie. "What are you after, you scheming little rosebud? What do you want?"

Rosalie met her stare for stare. "I want only that which any person would want: a choice. You cannot declare to a room full of people that I am your ward without first hearing *me* say the words. If I stay, it must only be *my* choice."

The duchess scoffed. "And what makes you think I will have you within fifty feet of my home after this disgusting display? I would see you set out on the curb with the rest of the trash."

Now James stepped forward. He barreled around the back of the sofa and came to Rosalie's side. "Speak to her like that again, and I will not be responsible for my actions."

Rosalie's heart was in her throat. She could feel the rage simmering off his skin, hot as a flame.

The duchess just laughed. "Oh, this is precious. Are you declaring yourself for her?"

"No," James grit out. "But nor will I let you bully her. Or Burke."

She turned all her attention on him, eyes flashing. "Now we come to it at last. This is what has you so upset with me. You still think I did wrong by Burke. All this anger is because you don't want to lose your friend in marriage." She laughed, and the sound made Rosalie's stomach twist. "Well, grow up, James."

"His marriage will not be moving forward," James declared. "Start whatever scheming necessary to undo what you've done. He will not marry Lady Olivia."

The duchess put her hands on her hips. "Unless you want to ruin the lady, she must go through with the match. And I told you what would happen if you went against me on this. I will cut you off without a penny, James. Do not test me."

He stepped closer, his face now inches from hers. "Then *do* it."

A long moment stretched between them. Finally, the duchess snarled and leaned away.

James barked a hollow laugh. "We both know your threat is empty. I am a viscount in my own right. The land, the title, the income associated with it—it's all mine. You cannot touch it." He placed himself squarely between Rosalie and his mother. "Threaten me again, and watch how fast I leave. Once I am gone, you and George can shatter the dukedom into pieces. Perhaps I might acquire a shard for myself when it is inevitably sold off."

"You would watch your family crumble?" the duchess cried. "All for the sake of winning a contest of wills with me?"

"Burke is my family," he parried. "I am not the Duke of Norland, as you so regularly remind me. If you decide to follow through with your threats against Burke or myself, I will leave you." He glanced at the duke and added, "Both of you."

"James . . ." the duke murmured, finding his voice at last.

There was a desperate glint in the duchess' eye. She'd bullied her way into a corner, and now there was no escape. Her gaze landed on Rosalie, and she smirked. "Go if you must, you ungrateful boy. Take Burke with you . . . but Miss Harrow stays."

Rosalie's heart clenched tight.

James stepped in close. "I will not leave her here to be abused by you."

The duchess laughed, a flash of triumph on her face. "You cannot possibly think to move an unmarried young lady into your bachelor's den. You would ruin her reputation for certain, what little she has of it," she added with a sneer. "And we all know she will not marry you. She doesn't want you, James."

Rosalie couldn't take this another second. She stepped forward, her hand brushing James' as she faced the duchess. "You cannot keep me here."

"You have nowhere else to go," the duchess replied. "Without my generosity, you will be on the street—"

"*Enough*!"

They all turned as the duke approached. So far, he'd merely watched them all tear at each other with their talons. Now he looked furious, his cheeks pink.

"George, darling—"

"I said enough," he barked at the duchess. "This has all been more than enough." He rounded on his brother, pointing a trembling finger in his face. "James, you are not dismissed. I do not give you leave of me. You will stay in this house, and you will do your job, which is to say you will do *my* job. Threaten to leave me again, and I will ruin you. You may be a viscount, but I am a duke. I breathe air reserved for kings. Just try and escape me, little brother."

Then he turned on their mother. "As for you, Mama . . . speak to my brother with such violence again, and I will turn you out on the street. See how you like living outside the warmth of any familial love."

She gasped. "George, you can't—"

He ignored her, turning his gaze on Rosalie. "Now for you, Miss Harrow . . . do you like living here? I mean, this disastrous and horribly uncomfortable conversation aside," he said with a wave of his hand.

Rosalie blinked, glancing from the duchess to James. "I . . ."

"Don't look at them, look at me," he pressed. "I asked you a question. Do you like living at Corbin House? Would you like to stay here? Or Alcott Hall . . . or the townhouse in Bath—any of my properties, really."

She held his gaze.

"You said you want a choice, and I'm giving it to you now," he said gently. "Do you want to be a ward of the Corbin family?"

She swallowed down all her fears, looking only at the duke. "Yes," she whispered.

He clapped his hands once, a broad smile on his face. "Well, then that settles it. Rosalie Harrow is *my* ward now."

27

James

JAMES STOOD THERE, dumbfounded, watching as George claimed Rosalie as his ward. Never in his life before had he witnessed his brother take such a stand. He didn't care about other people. He didn't lift a finger to fight for anyone but himself. He certainly never stood up to their mother in any way beyond the occasional spewing of curses or empty threats. No, James weathered every battle alone.

So, what happened to make George step in at last?

James knew the answer without hesitation. *Rosalie.* It was all coming down to this beautiful, frustrating, intoxicating woman. In one short month, she'd managed to have even George Corbin bending to her magnetic pull. Christ, would any of them survive her?

"George, you can't be serious," their mother huffed.

"Oh, I am deadly serious," George countered. "Miss Harrow is under my protection now, and she will serve the family at *my* pleasure, not yours." He turned to Rosalie and waved his hand in a gesture that looked curiously like the sign of the cross. "I hereby revoke any and all previous arrangements you made with my mother."

"This is ridiculous—"

He spun to face their mother. "Are you still here? Be gone. We have no more need of your poison tonight. And since you are clearly so overtired, I'll be sure Wilson brings a dinner tray to your room."

"You would order me about in my own home?" she shrieked.

He puffed himself up to his full height, eyes blazing. "It is *my* house. I am the fucking Duke of Norland. *Me!*" To make his point, he waved his signet ring in her face. "You wear my jewels and sit at my table and eat my food, Mama. Never forget it is my generosity that keeps you so comfortable in your luxurious dotage."

George picked his needle well, for there was nothing their mother hated more than to be called old. Her face turned three shades of pink before she shrieked, ready to strike George, but he moved before James could step forward, grabbing their mother by both wrists. "Claws in, you cat!"

"You ungrateful boy," she cried, tugging at him to free herself. "You worthless creature!"

"*Guards!*" he squawked.

James blinked. Guards? Did George think he was at the Tower?

Harris the footman peeked his head around the open doorway. His eyes blew wide as saucers when he saw the duke in a scuffle with the dowager.

"Mother, that is enough," James muttered, embarrassed for her.

With an angry sob, her eye fell on the footman and she stopped struggling.

Panting, George let her go, taking a step back and smoothing a hand through his tousled hair. "Harris, my dear mama is overtired," he called. "Please see that she makes it safely to her room and have her maid tend to her there."

"Of course, Your Grace." The footman stepped forward, ready to escort their mother out.

"This isn't over," she hissed at George.

"For tonight at least, it is."

Snarling under her breath, she swept from the room, not looking back. Harris quickly followed, pulling the door shut with a soft click.

A moment of silence stretched between the three of them. James glanced from Rosalie to George, unsure of what to do next.

"HolyfuckingChrist, that was so stressful." George sank onto the closest empty chair.

Rosalie stepped around James, dropping to her knees by George. She reached for him with one hand. "Are you alright, Your Grace?"

"James, I think my arse is sweating," George cried, glancing at him with an anxious look.

James took the chair opposite his brother. "George, you didn't need to do that . . ."

"I did," he replied, fanning himself with his hand. "I should have done it years ago. God, it felt so good to see her squirm. Did you see her? I really think she thought I meant it when I said I'd throw her out."

James raised a brow. "Did you not?"

"I can't even dismiss a servant when I know they're stealing from me. You think I could toss my own mother to the street?"

For a moment, James caught Rosalie's eye. He had to quickly look away as he saw her lips curl into a smile. George was certainly an odd kind of champion for them both.

"Did you mean what you said?" he asked. "Do you really want me to stay?"

"Of course, I want you to stay," George replied, sitting forward. "You're my brother, James. You're a Corbin. As things stand now, you're my heir. Your place is here. Always." James couldn't deny the small fluttering he felt in his chest when he heard his brother say the words. It was small . . . but it was there. He glanced at Rosalie fast enough to watch her head turn as she wiped a tear away from under her eye.

"And me, Your Grace?" she murmured. "Are you certain I'm not more trouble than I'm worth?"

George faced her. "Hmm . . . that remains to be seen. You certainly have caused quite the stir. But anyone who is willing to stand up to my fearful mama is a friend worth having, eh James?"

She laughed. It was a soft sound, low in her throat. She covered her mouth with her hand, her eyes going wide as if the sound surprised even her.

"I've never actually had a ward before," George went on. "I'm not sure of the protocol. What do I do with you? Dress you? Do you need a spending allowance? Feed you, of course. Dancing lessons or . . . you're probably too old for a French tutor. Do you want to learn German?"

"I don't need anything, Your Grace," she said with another soft laugh. "I thank you for your generosity, and I'm willing to help you in any way I can. I mean to earn my keep."

George's eyes lit up as he glanced from James to Rosalie. "This is fantastic," he cried. "You'll be like my own little shadow. Oh Cabbage, there's so much fun we can have together!"

"George, be serious," James warned. "Just because she is your ward, that does not entitle you to treat her like a servant. What if you simply live and let her live—"

George held up a hand. "Quiet, James. This doesn't concern you."

Rosalie gave James a sympathetic look before turning her attention back to George. "I am in your debt, Your Grace—"

"Say nothing of that," he replied with a wave of his hand.

Loud voices and laughter in the hall alerted them right before the door to the study was flung open.

"No, I don't know where—*oh*—there you are, darling. Prue, I found them!" Piety Nash stumbled into James' study. She hung on the door, glancing around the room at the three of them.

"Are you lost, sugar plum?" George called.

The forced sweetness between the pair was enough to make James want to gag.

Piety blinked, still holding onto the door. "You've been gone for ages, Your Grace. You said you'd play cards with us." She narrowed her eyes on Rosalie, forcing a smile. "Ah . . . and Miss Harrow is here too. How nice. We hoped you might indulge our desire for miniature portraits before dinner."

Rosalie got to her feet, smoothing down her skirts. "Of course, Miss Nash." She bobbed a little curtsy to them both before making her escape.

"I'll be along soon too, my candied apple," George called after them.

Piety gave him a winning smile before she, too, disappeared. The door clicked shut once again, leaving the brothers alone.

"Heavens," George muttered, breaking the awkward silence. "That was . . . she stood up to our mama."

James let out a slow exhale. "I know."

"She just . . . she didn't flinch or anything. She held her ground. She fought like a lioness." The incredulity was written across his face, and the awe.

"I know," James repeated.

"Damn . . . I think my cock got a little hard."

James growled. "George, I swear to Christ—"

George laughed. "Easy, little brother. I enjoy my fingers right where they are, thank you very much. That rabid little cabbage would bite them clean off if I dared to approach. She's all yours."

Those three words settled inside James like a punch to the gut. No, she wasn't. Not even close. James feared there was no world in which he could ever change that fact. She didn't want to belong to anyone. No cages. No marriage.

She doesn't want you.

His mother's words echoed in his mind. Rosalie was attracted to him, certainly. Their physical attraction was more than mutual. He could hardly be in the same room as her and still find breath. She would give him her body, but he wanted more. Needed more. The things he wanted most were the very things she refused to ever give.

George shifted off the sofa, and James was sure he would leave. He glanced up to see his brother watching him with an odd look on his face. He frowned. "What now?"

"You were right. She doesn't see you. But I do."

James' frown deepened as he sat back, holding his brother's gaze. "You were listening."

"Your voice carries," George replied with a shrug. James looked away, staring into the empty fireplace.

"I see you, James. And so does that sweet little cabbage." James stilled.

"I meant what I said," George murmured. "She is my ward now. She's under my protection." He paused at the door, one hand on the knob. "And I know you care nothing for my advice, but I'm going to give it all the same."

"Please don't."

"She's knocking at your door, James. Let her in . . . or let her go."

George left, and James felt the hold on his walls crumble at last.

Let her in, or let her go.

For perhaps only the third time in his life, James had to admit that his brother was right about something. James had to learn to let Rosalie in, or he had to let her go. So why did he feel so completely incapable of doing either?

28

Rosalie

ROSALIE WAS SWEPT to the drawing room on Piety's arm and thrust into the middle of the boisterous house party. For several hours, the group played cards and charades. A young lady was always at the piano, plinking out a merry tune. She was forced to satisfy the curiosity of the other young ladies, answering repeated questions about her odd departure with James from the Michaelmas ball. While she kept the details brief, she couldn't avoid the judgmental looks cast her way.

After tea, the Nash twins set Rosalie up in the corner with a sketchbook and insisted that she take their likenesses. The twins looked as beautiful as ever, their golden curls arranged in matching tight rows around their oval faces. They were identical down to the last freckle, their big brown eyes framed in long, dark lashes. Rosalie was grateful to be sat in the corner, away from all the prying eyes. She sketched the twins, the Swindon sisters, and Peanut, Piety's spoiled lap dog.

Just as Rosalie prepared to take her leave, desperate for a few minutes of peace, Piety stood and clapped her hands.

"Right, if we don't all get ready, we'll miss the start of the concert!"

That's how Rosalie found herself dressed in one of her new evening gowns, white gloves pulled up to her elbows, the duchess' pearls at her neck, wedged between Renley and Mariah Swindon at a public concert. Before her, a string quartet played the selected works of Joseph Haydn.

She hadn't had a chance to speak to Burke or Renley since their return to the house, but she could tell from the way Renley leaned in with a furrowed brow that he knew something was wrong. A row behind them, Burke sat between Blanche and Lady Oswald. Rosalie could feel his eyes on her. Her skin felt so warm under his gaze that she was forced to fan herself with her concert program.

"Are you well?" Renley whispered.

"Perfectly," she replied, stirring the air with a flick of her wrist.

In fact, nothing about this situation was perfect. Rosalie had sailed right into perilous waters. Perhaps it was just her imagination, but she felt Burke wasn't the only one with his eyes on her. Each time she glanced around at the crowd of concertgoers, she made eye contact with someone. More than once a lady turned to her neighbor, raising her feathered fan, and whispered some remark that had them both looking her way. It was torture. She fought the urge to squirm in her seat.

And James was being no help at all, keeping himself as far from her as possible. In fact, she wasn't even sure if he was still in the concert hall. This apparently was his way of disproving any rumors swirling about them.

She took a steadying breath, grateful that Renley at least was at her side. He filled the space next to her, looking so dashing in his officer's uniform. The navy blue of his coat brought out the blue in his eyes, and the white contrasted with his tanned face. She dared to glance up, offering him a smile. He returned it, shifting his arm so that it might brush ever so gently against hers. The contact made her sigh. It was the best they could manage for now.

After an hour of music, the quartet took a break, and the concertgoers were treated to punch in the ornate entry hall. It was a beautiful space, with a wall of mirrors on one side that cast dancing candlelight all around. Peals of laughter and overlapping voices created a hazy hum that was punctuated by the clinking of glasses.

She took Renley's arm as he escorted her towards the punch table.

When he was sure no one could hear them, he leaned in. "How are you managing?"

"They scorn me with such delight," she replied, noting how several sets of eyes watched them together.

He gave her hand a gentle squeeze. "Just give it a week. It will soon blow over."

"Not soon enough," she murmured.

"Renley?" An older gentleman in a navy uniform approached. "Good God, I *knew* it was you. Tom Renley back in England? How the devil are you, sir?"

Renley let out a barking laugh. "West Price, you old sea dog! You've gone greyer than the cliffs of Dover!" He stepped away from her to shake the sailor's hand. The men were soon lost in a conversation full of nautical terms and sweeping hand gestures.

Without Renley on her arm, Rosalie felt naked, but she resolved to get them both a glass of punch. It didn't escape her notice how each time she took a step, the crowd seemed to move away, unwilling to acknowledge her presence. How was it possible to feel so alone in such a crowded room?

"Miss Harrow . . . what a surprise to see you here," came a sweet voice to her left.

She turned to see Marianne Young standing along the wall of mirrors. The lady was as beautiful as ever, with her dark curls and icy blue eyes. She was flanked to either side by a pair of equally impressive ladies adorned in their jewels, with plumes of feathers in their powdered curls.

Rosalie worked quickly to put a society-approved smile on her face and dipped into a curtsy. Rank is rank, after all. "Good evening, Mrs. Young. I trust you are well?"

"Perfectly well," she replied. "Oh, but I hope *you* have recovered, dear."

Rosalie held her smile on her face. "Recovered?"

"Yes, from your frightful ordeal. The *ton* has been quite ravenous over it." Marianne glanced to either side to simper at her friends. "Rushed to London in the dead of night in the arms of the Viscount Finchley. Was it medical, dear? A death in the family, perhaps? For I can't imagine it was as scandalous as the gossip columns claim."

Rosalie's breath caught in her throat. "Gossip columns?"

"Oh dear, you didn't know?" Marianne laughed, patting her shoulder like a child. "It's all over the papers, Miss Harrow. There was that column in *The Morning Chronicle*," she said to her friend.

"I read it in *Lady Whisper*," her friend replied with a haughty sniff.

"I wouldn't be surprised if you're featured in *The Times* itself by the end of the week," Marianne added. "You sure know how to make an entrance into high society. I only fear that your entrance might also mark your exit."

Rosalie was going to be sick. Whispers and rumors were one thing, but her trip to London had been printed in the papers? *Multiple* papers? Frustration coiled in her gut. Frustration at herself, which was wholly deserved. But she was frustrated with James too. He had to know. Every morning she watched him at the breakfast table unfurl and read his stack of papers. He knew and said nothing, she was sure of it.

Did Renley know too? Did Burke? Had they all been keeping it from her for days?

"The truth is hardly worth noting," she said, doing her best to hold her head high.

"No one cares about truth in this town," Marianne replied with a flick of her fan. "All we want is a good story."

"Either way, I shall leave the *true* story with you," Rosalie countered. "The viscount had urgent business in town to prepare for His Grace's wedding. They mean to marry within the month. Surely you must have heard?"

"Oh yes, we know. The soon-to-be Piety Corbin, Duchess of Norland," Marianne replied. "Oh, how the climbers will climb," she added under her breath, taking a sip of her bubbly pink punch.

The other ladies snorted with derision.

"Speaking of social climbers, I hear I am to congratulate *you* on your official position at Corbin House," Marianne went on. "You are the new governess now, yes? Oh, wait . . . that makes no sense, for there are no children in the house." She looked to her friends in mock confusion. "I must be misremembering what Tom told me. Tell us Miss Harrow, what *is* your role there?"

Rosalie let out a slow exhale, saying nothing as the other ladies sneered. She was too busy focusing on the way Marianne's mouth had shaped the word "Tom."

"Miss Nash will have to watch out for you," Marianne goaded, knowing she'd hit her target. "I hear the Duke of Norland suffers from a most pernicious case of the wandering eye. With such a treat before him, however will he look away?"

"I'd hate to be Miss Nash," huffed the lady on the left.

"Forced to compete for attention in my own home? It is not to be borne," the lady on the right replied.

Marianne took a sip of her punch. "Some men just prefer dross to gold."

"Hmm, too true, Mari," cooed the lady on the right. "And some people need to be reminded of their proper sphere."

Rosalie could feel her heartbeat in her ears. It mixed with the hum of conversation around the room. Too much noise. Too many people. Too everything. She blinked. Were her eyes wet? Was she about to cry in front of these women?

Never. Pull yourself together.

Trying her best to recover her dignity, she lifted her chin and smiled. "I must go find Lieutenant Renley before the concert resumes. He'll no doubt be wondering where I am." She dipped into a little curtsy. "Excuse me—"

Marianne stepped forward, clutching Rosalie's gloved wrist. "No, he isn't," she hissed in her ear. "He isn't wondering that at all. Because Tom doesn't think of you. He will tire of you, and he will cast you aside as just another gossip column skivvy."

She raised her free hand, brushing it along Rosalie's jaw. This was the second time this woman had dared to touch Rosalie in such a familiar way. Rosalie stiffened, feeling the satin of the glove against her skin like it were sandpaper.

"Such a pretty little rose," Marianne murmured. "So soon to wilt."

"Take your hand off me," Rosalie said, enunciating each word.

"Gladly." Marianne dropped her hand away.

Without waiting another second, Rosalie slipped between the crowd, moving as far from Marianne Young as possible. She left the hall, following a sign for the ladies' dressing room. Tugging open the door, she stepped inside, closing it with a snap. Thank heavens, the room was empty.

Sagging against the door, she let out a shaky sob, putting her gloved hand over her mouth. She leaned against the wood for a minute, trying to control her breathing. Then she stumbled forward, reaching for the drink cart like it was a lifeline. She gripped it with both hands, pouring herself a glass of tepid lemon rosemary water.

Before she could raise the glass to her lips, a deep voice spoke behind her.

"Oh, Cabbage, that was embarrassing."

29

Rosalie

ROSALIE SPUN AROUND with a gasp. The duke was standing by the door. "Your Grace," she said on a breath. "This is a ladies' dressing room."

He glanced around, noting the sparse furniture, the row of vanities along one wall, the painted screen in each corner. "So, it is."

"You should not be in here."

His eyes narrowed. "Neither should you."

She held his gaze, feeling her lower lip start to tremble.

The duke just watched her. He wore a black evening coat with black breeches that came to the knee, and crisp white stockings. His double waistcoat was a mix of blue and gold, and his cravat was a handsome burgundy patterned silk. His only adornment was his signet ring, which he twirled round and round on the smallest finger of his left hand.

She took a shaky breath. "You heard."

He shrugged. "I wasn't close enough to hear it all but I saw."

She gave a little nod, her gaze dropping to the carpet.

He leaned against the door. "I've known Marianne Young all her life. I've never seen her sharpen her claws on another lady before. Your mere presence made her go feral. Why?"

She turned away.

"*Ohh* . . ." He chuckled. "She used to hold a candle for Renley, did she not? Yes, I remember them together," he mused.

Rosalie stiffened.

"Have I hit the mark? I can see that I have. She doesn't like to see our dear Lieutenant Renley chasing after your skirts. Certainly not while the rumors about my brother spread all over town."

She spun around. "He is not chasing after me—"

"Oh yes, he is," the duke countered, pushing off the wall and crossing the room towards her. "There can be no secrets between friends, Cabbage. If you think I don't know exactly how eagerly the men in my house are chasing after you, then you've grossly underestimated my ability to sniff out sexual tension, and I take great offense."

She was sure her cheeks must be flaming crimson. "So, tonight you didn't fight back when Marianne attacked you. But this morning, you fought off my mother with the ferocity of a lioness. So it's certainly not a question of whether you *can* fight . . . but whether you *choose* to fight."

She didn't dare meet his eye.

He barked a laugh. "Of course, you only stepped in with Mama when she threatened James. I have unraveled the mystery," he said, clapping his hands together. "This morning you were protecting James and . . ." He glanced up in time to see her wipe a tear from her eye. He sobered, his voice softer. "You were protecting James, but no one was there tonight to protect you."

She focused again on the carpet.

"That's it . . . isn't it? You'll defend another, come hell or high water. But when you're the one under attack, you take the hits. You wait for it to end." He let out a long sigh. "Who taught you that trait? A former lover, perhaps? A parent? Is this the work of Francis Harrow?"

She sucked in a breath, raising her eyes to him at last. "How did you . . ."

"I'm a duke, Cabbage. I know everything," he replied with a wave of his hand. "Here's the thing . . . if you and I are going to be friends, you can't embarrass me like that. Not in public. We need the lioness to sharpen her claws."

She glanced up. "And are we friends?"

He chuckled. "Oh, yes, I've decided I want that to be one of your duties."

"As your ward, you're requiring that I be your friend?"

"Yes."

She waited for him to laugh or break, but he didn't. "But that is not how friendship works."

He tipped his head to the side, a petulant frown on his lips. "Why not?"

"Because it's unnatural. You cannot force a friendship," she reasoned.

"I'm a duke," he said with a shrug. "I can do whatever I want."

She lifted her chin and crossed her arms over her beaded evening gown. "No. You cannot make me be your friend."

He stomped his foot like a spoiled child. "Well, what am I supposed to do, then?"

"Well, you have to *be* a friend, Your Grace. You can do nice things for them or help them. Offer advice . . . comfort."

He glanced around the room, brows lowering over his blue eyes. "Let me help you out of this mess."

She blinked. "What mess?"

"Well, you can't possibly go back out there," he said, moving past her towards the window. He tugged back the curtain, looking out.

"I must go back," she cried. "Renley is probably looking for me even now—"

"So?"

"So I must return to my seat."

"Absolutely not." He moved behind her and helped himself to the drink cart, pouring himself a generous measure of wine.

"Why not?"

"You just said that as my friend, I must help you and offer advice. So here it is: You have to learn to fight for yourself, not just for others. That is the first and last time the likes of Marianne Young gets to make you cry. Do you understand me?" He drained the glass of wine in two gulps, smacking his lips as he pulled it away. "You retreated, and in so doing, you gave her the field. The battle is lost."

She stifled a laugh. "Am I at war then, sir?"

"All life is war," he replied somberly, refilling his glass.

His words hit her right in the chest. She knew how much truth they contained.

He stepped forward and put a brotherly hand on her shoulder. "If you go out there now, I guarantee you that Mrs. Young and all those sparkling ladies will be waiting for you. The gossip rags have not been kind. You and James were careless, and you must pay the price. He won't. Men never do," he added. "Only *you* will pay."

"What will they do to me?" she whispered, eyes wide.

"Do?" He snorted. "They won't *do* anything. That's the whole point. If you go out there, they will sneer and snarl and do nothing. And by doing nothing, they will know they have beaten you. There is no regaining the ground you've lost tonight. All you can do is retreat and return to fight another day."

She raised her gaze to him, desperate to puzzle him out. "Is that how you survive in society, Your Grace?"

He was quiet for a moment. "If you want to beat them at their game, you must learn to do as I do."

She raised a wary brow. "And what is that?"

"Refuse to play," he replied. "If they want you to fight, retreat. If they want you to run, stand your ground. If they're playing whist, well then strip off all your clothes, do a merry jig, and play hazard instead. Keep them guessing. Keep them confused. And by all the gods, keep them entertained." At this, he raised his glass and gave her a wink.

She couldn't help but smile, but it quickly fell. "You know . . . your position in society is far more enviable. You have a power none of the rest of us can wield," she challenged. "As a duke, you can *set* societal expectations."

He poured himself another glass of wine. "Hmm . . . I'd never thought of it that way."

She dared to take a chance. "You want me to be bold. You say your friends must stand up for themselves. But do you follow your own advice? Do you fight for yourself and what you want, or do you leave it all in your brother's hands?"

He frowned, his entire mood swinging to dark and brooding in an instant. "Are you calling me a coward, Miss Harrow?"

"Your Grace, no—I—"

"Because you can save it," he snapped. "I know I'm a coward. I know I disappoint everyone. I know I am the worst duke to ever live."

"Only because you choose to be," she replied, her voice soft.

He huffed, drowning himself in more wine.

"But you're wrong in one respect," she murmured. He turned to face her, a glower on his face. She gave him a weak smile. "You've never disappointed me."

He blinked, as if he didn't understand her words. After a moment, he murmured, "Thank you, Cabbage." Suddenly, he offered out his hand. "Now, leave with me. I've heard enough Haydn for a lifetime. We shall seek our entertainment elsewhere."

Her heart fluttered. "You told me I can't leave the room—"

"I said you can't rejoin the vultures. I never said you can't leave," he corrected.

"How would we leave without showing our faces?"

But he was already moving to the door. "We'll go out the window, of course."

"The—*what*—"

He flung the door open, barking for a footman.

"Yes, Your Grace?" said a young man with a freckled face.

"I have urgent business to attend to and must depart," he said, suddenly all authority. "In ten minutes' time, I want you to alert my brother to my leaving and tell him I have taken my ward with me. Not a minute sooner, understood?"

This was absolutely ridiculous. If riding with James in a carriage at midnight was enough to get her in the society papers, what might climbing out a window with the duke do to her reputation? That was to say nothing about how the men would respond on learning she was gone. But His Grace was right: No force on Earth would compel her to face Marianne again tonight.

The footman took off and the duke shut the door, crossing the room back over to her. "Well? A new adventure awaits. Shall we?" He held out his hand again.

She took a step back, shaking her head. "This is crazy. This is—we can't go out a window. You're mad!"

He grinned. "Yes, but you already knew that. It didn't stop you from agreeing to be my ward. My madness is yours now, Cabbage."

"I can't—I—I don't want the papers to write about me," she whispered. "I don't want to be an object of scorn. I don't want to embarrass your house, your family . . . any more than I already have—"

The duke placed a finger under her chin. "Look at me, Cabbage."

She met his gaze, seeing so much of James in the shape of his brows, the lift of his cheekbones.

"Do you know why your business is being splashed across the gossip rags?"

She nodded, sucking in a breath. "Because I was reckless—"

"No," he countered. "The whole *ton* is gossiping about you because you are *worth* gossiping about. You've arrived, Rosalie Harrow," he said with a widening grin. "You are the mysterious, beautiful, enchanting new ward of the Duke of Norland. Through your connection to me, you will take tea with royalty. You will breathe the rarified air of Kensington Gardens. You will walk into rooms on my arm. You will be served first, you will always have the best seat, and you will not give a bloody *damn* about all the noise that echoes around you."

Fresh tears filled her eyes.

"They will talk about you," he admitted with a slow nod. "They will talk about you, because they cannot *be* you. But their envy is not yours to bear. Live your life on your terms." He paused, searching her eyes. "There, was that friendly advice?"

She laughed. "Yes, Your Grace."

"Good. Now, are we going? Because I don't know about you, but I'm bloody starving." He held out his hand a third time.

Throwing caution to the wind, she took it.

30

Burke

"WHERE THE HELL can they be?" Burke growled. "It's nearly midnight!"

He was pacing before the fireplace in the drawing room. He had been for over an hour. If he wasn't careful, he might just wear a hole in the carpet. The ladies had all retired hours ago, and James had dismissed the servants, so they were blessedly alone.

"We're talking about George," James replied. "There is quite literally no way to know where he might go or what he might do."

Tom rose to his feet. "I can't just keep sitting here."

"Well, you can't go wandering the streets calling her name either," James replied. "Just sit down and wait. They'll return soon, and you'll have your answers."

Reluctantly, Tom paused halfway between the sofa and the door.

"You mean *we* will have answers," Burke countered, turning on the carpet to face his friend. "Don't pull back from this, James. Stay with us."

James scowled, gesturing to his position on the chair. "I'm sitting right here, aren't I?"

"You're here, but you're not *here*," Burke replied. "Don't shut us out, and don't push her away. You must give her a chance to explain."

"No one is saying we won't," Tom assured him.

Burke gave a curt nod, knowing he was saying the words for his own benefit as much as theirs. He was more unsettled now than he had been upon first learning Rosalie fled Alcott. At least then Burke knew she was with James, and thus safe. George was an entirely different story. Why the hell would Rosalie agree to leave with him?

It was the not knowing that was driving him mad. For the hundredth time that night, he dragged both hands through his hair. The sound he made in his throat was somewhere between a moan and a groan.

"Burke, come sit," Tom said, voice low. He was back on the sofa.

But Burke couldn't possibly sit still.

Rosalie Harrow burst into his life, swinging her left fist at that drunkard like any back-alley brawler, and Burke had been lost. He should have dropped to his knees then and proclaimed himself hers. At this point, walking away from Rosalie was an impossibility. He wanted to be entangled in her in every way. Always. Not just her body—which was goddamn perfection—but her clever mind, her goodness, her resilient spirit. She was meant for him, and he for her.

He huffed. The Lord clearly had a sense of humor, for the woman who set Burke's heart aflame was also an angsty, complicated, obstinate siren who was going to challenge him every day for the rest of his life.

"Did you hear that?" Tom muttered.

Burke spun to face the door. The sound of George's muffled laughter had him on the move. If Tom and James were following him, he didn't care. He burst through the drawing room door, leading the way to the entry hall. His heart clenched tight as he saw her, magnificent in her glittering evening gown. It reminded him of champagne, the way it caught the light like bubbles in a glass. George was removing his evening coat from around her shoulders. She glanced back at George as he said something too low for Burke to hear. Whatever he said made her laugh. The sound pierced Burke straight through the heart. He watched as George's fingers brushed along her arms as he dragged the coat down.

Burke's mind went blank as he launched himself across the entry hall. "Get your hands off her," he growled.

George spun around. His eyes went from narrowed with a laugh to wide with surprise.

"Burke," Rosalie cried. "Burke, *no*—"

His hands were within an inch of grabbing onto George's waistcoat when a pair of thick arms wrapped around his shoulders, dragging him back.

"Easy, Burke. Leave him," Tom panted.

In moments, James was on him too, hooking an arm around his middle. Together, the men held him back from George. The insufferable arse just laughed. He even took a half-step closer to Rosalie, who stood still as a statue, eyes wide with shock.

"Burke, what are you doing?" she cried.

"Didn't I tell you, Cabbage? Your men waited dutifully for your return," George jeered. "They're such good little guard dogs. Such loyal chaps."

Next to him, Burke felt James stiffen.

"Where the hell have you been?" James barked.

"*Shh*," George replied, raising a finger to his lips and pointing up the stairs. "Do you want to wake the whole house?"

"Why did you take her?" Burke pressed.

"Take her?" George gave an affronted look as he turned to Rosalie. "Cabbage, did I take you against your will like a Saracen knight and drag you away to some unspeakable fate?"

"No," she replied softly.

Tom and James loosened their hold on Burke, and he shrugged himself free.

"Someone better start talking," James demanded. "Do you have any idea the damage you've both caused tonight? Do you know how hard it will be to keep it contained?"

"So then don't," George said with a shrug. "I can see it now: 'Duke of Norland leaves boring concert early to attend to his business affairs, personal assistant assisted.'"

"That will not be the headline and you know it," James countered.

"Don't we own one of the papers? We can make it say whatever we want—"

"That is not the point!"

"Why own a paper if we can't control what it prints?"

"Rose . . ." Tom's deep voice cut through the brothers' bickering. "Are you alright? Please just tell us that much."

She met Tom's gaze, and several emotions flickered across her face at once. Burke tried desperately to read them. Longing, of course. She was mad for Tom, and he for her. Their chemistry was electric. But there was something more . . . resentment? Mistrust? She schooled her expression too fast for him to get a clear read.

"I'm fine," she murmured.

Tom took another step closer, but George gave an exaggerated stretch and a yawn.

"Well, I'm beat. You"—he snapped his fingers at the footman—"Go get my valet. Have him meet me upstairs. I require a hot bath and a hot chocolate."

"Yes, Your Grace," the footman replied, darting away down the hall.

George glanced at Rosalie. "Shall you be quite safe with them, Cabbage? Or shall I order the other footman to stay as your guard?"

"Why wouldn't she be safe with us?" James snapped.

"Because after tonight, it's clear you three don't know how to provide our Cabbage with the proper care she deserves," George replied.

This sent Burke's mind spinning like a top. What the hell happened at that concert?

"As her friend, I am heartily ashamed of you all," George finished with a frown.

James huffed. "Since when are you two friends?"

"Since tonight," George replied. "I made it part of her official ward duties."

Burke groaned at the same time as James.

"That's not how that works," Tom muttered.

Rosalie was still looking at him strangely. Burke knew Tom had noticed from the way his hands were twitching to reach out for her. But he wouldn't dare show that kind of tenderness in front of George and the servants.

"Rose . . . what happened?" Tom asked.

"It doesn't matter," she replied, her expression closed off.

"Tonight, you left her to the wolves. That's what happened."

George pointed a finger at each of them. "If any of you mean to deserve her, do better." He gave her a quick peck on her temple. "Good night, Cabbage." With that, he spun on his heel and headed for the stairs.

Finch, the remaining footman, glanced anxiously from George's retreating form to James. "My lord, shall I . . ."

James frowned, rubbing the back of his neck. "Go to bed, Finch. It's been a long night. Please have a maid meet Miss Harrow in her room."

"Yes, my lord," Finch replied, disappearing in the same direction as the other footman.

Burke was the first to turn to Rosalie.

"I need a drink," she said quickly. Stepping around all three of them, she walked away towards the drawing room.

"You need to tell us what the hell happened tonight," James called after her.

Burke put a warning hand on his shoulder. James was quickly losing his temper. "Go gently," he muttered in James' ear.

James shrugged him off.

The three of them entered the drawing room to find Rosalie at the sideboard, pouring herself a drink. Damn, but she looked beautiful in that dress.

"Rose, for the love of God, I'm dying here," Tom said, crossing to her side. "What happened tonight?"

Her body was stiff. No playfulness, no romance. She turned to James. "Did you know?"

"Know what?"

"The gossip columns," she replied. James stiffened, saying nothing. "You did, then," she murmured, taking a small sip of gin. "Were you ever going to tell me the papers were writing about us?"

"Whatever George told you, I guarantee you it is not that bad," James hedged. "It was a few articles in some of the rags."

"The papers love to make trouble," Tom added gently. "It will pass in a few days. George was wrong to stir you up like this."

Reaching out, he brushed her shoulder with gentle fingers.

She shifted away from his touch. "George only confirmed it for me."

A stone sank in Burke's stomach. This was bad . . .

"Then who told you?" James pressed.

Rosalie's eyes didn't leave Tom's face. "Your darling friend Mrs. Young."

Goddamn it, Burke was going to *bury* that scheming bitch!

Tom reached for her again. "Rose, I'm so sorry—"

She stepped away, holding her little glass of gin like a shield. "Yes, she cornered me with a few of her lovely friends. They said the most horrid things."

Burke turned his fury on Tom. "Where the hell were you? We agreed you would be the buffer tonight! You were to stay by her side and keep the worst of the gossips at bay. It wasn't bloody difficult—"

"I got distracted for *one* moment," Tom replied. "West Price was there. I blinked, and she was gone."

"It was clearly a mistake to use Renley," James muttered. "He's too popular here in Town. It should have been you, Burke. Next time, it will be."

Burke nodded, even while Tom hung his shoulders with frustration.

"Hold on." Rosalie glanced from James to Tom, her eyes settling on Burke. "You *all* knew, didn't you? Was that your plan, then? To use Tom as a shield against insult? You think I intend to spend the rest of my life with one of you on my arm so the high-society vultures cannot peck out my eyes? I am not yours to protect!"

Burke was by her side in a moment, holding her shoulders. "Yes, you bloody well are!"

"Let me go," she hissed, nearly tipping her drink on them both.

"You think we didn't know there would be gossip? Of course, we did. This is *our* world, Rosalie. You are an innocent, uncorrupted by these social politics. We are trying to keep you safe."

"I'm so sorry about Marianne," Tom said from behind her. "What did she say?"

"It's not worth repeating," Rosalie murmured.

"It *is*," he pressed, stepping around her to stand at Burke's side. "No secrets, Rose. Not here, not with us."

She huffed an empty laugh. "No secrets? That's rich seeing as you've all just admitted to gossiping without me . . . *about* me . . . again!" She struggled in Burke's grasp, and he let her go. She stumbled back, clutching her glass of gin as she moved towards the fireplace. "You want me to open up, but the three of you constantly keep me on the outside. How can I trust when you don't let me in?"

"How can we trust when *you* let no one and nothing in?" James countered, finally crossing the room.

She turned her anger on him. "Don't you dare take the high road, James Corbin. You plot and plan, making decisions for me, dressing me like your little doll," she added, gesturing to her gown. "All the while, you are a mighty fortress with thick walls a mile high. *You* are the one who cannot let anyone in! And my opinion clearly doesn't matter to you. To any of you!"

"That's not true," said Tom.

But James was steaming mad now. "Why would I trust you when you pull stunts like this? Climbing out a window with my brother? You're mad! Where was the consideration? Where was the discernment that we might have been able to help you, defend you, *protect* you—"

"I don't need your protection—"

"No, of course not," he barked, cutting her off with a wave of his hand. "You don't need our protection. You're a one-woman bloody army!"

Tom took a step closer to Rosalie, sensing she was about to break. "James—"

"You're reckless, Rosalie Harrow," James bellowed. "Reckless and fearless, and I do not trust you. I don't trust you in my house. I certainly don't trust you with my friends." He stepped closer, eyes narrowed. "You're going to break them. You'll shatter them when you inevitably leave, and I will be left picking up the pieces."

Burke's heart was in his throat. He was losing it—his bright, shining vision of the future. It was slipping away before his very eyes. How did he hold the four of them together if two were determined to pull them apart?

"James, please—"

"I will not lie to her," James threw at him. "You know honesty means everything to me. And you are not honest," he spat at Rosalie. "You hide yourself away. Your thoughts, your intentions. You act alone—"

"That is not fair—"

"You may think you know me," he went on. "You think I am a fortress, and none may enter, but it is only *you* who cannot enter. You stand outside my walls, unable to look in, and assume I must be alone. But Burke walks freely through my gates. Renley too. Do you know why? Because they have *earned* my trust through years of fidelity and honesty. You are on the outside, and I shall keep you there until you prove worthy of being let in."

Eyes filled with tears, she held James' gaze. "What you say is true," she said softly, setting her glass aside. "I am guarded. I walk alone because I've never had anyone willing to walk beside me. My family was small, scattered to the four winds. An ailing grandmother in Richmond, an uncle in India, Aunt Thorpe here in Town. My father was only at home when he needed food or pocket money or someone to kick around. My mother tried to be there for me, but she had her own demons."

She lifted her chin. "So yes, James, I fight my own battles—" She stifled a cry with her gloved hand, batting Burke away when he reached for her. "Tonight, members of your social set, former lovers . . . they mocked me and jeered, they called me a wilted rose, a distraction, a gossip column skivvy."

"Fucking hell," Tom groaned.

Burke wanted to find Marianne Young and string her up by her ears.

"You are the great lords here," Rosalie went on, gesturing to each of them, her gaze landing on James. "I am nothing to you, I know that. I'm not worthy of you, you've made that clear. Can't you see it, James? *You* will be the ones to tire of me, not the other way around."

Burke felt like his heart had just dropped through the floor. Forcing his chest to rise, he took a sucking breath. He glanced at Tom and knew he was experiencing the same emotions. Rosalie thought she was nothing? She thought they intended to use her up and set her aside? What was it going to take to convince this goddess that she was the orb by which they meant to set all the functions of their lives? She was everything. *Everything*.

He took a step closer. "Rosalie . . . please, love—"

James' voice stilled him. "What did my mother say to you?"

Rosalie blinked back her tears. "What?"

Burke turned from one to the other. "James—"

"She knows something about my mother," he snapped. "Some secret." He turned back to Rosalie. "If you want on the inside, there's a place to start. Tell me what you know."

"Please, don't ask it of me," she whispered, wrapping her arms around her middle. "Ask me anything else—"

"Why are you protecting her?" James challenged, closing the distance between them.

"It is not my truth to tell. It was spoken in confidence, and that is not a lie—"

"It is withholding," James countered. "Which is the same as a lie to me."

She tipped her head back, holding his gaze. They were standing so close, their noses almost touching. Suddenly, James dropped his forehead down to hers, his arm wrapping around her waist as he pulled her close and breathed her in, his nose buried in the curls at her temple. Her hands raised to fist the lapels of his evening coat.

"James . . ." she whimpered, clinging to him.

The sound pierced Burke's soul. He wanted to go to them,

hold them in his arms and keep them like this forever. Oh God, he could taste it.

Please, James . . . say the right thing.

"I may want you, Rosalie," James whispered into her hair. "I may *ache* with the pain of this wanting." He lifted his head away to meet her eye. "But until you give me this." He tapped her forehead with a gentle finger. "And this." He splayed his hand over her heart, right over the exposed swell of her breast. "All the rest is meaningless to me." He lifted both hands to cup her face. "Can you give me what I want?"

They stood there, suspended in time before the fireplace, gazing into each other's eyes. Her lips trembled. "I . . . you can't just ask this of me all at once—"

James dropped his hands away so fast she was left swaying on the carpet. He took two steps back. "I bid you all a good night," he muttered. Turning on his heel, he stalked away.

"James, stop," Burke called, desperate that they all stay in this room.

"Let him go," Tom said, putting a firm hand on his shoulder.

Burke watched as the drawing room door shut. Then he spun around to face Rosalie. Tears fell silently down her cheeks as she stood alone by the fireplace in her beautiful ball gown, James' mother's pearls at her throat. Burke didn't miss the way James' fingers unconsciously found them, stroking the strands as he held her close, his hand splayed over her heart.

"Oh, my love," he murmured. Going to her at once, he wrapped her in his arms and she fell apart, crying against his chest.

Tom was there in an instant, framing her from behind, shoring her up. He wove his arms in with theirs, holding onto

Burke as much as Rosalie as he dropped his face to the curve of her neck. "I'm so sorry," he murmured. "I'm sorry, Rose. You don't have to be so strong all the time. Let us help you. Let us hold you. Let us *in*."

She stiffened in their arms, her face still pressed into Burke's cravat. "I don't know how," she whispered, her voice breaking.

Burke felt the humility of her declaration down to his very bones. This beautiful creature had known nothing but violence and rejection and dismissal all her life. She didn't know how to let them in. She didn't know how to let them love her. Still holding tight to her and Tom, he lowered his head to kiss her temple. "Let us teach you."

31

Rosalie

THIS AUTHOR CAN *confidently report that the illustrious V— F— recently returned to town. He was spotted in the early hours of Saturday arriving at C— House. Rumors abound as to the identity of a certain lady seen on his arm . . . and sporting his evening coat.*

Rosalie set the folded newspaper aside. "Is this the last one?"

Renley nodded, his hand rubbing small circles on her back over her chemise. "There may be more in the coming days. Though your window escape will cause a bigger splash," he added.

"George makes the papers so often, the *ton* will hardly see it as sensational," Burke said from her other side. "He's always been an eccentric."

She considered this for a moment. "Meaning the focus will be on me entirely. No one will care about his behavior. They will only mark mine."

Burke shrugged. "The *ton* always marks a lady's conduct more harshly than a lord's."

They were sitting on her bed, the early morning sunlight

peeking in through her cracked curtains. Last night, they'd been so gentle with her, holding her and murmuring soft words as she fell asleep in their arms. She woke to find Burke's place empty, but he'd returned before she could question his absence, the small stack of papers in hand.

The gossip wasn't as bad as she imagined—half a dozen pieces announcing the arrival of Viscount Finchley. Her name wasn't referenced in any of them, but two made mention of her dark hair. It wasn't hard to piece the rest together.

She handed the papers back to Burke. "We need to talk about Olivia."

He set them aside. "I don't like having other women mentioned when I'm in your bed," he replied, pulling her closer.

"In this case, sir, *I* am the other woman."

He stiffened, his forehead pressed against the nape of her neck.

"She is your intended. Even if you don't mean to follow through with the wedding, you still shook hands with her mother. You agreed—"

"Under duress," he growled.

"All the same . . ." She shifted away from him, turning to meet his stormy grey eyes. "You need to speak with her. Alone. Do it today. You need to make her understand your intentions. She deserves the truth, Burke."

He raised a dark brow. "You think it wise to tell her about us?"

"If she is half the lady I think she is, she'll already be hard at work recruiting gossip from the staff here. And you have not been discreet," she reminded him. "I imagine there is little else on this Earth surer to upset her than humiliation. Tell her that we mean to see a way out for her."

Burke glanced at Renley, seeking confirmation.

She looked back to see Renley stretched out, arms tucked behind his head and his broad, muscled chest on display. Each time she saw his tattoos, she fought the urge to trace them with her fingers, her lips . . .

"I agree with Rose," he said. "Secrets and lies make me edgy. I may think the gorgon deserves to be brought down a peg, but not like this. And certainly not in any way that will reflect badly on Rose."

A sound down the hall of a shutting door made them all twitch.

"Heavens, the servants will already be moving about," she whispered, checking the time on the mantel clock. "You both have to go. Now."

They wasted no time getting out of the bed. Renley slept in his breeches, but his shirt was left discarded on the floor. He tugged it on, while Burke worked himself into his robe. Apparently, the man always slept naked, company or no. Rosalie felt a little flutter in her chest knowing she was learning these intimate habits.

"We may not see you again until dinner," Renley said, coming around the end of the bed. He wrapped her in his arms, kissing her twice. Her senses swam. Each time he kissed her, she felt it everywhere.

No sooner had she recovered than Burke was there. He cupped her face with both hands. "Don't think I will soon forget your comment about being the other woman," he said. "Add it to the list of things I intend to punish you for . . . soon."

With that threat, he kissed her, nipping her bottom lip hard enough to make her wince. He pulled back, brushing his thumb lightly over the abused lip. "There is no other woman, Rosalie Harrow. There is only you."

An hour later, Rosalie was dressed in her favorite new walking gown—the pretty, long-sleeved French design with the forest green overlay and pink patterned skirt. She paused at the top of the stairs, one hand on the banister, as she spotted Piety and the duke on the middle landing.

"Oh, Miss Harrow, what a relief," Piety called. She was a vision in sapphire blue, her blonde curls piled high in a style not unlike the one typically worn by the duchess. "My *fidanzato* and I are having a disagreement. You must come arbitrate." She waved her hand airily over her shoulder, already turning back to the apparent object of their tiff.

Rosalie came down the stairs and stood at Piety's side.

"I think it is grotesque, and want it boxed away," Piety explained, pointing up at a large painting on the wall. "But His Grace believes that art must be allowed to be art. What is your opinion?"

"Cabbage is an expert in pencils," the duke complained. "What can she know about oils?"

Piety giggled. "Did you just call her a cabbage?"

"Hmm," he replied, still looking at the painting. "Don't the lower classes eat cabbages?"

"Oh, Your Grace, you are cruel."

"Thank you," Rosalie murmured, to which the duke just shrugged.

"Well?" Piety gestured at the painting. "What are your thoughts, Miss Harrow?"

Rosalie took in the life-sized portrait of . . . well, he was surely a man, a lord, perhaps? But the proportions were off—his torso too narrow, and his thighs longer than his calves. The details of the face were so obscured by the heavy-handed application of thick paint, it made the features seem almost deformed. If the sitter actually paid for this portrait, he was grossly abused.

She pursed her lips. "Well, from a certain angle, perhaps . . ."

"It is horrid," Piety whined. "It shall haunt my dreams, Your Grace. It should have no place on the walls of a house as great and noble as this. Whoever put it in such a spot of honor must have been playing a cruel joke."

The duke just chuckled. "I had this piece hung here. It may be one of my favorites in the house."

Rosalie fought her laugh as Piety sputtered. "But—you have an original Reynolds," she cried. "A Gainsborough portrait sits in your drawing room. There is a Vittore Carpaccio in your dining room, Your Grace. How can you even compare—"

"I never said I was trying to compare them," the duke replied.

"But—"

"My darling lemon drop, if it bothers you so much, simply avert your eyes," he said, patting her on the shoulder.

"Avert my eyes on the stairs? Do you wish me to tumble to my death?"

Turning sharply, he wrapped his arms around her, nuzzling her neck and cupping her bottom in a display that had the lady squealing.

"Your Grace, not in front of Miss Harrow," she said with a giggle.

Yes, please God, not in front of me.

Rosalie took a step back as the duke growled into Piety's neck. "I shall build a litter for you with silk curtains, and my footmen shall carry you down the stairs past the offensive painting every morning and every night."

"You are impossible," Piety cried.

"Nothing is impossible for a duke." Over her shoulder, he caught Rosalie's eye and winked.

Rosalie grimaced. "I shall just . . . leave you, then." She inched around them, trying to blot out the sounds of panting as she escaped down the stairs. No sooner had she turned the corner than she paused in her steps with a gasp.

The duchess stood before her, resplendent as ever in a blush pink gown. A little lap dog sat curled in her arms. "Are they still there?" she said, her mouth tipped into a frown.

Behind Rosalie, peals of laughter echoed down the stairs, followed by a squeal of "Oh, Your Grace!" She shifted awkwardly. "It would seem so."

The duchess tsked. "Apparently, Mr. Nash has not managed to buy any class with his buckets of new money. The girl is offensive."

"The girl will be duchess of this house," Rosalie replied. "Perhaps if we are all to live happily together, we might look for her merits rather than her faults."

The duchess held her gaze, those blue eyes the same shade and shape as her eldest son's. "And what of me, Miss Harrow? Are you to look for my merits rather than my faults?"

"I don't typically look at people to find fault with them, Your Grace. I prefer to find the beauty in things. It is the artist in me, the ever-reluctant optimist."

The duchess huffed at that.

Rosalie decided to offer an olive branch. "In your case, I need not look very hard . . . your merits being so evident in the running of this house, the quality of your staff, the generosity of your sons." She paused before adding, "As well as your demonstrated generosity towards me. You paid my family's debts. I have not forgotten."

"And yet, yesterday you threatened to expose me in front of my children," the duchess snarled. "I confided in you, I helped you, and you were ready to use it against me. You think after three weeks in this world you're ready to take on a duchess and win? You think to put me in my place?"

Rosalie just shrugged. "I think, to quote your son, I am a lioness. I will fight for those I love and for those too weak to fight for themselves."

The duchess narrowed her eyes. "And James is weak in your eyes?"

"I said nothing about James," Rosalie replied. "His Grace calls me the lioness. You fought so hard to earn him his title, schemed so beautifully, and I think part of you now resents him for it. You are cruel to him, and I will not tolerate it. As his ward, I issue you this warning: Hurt him with unkind words in my presence again, and I will tear at your throat until no words are left."

The duchess blinked, unshed tears in her eyes. Slowly, she nodded her approval. "He doesn't deserve you, you know," she whispered.

A faint smile tipped Rosalie's lips. "True, but he has me all the same."

The ladies held each other's gaze for a moment before the duchess leaned in and whispered, "Will you tell him what you know?"

Rosalie didn't need to ask which son she referred to now. "No, but perhaps you should. About the money . . . about everything. James values honesty above all else. You will not keep him close to you if you cannot learn to be honest with him."

Even as she said the words, she saw them for the cruel joke they were. But she'd given her promise, and she meant to keep it. James would not be hearing about his mother's past from her lips. And if he couldn't respect her decision to honor her oath, well then perhaps they were too incompatible to ever work.

The duchess squared her shoulders, giving her little dog another pat. "I think I shall take a walk in the garden. Moppet needs some fresh air. Will you join me, Miss Rose?"

Rosalie smiled. "I would be happy to, Your Grace."

32

Rosalie

THE DUCHESS' PLAN to stroll the back gardens quickly turned into a morning promenade at the park. All the ladies opted to join in. They put on their fanciest hats and most fashionable dresses, carrying an odd collection of muffs and parasols between them, for it was a cool and windy day, but sunny.

Rosalie walked alongside Prudence, who let her little corgi trot between them on a leather lead. Olivia walked just ahead with Elizabeth. She looked austere in a dark velvet cap trimmed with feathers and a plum pelisse. In contrast, Elizabeth looked like the sun itself in a bright yellow ensemble that clashed spectacularly with her mane of fiery red hair.

The park was busy, as all of London seemed to share the idea of enjoying one of the last truly fine days of autumn. The strong breeze had several families flying kites on the long stretch of green lawn. In their excitement, Blanche and Mariah were already several yards ahead of the rest of the group, waving down a man selling sugared almonds.

The arrival of the Dowager Duchess of Norland and her retinue caused quite a stir. Rosalie couldn't help but be impressed. Any hint of the scheming, snarling creature from the day before was locked tightly away. Now the duchess was all smiles, flanked by the countess and marchioness, the bevy of young ladies trailing in their wake. All down the promenade lane, other ladies not-so-subtly corrected course so that they might pass by, hoping to spy something of the latest fashions and receive a public acknowledgment from the duchess.

But Rosalie didn't care about the social politics of promenading. She eyed Olivia carefully, trying to note her mood. She meant what she'd said this morning—Burke needed to talk to her, and soon. Perhaps if Rosalie laid a bit of a foundation with the lady now, his way would be easier later.

The trouble was, since her arrival to Corbin House, Olivia had kept herself even more aloof and apart. It made sense, seeing as the duchess was effectively blackmailing her. Rosalie could only imagine how the Rutledges felt, forced to simper and smile. All the while, a Sword of Damocles hovered over their heads.

The group congregated near a new art installation, and Rosalie took her chance. She stepped up next to Olivia. "It's lovely, isn't it?" she said, gesturing to a sculpture of two lovers sharing an intimate embrace.

Olivia just sniffed. "I have no eye for sculpture."

Rosalie glanced around. "Then might we take a turn over by the flower garden?"

With an indifferent shrug, Olivia began walking in that direction. Rosalie fell into step beside her, making sure to keep the rest of the group in sight. The wind gusted at their backs, billowing their skirts forward. As soon as they were clear of the others, she glanced at her companion. "And how are you this morning?"

"Come now, Miss Harrow," Olivia said with the hint of a smile. "You have me alone and that is your great query?"

Rosalie smiled. She was determined to think of this lady as the personification of a hedgehog—prickly on the outside with a soft underbelly. Rosalie just had to find her way in. She opted for sarcasm, meeting her companion barb for barb. "Yes, you saw through my clever ruse. I worked quite carefully to extract you from the others."

"Just ask your question, Miss Harrow."

They stopped at the edge of a sprawling flower bed, still bright with fall colors. Claret-colored dianthus mixed with purple asters, sprays of bright yellow goldenrods, and soft pink shrub roses. It was pretty as a painting.

Rosalie focused her attention back on her companion. "How are you? Since the ball . . . since the engagement?"

Olivia stiffened, both hands holding tight to her parasol. "It's not made the papers yet, which is a small mercy, I suppose."

"You don't want to marry Mr. Burke." It wasn't a question.

"Of course, I don't," Olivia huffed. "Marry a man with no social standing, no name, no title or wealth? It is unconscionable."

Rosalie held her breath, even as her heart thrummed nervously. She had to know. "That is your assessment of his social status. What of Mr. Burke the man? Is he wholly disagreeable to you?"

Olivia turned her gaze on Rosalie. "Do you mean to ask whether I find the penniless, bastard son of a disgraced steward to be otherwise charming and handsome enough to marry?" She laughed. It was an empty sound, full of bitterness.

"So, for you, status is all that matters," Rosalie probed, feeling a flutter of relief. "You would marry a man of status, even if he had a cloven hoof. With big enough pockets, all personality failings can be ignored . . ."

Olivia gave her an incredulous look. "You think I get to select from a cornucopia of handsome lords with healthy estates and witty personalities? I'm sorry, Miss Harrow, but that cornucopia does not exist."

"But what if—"

"It does not exist," Olivia snapped. "Not for me anyway," she added under her breath. "And why should you care? We are not friends. Why are you so curious about my plight?"

"Mr. Burke is my friend," Rosalie replied. "Lord James is my benefactor. This is hurting them as much as you. And you and I . . . we have an understanding. I understand—"

"You understand nothing. How can you?"

"Don't treat me like I'm simple," Rosalie countered, not backing down. "I was there on the floor with you in that water closet. I held you as you cried—"

"Quiet, you fool," Olivia hissed, glancing around with sharp eyes. "I'll thank you not to speak of my business again. I can't believe I was so unguarded," she muttered. "I don't even know you."

"I will not betray your confidence. Olivia, I mean to help you—"

"No one can help me. Lack of marriage for a lady is a slow kind of death. I must—" She took a steadying breath, blinking back her tears. "I must marry, and there's an end on it. I've run out of all my good chances."

Rosalie was trying desperately not to let her own mistrust of matrimony cloud her judgment. Did Olivia truly believe there were no single men of quality worthy of marriage? Or was the lady revealing some deeper sentiment, perhaps a fear that she could never hope to win such a man?

The wind picked up a bit, whistling through the trees. Rosalie put a hand on her bonnet, holding it in place as she studied Olivia's expression. "What if there was a way out? You don't have to marry him, Olivia. I promise you, the duchess can be persuaded—"

"You have known the duchess for thirty days," Olivia snapped. "I have known her for nigh on thirty years. She is as cold as she is ruthless. She'll follow through with her threats if I don't marry Mr. Burke-Corbin-whatever his name is now. Besides," she added, "word is already spreading of the engagement. The papers will soon seal my fate. No, I must marry him, or I am ruined."

Rosalie took the lady's arm. "Please, Olivia—there is a way for you both to get what you want. If you will but trust me, I think I can see you clear of this."

Olivia turned, her fair brows raised in curiosity. Quickly, the brows lowered. "Miss Harrow . . . what are you scheming in that pretty little head of yours?"

Before Rosalie could reply, a huge gust of wind swept over the flower beds. It knocked Rosalie's bonnet back. Only the ribbons tied under her chin kept it from flying away. She scrambled to right it as Olivia screeched.

"My parasol!"

The wind had plucked the fancy lace parasol right from Olivia's hand. The ladies watched as it was swept away on the breeze, tumbling across the grass. Olivia ran after it in a flash, her hands fisted in her skirts.

"Olivia," Rosalie called. "Wait—"

"It was my grandmother's," Olivia cried.

"Be careful!" Rosalie's bonnet flopped down her back again as she followed Olivia's zig-zagging pattern through the grass.

"Oh no," she huffed, glancing up. "Olivia, the trees!" Olivia shrieked, reaching for the parasol with both hands, but another gust of wind tumbled it higher. Riding the wind, it flew up into the branches of an obliging chestnut tree.

"No!" Losing all sense of decorum, Olivia did a few little hops, snatching for the handle that hung just out of reach.

Rosalie came to a halt behind her, chest heaving from their short sprint. She covered her mouth with her hand to stifle her laughter as Olivia did another jump. "Olivia, please." She put her hand on her shoulder. "Let me go for help."

"I've nearly got it," Olivia said through gritted teeth. "If the wind would just dislodge it a bit more—"

Suddenly, a deep voice chuckled behind them. "Why are you always losing things up trees?"

Rosalie and Olivia both spun around. Rosalie gasped. Standing before her was a giant of a man in a navy captain's uniform. He had deeply tanned skin and dark eyes, with a square jaw. His hair was trimmed unfashionably close on the sides, with the rest hidden under his hat. A long, thin scar marred his right eye in the corner, extending down to mid-cheek, giving him a rugged, dangerous look.

He smiled at Olivia, his eyes flashing with mirth. "Hello, Livy. It's good to see you again."

Rosalie's mouth opened in surprise as she glanced from the mysterious captain to Olivia, who was now white as a sheet. Not wasting another breath, Olivia stepped forward and slapped him across the face.

33

Rosalie

THE CAPTAIN BARKED a deep laugh, rubbing his jaw. "Aye, I suppose I deserved that."

"That and more," Olivia hissed.

"Olivia—" Rosalie put a hand on her arm as the lady dared to wind up for another strike. "Come away," she whispered. "Leave him and come away."

Olivia's antics with the parasol had already drawn attention. Several people were watching, whispering to their neighbors with narrowed eyes. Rosalie forced a smile, adjusting her bonnet with her left hand while still holding onto Olivia with her right.

Olivia stepped back, chest heaving and eyes glassy with angry tears.

The captain grinned, dropping his hand from his jaw. "I knew you'd remember me. I certainly remember you."

His smile put Rosalie in mind of a hungry wolf. She fought a tremor as she tightened her hold on Olivia's arm. "We should rejoin our group," she murmured.

"Is Henry here?" He glanced over his shoulder with

interest as he surveyed those on promenade. "I'd love to see him."

Olivia spoke at last, her voice clipped. "Henry is in Deal." Rosalie could only assume Henry must be her brother.

She was starting to put the pieces together. This captain couldn't be more than five and thirty. No doubt, they all grew up together in some way. All that was left to discover was whether Olivia's animosity for this man was rooted in some childhood dislike . . . or the reverse.

"I heard he's married now," said the captain. "I was sorry to have missed it."

"That was six years ago," Olivia replied. "He has three children."

"Aye, well I've been abroad for quite a long time." He glanced at Rosalie and smiled again. "I'm sorry, miss. It doesn't appear that Livy's going to introduce us—"

"Stop calling me 'Livy,'" she hissed.

"Captain William Hartington, at your service," he said with a tip of his hat.

With a huff of indignation, Olivia crossed her arms.

"Rosalie Harrow," Rosalie replied automatically.

"It seems as though you ladies are in a bit of a situation." He gestured to the parasol. "May I assist?" Not waiting for their answer, he stepped between them and reached up, wrapping his huge hand around the slender handle of the parasol. He jiggled it gently, freeing it. Then he turned with a smile, offering it out to Olivia.

She took it wordlessly, snapping it closed.

His mouth tipped into a wry grin. "Is this all the welcome I am to receive, then? Surely, after ten years, you can't still be salty—"

"I am not salty," Olivia replied. "What I am is *leaving*. Come, Miss Harrow." She looped her arm in with Rosalie's, determined to drag her away.

Before they could take a step, new voices called.

"Olivia!"

"Miss Harrow!"

Both ladies turned to see Mariah and Blanche crossing the grass towards them. Mariah's bright red curls were loose under her bonnet, whipping in the wind as she hurried her steps. "This wind is murder," Mariah panted with a laugh, flicking her curls away from her freckled face. "The duchess wishes to return now."

"Hello, sir," said Blanche, eyeing the captain with interest.

"Good morning, ladies," he said with a smile.

Rosalie glanced from Olivia to the captain, waiting for the lady to remember herself. When Olivia stayed silent, Rosalie sighed. "Lady Mariah Swindon, Miss Blanche Oswald, this is Captain Hartington . . . Olivia's friend."

"We are not friends," Olivia said at the same time the captain said, "Charmed."

Hearing his name, both the young ladies gasped. Blanche lifted a gloved hand to her mouth. Mariah clung tighter to her friend's arm and said in a rush, "Oh, but you must join us, Captain Hartington. The duchess is hosting tea for the Marchioness of Marlborough, and I'm sure she'd be delighted if you joined as well—"

"Mariah, you cannot make invitations on behalf of the duchess," Rosalie warned under her breath.

"Whyever not?" the girl laughed.

"Which duchess can you mean?" asked the captain.

"The Dowager Duchess of Norland," Blanche replied, still

batting her lashes at him. "We are all her particular guests for the autumn season."

"The captain is far too busy to attend a lady's tea party," Olivia declared.

"The captain is famished, actually," he replied, patting his trim stomach. "I'm sure nothing could hit the spot quite like a slice of fresh seed cake."

The young ladies giggled, while Rosalie felt Olivia stiffen on her arm.

"Then let us lead the way," Mariah cooed, pulling Blanche back in the direction of their group. They walked with a new spring in their step, the captain strolling at their side. Rosalie could only describe Olivia's walk as a funeral march.

By the time they were all settled back at Corbin House, the drawing room was full with over twenty people—all eager lords and ladies on promenade who'd managed to snare the duchess' attention. Tea was served, along with trays of finger sandwiches, egg quiches, and yes, seed cake.

On the walk home, Rosalie discovered more about the mysterious Captain William Hartington. Blanche and Mariah were all too eager to laugh at her expense when they learned of her ignorance and filled her in at once.

Captain Hartington was none other than the eldest son of the Fifth Duke of Devonshire. Rosalie knew that the Cavendish family was perhaps the most illustrious peerage in the land; however, she'd never heard of the captain, and for good reason. Like Burke, Captain Hartington was a bastard, his mother being a maid in the late duke's household. But the duke had denied his son nothing, including giving him use of his own name and providing for him a surname in honor of his subsidiary title as Marquess of Hartington. As a bastard, Captain Hartington could have no claim on his father's title. His younger half-brother assumed it last year upon their father's death.

Rosalie learned from the captain himself that he'd joined the navy young and spent the better part of the last thirteen years on the far sides of the world. She was curious to know whether he was acquainted with Renley, but the other ladies had too eagerly snared all his attention for her to get another word in.

She watched with curiosity as he moved about the drawing room, making small talk with the other guests, giving all the right smiles and paying all the right compliments. He was clearly an expert at sailing these high-society waters. And yet, she couldn't shake the feeling of him being an untamed wolf at heart.

Meanwhile, Olivia had retreated in on herself, doing her best to say nothing to the captain or even acknowledge him. But Rosalie saw the way her eye kept slipping over to him. She saw the way Olivia held too tightly to her cup and saucer, the way she chewed her bottom lip. Unless Rosalie was very much mistaken, Olivia Rutledge did not despise the captain as much as she let on. Rosalie didn't know the details, but she was desperate to find out. Might this not be a possible solution to all their problems?

Before she could question the lady about it, a footman opened the drawing room door and announced, "Lord Darnley, Lord Seymour, Lieutenant Renley, and Mr. Corbin."

"Ah, excellent timing," said the duchess from her seat in

the middle of the room. "Let them come in, Finch," she added with a wave of her hand.

Rosalie's stomach flipped as she set her cup back on its saucer. Darnley and Seymour were two of the names on the top of their list of eligible bachelors. Apparently, Burke meant to try and shove them under Olivia's nose today. His timing could not possibly have been worse. He was the first in the room, his eyes scanning quickly until they fell on her and he smiled. He made a move as if to come to her but was distracted when Captain Hartington launched to his feet and spun to face the door.

Renley was frozen in the open doorway, eyes wide. His look of shock quickly morphed into delight. "Hart—bloody hell—"

Captain Hartington barreled over, wrapping Renley in a tight embrace, nearly lifting him off his feet. The two sailors laughed, both talking at once as they cuffed each other's shoulders, wholly oblivious to the presence of others in the room.

"When did this happen?" Renley cried, fingering the epaulets on Hartington's shoulders.

"Eight months back," the captain replied.

"And how long have you been in Town?"

"Just a fortnight. I've been in Greenwich—"

"The hospital?" Renley's voice was suddenly tight as he gave his friend a once over, looking for any obvious injury. Rosalie knew there was a notable hospital for seamen in Greenwich.

"Aye, but not as a patient. I've been giving lectures, actually. Don't know why they'd let me behind a lectern, but I can't argue with orders."

Both men laughed again.

"Are you going to come in, Lieutenant, or should we all just learn to live with this ghastly draft of air?" called the duchess from her spot on the sofa.

"Sorry, Your Grace," Renley replied, still holding Hartington's shoulder as he moved into the room to let the footman shut the door.

Rosalie hardly noticed that Burke was standing behind her chair, a cup of tea already in hand. "How the hell did Will Hartington get invited to tea?" he muttered.

"That's partially my fault, I suppose." She looked over her shoulder at him to see his confused frown. "We met him in the park. He pushed his way in, as a matter of fact."

Burke just grunted, taking a sip of his tea. "Sounds about right."

She didn't know why, but Burke seemed displeased. "You know the captain?"

"Only by reputation," he muttered, his eye still on the sailors.

Rosalie turned her attention to the lords at the tea station. "Which is which?"

"Darnley is the one on the left," he replied.

She took in both gentlemen. Lord John Darnley was the eldest son of the Earl of Whitby. He was tall and narrow through the shoulders, not unattractive, with dark blond hair and dark eyes. The other gentleman was Lord David Seymour, third son of the Marquess of Hertford. He had an athletic build and dark features, with a prominent nose and hooded eyes.

"Your timing is not ideal," she whispered, bringing her cup of tea to her lips.

"No time like the present," he replied. "I need this over and done with."

"You need to *talk* to her first," Rosalie countered. "She's in a fragile state, Burke. If she finds out we're trying to manipulate her or pawn her off on strange men, she'll dig her heels in. Please, talk to her before this gets out of our control—"

"Alright," he soothed, his hand itching with the desire to give her comfort. She watched him curl it into a tight fist. There were too many eyes here, this was too public.

She gave him a little nod of understanding.

His eye darted over to the pair of lords now in conversation with the Swindon sisters. "Seymour and Darnley are staying through luncheon. I've arranged it with James to seat them by Olivia. I'll get Renley to invite Hartington to stay to better balance the numbers. And I *will* talk to her," he said again. "I swear to you, I'll talk to her before the day is done."

34

Burke

THE GORGON WAS looking at him again. To be fair, Burke had the sneaking suspicion he wasn't actually the object of her interest. He happened to be sharing a sofa with Tom and Captain Hartington. Olivia sat on the sofa opposite them, wedged between Rosalie and Prudence Nash, adding very little to the conversation.

But those looks . . . every few minutes she couldn't seem to help herself, and she had to glance his way, her eye roving from him over to the captain and back. Was she measuring him against this officer and finding him wanting? *Good.* Anything to convince her to go her own way.

Tom and Hartington were carrying the conversation, regaling the ladies with countless stories of their adventures in the Caribbean. Burke had listened to Tom sing the praises of Will Hartington for nigh on ten years, but this was his first time meeting the man in person. Did he have to be so bloody tall? And how did he get that ugly scar? And why was Rosalie laughing so hard? His jokes weren't that funny.

Christ, but Burke was in a sour mood.

Hartington said something else that had the group laughing again. On the far side of the couch, Tom wiped a tear from his eye. Burke couldn't help but feel a twinge of jealousy. When Tom left for the navy, a wall started to grow between them. On one side, there was the life Tom shared with Burke and James, the country gentleman's life of fishing, riding, hunting, and farming. On the other, there was his navy life, and Burke shared no piece of it. Hartington knew Tom in ways Burke never could.

But it was pointless to feel jealous of this captain, he reminded himself. Tom belonged to Burke. They belonged to each other. Since their moment in the alley, he buzzed with a thirst he couldn't sate. He wanted Tom. *Needed* him. The ache was nearly as strong as his constant ache for Rosalie. He watched this confident, brash Captain Hartington with an easier smile. He wasn't a threat. Burke could relax and enjoy the conversation.

"So, tell me of your life now, Livy," said Hartington, addressing Olivia directly. "I can't believe you're not yet married. You always held such high regard for the institution."

Shit.

Across from them, Olivia went stiff. Next to her, Rosalie's eyes darted to Burke, her expression impossible to read.

"No," Olivia murmured. "I am not yet married."

If anything were to ruin his mood today, it would be this conversation. *No one say it.*

"Oh, but she is engaged," Prudence cooed, all smiles as she completely ignored the tension around her.

Burke stifled a groan, while Hartington leaned back on the sofa, schooling his features. "Oh? And who is the lucky man? Would I approve of him?"

Olivia chewed her lip, unable or unwilling to look at Burke. Next to her, Rosalie was still as a statue.

Prudence twittered a laugh. "You're sitting right next to him."

Goddamn it.

Hartington's head swung around as he gaped at Tom. "You're engaged to Livy?"

"No," Tom replied, at the same time Olivia balled her hands into fists in her lap and hissed, "*Stop* calling me 'Livy!'"

Prudence looked between the two of them in confusion. "I'm sorry but do you two know each other?" She pointed between Olivia and the captain.

"Not since we were children," Olivia replied.

Hartington was still distracted. His eye settled on Burke. "*You're* engaged to Olivia?"

Burke took a deep breath. "Well . . ."

"It's a bit complicated," Tom said, putting a hand on Hartington's shoulder.

Hartington frowned, shrugging away from him. "What's complicated about being engaged? You either are or you're not." He turned to Olivia, one brow raised in question.

"They are," said Prudence, because apparently it was impossible for her to read the tone of a room. "It was just announced at the duke's Michaelmas ball. You looked so lovely dancing together," she added with a smile at Olivia. "You'll have such beautiful children."

God in heaven, someone shut this woman up.

Hartington was still looking at Olivia, waiting for her to confirm it. "Is it true?"

Burke cast Tom a pleading look and Tom sprang into action. He gripped the captain by the elbow and pulled him to his feet. "Rose, why don't we show Hart the back gardens before lunch?"

Rosalie cast a nervous eye at Burke before nodding. "Yes . . . yes, I'd love another walk. Prudence, will you come?"

"But it's too windy," Prudence replied, confused that she should even suggest it.

In that moment, divine providence intervened. Piety called from the far side of the room. She and the other young people were playing whist at two card tables. "Prue, darling, come take my place. The duchess is asking for me."

Prudence floated away, wholly oblivious to the awkward tension she'd created.

"Come outside with me," Tom soothed at Hartington. "I'll explain."

Olivia couldn't look at them. Indeed, she seemed on the verge of tears. Burke's heart broke for her . . . for who could better sympathize with her plight than her wholly reluctant bridegroom?

Clenching his jaw, Hartington let himself be led away.

Everyone on the far side of the room was too immersed in their game to realize Burke was now sitting alone with Olivia. It helped that Tom and Rosalie made as much commotion as possible. They declared their intention of showing Hartington the topiaries, rebuffing all the ladies who chimed that it was far too windy for a stroll. In all the flurry of activity, Olivia raised her eyes to Burke, waiting for him to speak.

Taking a deep breath, he gave her a weak smile. "I really think we need to talk."

35

Rosalie

CAPTAIN HARTINGTON LET himself be dragged into the back gardens, following between Rosalie and Renley as they made for the box hedge maze. There, at least, they might get a bit of a reprieve from the gusting wind.

Rosalie didn't bother fetching a bonnet. She didn't want to fight to keep it on her head. And instead of a pelisse, she snatched Mariah's shawl off the back of her chair. She wrapped herself in the soft purple silk, following along after the pair of brooding, long-legged sailors.

As soon as they passed into the hedge maze, the wind died down and she brushed the tangle of loose curls from her face. She caught Renley's eye and her cheeks warmed at his heated gaze. She looked pointedly away.

"So, how do you two know each other?" Captain Hartington muttered, the corner of his mouth tipping into a grin.

"We met back in September at Alcott Hall," she replied.

"Ah, yes, the famed Alcott Hall. I've heard much about its beauty from Renley over the years."

She smiled. "None of it is exaggerated."

It pained her to admit just how much she missed the place already. It was dangerous to think of it as her home, even if her position with the duke seemed to be more settled. A social nobody like Rosalie could never be too careful, nor get too attached.

The captain sighed, tucking one hand in the pocket of his waistcoat. "And what do you make of our Lieutenant Renley here?"

"Easy now, Hart." Renley laughed. "We can't ask the lady to spill all her secrets upon a first meeting."

The captain jabbed Renley with his elbow. "I'm just trying to get the lay of the land. It's been nigh on three years since we last met, Ren." He turned to Rosalie. "Are all the ladies falling over themselves to make him a good and proper wife?"

Her smile strained as she glanced to Renley. "I . . ."

"I see I've stuck a nerve." He glanced between them, his grin lifting the corner of his mouth. "Is there a secret understanding between the two of you, then? Can we expect a letter from Gretna Green?"

"Christ, you always dive right in, don't you?"

"You know you can tell your old friend Hart. I am a veritable vault of other people's scandalous secrets."

At the sound of Renley's laugh, Rosalie blushed anew. "That is quite enough," she pressed, tugging the ends of Mariah's shawl tighter around her shoulders. "Lieutenant Renley and I are just friends. All those in the Corbins' inner circle have been very good to me," she added, not daring to look at Renley, lest it give them both away.

"Fine, keep your secrets," the captain said with a shrug.

"Tell me about this engagement, then. Why does Livy seem so miserable over it?"

She glanced over at Renley. His expression was veiled, his smile gone now that they had a grave matter to discuss. He gave her a nod, his meaning clear. It was safe to confide in this man. "Suffice it to say the match may be wanted by certain parties, but it is assuredly *not* wanted by the pair themselves," she explained.

The captain paused in his steps, turning to meet Rosalie's eye. "She's not in love with him, then?"

From his other side, Renley huffed a dry laugh. "The gorgon in love with Burke? She despises him. She hates everyone."

"Gorgon?" Captain Hartington repeated.

"Aye, that's what we call her," Renley muttered. "A bit of an inside joke. Sorry, Hart."

"Livy the Gorgon." The captain chuckled. "It fits."

Renley smirked. "Christ, does it ever."

"Enough, Tom," Rosalie chastised. These two may be intimate friends, but she still didn't like them speaking of Olivia in such a way. She glanced back at the captain. "Lady Olivia does not want the match. Anyone would be upset in her position."

Hartington growled, cracking the knuckles on each of his massive hands. "Henry would never stand for his sister marrying someone she despised." He let a slow breath, thinking it over. "I'll write to him tonight. If it's the marquess putting pressure on her, maybe Henry can head him off."

A fresh gust of wind blew down the lane, and Rosalie held tighter to the ends of her shawl. "It is not the marquess who conspires," she said. "If the Rutledges could be free of this match, they would already be gone from this house."

Captain Hartington scowled. "So, it comes from Norland, then. Or is it the brother? Finchley?"

"James is the best of men," Renley declared from his other side. "He is Burke's dearest friend and is doing everything in his power to break this engagement . . . with minimal damage to the lady's reputation."

"Wait a goddamn minute," the captain snapped. "Does this Burke-Corbin character mean to jilt her, then? Leave her high and dry before the whole *ton*?"

Rosalie glanced from Renley back to the captain. "He respects the difficulty of her position. He means to help her if he can, but he will not marry her."

The captain's scowl crinkled his ghastly facial scar. "This is preposterous. What kind of gentleman in his position turns down someone like Livy? Is her dowry too great? The lure of a title too overwhelming? This Burke must be slow in the head!"

"Christ, Hart, look at me." Renley took the captain by the shoulder and turned him. "Burke is taken, alright? There is no question of him marrying Olivia Rutledge."

The captain's back was now to Rosalie, and his broad shoulders blocked Renley from view, so she couldn't read either man's expression. Slowly, his shoulders stiffened under Renley's hand.

"Taken?" the captain muttered.

"Aye," came Renley's soft reply.

The wind whipped around them, tugging at her dress. She was about to speak when the captain's shoulders relaxed. "Fine," he muttered, shifting away from Renley's touch. "Well, it sounds like you're all working on some kind of plot to get them out of this."

"Quite right," Renley replied. "The plan was all Rose's idea."

The captain glanced at her. "And what is this great plan?"

"She wants to be married," Rosalie replied. "She wants it all—the husband, the children, the life. So, we are finding her a suitor worthy of the name. Someone more respectable than Burke, so she can jilt him without harm to her own reputation."

Captain Hartington eyed Renley again. "There is no question that Mr. Burke agrees to be jilted?"

"None whatsoever," Renley replied firmly. "In fact, it is his greatest wish. And we fear we need to move quickly. The forces pushing them together are quite determined. She needs to find a better match, and soon."

The captain let out a slow whistle. "Well, this is certainly a Herculean task."

"Perhaps not," Rosalie replied, even as Renley nodded. "There is an innocence to Lady Olivia that she keeps hidden. I see it in her. I think you do too," she added with a smile. But she couldn't lay this on too thick. Not until she was surer of the captain and his shared history with Olivia. "She is strong because she must be. Her life and her status demand it of her. We aim to find her a partner who can be strong with her . . . strong *for* her."

Captain Hartington flashed Rosalie a curious smile. "Yes, I can see why Renley likes you so much." Before she could reply, he clapped his hands together. "Right, very well. I'm in. Tell me what you need me to do."

36

Burke

"I'M SORRY." THOSE were the first words that came to Burke's mind. The only words.

Across from him, Olivia sniffed. "Why should you be sorry? This is the perfect situation for you. A new name, a title, a fortune, a wife. Any man would be pleased—"

"I am not any man," he replied sharply. Taking a breath, he scooted to the edge of the sofa, his elbows on his knees, hands clasped together. "Lady Olivia, it is very important to me that you know that I had nothing to do with this."

She scoffed. "That's hard to believe."

"You *must* believe it," he said, crossing the narrow expanse of carpet between them to sit at her side, his back to the card players. "Not ten minutes before I approached your mother in that ballroom, I was being harangued in the music room by the duchess, threatened into agreeing to this foolish scheme. If you don't believe me, ask James. He knows every particular. You could even ask George," he added, "if I thought he'd tell you the truth."

"I'll not be speaking to the duke again," she murmured. "I

may be a captive in this house while the duchess has her way with me, but I've not completely lost hold of my dignity."

He blinked, surprised she would admit so much to him.

She just rolled her eyes. "Lord James is your closest friend, and your infatuation with Miss Harrow has not gone unnoticed. You know what they know about me . . . don't you, Mr. Corbin?" She narrowed her eyes at him, her lips pursed as she waited to detect a lie.

"Please don't call me that," he said. "My name is Burke. The duchess can try to make the Corbin name stick, but I will never be a Corbin. And I'll never be Baron Margate either."

Olivia sucked in a breath. "You can't be serious." For once, her mask of anger dropped. All Burke saw was fear. "Do you mean to jilt me, sir?"

Burke reached instinctively for her hand, wrapping his fingers around hers. "It doesn't have to be that way."

"Oh, God." She jerked her hand out of his grasp. "You do. You mean not to honor the engagement."

"Olivia, *no*—" He paused. "Damn it—well, *yes* . . . but only if I have to, and I don't think I will—"

"I can't do this." She braced her hands on her knees. "No, not again."

"Olivia, I will only jilt you if we cannot come up with a better alternative *together* that is not matrimony—"

"Were you kicked in the head today?" she snapped, glaring at him. "I thought you were a clever man, Mr. Corb—Burke. There is no way out of this other than the altar."

"Yes, but it doesn't have to be *me* waiting at the end of it," he blurted.

She blinked, eyes wide, her mouth open in a shocked little "O."

"Just try and hear me." He scooted an inch closer to her. "If you trade me in for someone better, then no one will bat an eye when you jilt me."

She let out a breath, her chest rapidly rising and falling. "This is . . . you're mad. You know what the duchess will do if she doesn't get her way—"

"Leave the duchess to me," he replied. "She will not hurt you, Olivia. If she tries, then James, Renley, your mother, Miss Harrow—we will all refute her claims."

"You are lucky, sir . . . to have so many people close to you who are willing to fight on your behalf."

"And yours," he pressed. "Look, I brought Darnley and Seymour here for you. They are both highly eligible and—"

"You did what?" she hissed, rage flashing in her eyes as she glanced over his shoulder towards the lords currently playing whist. "Do you think I'll just say 'yes' to any man with a title and a beating heart who stumbles into the drawing room? It's despicable. I am not for sale!"

"We have very limited options here," Burke countered. "As I see it, the only one where you keep your social standing intact is to jilt me for a better man. I have brought two for your consideration. So why don't you put your claws away, flash a little smile, and go talk to Lord Darnley."

Her eyes blazed. "I would not marry John Darnley for all the tea in England. The man only cares about horse racing and whores! You think he wasn't already on my mother's many lists of eligible suitors?"

"Then I will help you find a different one! Just tell me what you want. Make a list of attributes, and I will find you that man."

Her eyes narrowed. "You will, or Miss Harrow will?"

He sucked in a breath and leaned back. "What?"

She scoffed and rolled her eyes again. "Of course. I knew she had to be up to something earlier. All that talk at the park." She leveled her gaze at him. "You all think to manage me? To make me go away quietly?"

"Olivia, please—"

"What if I counter your offer with one of my own?"

A stone of foreboding sank into his stomach. "What do you mean?"

"Perhaps I don't need to jilt you by marrying another," she replied with a little smirk. "What if I just tell the whole *ton* about your unsavory relationship with your benefactor's ward?"

"I don't know what you're—"

"Don't play with me, sir," she hissed. "You think I can't see the way you look at her? The way you watch her? The way you have to stop yourself from touching her? It's clear you've been granted such liberty before. Could anyone blame me if I chose not to marry a man who was already involved with another?"

"You will leave her out of this," he growled.

"The papers have already linked her to both the Corbin brothers," she went on, because she apparently had a death wish. "Heavens, what kind of den of iniquity exists in this house, sir? Is she at the center of it? Perhaps the *ton* will applaud me for unmasking such debauchery." She lifted her chin, giving him a little imperious smile. "And thus falls the House of Corbin, undone by a licentious ward."

Burke's voice was deathly quiet as he said, "If you dare speak a word against her, I will *ruin* you." He leaned in closer. "I will hound you to the ends of this Earth, and when you reach the very end, I will push you over the edge."

She smiled in satisfaction, clearly enjoying his heated

response. "And here I thought you meant to help me. How fickle you are. How false."

He let out a slow breath, squeezing his hands into tight fists to control their shaking. "I will help you find another unsuspecting mortal to marry, you charmless gorgon. But threaten Miss Harrow in my presence *ever* again, and like Perseus, I will rip off your fucking head and mount it on the wall. Now, do you want my help, or not?"

37

Tom

"SO, TODAY was a bit of a disaster," Tom muttered.

He stretched out his legs towards the fire, leaning back in his chair. They were in Rosalie's room. She sat with her legs curled under her at one end of the small sofa, while Burke brooded like a gargoyle in a chair opposite. Both men had a glass of whiskey balanced on their knee.

"She's going to make this as hard as possible," Burke growled.

Tom and Rosalie had returned to the drawing room with Hart to find Burke and Olivia snarling like cats on opposite ends of the sofa. By the time lunch was called and Olivia took her place between Lord Darnley and Lord Seymour, she chose to be as pleasant as a famine. After an hour in her company, they couldn't flee the table fast enough.

Hart at least seemed to find it riotously funny. "I'd say she won that round," he said, as they all exited the dining room. He stayed through dinner but left before he could be dragged by the ladies into a drunken game of charades.

Tom, Rosalie, and Burke each found an excuse to retire

early and were now blessedly alone. The fire in her room was warm and inviting. Burke had shed himself of his coat and cravat, unbuttoned his waistcoat, and kicked off his shoes.

Rosalie watched Burke with a worried expression on her face. "Won't you tell us what happened?"

"She's a gorgon," Burke muttered. "She doesn't want to be happy, and she's going to try to drag us all down with her."

"You told her you wouldn't marry her?"

"Aye, and she accused me of trying to jilt her. Then, when I said I could help her find someone better to jilt *me*, she threatened *you*."

Tom let out a low curse. "Olivia threatened Rose?"

She sat up, swinging her feet off the sofa. "Why would she threaten me?"

Burke grimaced. "It is a threat on both of us . . . all of us, really. She means to paint you as the jezebel in the House of Corbin. She claims she can jilt me by calling this a den of iniquity."

"She didn't," Tom growled.

"She did," Burke replied, eyes on his glass of whiskey.

"This is my fault," Rosalie whispered. "This is . . . I haven't been discreet enough. I . . . Burke, I'm sorry—"

"Don't," Burke snapped. Setting his glass aside, he dropped off the chair to his knees. He cupped her face with both hands. "Look at me."

Rosalie met his gaze.

"This is not your fault," Burke said. "Do you hear me? I will protect you from scandal. She will not spew any venom about you or this house."

"How can you be sure?" she whispered.

"Because she would be tainted by association," Tom replied,

leaning forward in his chair. "To claim this house as some kind of den of sin would be to implicate herself. Everyone would easily refute her claims, including Burke and myself, James. Hell, even George. She would be painted as the scheming one who said 'yes' to an engagement, and then fabricated a lie to get herself out of it when it no longer suited."

Rosalie glanced from Burke to Tom. "But it is not a lie . . . not completely. The duke knows, he teases me about it. Olivia knows. And you heard Hartington today . . ."

Tom clenched his jaw, an uncomfortable feeling twisting in his gut. "Aye, I heard."

Burke let go of Rosalie, joining her on the sofa. He looked from her to Tom. "What did Hartington say?"

"He claimed to know that Tom fancied me," Rosalie replied.

Fancied her? That's not quite how Tom would describe it. He grimaced, feeling that same pang of discomfort he'd felt in the garden.

"What's wrong?" Rosalie murmured.

He glanced up to see she was watching him, those dark eyes full of questions.

"Nothing." He took a sip of his whiskey, letting it burn the back of his throat.

"You're lying." She sat forward, one hand on Burke's thigh. "You've been in an ill humor all afternoon."

He rubbed his thumb over the decorative nubs on the edge of his glass. "You called me your friend."

She blinked. "What?"

"With Hart . . . in the garden. You called me your friend."

"And so you are," she replied, her cheeks going pink. "Are we not friends?"

"It's the way you said it," he muttered. "So casually, it was almost dismissive. 'Oh, that's just Renley. What a good friend.'"

She huffed. "I can hardly call you my beau, my lover, my paramour."

"No, you can't." He tried to keep the disappointment from his tone.

Rosalie's gaze softened. "But you *want* me to call you those things, don't you?" She looked close to tears now. "Tom, you know I can't. I won't risk your reputation. And clearly, with people like Olivia about, we must be even more careful—"

He set aside his glass. "I know you can't tell anyone what we are to each other. It's just . . . the only thing I hate worse than a secret is a lie."

"I don't want to hurt you, Tom, but we *are* friends—"

"Enough," he growled, rising to his feet. He held out his hand. "Rose, come here."

"What?"

"Just come here, you stubborn creature."

She crossed the space with a huff. "Well, sir? You have me standing. Now what?"

Tom couldn't hold back for another second. Not when every moment in her presence felt like one excruciatingly long exercise in self-restraint. He cupped her cheek with his hand, the other wrapping around her waist, and pulled her in close, losing himself in the divine taste of her mouth.

At the first movement of her lips, his body erupted in fire, blood racing to his cock. It hardened against her. He knew she felt it too, because she tipped her hip forward with a little moan, tugging his bottom lip between her teeth.

Burke was right—she was a goddess. He couldn't get

enough. She was so warm and smooth. He wanted to taste and touch every inch of her. He dug his fingers into her hair as he tipped her head back, letting his tongue dance with hers. She made the sweetest little whimpering sounds as she clung to his open waistcoat.

He traced the gentle curve of her shoulder, sliding inside the open "V" of her dressing gown. She gasped as he cupped her breasts over the chemise. They were so perfect—round and full, with rosy pink nipples as sweet as her name. He slipped one hand inside, needing to feel her hot skin against his palm.

She arched into him, her own hands working diligently to shed him of his waistcoat. He kissed her neck, caressing her breast as she panted, tugging at his braces next. They slipped down over his shoulders, and she helped him get his arms free.

"I want you. Please, Tom—"

He broke their kiss, pushing her a step away. Her eyes were dark with desire. "Christ, Rose, is that how a friend makes you feel?"

She inched closer, reaching for him with both hands. "Tom—"

"Answer me," he growled. "Do all your friends make you feel as I do? Do they set you on fire with a touch? Burn you from the inside out?"

"No," she whispered, dropping her hand so it grazed against his hard cock.

He sucked in a breath. His whole body was on fire. He needed release. Needed to channel this frustration, these hurt feelings of rejection. He brought his face closer, his lips brushing against hers. "Get on your knees."

She gasped. "What?"

He cupped her face with both hands, tipping it up so he could see her eyes. "I said get on your knees."

Behind her, Burke shifted on the sofa. Tom prayed he didn't attempt to move. This was between him and Rosalie.

"What are you going to do?" she whispered.

He brushed a thumb over her parted lips, pressing down to wet the tip. She gave it a little flick with her tongue and his cock twitched. He leaned in, his body burning with desire. "I am going to fuck the word 'friend' from this perfect mouth."

38

Rosalie

AS IF ROSALIE wasn't already at the edge of sanity, Renley's words pushed her over. Heat flooded her entire body, and she knew if he touched her once she'd likely come apart.

Renley loved her. Perhaps he hadn't said it yet, which was probably her fault, but she knew it with a surety that ran marrow deep. He loved her, and she loved him. Heavens, she wanted to tell him. Could she say the words now?

She looked up at him and her breath caught. His beautiful blue eyes were warm with longing. His calming scent filled her senses—sunshine and sea salt on a warm summer's day. Renley was her safety, her comfort, her friend. He may not like the word, but it was true. She could tell him anything and he'd understand. She never wanted to feel herself standing outside the warmth of his friendship.

But now he needed something else from her. He didn't want to be Renley the friend. He wanted to be Tom, the man who held a piece of her heart, the lover who set her soul on fire. She was his caged phoenix, and he wanted her unleashed.

Something about submitting to this man made her feel

powerful. His passion made her bold. She slipped her dressing gown and chemise from her shoulders, letting them fall to the floor. Tom's eyes flashed with hunger as he took in her nakedness.

Behind her, Burke groaned. But he'd have to wait his turn.

Holding Tom's gaze, she smiled and dropped to her knees.

39

Tom

TOM WAS DEAD. This was death, and he was in heaven. Rosalie was naked on her knees before him, her hands at the fall on his breeches, fingers working the buttons. His cock was aching with the desire to feel the heat of that perfect mouth. He glanced over to Burke on the sofa. The man sat still as stone, taking in the scene. Tom caught his eye and smirked. When Burke nodded, he knew his message was received. Burke wouldn't interfere . . . yet.

As Rosalie loosened the last button, Tom wasted no time tugging his shirt off over his head and tossing it aside. He raised his arms and Rosalie's soft hands were on him, smoothing over his stomach. She inched closer. When her mouth touched the sensitive spot over his hip bone, he wanted to die all over again. Instead, he fisted his fingers in her dark hair.

She trailed kisses from his right hip, across the top of his breeches, to the other side. While she kissed him, her warm hands caressed his skin, sliding up his sides. Gooseflesh spread down his arms.

When she nipped playfully at the skin right above his

crotch, he groaned. He was done being teased. Gripping his breeches, he shoved them down. His hard cock sprang free before her face. He watched her breath catch as she reached for him, her soft hand making him dizzy with desire.

"Tell me what you want," she murmured, looking up at him with hooded eyes.

His tip was already weeping for her. "Taste it."

Holding his cock with one hand, she leaned in close and licked the tip. At the first touch of her warm tongue, fireworks went off in his chest.

"Don't stop," he grunted. "Take me in your mouth."

She shifted a little on her knees and took hold of his hips with both hands. Then she stretched her pretty pink lips around him. Christ, it was perfection. He watched every inch of his cock disappear into her hot, wet mouth. The vision of it was eclipsed by the physical sensation. She was playful, using her control of his hips to help her move.

It was all he could do to let her stay in control. He wanted to rut. He wanted to *claim*. He smoothed a hand over her beautiful, dark hair to remind himself that she was precious. "Please, Rose—"

She made a little sucking noise as she let him go, glancing up with wide eyes. "Please what?"

He blinked. Had he said that out loud?

"What do you want?" The dark eyes reeled him in.

"I can't—" he muttered, not even knowing what he was trying to say.

"Tell me." She kissed his thigh.

"He wants control."

Rosalie glanced over her shoulder.

Burke, who'd been watching silently, flashed Tom a smirk.

"He wants to own your mouth, love. He wants to rut into you until you're choking on his cock, and he wants to come down your throat. He wants to taste himself on your tongue. Isn't that right, Tom?"

Tom let out a shaky breath. "Yes."

Rosalie turned back to him, eyes wide. It wasn't with fear, but desire. She wanted it all. Everything Burke described. Fuck, this woman was made for them.

"Take control, Tom," she murmured, kissing one side of his hip, then the other. "Take anything you want. I'm yours."

The words echoed around inside his head. *Take control . . . I'm yours.*

"Hold on to me," he ordered.

Her hands went to his hips, and he got rougher, his fingers digging into her hair again as he tapped her parted lips with his cock. "Take it," he said, his voice a growl.

Her mouth opened wider, and he slid inside, greeted by her fluttering tongue as she took him deep. Holding her still, he gave a few short thrusts, letting her feel with her hands and mouth how he wanted to move. She squeezed his hips in encouragement, letting out a little moan of pleasure.

With a muttered curse, he unleashed himself on her. He thrust into her mouth again and again, until he was tapping the back of her throat. She was so wet, so warm. It was a pleasure verging on pain to feel her give way to him, letting her mouth be claimed so completely. He let go of everything—his fears, his frustrations. He put all of himself in her hands, every piece, and she took it, shaking with need, asking for more. God, he could stay here forever. Stay inside her. Never leave.

Her hands tightened on his hips, her fingernails digging into the flesh of his arse. She looked up at him, tears in those dark eyes. He cupped her head with both hands, holding her gaze. She was ready for him.

"I'm gonna come. Rose, I'm—"

She sucked him deep and he cried out his release, holding her still as he gave her everything. It felt like he was being split apart. He was hot and cold, aching and euphoric. He'd never come so hard. Her tongue fluttered against the underside of his cock as she swallowed.

After a few moments, he released her and she sank down, panting for breath. He dropped to one knee and took her face roughly with one hand, tilting her chin up to meet his eyes. The open affection reflected on her face made his heart ache.

"I am not your friend," he said, unable to control the tremor in his voice. "Stop calling me Renley. Call me Tom, call me darling, call me lover divine, but *never* friend." He squeezed her jaw tighter. "Say it."

She wrapped her hand around his wrist, nodding. "You're Tom. My Tom."

He turned her head, pointing with his free hand at Burke. "He is not your friend either. He has enough friends. And calling yourself his friend is an insult I'll not abide." He leaned in closer. "You are the air in his lungs, the north star guiding him home. Do not sell yourself short by using that fucking word again. Tell him who you are."

A tear fell as she looked at Burke. "I'm your siren," she said. "You belong to me."

"Yes," Burke replied, his voice heavy with want.

Tom leaned in. "In public, you may call us 'friend,' and we will grin and fucking bear it. But in private, that word is banned. Understood?"

She nodded, still looking at Burke. Tom pulled her to her

feet and kissed her, replacing all the hardness of his thrusts with the gentleness of his soft lips and teasing tongue. He ended the kiss quickly and turned her around. "Our Burke has been patient long enough," he murmured. "Go to him. Show him to whom he belongs."

Without hesitation, Rosalie crossed over to Burke, climbing naked into his lap. Their mouths clashed in a passionate kiss, with Burke's hands wrapping around her perfectly rounded arse. Rosalie moaned at the contact, moving her hips as she sought to relieve her ache. Christ, watching them together was going to have Tom hard again in minutes.

Burke broke their kiss, his hands smoothing back her hair as he murmured. "Wait—love. Rosalie, look at me."

She sat back, her chest rising with each short breath.

"I want you," he said, kissing her again. "I will always want you."

"I want you too," she replied, nuzzling his neck. "My Burke, my Horatio, I want you."

The word buzzed through Tom, jolting him like a zap of lightning. His heart was aching, his need for both of them tearing him apart.

Burke looked over Rosalie's shoulder, his eyes locking on Tom. Slowly, he smiled, his gaze heating as he said, "I want Tom too."

Tom's heart stilled. Oh hell, they were apparently doing this now.

Rosalie perched on Burke's lap with her hands on his shoulders. "What do you mean?"

Burke tucked her hair behind her ears. "If we're going to be together, I want us all to be together. You're it for us. I know it. Tom knows it. James knows it too, even if he's being a damned pain in the arse. We belong together."

She glanced over her shoulder at Tom. The warmth of feeling in her eyes had him aching all over again. She raised a brow. "Tom?"

He stood there, looking at his future. There'd be no going back from this. He didn't want to go back. "I want you both. I'm drowning in an ocean of need, and you are my air."

With fresh tears in her eyes, Rosalie held out her hand.

Tom went eagerly, his pulse racing as Burke reached for him too, pulling him down on the sofa next to them.

Burke leaned in, his mouth inches away. "Tom." He said his name like a prayer, infusing the word with a need that made Tom ache down to his very bones. "You have to stop me if I go too far or—"

"Shut up and kiss me," Tom growled, crashing his lips against Burke's. Each time felt more amazing than the last. Rosalie's lips were so soft and tender. Burke's were soft too, but there was nothing of tenderness, only raw passion. His hand curled tight in Tom's hair, holding him close as he teased with his tongue. Tom opened to him. Burke tasted like whiskey and Rosalie. It was a heady combination that had fire burning through him, licking down his spine.

Then Rosalie's hands were on him, sliding up his bare arms. Oh God, her soft lips were on his collarbone, his shoulder. Her sweet tongue traced the lines of the cross tattooed on his chest. Then she was kissing his neck, sucking at his pulse point. The sensation sent a cresting wave of desire straight to his cock.

Burke broke their kiss and pulled Rosalie off Tom, claiming her mouth with his own. He poured his passion into her until she was trembling. When he finally let her go, she was squirming on his lap, desperate to chase her own release. Burke gave a little chuckle. "Not yet, love. You looked too good on your knees. I want to feel your mouth on my cock while I make our darling Tom moan."

Their perfect goddess was up for anything. With a smile, she slipped off his lap and helped Burke with his breeches. Tom watched as together they got him free. Burke's cock was long and proud, the tip glistening. Rosalie smoothed her hands up his thighs as she sank down on him with her mouth.

Burke leaned back. He looked at Tom with such fire that Tom was sure he'd been scorched. "Give me your mouth, Tom."

Careful of Rosalie, Tom pressed himself closer into Burke's side and met him in another heated clash. As they kissed, a hand wrapped around Tom's half-hardened cock. It wasn't Rosalie's hand.

"Bloody hell." Tom broke the kiss, sinking back against the sofa as Burke stroked him. Tom looked down to see Burke matching his strokes to Rosalie's movements.

With a growl, Tom slapped his hand away and dropped to all fours on the narrow sofa. It took some maneuvering, but he lowered himself until he could reach Burke's cock. Rosalie smiled, lifting her mouth to just the tip, giving it a playful suck as Tom stroked the base with his tongue. Their mouths were close, sharing breath, as they teased Burke together. Tom's own cock was painfully hard again.

"Touch yourselves," Burke panted. "Please, *God*—come with me."

Rosalie eagerly slid her fingers through her wetness, riding her hand as she moaned. Her sounds spurred Tom on, and he wrapped his hand around his cock, stroking it as he continued to lick and tease Burke. Rosalie shifted on her knees, reaching out blindly with one hand. Tom curled forward on the sofa, guiding her hand around his cock. She gave a little sigh of relief, working both her men together.

Burke's hand was fisted in his hair, Rosalie's hand was around his cock, and Tom's mouth was pleasuring his best friend. He was gone. He was destroyed. With his heart fit to burst, he came again so hard he saw white spots dancing before his eyes. His release filled Rosalie's hand, leaking between her fingers.

He groaned in ecstasy as Burke came too, thrusting his hips up against them. Rosalie opened her mouth on his tip and some of Burke's warm release leaked down his shaft. Tom licked it up, letting the salty taste coat his tongue. Meanwhile, Rosalie pumped him with her hand until his legs were shaking. Then, in a move that had Tom ready to come all over again, Burke took Rosalie's hand off Tom's cock. Holding her by the wrist, his eyes on Tom, Burke raised her hand to his lips and licked Tom's release off her fingers.

A piercing ache shot through him. He made a whimpering sound, wholly undone by the heat in Burke's eyes. Then Rosalie was arching up, taking her own thumb in her mouth, tasting Tom with Burke. The pair of them sighed, ending their erotic feast with a hungry, open-mouthed kiss.

As Burke relaxed, his hand loosened in Tom's hair, soothing him with slow strokes. The gentleness had Tom blinking back tears. He was afraid to move, knowing the moment he did this feeling of perfect happiness would begin slipping away.

Rosalie sagged back to the floor, resting her head on

Burke's thigh. She looked over at Tom and smiled before her eyes fluttered closed.

Burke was splayed out beneath them, one arm stretched along the back of the sofa. He hummed in contentment. "That was . . ."

"Yes," Rosalie replied, placing a soft kiss on his leg.

"You were both perfection," Burke muttered. "Tom, we should have done this years ago."

Tom relaxed into him. "I'm glad we didn't," he admitted. He reached out and stroked Rosalie's face. She leaned into his touch like a flower seeking sunlight. When she looked up at him, he smiled. "She was worth the wait."

"Agreed."

Rosalie smiled, turning her face into Tom's hand to kiss his palm.

"I hope you don't think we're finished with you," he said, tucking a dark strand of hair behind her ear.

She gave a little laugh. "My mouth begs to differ, sir. I wouldn't be surprised if it bruises by morning."

Even as she said the words, he noted the pleased smile she wore. She loved every second of it, the wanton goddess. She was perfect for them. He'd marry her this moment if he thought she'd ever say yes. Then they could spend every moment of the rest of their lives naked and happy.

He slipped off the sofa and sank down onto the floor behind her, wrapping her in his arms. He kissed her shoulder, her neck. "You were more than generous, sweet girl. This beautiful mouth is done for the rest of the night," he said, tracing the shape of her lips with his fingers. "We don't need it for what I have planned."

A little shiver ran through her. "Oh? And what do you have planned?"

He cupped her breasts, giving her nipples a tweak that had her arching into him. "This is a den of iniquity, is it not?"

She hummed her assent, eyes closed as she dropped her head against his shoulder.

"Get on the bed, and spread those pretty legs," he whispered in her ear, loud enough for Burke to hear. "I'm going to show you how generous I can be. And if you're very good, Burke and I will show you together."

40

Rosalie

ON MONDAY EVENING, *Hoxley House hosted a concert featuring the works of Haydn. While most attendees enjoyed the musical selection, one graceful lord was so displeased he left mid-sonata by way of a window. And he was not alone. The identity of the mysterious ward at C— House is not yet known, but one can only wonder if Miss P— N— is aware of her new competition.*

"Well, Miss Harrow? Have you seen today's news?"

Rosalie slapped her gossip pamphlet shut as Piety sat down next to her at the breakfast table. She tucked the rag under the table on her lap, placing her napkin over it. At the same time, Piety unfurled a copy of *The Times* and laid it atop Rosalie's half-finished plate of eggs and sausages.

"What do you think?" Piety cooed, tapping the top article. Rosalie read the headline announcing the Duke of Norland's upcoming marriage. "Well, it's . . ."

"It's absolutely wonderful," Prudence cried.

Piety took back her paper, folding it with a satisfied smile. "I know two weeks isn't a lot of time, but when two people are so much in love . . ."

"Two weeks?" This was news to Rosalie. She imagined the duke might drag this out into a much longer engagement.

Piety's smile widened. "Oh, you hadn't heard? Yes, Papa settled it all with Her Grace yesterday. We'll be married the week after our engagement party. Then it's to be Lisbon for Christmas and Greece in the new year!"

"Long engagements are not to be borne," chimed Prudence.

"Too true," Piety replied. "And Lord James assures me you're skilled at event planning, Miss Harrow. The Michaelmas ball was so lovely."

"Oh, but I didn't—"

"I'll need you by my side through this," Piety pressed, narrowing her eyes.

"And me too," Prudence cooed.

"Yes, of course, dear," said Piety, patting her sister's hand. But then she focused her gaze back on Rosalie and let her eye drop pointedly to Rosalie's lap.

Rosalie stilled, one hand over the napkin hiding the gossip rag.

Piety's mask of perfection slipped as she lowered her voice. "I will not have this go wrong, Miss Harrow," she hissed. "Do you understand me? I *will* be the next Duchess of Norland."

"Of course," Rosalie murmured. "The duke knows how lucky he is to have you."

The lady raised a brow. "But does he truly need me if he has you?"

Rosalie clenched the pamphlet. "I am his ward," she whispered. "There is no romantic attachment between us."

"Thank you, Miss Harrow. That is all I needed to hear." With a curt nod, Piety slipped off her chair and floated away.

Rosalie took a breath, watching the lady go. The last thing

she wanted was to make an enemy of the future mistress of this house. She'd need to make a point to distance herself from the duke publicly to ease this tension. The engagement party was well-timed, for she could be sure to dance with Burke and Tom and any other eligible man . . . except James. She could not let the public see her in the arms of either Corbin brother.

By ten o'clock, the house was blissfully quiet. Even the men were out. Rosalie could sit comfortably in any room she chose and not be bothered. She decided to search out a new book from the library. She didn't get far before a commotion had her pausing in her steps.

A slamming door. Shouting.

At the end of the set of en suite rooms, James stood leaning against the open door to his study, his eyes downcast on a letter in his hand.

"Burke!" he shouted again. "Where the bloody hell is everyone?"

41

Rosalie

THE LAST TIME Rosalie and James spoke, he had been shouting at her in the drawing room. In the past two days, she'd only seen him at mealtimes, and even then, he'd been missing both last night and this morning.

He looked haggard. Not at all his usual polished self. His coat was off, his cravat loose. Dark circles under his eyes belied the likely source of his current distress.

"Can I help, my lord?" she called, alerting him to her presence.

His eyes shot up as his shoulders stiffened. He took her in from head to toe. "Where is everyone? Even the bloody footmen have deserted me."

"Her Grace is at the Queen's tea," Rosalie replied. "The young ladies are shopping, the lieutenant is with Captain Hartington, and I couldn't begin to guess at where His Grace might be," she finished with a small smile.

James just grunted, his eye back on the papers in his hand. "Where is Burke?"

"I imagine he's not back yet."

"Back? Where did he go now?"

Concern twisted in her gut. "He . . . you sent him on an errand after breakfast, my lord. Do you not remember?"

"That was hours ago." He turned sharply and retreated into his study.

Taking a deep breath, Rosalie followed him into the lion's den.

The study was a mess—stacks of papers on the desk, more on the floor, account books splayed open. Then there was the tray of cluttered tea things, another with an uneaten meal. This mess had accrued in two days? Had the man slept at all?

She leaned against the open doorway. "My lord, what time is it?"

"I haven't had a moment—" He glanced at his clock, rubbing his eyes. "Christ, does that say ten?"

This confirmed her suspicions. "Can I help, sir?"

"No." He slapped down the papers in his hand, snatching up a different set.

"Oh, I think I can," she replied with a frown. "Put that down."

He glanced up sharply. "What?"

"The paper in your hands, James. Whatever it is, put it down. It's not what you need right now."

He narrowed his eyes. "You presume to know what I need?"

"I do." With more confidence than she felt, she shut and locked his door.

James went still as stone. "What are you doing?"

She pointed to the window. "Make yourself useful and close the curtains."

"Miss Harrow—"

"Don't 'Miss Harrow' me, James. The stairwell rule now applies to your study. I have decreed it."

He raised a brow. "You decree it?"

"Yes, I do. Now close the curtains."

He opened his mouth then shut it again, his brows lowered in confusion. "What happens when I do?"

She smiled. "Close them and find out."

With a frown, he turned away and went to the window.

"Not all the way," she directed, wandering over to his bookshelves. "Do you have any novels in here?"

James stilled, one hand on the curtain. "Novels?"

"Yes, James. Novels. Works of fiction, often with fantastical settings. Perhaps a story with a windswept castle on a moor. I'm in the mood for something brooding. It seems fitting for this atmosphere."

"To the left," he muttered. "Are we going to read in the dark?"

"Oh, perfect." She tugged loose a copy of *The Castles of Athlin and Dunbayne* and tucked it under her arm. "*I* am going to read," she corrected. "*You* are going to nap."

"What?"

She sank onto the end of his sofa. "I'm starting to feel like you're being obtuse on purpose. Is my English incorrect? A *nap*, James. It is the act of sleeping during the day. Hounds do it, children do it, and now so will you."

"I can't possibly nap," he said with a huff of indignation.

"Of course, you can. Close the curtains and come here. Take off your boots."

Grumbling, James pulled the curtain halfway closed. The effect was immediate, creating a darker, more intimate space. He tugged loose his cravat. She watched the flash of skin at his throat as he swallowed. He sat on the other end of the sofa and made quick work of his boots. "This is ridiculous," he muttered.

She set her book on the arm of the sofa, propping her feet up on the little pouf. "Yes, I am ridiculous and impossible and full of deceit, James, I know."

"Rosalie—"

"With any luck, we have two hours before the others return, if not three," she said over him. "Either way, until I hear the sounds of return, you will lie here in my lap." She put a pillow over her legs, patting it with a smile. "Sleep or don't sleep, I don't care. But you *will* rest, James. You're not moving from this sofa until I say."

His lips twitched. "You're a tyrant, and this will not work."

She gave him her best steely, determined look. "Put your head in my lap, James."

He flopped down, his weight pressing into her. Feeling him so close had her heart pounding. She swallowed it down before it dared to fly away. Could he hear it? Could he *feel* it? Oh heavens, was this a mistake?

He lay there on his side, his legs half-curled up on the sofa. His body was stiff as a board.

"I can feel your eyes open," she murmured. "Close them." He let out a slow breath, his shoulders relaxing a little.

"God, you're exhausting."

She smirked. "I'm not exhausting, you're exhausted. There's a difference. Now, close your stubborn eyes."

He relaxed a little more and she moved one hand to his hair. She liked the auburn color, how it went darker at the tips. It only curled around his ears. At the first stroke of her fingers, he let out a soft groan, sinking deeper into her. She petted his hair, humming a little tune under her breath. As he relaxed, his breathing slowing, she opened her book one-handed and began to read.

"What are you humming?" he murmured.

"A lullaby. I think it might be Italian. I only know the tune. My mother favored it."

He was quiet for a moment. "Do you miss her?"

She buried the ache deep in her chest. "Yes."

He shifted a little. "I miss my father . . . but I can't say it without facing rebuke. The longer he's dead, the more my mother tries to poison his memory, and I begin to doubt. He was cold and demanding, it's true. But, while he lived, I never worried that Alcott was being managed."

Her hand stilled in his hair. "It's wrong of your mother to try and take what was good away. He can be imperfect *and* your father. You can mourn his loss."

"Is it wrong that I mourn my ignorance more than his loss? I mourn my lack of worry. I never worried before."

"And with George at the helm you worry," she intuited.

"Constantly." She went back to smoothing her fingers through his hair. "Do you resent him? George?"

He sighed, shifting his head. "I resent the rules. I resent that he inherits based on the whims of nature. He was born first, he was born a man, so he gets everything."

"Thus spoke every sister who ever lived," Rosalie mused.

They were both quiet for a moment before she added, "I think he resents the rules too. One more thing you have in common."

"We have nothing in common," he muttered. She just hummed, stroking his hair from brow to nape. "What else in common?" he asked.

"Hush, now. You're meant to be sleeping."

He turned his face to look up at her. "What else do we have in common?"

"You're both pests determined to get your own way. A worse pair of horseflies, I've never known. Now rest, before I get cross."

He rolled back on his side. "You barge into my study, order me around, force me on my belly like a dog. Who is the bigger pest?"

She gave the hair at his nape a sharp tug. "*Ouch.*" He slapped his hand over hers.

"Rest, James. Or I shall take my lap with me and find a quieter corner of the house in which to read." She made like she was going to get up.

"No." His arm curled around her. "Stay."

She smiled, settling back down, her hand going back to his hair.

They were quiet for a few more minutes. "Where did you go?" he murmured.

"Hmm?"

"With George the other night . . . where did you go?"

She smiled, setting her book aside. She'd wondered when one of them was going to ask. Burke and Tom had been too preoccupied with comforting her. "He took me to a house party hosted by his friend. She was a lovely lady, very obliging and kind. We had dinner and played cards."

James stilled. "Where was this house party?"

"Leicester Square, I believe." James groaned. "James?"

"What was her name, the lovely lady who hosted you?"

"Helene Trudeau."

Then he was laughing. It was a deep sound that vibrated through him into her.

"James—"

After a minute, he relaxed. "Goddamn George straight to hell," he muttered.

She didn't like this feeling of jealousy creeping up her spine. "Who is she to you?"

"To me?" He gave another dry laugh. "She is nothing to me. I've only met the woman once or twice in my life. She was my father's mistress. She used to live here in this house until he died. Then my mother forced her out. George still provides for her."

Rosalie wasn't sure what she had expected him to say, but it certainly wasn't that. "Oh . . . I . . . are you upset that I met her?"

Reaching up, he took her hand, entwining their fingers together. He rested their joined hands on the pillow by his face. She could feel his warm breath on her skin. "I'm not upset that you met Helene. I'm upset you needed comfort and turned to George instead of me."

Tears pricked the corners of her eyes.

You are the one with high walls. Let him in.

She bit her lip before admitting the truth. "I want to turn to you, James."

He pulled her hand closer, kissing the joint of her thumb. "I want to be the one who protects you."

"You do," she replied, curling towards him. "You make me feel safe."

"Good," he muttered, kissing her first finger, then her second. Suddenly, he stilled. "And stop fighting me about the bloody clothes. I'm not trying to own you, I'm trying to care for you."

"I know. It's forgotten," she whispered. "Forgiven. I love the clothes."

He kissed her palm, sucking in a breath with his face pressed to her skin. Oh God, he was scenting her. Such a simple act, but so sensual she fought the need to moan. She looked down at the man in her lap and made her own request. "Stop avoiding me. James, I can't bear it. If you're angry with me then scream, pull your hair, throw glass until it shatters . . . only don't abandon me."

"I'm here," he murmured. "Rosalie, I'm right here."

She put both hands on him, one in his hair and the other rubbing small circles on his shoulder. They relaxed into each other. Rosalie tipped her head back on the sofa, closing her eyes, letting herself feel every inch of him all around her.

It didn't take long before his breathing finally slowed, and James was asleep.

42

Burke

It should have been a perfect day. Burke got to wake in the arms of his lovers, sated from a night of vigorous lovemaking. Tom's pretty words to Rosalie about retiring her mouth had been pure fantasy. Their wanton siren took them to hand and mouth again and again until they were begging for mercy. They reciprocated in full, worshipping her body, teasing and sharing her sweet cunt until each kiss tasted only of her.

God, he'd never wanted to wake. Day should be abolished. It should only ever be night, and he should be naked between his lovers forever.

But day came, and with it came all the demands of the world outside their bed.

He started his morning being forced by James to run an errand on the opposite end of Town. He waited for two hours for the gentleman to show, but he never did. On his way back to Corbin House, he stopped by the stable yards and was told that, not only did one of his favorite broodmares die of colic in the night, but one of his most promising new racing stallions took a tumble during a training run and shattered his front leg. The poor animal had to be put down.

So, when Burke entered the library to find Tom alone with Captain Hartington, the two of them standing together in the window, his patience snapped.

"Burke," Tom said with a smile. "We were just talking about you. Good outing?"

"No," he muttered, crossing over to the sideboard to pour himself a glass of port. He didn't need Tom to confirm what he already knew. Tom and Hartington had history. It was in their shared looks, the way they could finish each other's sentences. Hartington knew Tom the way Burke knew Tom . . . the way Burke was learning to know Tom. He squeezed the glass tight, not turning around as he took a sip.

"Renley here tells me you can box," called Hartington. "You trained at Oxford?"

"Aye," he replied, setting the glass down. Did the captain want a demonstration?

"I was just telling Renley about a charity bazaar Greenwich Hospital is hosting on Sunday," Hartington went on. "There'll be stalls for jams and pies and the like. But we're trying to make it a bit more of a show. We've landed on the idea of hosting a few sparring matches."

"It's brilliant, eh?" Tom said with a smile. "People can make bets and part of the winnings will go to the hospital."

"Brilliant," Burke replied.

Tom's smile fell, his eyes narrowing on him. He glanced at the captain, then back to Burke. Tom and the captain might have a language of looks they shared, but so did Tom and Burke, and Burke was making no mystery of his current thoughts. Tom frowned and shook his head.

"Well?" called the captain, oblivious to their silent conversation. "What say you, Mr. Burke? Care to try your luck in the ring against a navy man? It's all for a good cause."

Burke tore his eyes away from Tom. "You want me to fight?"

"Aye, it would be good to have a few men with some proper training," the captain replied. "If you leave it to us old sea dogs, it may be little more than a rowdy slinging of fists. But there's an art to boxing, as you well know."

Damn it, why did Hartington have to be so likable?

Sensing Burke's thoughts, Tom smirked.

Burke looked pointedly away. "Who would I be fighting, then?"

"You could have your pick," Hartington replied. "We've got a retired captain, Yates. Tall as you, a bit broader in the shoulder maybe. Hits like an anvil. A few of the lads are wirier, but they're fast. They'll take your head for a spin if you let your hands down."

"Hmm," Burke replied. It had been a while since he'd had a proper match in a ring. He couldn't deny the prospect interested him. It would be good to let loose some of this tension. "When do you need an answer?"

"Soon as you can give it," Hartington replied. "The lads hoped to make some pamphlets to drum up more interest."

"I think it's a brilliant idea," Tom replied. "Even if Burke's out, consider me in." He cuffed the captain on the shoulder and Hartington laughed, cuffing him back.

Burke had to fight the urge to stomp forward and slap his hand away. He was saved by the chiming of the mantel clock. Five o'clock already.

"Christ, is that the time?" Tom muttered. "Sorry gents, but

I'm afraid I must be off. I take dinner at my captain's house tonight."

"I'll walk out with you," Hartington replied.

"Wait." The word was out of Burke's mouth before he even had time to think it.

Tom and Hartington both cast him a curious look.

"I would speak to Hartington about something."

Tom raised a wary brow. Slowly, he crossed the room to Burke's side. "Should I stay? I can be fashionably late."

"Not necessary," he replied.

Tom gave Burke a warning look. But Burke was never one for heeding warnings. Feeling rash, he pulled Tom to him by his coat lapel and kissed him square on the mouth. Tom pulled away with a startled gasp. He narrowed his eyes, more irritated than upset. "Was *that* necessary?" he whispered.

Burke smirked. "Yes."

Tom glanced over his shoulder at Hartington and back at Burke, his voice low. "Nothing happened," he murmured.

"I know."

"Nothing would have happened," he added.

Burke raised a hand and stroked Tom's jaw with the back of his fingers. A quick touch. A statement. A promise. "I know. Now go."

With a frustrated sigh, Tom stepped past him and left.

Hartington still stood framed by the bright window. "Is that what you needed to tell me, Mr. Burke?"

Burke crossed his arms, not moving from his spot by the wall. "It's part of it."

The captain chuckled. "There's no need to be jealous of what Renley and I once shared. It was another life for me."

A muscle twitched in Burke's jaw. "I generally find jealousy to be a useless emotion," he replied. "It implies a deep dissatisfaction in wanting something I cannot have. In this case, jealousy is wholly absent from my feelings."

"Is that right?" the captain mused.

"Why would I be jealous of you, Hartington? You have nothing that I want."

It was Hartington's turn to cross his arms. "Then why the big show?"

"Because I am territorial. I know what I have. I fought hard for it, and I intend to keep it."

Hartington smirked. "Am I a threat, then?"

"*I* am the threat," Burke replied. "Touch Tom again, speak a soft word in his ear, so much as look at him in a way I find overly familiar, and I will rip out your goddamn throat."

Hartington gave him a measured look. "You know I am a decorated naval captain, right? Scratch that. You know I am the son and brother of a duke?"

Burke wasn't intimidated. "What you are is a bastard, Hart. Same as me. The rules are different for us. We're not really part of their society. The only way we survive is by staking our claims and holding to them with everything we have. So, bastard to bastard, hear me when I tell you that Tom Renley is *mine*. And in a fight to keep him, I have absolutely nothing to lose."

The men held each other's gaze for a moment before Hartington's mouth tipped into another grin. "Is it wrong for me to admit I hoped never to meet you?"

Burke blinked. "What?"

"I didn't want to put a face to the name and hate you even more. Damn, but you're handsome," Hartington said with a dry laugh. "It's unfair to the rest of us bastards." He absently raised a hand, stroking the bottom edge of his scar. "Worse still would be to meet you and like you, which is exactly what has happened."

"I'm not looking to make an enemy of you, Hart. Any friend of Tom's can be a friend of mine. I trust his taste . . . usually."

The captain laughed again. "Your message is received, Mr. Burke. It was received years ago."

"Years ago?"

Hartington raised his scarred brow. "Do you know how often he talks of you? Do you know how hard it was to know another charming bastard claimed a piece of him?"

A warm feeling spread through Burke. Tom spoke of him with Hartington?

"I am no one's second choice, Mr. Burke. I walked away from him long ago . . . when it was clear he would never walk away from *you*."

Burke smiled, feeling those words sink down to his very bones.

Hartington cleared his throat. "Now, is that all you wanted?"

"Actually, no," Burke replied. "I wanted to talk to you about Olivia."

43

James

"JAMES, WE NEED to talk."

Sucking in a breath, James bolted upright, blinking in the dark. "George—what—"

"I'd resolved to keep this to myself, but it's clear you need the push, so . . ." George blinked, looking around the room. "Why are you sitting in the dark? What . . . are you ill?"

"No." James was still trying to clear the fog from his mind. He'd fallen asleep in Rosalie's arms, hadn't he? Did he dream it all? He was alone on the sofa, the curtain half-closed. No candles lit. No fire. The sky outside was nearly dark.

George still stood in the middle of the room. "Were you *sleeping*?"

James dragged a shaky hand over his face. "What does it look like?"

"But you never sleep. Oh God, you're ill, aren't you? Is it catching? Should I call for Fawcett?"

"George, please just shut up for a minute." James shifted off the sofa and moved over to the mantel in his bare feet. The fire in the grate was already set—it just needed a light. He lit a taper and held it beneath the logs, letting the fire papers catch. Soon, a soft yellow light flickered around the room. He sat back on the sofa, tugging on his left boot. "What time is it?"

"Just after six—"

"At night?" James nearly cricked his neck turning to look at the clock on his desk.

"Of course, at night," George replied with a huff. "I wouldn't be parading in here at six in the morning, would I?"

Sure enough, the clock showed the time as a quarter after six. That little schemer lured him to sleep, then left him for nearly eight hours. He'd lost an entire day, thanks to her meddling!

To be fair, he couldn't remember the last time he'd gotten such good sleep.

George tipped his head to the side. "James, you're worrying me. Have you been in here all day? The staff said you were out."

James tugged on his other boot. "George, for the love of God, please just tell me what you want."

George shrugged away his confusion. "Right. Well, it's difficult to know where to begin."

"Heaven, help me," James muttered, snatching up his coat and cravat as he moved around to sit behind his desk. He gestured to one of the empty chairs. "Should we both be sitting for this?"

George considered before taking a seat. "Yes, perhaps that would be best."

James shuffled a few things on his desk. "Alright, out with it."

"Fine," George huffed. "But just know that, when I confide in you what it is I'm about to confide, you're going to become cross with me. You'll accuse me of meddling, which might be accurate, but please know I do so with your best interest at heart."

"I swear to Christ, George—"

His curse died on his lips as George reached into his pocket and took out a stack of letters tied with a blue ribbon. He slid them across the desk at James. The last time James saw those letters, they were clutched in Rosalie's hand as she tried to tuck them behind her skirts.

"What are those?" he muttered, heart in his throat.

"Why do I get the feeling you already know?"

James scowled. "Where did you get them?"

George drummed his fingers on the desk. "I think you already know the answer to that too."

He slapped the desk with his hand. "Goddamn it, George! You went through her things, didn't you?"

"Of course, I went through her things! I am the duke, and her welfare is my responsibility."

"Oh, spare me," James growled.

George pursed his lips, crossing his arms over his chest. "Fine, I snooped, alright? Are you happy? The minute you left, I charged into her room and tossed her trunks, and I found *these*." He waved his hand at the offending stack of letters.

"You know, there is such a thing as personal property—"

"Not for a duke—"

"A court would disagree!"

"What was I supposed to do?" George cried. "This sweet little apple falls from the heavens into our midst, and we're to ask no questions? You might suffer from a chronic case of disinterest, but I can't live like that, James. I'm a curious person!"

"So, you stole a lady's private correspondence?"

"They're not correspondence . . . not exactly. And they're not hers."

"That's not the point—wait—what?"

George leaned forward. "Don't you want to know what they are?"

God, yes. Rosalie, what secrets are you keeping?

"No."

"It's scandalous, James. Our dear mama has much to answer for," George teased.

"Our mother? What does she have to do with this?"

"Tell me brother . . . who is Francis Harrow?"

James clenched his jaw. "I believe that is the name of Miss Harrow's father."

"And why would our mother agree to pay all his outstanding debts?"

"What?" James hissed, his eyes back on the stack of letters.

"Oh James, this is a stack of pure sin." George stroked the satin bow. "Mr. Harrow lived outside his means in every sense of the word. Each bill in the stack is worse than the last. Unpaid debts to multiple banks, outstanding business loans, lines of credit denied at establishments across London, Richmond, Bath, York . . ."

James took a deep breath. "How much was the debt?"

"You really don't want to know," George replied somberly.

James' mind went wild as he calculated a figure. How had she managed it? He'd worked hard to rein in all their mother's spending. So how could he miss her making a large payment . . . or a series of payments as large as this stack? God, help him, he had to know. He glanced across the desk at his brother. "Was it . . . five?"

George gave him a sympathetic smile. "More."

"Ten?"

"More."

James needed a drink. He needed the whole bottle. Hell, the whole vineyard. Maybe his mother bought one without his knowledge. "Just tell me."

"Seventeen."

Rage filled James until he thought he might choke on it. "Seventeen? Our mother paid seventeen *thousand* pounds to cancel Harrow's debts?"

"Well, the father's debts only totaled about fifteen thousand," George replied. "The remaining two thousand was paid directly to a Mrs. Beatrice Thorpe."

James leaned back in his chair, dragging both hands through his hair. Seventeen thousand pounds was roughly what it cost to maintain Corbin House each year. Where the hell had their mother found such a sum without James knowing of it? He scowled at his brother. "How did she manage it? Are you sneaking her money?"

"You're asking the wrong question. The more interesting question is not how, but *why*." He leaned forward, tapping the stack of letters. "Why would our mother pay all Harrow's debts?"

James wasn't ready to contemplate the why of it all. The family accounts hemorrhaged seventeen thousand pounds and he hadn't noticed. As the manager of Alcott, the *how* is what mattered most to him.

But George was looking at the stack of letters like they held the answers to existence. "Our dear mama is motivated by only two forces: greed and guilt. Which do you think is the more likely driver behind this act of gross generosity?"

James sighed. "Guilt."

"Exactly. And what would our mama have to feel *so* guilty about that she would pluck a young lady out of obscurity, pay all her family's debts, and offer her a permanent place in our household?"

James frowned. "You clearly have a theory."

"Aye, but you're not going to like it."

"I haven't liked a word you've spoken yet, so why stop now?"

George took a deep breath. "Right. Bear with me on this, but . . . love child," he said with a dramatic wave of his hand.

James felt a faint echoing in his ears. George was speaking, or at least his mouth was moving. But James heard nothing. Ignoring George's odd hand gestures, he moved around his desk to the corner and poured himself a glass of scotch. He downed it in one and poured another. He downed it, feeling the spicy burn of it tingling in his mouth and down his throat.

George was right behind him, one hand on his shoulder. "Easy there. Let's just slow down, shall we? You can't be drunk for what comes next."

James blinked, looking over his shoulder at this brother. "Next?"

"You know what you have to do next, right?"

"Aye, I need to drag our mother down here by her hair and turn out her pockets," James snarled. "I mean to collect every last coin from her. She will no longer be allowed to spend the family's money. Not a single farthing, George. Agreed?"

"Agreed," George said. "Drag away, little brother. After you talk to Cabbage." He slipped the full glass of scotch from James' hand and backed away with it.

James' heart was racing out of his chest. Yes, he had to talk to Rosalie. Oh God, was it true? No. Rosalie would never knowingly engage in such deception. She wouldn't lead him on like that. "It's not true," he muttered. "Rosalie wouldn't . . ."

"Wouldn't what?" George pressed. "Wouldn't accept the cancelling of all her family's debts as a buy off for keeping our mother's dirty secrets?"

James considered this. Seventeen thousand pounds was a hefty sum, even for a duke. As a one-time payment, it was manageable, but the estate would certainly feel it. James was desperate to understand how his mother was manipulating the accounts.

As for Rosalie . . . Christ, how would she have been expected to repay even a quarter of such a sum on her own? It was unfathomable. She would have drowned in that debt. No wonder she accepted a lifeline when it was offered. Any sane person would have done the same. But James had to understand what strings were attached. Why did she take it? What had she agreed to do to earn it?

"Ask her," James said, moving over to his desk and snatching up the letters. "Give these back to her and ask her what she knows. Please, George—"

"Absolutely not," George replied, backing away. "*You* must be the one to get the answers."

"I'm not the one who stole these from her in the first place!" James barked, shaking the letters in his brother's face.

"And *I* am not the one who'd like to take a stroll down her sweet little cock alley," George replied, raising the glass of scotch to his lips with a satisfied smirk.

James lunged forward and slapped the glass from his brother's hand. It glinted in the air before smashing to the floor, the glass shattering like a bag of spilled diamonds.

"Disrespect her again, and I'll make you eat that glass," James growled, pointing to the mess on the floor.

George's grin widened. "Spoken like a true beau."

James huffed and turned away. He couldn't breathe. Couldn't think. The stack of letters was still in his hand. He paced behind his desk like a caged animal.

George stood there watching, an oddly sympathetic look on his face. "For the record, I don't think she's a secret love child either."

James paused in his pacing, turning sharply to face his brother. "Then why the hell did you say it?"

George just smirked. "I wanted to see your reaction, and it was even better than I hoped."

"Lick my bollocks, George."

"No thank you," he replied, still smiling. "You're in love with her, aren't you?"

"I will not discuss Miss Harrow with you."

"She may not be a love child. In fact, the idea is absurd," George said with a little laugh. "But those bills were paid by our mother all the same," he added, pointing to the stack in James' hand. "There *must* be a reason, and Cabbage knows what it is."

James groaned, knowing his brother spoke the truth.

"I know you, James. You like to think I don't, but I do. You cannot abide a secret. You'll punish Cabbage all her days for keeping this one from you. Will you ruin your chance with that girl over your own damned pride?"

James stilled. "Careful, George. If I didn't know any better, I'd say you cared about a person other than yourself."

George just smiled. "For once in your life, take your elder brother's advice, and *talk* to the woman you love. Shed light on this secret, so you can both move on with the business of being happy." With a nod, he turned for the door.

"George," James called.

His brother paused, glancing over his shoulder.

James took a deep breath before saying the words he'd been mulling for days. "You deserve to be happy too. Plenty of dukes in the past were lifelong bachelors. You don't have to marry and sire children for the sake of the family. That is not your sole purpose in life."

George's mouth quirked. "Thank you for saying that, James."

"I will support you either way."

"Good to know." His smile widened as he wiggled a finger between them. "Oh, and this little heart to heart never happened. I have a reputation to maintain. Understood?"

James sighed. "Understood."

With that, George left, and James stood alone with the stack of pilfered letters, an aching head, and no plan for how to get Rosalie alone to ask her the question that was now burning him alive.

44

Rosalie

"A BOXING MATCH? But wouldn't that be dangerous?" Rosalie murmured.

Burke laughed. "Hardly. And it's for charity."

They were sitting together in the corner of the drawing room. The mood was festive tonight as the group waited for Wilson to announce dinner. Everyone was getting excited for the engagement party. Rosalie had her last gown fitting earlier that afternoon and had only just made it back to the house in time to change for dinner.

Across the room, Olivia actually seemed to be making an effort at civility as she chatted with the handsome Lord Talbot, eldest son of the Viscount Roydon. Rosalie counted as the lady flashed him a smile no less than three times.

"What do we make of that?" she murmured, raising her glass of sherry to her lips and pointing with her eyes.

Burke followed her glance and frowned. "About that . . . I may have done something today you would call meddling."

Rosalie swallowed her sip of sherry with a grimace. "Oh Burke, what did you do?"

"I spoke to Hartington."

Rosalie blinked, letting herself absorb those words. She couldn't deny that she'd had the thought herself. She was desperate to know what went so wrong between them. "And?" she whispered, scooting to the edge of her chair.

"And I think he's in love with her," he murmured.

Her heart pounded in her chest. "Oh Burke . . . oh, this could change everything. This could be a real chance for them. A love match. Surely, she will consider him as a suitor. We must add him to our list—"

"Don't be too hasty to start ringing wedding bells," he muttered.

Her excitement vanished. "Why?"

"Apparently he proposed to her once before—"

She gasped. "What?"

"Easy," he warned, his eyes darting around the room to make sure no one was watching them too closely. "Aye, he was leaving for his first tour. He proposed, she declined. And today he said, and I quote, 'Hell will freeze over before I bend the knee again. If Livy wants me, she'll ask me.'"

"Oh Burke . . ." Rosalie's eyes trailed over towards Olivia, all her hopes vanishing like a puff of smoke. In what reality would the headstrong, self-important Lady Olivia Rutledge ever bend her knee and propose to a bastard sailor? As her hope diminished, frustration had room to bloom. "Would she really rather marry Lord Talbot and become his drawing room ornament, when she could have a life of travel and adventure with a handsome and daring sea captain?"

"Christ, help me. Not you too," Burke muttered. "Did you just call him handsome? Don't make me drag you out of here and claim you in the hallway."

Before she could respond, the drawing room door opened, and Wilson announced dinner. The room chattered with excitement as everyone got to their feet.

Rosalie stood, taking the hand Burke offered. They didn't make it out of the room before James came pressing in.

Burke smiled at his approach. "All well?" His smile fell as he took in the determined look on his friend's face.

"I need to speak to you," James muttered, eyes only for Rosalie.

She glanced around the emptying drawing room. "What . . . now?"

"Now."

Burke's hand curled protectively over hers on his arm. "Can't it wait until after dinner? People will notice—"

"Make her excuses," James ordered. "Tell them she's overtired and returned to her room."

Burke glowered at him. "Tell me what this is about."

James glared right back. "Burke, go. You know one of us will fill you in later."

Burke glanced between them, a brow raised to Rosalie in question.

She tried to give him a reassuring smile, even as her pulse raced. Something was wrong with James. He wouldn't make this kind of show otherwise. Something was definitely wrong, and she desperately needed to know what it was.

"I'll be fine," she murmured.

Giving them both a last look, Burke dropped her arm and stalked off after the retreating dinner crowd.

Wasting no time, James held out his hand. "Come with me."

45

Rosalie

ROSALIE FOLLOWED AT James' side as he led her down a back hallway of the house. It was clear he wanted to get as far from the dining room as possible. "Where are we going?"

"In here," he replied.

She gasped as he turned sharply to the right and opened a door, leading her into a small, unused parlor. It was dark inside, the curtains shut tight, and the furniture covered with white sheets. James walked over to the window and tugged back one of the curtains enough to let autumn moonlight filter into the room. It gave all the white sheets an odd, silvery sheen.

Rosalie suppressed a shiver that raised gooseflesh down her arms. She wasn't dressed for autumn without a fire. She wore only a red satin evening gown. The cut was such that she wore no chemise, only half stays and a pair of silk drawers over her stockings.

James stepped past her over to the fireplace. After a moment, a little pop of yellow flame danced to life on the tip of a taper, and he lit a few candles. The mirror hanging above the fireplace reflected the light, making the room glow a little brighter.

"Could we light a proper fire?" she murmured, giving her evening gloves a little tug at each elbow.

"It's not set for a blaze," he replied. Instead, he shrugged out of his evening coat, handing it out to her.

She kept her arms crossed. "I'll be fine."

"Don't be stubborn," he growled.

"If I'm about to be excoriated for something, I'd rather not be wrapped in the comfort of your coat."

He tossed the coat on the back of one of the sheet-wrapped chairs. "I don't want to fight. I just need us to talk with no prying eyes or ears."

"Then talk," she pleaded. "I can't stand this. Are you angry, are you not? Am I sorry, am I not? Are we fighting, are we not? I'm exhausted. Please, just *talk* to me."

He reached into the "V" of his waistcoat and pulled out a stack of letters. He set the stack down on the edge of the side table.

She glanced down at them, a shiver of warning racing down her spine. She recognized the blue ribbon tying the offensive little bundle together. Her heart thundered in her ears as she gripped the back of the closest chair. "Did you—"

"No, Rosalie. I did not rifle through your things." He pointed at the stack. "This was all George."

Relief was quickly replaced by annoyance. "Why would he go through my things?"

"Because he has no understanding of the laws that protect for things like personal property." He raised his eyes to her, his gaze sharp as glass. "And because, like me, he knows there are things you are keeping from us."

"James—"

He took a step closer. "Why did my mother pay all your family's debts? She spent seventeen thousand pounds without asking me. I need to understand why."

Seventeen thousand? Heavens, the duchess never told her the actual figure, and Rosalie had been too much of a coward to look. She gripped tighter to the chair in front of her as hot tears of shame burned in her eyes. "James . . . I'm so sorry."

"I don't want apologies, I want an explanation," he growled, taking another step closer. "On my watch, my family estate hemorrhaged seventeen thousand pounds. I have to understand why. Please, Rosalie . . . tell me something."

"I didn't know the full figure," she whispered. "I couldn't bear to know." She paused, desperately trying not to break. "You've read them?"

"Not all of them."

"But you read enough."

He gave a slow nod.

Shame burned through her. "Then you know what he was. You know how we lived."

"The bills paint a picture, yes."

She took a deep breath, pulling her eyes away from the stack and back to his face. "Your mother never knew Francis Harrow. Her generosity is all for the sake of my mother . . . and me."

James was close enough now that she could touch him. She felt the way her body ached to lean in. His cold gaze held her at bay.

"My mother does not understand the meaning of the word generosity. This is a gesture of apology or guilt. Both. What did she do that you are owed seventeen thousand pounds?"

She closed her eyes, unable to look at him.

"George has a theory," he said.

She blinked her eyes open. The trio of flickering candles on the mantel cast a shadowy light over both their faces. "A theory?"

James narrowed his beautiful green eyes, now so hard and unfeeling. "Aye, George believes you're a secret love child. You came here to extort your position, claim an inheritance. But are you the child of my womanizing father? Or my frigid mother?"

Rosalie gasped. "That is preposterous," she cried. "I am my mother's mirror. Ask anyone who knew Elinor Greene. Ask my aunt. Heavens, ask your own mother! I am a Greene—"

"But are you a Harrow?" he pressed.

She wrapped her arms tightly around her middle. This was more than humiliating. "I would give anything to say Francis Harrow was not my father, but I have no reason to doubt my mother's fidelity. She was once your father's sweetheart, it's true. But that was many years before I was born. Their affair ended when he married your mother."

James stared her down for a few more seconds before he broke. His shoulders sagged, and he dropped his hands to his knees, almost doubling over. "Thank fucking Christ."

Her anger overflowed. "James Corbin, did you honestly believe I pushed my way into your life knowing I was some kind of secret half-sister? Did you . . . oh God . . . did you think I would *kiss* you if I knew?" she shrieked, shoving at his shoulder. "That I would want—" She stopped herself, not needing to go into more detail of the time they nearly ravaged each other in the library.

"No," he said, reaching for her. She took two steps back. "I swear to you, Rosalie, I didn't believe George when he said it. But to have you confirm it . . ." He pressed a hand to his chest. "Christ, it's like I couldn't breathe."

"Well, it's a ridiculous falsehood, and I'll be thrashing him for it!"

"Not if I get to him first," James muttered. "But something must account for all this madness. Rosalie, I *need* the truth. We cannot move on from this otherwise."

She raised her chin in defiance. "Are you saying I tell you, or I lose my place here?"

"Rosalie, please—just—can't you understand why I need to know?"

"I understand you think you're entitled to another's secrets, but you're not—"

"I am if—"

"You are *not*. And before you keep pushing me, I will say this: I have no secret I will keep from you regarding my own life. You demand honesty, and you will have it. Ask me anything—*anything* except to reveal the secrets of another person."

"So, you will not tell me why she paid all your family's debts?"

She wanted to tell him everything. She wanted to be so deep inside his walls she became like the princess Ariadne, lost in a maze of her own design. But she'd given her word to the duchess. "I'm sorry, James, but your quarrel is with your mother."

He grimaced, his eyes flashing in anger.

"I am not lying to you, and I am not withholding," she added. "I am simply keeping my word. Hate me if it helps. Kick me out. But all I have in this world is my word and my pride. In keeping one, I safeguard the other."

"Fine," he muttered at last.

She let out a little breath. "Fine? What does that—"

"I said it's fine," he repeated. "I will just have to try and pull the truth straight from the source." He said this as if he were suddenly Heracles preparing to descend into the Underworld to capture Cerberus.

"But it's *not* fine," she murmured. "You can't even look at me."

Without looking up, he tucked the letters back inside his waistcoat.

Fresh tears stung her eyes. "You told me you require honesty, but you've picked the one thing I'm not at liberty to tell you. And now you can't look at me—"

His head shot up, his face a mask of frustration. "I'm looking at you. Alright? I'm *always* looking at you. I can't look away."

On instinct she reached out, her hand curling around his arm. To feel him stiffen made her heart ache. "Please, James. You said it yourself, we must move past this. My walls are down, I swear it to you." He tried to pull away but she tightened her hold on him. "Head and heart, James. I will tell you anything you want to know. Please, just ask me. *Please*—"

His eyes darted as he took in the features of her face. "How many men?"

She blinked, dropping her hand away from him. "What?"

"How many men have you been with? You want to play the truth game? Well, that's what I want to know."

No walls. No lies. She closed her eyes for a moment, praying she was doing right. "By choice?"

It was his turn to blink in confusion. He quickly recovered. "God*damn* it," he cursed, dragging both hands through his hair instead.

"Well . . . which number do you want? You must be more specific."

"Choice," he muttered, not looking at her.

"Five," she whispered. "Burke and Tom you already know."

He swallowed. "And did you love them? The other three?"

She sniffed, crossing her arms again. It was the smallest kind of comfort, even if all she could do was hold herself. "I thought I did. With two of them, at least. But I was young and foolish and very alone. It never lasted long." She blinked back the memories, letting warmer ones fill her mind. Slowly, she let herself smile. "There is no comparing what I had then to what I have now. It's like having droplets of fresh rain land in your palm and then claiming to hold the ocean."

"Burke is your ocean, then?"

"He is part of it, yes," she replied, willing him to look at her.

"And the other number?"

"Two."

He made a noise in his throat. "How old were you when . . .?"

"Fifteen," she whispered. "It was in the months just before my father died. That's when he got the most creative . . . the most desperate in how to buy time with his creditors and try to cancel debts."

James cursed again.

"I couldn't read the bills," she admitted, gesturing to the bulge in his waistcoat. "I was afraid I might find one from . . . I didn't want to find any proof of a canceled debt."

James looked down slowly at his chest. In a flash, he reached inside his waistcoat and pulled out the stack of letters. He turned and dropped to one knee in front of the hearth, placing the stack on the grate.

"What are you doing?"

He stood and snatched a candle off its stand.

"James, don't—" She watched James touch the flaming tip of the candle to the edge of the stack. In seconds, the top letter caught fire. Smoke billowed up the chimney as all the evidence of Francis Harrow's wasted life burned to ash.

James stood and replaced the candle. Giving his waistcoat a little tug, he watched the letters curl and burn.

"That was evidence," she chastised.

"I don't give a damn. The debts have all been paid. You're free of him. He and all his creditors can burn in hell." Slowly, he turned, reaching out for her.

"*Don't*—touch me," she rasped, backing away.

He lowered his hand, his features now impossibly soft. "Rosalie . . ."

"Don't ever touch me out of pity, James. I can't bear it. Not from you."

A muscle ticked in his jaw. "Tell me their names, and I will purge them from this Earth."

"I will never tell you. They're already dead to me. You asked for my truth, and I said I will not lie. Please don't hate me for my past—"

"Hate you?" He looked horrified at the idea.

"Don't judge me, then," she corrected.

"Rosalie, you were a child! You deserved protection, a safe home, a guardian worthy of the name. If he was not already dead, I'd kill him myself. Tell me where he is buried, so I may spit on his fucking grave."

"No," she whispered. "The ghosts of my past shall not claim any part of my present. Let it go, James. For your own sake, if not for mine."

A quiet moment stretched between them as she watched

an array of emotions flash over his face. He was angry, confused, disgusted. At her? At her past? At their current confusing present?

Suddenly, he stepped forward. "I need to touch you," he admitted, his voice pained.

She backed away. "Not so long as I can still see pity in your eyes."

"Then look again," he growled.

She sucked in a breath, noting the heat in his gaze. The longing. The aching need. Why must this man spin her up so completely? "James, I must know . . . in the library you said—am I still just a passing infatuation? Do I hold any interest for you other than your need to protect people?"

"Damn it, Rosalie, you are the *only* thing that holds interest for me!"

His words sent a jolt of desire straight through her. She wanted to feel bold, to put the pain of the last few minutes behind them both. "And . . . what is it about me that interests you? My eyes, perhaps?"

"Yes."

"What color are they?" she whispered.

He let out a slow breath. "Brown . . . in the right light, they have flecks of gold. In this light, they are dark as night. Pools of blackness I want to swim inside. A starless sky."

"And what about my arms?" She smoothed her hands up the length of her silky white gloves. "Do they interest you as well?"

"Yes."

She held out her left hand, turning it over to expose the buttons at her wrist. "Why don't you come get a closer look?" He closed the space between them in two steps, his hands going straight for the delicate pearl buttons. He popped each button and glanced up at her with hooded eyes, waiting for her permission to act. She dragged the glove down her arm.

His eyes were fixed on the movement, watching as she exposed her skin.

"What about my hands?" she whispered. "Do you find those interesting?"

He nodded, reaching out with the lightest of touches, his bare palm skimming along her gloved one. Even through the fabric, she felt the heat of that touch burn straight through her.

He glanced up at her again and she gave a little nod. That was all the direction he needed. Using both hands, he peeled her glove off, tossing it aside. He pulled her in by the wrist, raising her hand to his lips. He kissed her palm, his lips soft.

She leaned in, letting a whimper escape as he kissed down her thumb, nipping the tip. Her gloved hand went to his shoulder as she stepped into him. He pulled her closer, sucking her finger into his mouth.

"Oh, God." She watched her fingers disappear. First one, then two. She pulled them out and gripped his face, tipping up on her toes with her chest pressed against him. "What about my lips—"

He claimed her with a kiss and then they were in a fight for dominance. He held nothing back, driving into her mouth with his tongue. She met his passion with her own, loving the feel of his hands on her, his hard cock pressed against her stomach. But she wanted more. "James, please—"

"What do you need?" His lips traced the arc of her neck. "Tell me what you need."

"I need you to make me forget everything outside this

room. Make me believe there is only you. Worship me until I beg you to stop—"

She gasped as he spun her around. His fingers feverishly worked the back of her gown. In moments he had it open, shoving the red satin off her shoulders to the floor. She turned as she stepped out of it, still wearing her stays and silk drawers. Her white stockings were tied with pink garter ribbons above the knee. Giving him a devilish smile, she raised her naked hand and brushed her fingers over the strands of pearls at her neck.

His response was immediate—a primal groan as he reached for her.

"You like seeing me in your family jewels, don't you?" she whispered, rolling the pearls at her collarbone.

"Yes," he growled, cupping her breasts over her stays.

"What if I was wearing *only* this? A Corbin at my neck . . . a Corbin in my cunt . . ."

That broke him. He worked fast, unfastening her stays as he kissed her senseless. As soon as the stays were loose enough, he shoved his hand between the laces, palming her naked breast for the first time. She arched into his touch, stifling the need to cry out as he pinched her aching nipple.

"Take it off," she pleaded, tugging on the strings herself. "Off—"

Together they jerked the strings loose and the stays dropped to the floor. She dug her fingers in his hair as he lowered his head, kissing the swell of each breast, licking her nipples. She whimpered, core clenching tight, desperate for more. As he kissed her breasts, she undid the buttons at her hip holding her drawers in place. The silk slipped down her legs, pooling on the floor. She stepped out of it, wearing nothing but stockings and the necklace.

James spun her around, one hand at her throat, holding her still while his other hand smoothed over her hip, pulling her tight against him. His fingers danced across her stomach, inching lower . . . lower. The anticipation nearly took her breath away. At the first slide of his fingers through her wetness, she moaned.

He dropped his forehead to her shoulder, panting with need. "You're so wet, angel. It's dripping down your thighs."

"For you," she sighed. "I'm wet for you. James, please—"

He stopped her plea with a hungry kiss, teasing her with his fingers. She felt no shame at her arousal. She wanted him. Any woman would be a fool not to want James Corbin. The sudden intrusive thought of another woman touching him made Rosalie feral. She reached around with one hand, gripping his hair as she opened her mouth to him in another claiming kiss.

She trembled as his fingers passed over the spot that ached, only to dance away. She tried to move her hips to get his hand where she wanted it. But then he curled two fingers inside her, lifting her up on her toes. With the first touch of his thumb on her sensitive bud, she shattered. Release rushed through her, weakening her knees as she sagged against him, clenching around his fingers.

"God, help me," he muttered in her ear.

They clung to each other, both panting for breath. "Stop . . . have to stop . . ."

She heard his jumbled words and stilled, wrapping her hands around the arm at her waist. "What?"

He groaned, his face pressed against the warm skin of her back. "I'm losing control."

She turned in his arms, placing her hands gently on either side of his face. One still wore an evening glove. "James, look at me."

He met her gaze. Emotions warred on his face—desire, pain, guilt. Each one pulled at something different in her, causing her doubts to spiral.

"Let me in," she whispered.

He let out a slow breath, running his hands down her arms, stopping at her elbows. "I'm not . . . I don't do this. I don't do casual sex."

She bit her lip, holding back any sound of pain that wanted to escape. Is that what this was for him? Casual sex? Is that what she meant to him?

As if he could read her thoughts, he put a finger under her chin, tipping up her face. His expression was so unguarded. He was in pain, and it made her want to weep. "You mean too much to me," he said fiercely. "I'm barely holding on."

His truth pierced her heart, making her feel weak. Her hands dropped from his face to his shoulders.

"If we have sex now, I will lose myself completely," he went on. "I'll want more than you can give. I'll want everything. And when you can't give it, I will resent you. I will resent my friends their ease that they can be with you without conditions. I will resent myself that I cannot be someone other than who I am. Please, let me stop. Please—" He buried his face in the curve of her neck.

She soothed her hands up and down his back, feeling the tautness of his muscles. "It's okay," she murmured. "We can stop."

"I don't want to stop," he rasped, his mouth on her lips, his taste on her tongue.

She pulled away, blinking back her tears. "No, we must stop." The words tore her apart, but she had to respect his wishes. "Living with your resentment of me would be hard enough," she murmured. "But watching you resent your friends would kill me."

"I wish I were different," he muttered, stroking her face with a gentle hand.

"I don't," she whispered. "Not for one moment."

He closed his eyes tight. "I need to leave before it's no longer an option."

She nodded, letting him go. "Then leave." Doing the bare minimum to protect the fracturing pieces of her heart, she stepped away first.

Snatching up his coat, he left.

46

Rosalie

FRIDAY MORNING WAS a blur of activity as the whole house prepared for the engagement party. Every entrance had the doors thrown open wide, with servants weaving in and out carrying fresh deliveries of flowers, tray after tray of delicate tarts and pastries, and stacks of chairs. Inside the house, footmen scurried everywhere. They climbed ladders to set each candle stand with eight-hour waxes, hung garlands, and fluffed and dusted every inch of the furniture.

Lunch was a chaotic affair with a buffet set in the hall, as the servants were still too busy converting the dining room into a party space. For some reason, Rosalie felt too nervous to eat, but she tried to scarf down a few slices of cold ham and an egg and cheese tart.

By seven o'clock, Rosalie was sitting at her dressing table. Fanny stood behind her, wiggling a few more pins into her pile of curls. She glanced over to the bed where her gown was laid out. It was a beautiful thing of goldenrod yellow. From the waist down, there was a sheer overlay in a pattern of leaves. The little cap sleeves had a ruff of lace to match.

The bodice scooped lower in the back than it did the front, exposing her shoulders in a way that felt daring.

"Alice says the performers arrived," Fanny said with a wide grin. "They're all dressing in the servant's quarters now. A magician and a woman who twirls with ribbons. She says there's even a man who breathes fire!"

Rosalie stifled a smile. In all the commotion of the last week, she'd nearly forgotten that she ordered the hiring of circus performers. She felt a momentary twinge of guilt thinking of James rubbing shoulders with a magician. But the guilt was quickly erased as she pictured him having a coin pulled from his ear.

A half hour later, she was floating down the stairs in her yellow dress, loving the silky feel of the fabric against her skin. The house glittered from so many candles. More mirrors had been strategically placed in each room, replacing some of the framed pictures to brighten the glow. Guests were already spilling through the front doors. An excited hum echoed off the walls, leaving Rosalie's skin prickling. The guests cooed in surprise as a woman dressed in jewels and feathers did a twisting flip high on a stand.

Rosalie had barely reached the bottom step before Piety was pulling her into her arms. "Miss Harrow, you've outdone yourself," she cried. "The performers were truly inspired. His Grace is beside himself. Look!"

Rosalie followed the line of her finger to spy the duke clapping as one of the performers juggled a seemingly impossible number of colored balls. She smiled. "And the fire-eater?"

"Oh, he's in the garden," Piety replied, looping her arm in with Rosalie's. "It's ever so strange. I whine if my tea is too hot, and he swallows down a flaming sword with the ease of eating a grape."

Piety led her through into the back garden, where a large set of guests were clustered in groups watching the performers who required more room to work. There was a trio of men doing amazing tricks of acrobatics, climbing each other like some kind of strange tower. A lady with hoops and ribbons was twirling about. A burst of hot fire had the back garden cheering as the fire-eater sprayed flames high up into the air. Rosalie clapped with the rest of the group.

"You clever little cabbage. This is brilliant," said a deep voice in her ear.

She turned to find the duke standing just behind her. She felt her smile fall as she crossed her arms. Piety had stepped away, now eagerly chatting with a group of ladies bedecked in jewels and feathers. Rosalie glanced back at the duke. "Good evening, *brother*."

He pulled his gaze from the fire-eater. "What?"

"Oh, is it still a secret? Am I not a desperate little deviant here to squeeze you for an inheritance?"

The duke just laughed, patting her shoulder. "So that's why James is in such a foul mood tonight, eh? I thought it was because the magician stole his pocket watch earlier."

Nothing about this was funny. Losing herself completely, she reached up and tugged sharply on his ear.

"*Ouch!*" He clapped his hand over his ear. "What the bloody hell was that for?"

"Why are you meddling in our affairs?"

His eyes narrowed. "So, there *is* an affair. Oh, I'm so

pleased to hear it. I couldn't bear to watch him be outpaced by Burke."

Heavens, how much did this man know? Did she dare bother to contradict him, or might that just make it worse? "Tell me why you're meddling," she demanded.

"Because James is hopeless," he said with a shrug. "Someone had to give him a push off this cliff."

"What cliff? What do you hope to achieve by upsetting him?"

The duke gave her shoulder another pat. "Cabbage, I already told you. I can sniff out sexual tension better than my best pointer, Ducky. You have those three wrapped around your cabbage-pulling fingers. Play your cards right, and you can have them wrapped around you entirely." He dared to give her a wink.

"Your Grace—"

"Now, I don't want to alarm you," he murmured. "But you should know that our delightful little friend Mrs. Young has been watching us from the arbor since the moment I sidled up to your back."

Rosalie stiffened, not daring to look behind her. "She's there now?"

"Yes."

"Is she watching us?"

"Oh yes . . . though she pretends she is not." He leaned in closer. "What did I tell you last time about embarrassing me?"

Rosalie swallowed, doing her best to square her shoulders. "I must keep the high ground."

"That's my girl," he said with a grin. "Now, go enjoy the party. Just be wary of any shadows dressed in a gaudy lavender gown."

47

Rosalie

ROSALIE MADE THE rounds of each room, taking in the general splendor. All the while, she glanced over her shoulder, expecting Marianne to descend. What the woman hoped to gain by antagonizing her, Rosalie didn't know. Tom was lost to her forever. Rosalie meant to see to it. As if thoughts of the man could conjure him, he appeared across the room in his handsome naval uniform. His curls were as unruly as ever. She wanted to run her fingers through them. His eyes were narrowed as he scanned the room. Once he found her, the tension in his shoulders eased and he was crossing to her side.

"Good evening, Lieutenant," she said at his approach, dipping slightly into a curtsy.

His steps faltered, as did his smile, but he quickly recovered. She understood his annoyance, but they were in public. Eyes eagerly watched their every move . . . and not all of them were friendly.

"Miss Harrow, you look devastating tonight. Yellow suits you." His eyes trailed down her form and back up, sending heat to her already warm cheeks.

"You were out very late last night, sir."

"All night, in fact," he replied. "Dinner ran long, and many drinks were imbibed. My captain's wife demanded we stay." He leaned in, turning his body slightly to step in behind her. "Why . . . did you miss me?"

"Parts of you," she teased with a smile.

"Tell me which parts, and I shall be sure you do not miss them again tonight."

Before she could reply, Burke joined them, two glasses of punch in hand. He handed her one, slipping along the wall on her other side.

"Where's mine?" Tom muttered.

"I only had two hands," Burke replied. "And you have two strong legs. Walk over and get it yourself."

"Not a chance," Tom said with a laugh. "You only want me to leave so you can monopolize her." Reaching out, he snatched Burke's glass and drained it.

"Hey," Burke growled.

Rosalie smiled, loving the feel of them to either side of her. So at ease, so friendly.

"Good God, that's Charlie Broadwood," Tom said, his eyes alighting on a tall sailor who had just passed the open doorway. "Excuse me a moment."

"Bring back more punch!" Burke called.

Tom strolled away with a wave of his hand, leaving Rosalie in the corner with Burke.

"Have you seen James?" she murmured.

"He was still greeting guests with the duchess last I checked." Slipping her glass from her hand, he took a sip and grimaced. "*Gah*, why does it even taste pink?"

She giggled. "Would you prefer a tall glass of beer?"

"Anything would be better than this." He placed the glass back in her hand, his fingers stroking along hers. "Will I be expected to dance tonight?"

"Only if you wish to," she replied. "There will be some dancing later. Only a few songs to close out the evening."

Before he could reply, James appeared at his shoulder.

Rosalie felt her heart squeeze tight. She didn't want him to feel guilty about what happened between them last night. She didn't want there to be any regrets. But now he was here, so close she could touch him. She remembered every kiss from his lips, every exquisite touch, his breath warm against her skin, his fingers buried deep.

Heavens, get ahold of yourself.

These men were murder for her self-control.

"Burke, I need you," he said without ceremony, without even a nod in her direction. That helped calm her fires. It all but put them out completely.

"What for?" Burke replied with a frown.

"Quentin is here. He has some papers that need signing and I need a witness."

"What . . . now? This is a party, James." He gestured around at the festive atmosphere. "Surely it can wait until morning."

James' eye darted to Rosalie and then back to Burke. "No . . . it can't. Come now."

Burke leaned in closer. "This won't take long," he murmured, moving away to follow James.

Rosalie watched them leave, their faces pressed close as they spoke quietly.

"Well, you certainly work fast, don't you," said a haughty voice, dripping with disdain.

Rosalie stiffened. She didn't need to turn around to know who she would find standing behind her. The ghoul in the lavender dress had her cornered.

48

Rosalie

ROSALIE TOOK IN the porcelain features of Marianne Young. The lady was alone this time. Apparently, she didn't want or need accomplices to drag her claws down Rosalie's back. "Good evening, Mrs. Young," she said with a tight smile. "It's a pleasure to see you again."

Marianne just pursed her lips. "I take no pleasure in your company, Miss Harrow. I only come to issue you a warning."

"And what might that be?"

The lady inched closer. "Be careful. The *ton* does not take kindly to grasping social climbers on the best of days, but a licentious harlot who merely wears the trappings of a social climber? They will obliterate you. There will not be a respectable house in England where you may take your tea."

"Heavens, you certainly have a very low opinion of me. I can only assure you that it is not deserved."

The lady snarled. "You think I have not watched you tonight? You flit about like a horrible little butterfly. Every man is a flower to you. First this great lord, then that one. I know you warm the duke's bed. I saw you in the garden just now.

Those brazen sensual touches . . . and his fiancée stood mere steps away. You disgust me!"

"Sensual what?" Rosalie's mind whirred. Oh gracious, did the lady consider a tug of the ear a sensual touch? "Mrs. Young, you mistook what you saw—"

"Don't tell me what I saw!"

"You saw the bickering of two friends who are as brother and sister. Ask the duke yourself, and I promise you he will be horrified to hear the words 'sensual' and 'Miss Harrow' spoken aloud in the same sentence—"

"And what excuse will you weave for your conduct with Mr. Burke? His behavior at least can be explained. I have never expected any better from his type," she said with a haughty sniff.

Rosalie felt a protective surge of rage coiling in her gut. "Mr. Burke is a dear friend. A better man, I do not know. He is worth a thousand of *your* type."

"If you care so much for the man, then why don't you marry him?" Marianne cried. "Or the duke? Or Lord James? Or any of the other men clearly under your harlot's thrall? Why do you continue to dangle Tom so cruelly?"

It all circled back to Tom.

Rosalie felt so tired. She let out a slow exhale. "There is no question of my dangling Lieutenant Renley—"

Marianne snatched hold of her arm. "Tom is *mine*. I will not abide competition. Do you understand me? Certainly not from the likes of such a three-penny upright. Why don't you crawl back to whatever Covent Garden alley you came from!"

Rosalie jerked her arm free. Every instinct told her to run. To hide. But then she glanced over Marianne's shoulder and locked eyes with a face in the crowded room.

The duke was watching her. With a wink, he gave her a little nod.

Be a lioness. Fight your corner. Hold the high ground.

If Marianne wanted to call her a harlot, that is the role Rosalie would play. She inched back, flashing the lady a false smile. "You know, just the other night, I asked Tom whether he still held any affection for you. Do you want to know what he said?"

Marianne was close to tears, but Rosalie didn't care. This woman had dared to take a bite out of her confidence for the last time.

Rosalie's smile widened. "He said nothing. You see, he couldn't speak with his tongue in my cunt—"

A feral scream erupted out of Marianne and then she was on her, scratching at Rosalie and slapping whatever part of her she could reach. In a panic, Rosalie tried to grab hold of her wrists. Loud voices echoed all around as Rosalie tried to get the demon off her. In moments it was over, strong arms pulling them apart.

"Alright, that's enough!"

She gasped, sucking air into her lungs as the duke dragged her to safety.

"I'll tear your tongue out!" Marianne shrieked. Another gentleman had her by the shoulders. She looked crazed, her face a mask of inhuman rage. "Whore!"

Next to her, the duke went still as stone. Suddenly, she was shifted behind him. He kept one arm raised as if to shield her. Turning, he addressed the room. "Let everyone bear witness that Mrs. Young has attacked my ward!" He pointed an accusing finger at the lady. "You will be gone from this place and never darken my door again!"

Marianne broke down in tears, trying to cover her face as the whole room went silent as the grave, watching the mild-mannered Duke of Norland castigate her.

"Any friend of mine will be no friend of hers," he called to the room. Turning to his footmen, he muttered, "Take her out. Make sure she doesn't come back."

The room broke into waves of whispers and gasps as two footmen took Marianne by the arms and pulled her away.

"This isn't over, you strumpet!" she shrieked. "You wretched, scheming whore! You'll tear his heart out! You'll ruin him for sure, and then what shall he do?"

One of the footmen had the good sense to wrap a gloved hand over her mouth to silence her, which left the lady squealing and thrashing in their arms. The whole room watched, utterly entranced as she was dragged out.

As soon as she was gone, Rosalie sagged on the duke's arm, letting out a ragged breath.

"No, no, no. Not here, Cabbage. Just hold on." He gripped her tight under the arms, and she let herself be led away. The sounds of the party turned into little more than a hum.

The duke shoved open the door to James' study with his shoulder. It was empty inside, but a fire crackled in the hearth and several candles were lit on the desk. He led her around the back of the sofa and set her down. She didn't even realize she was crying until he dropped to one knee before her and handed her his handkerchief.

"Should I go get a maid, Your Grace? Or Lord James?" asked a footman.

The duke tucked one of Rosalie's loose curls behind her ear. "No, get Lieutenant Renley. Discreetly, Finch," he called after the footman. "And keep Burke and my brother away. Tie them down if you must!"

The door shut and Rosalie let out a shaky breath, tears of shame stinging her eyes.

The duke disappeared into the corner. A soft clinking and rattling and he was back, curling her fingers around a glass of port. "Oh Cabbage, what did you do now?"

"I'm sorry," she murmured.

"Why are you apologizing?"

She glanced up, biting her lip. "Because you said not to embarrass you again and now look at what I've done—" She couldn't even finish before her voice broke with a strangled sob. This would be the last straw. If not for him, certainly for the duchess. Rosalie would be out on the street.

But the duke just chuckled. "You think I was embarrassed? Cabbage, that was amazing! You were better than the fire-eater. They'll be talking about this for weeks."

Rosalie covered her face with her hand. She was ready to drown herself in the port.

"I'm serious," he said, flopping by her side on the sofa. "Cabbage, you were brilliant. You really held your own. But I must know what you said. I really think she was ready to kill you."

"You exaggerate."

"Men on the battlefield have witnessed less malice," he countered, his tone one of awe. "You turned her feral with a word. What did you say?"

A fresh wave of embarrassment flooded her cheeks. "I, um . . . I may have said something rather crude. She took offense."

"I am quite literally on the edge of my seat," he said with a grin, leaning forward.

His eagerness made her smile despite the surge of embarrassment flowing through her. "If you think I'm going to reveal my disgrace to you, you're wrong, sir."

Before he could protest, there was a knock on the door that had them both turning. The footmen swung it open, and Tom pressed in, eyes wide as he locked his gaze on her. He looked as though he ran the length of the house. "What the hell happened?"

Rosalie couldn't bear to look at him. She bolted off the sofa, slapping the glass of port down as she crossed to the other side of the room.

"Rose, what happened?" Tom pressed, moving around the sofa towards her.

She spun around, holding up a gloved hand. "Stop. Don't come any closer." She couldn't bear it. She didn't trust herself.

Tom's heated gaze swept over her, his eyes narrowing with shock, then anger. "Christ, are you hurt?"

"Your little lioness got herself into a bit of a scrap," the duke explained.

"What?" Tom barked, eyes darting between them. "With whom? Why?"

She held his gaze, her emotions burning through her chest. Anger, want, shame, need. How could she feel so much at once? Her heart was pounding so loud she was sure they could all hear it.

The duke just chuckled, shifting around the sofa. He passed a side table and plucked a shiny black piece off a chess board, holding it up in the candlelight. "Because in chess, as in nature, my dear Renley, a queen must always protect her king." Smirking, he tossed it.

With the deft reflexes of a sailor, Tom snatched the queen piece from the air, glancing down at it with a frown.

The duke cuffed his shoulder. "I mean to see that my ward gets whatever she wants. And for some unknowable reason, she wants you."

Tom's eyes shot up to Rosalie, his gaze blazing hot enough to burn.

The duke cast a wink over his shoulder at Rosalie before glowering at the sailor. "Ruin this chance, and I will personally see to it that the grandest ship you ever captain is a dinghy." With that, he left.

Rosalie stood alone in the room with Tom.

"Rosalie, please tell me what the hell is happening."

49

Rosalie

ROSALIE PACED AWAY. She couldn't bear to look at Tom. She couldn't breathe. This torrent of emotions threatened to tear her apart. Since these men came storming into her life, she felt each bar that made up the cage of her heart rattled and tested for weaknesses. If she wasn't careful, the right word or look or gentle touch would become her undoing.

"Rose," Tom growled, slapping down the chess piece on the side table.

She ignored him with a shake of her head, pacing to the other side of James' study. She had to stay strong. She had to stay safe. She wanted more than bars on a cage. She wanted walls, walls, higher and higher walls.

Safer alone. Always alone.

"Christ, Rose, *talk* to me." Tom was quiet for a moment, watching her pace. "Oh shit . . ." And then she knew he knew. "It was Marianne, wasn't it?"

"Don't say that name in my presence again," Rosalie snapped, her eyes locking on him as she swept around the chairs. "It is unspeakable between us now. Do you understand?"

Tom snatched her arms at the elbows and pulled her close. His intoxicating scent enveloped her—salt and sea and sun. She bit back a whimper, even as she tensed at his touch.

"She is dead to me," he growled, his breath warm on her cheek. "She is not even a memory I hold. She is *nothing*."

The sincerity of his words washed over her like a cleansing rain. His arms wrapped around her as he pulled her close. "What can I do, Rose?" he muttered. "How can I remove this doubt once and for all? How can I prove to you that I love you?"

She stilled. "You love me?"

"We've been dancing around the saying of it for days—hell, it's been weeks for me," he admitted, his thumb brushing her cheek. "I swore to James and Burke I'd not push you. I'd let you lead and follow dutifully at the pace you set. But clearly, that is not working for us. I am near-mad with wanting to speak the words. I cannot breathe but think them at every moment. I feel them on the tip of my tongue, desperate to fly from my mouth."

She held his gaze and whispered, "Then speak them now."

He smiled down at her, eyes shining. "Rosalie Harrow, I love you. I am in love with you. I *ache* with love for you. I am consumed. I am burned down to ash and remade anew. I am yours, body and soul."

A broken cry escaped her lips as she felt the bars around her heart rattle and crack.

"No other woman has ever compared, *can* ever compare to you," he went on. "Your kindness and generosity, your fierce protection of others, your optimism in the face of adversity. Most importantly, you inspire me to be better, to be happier. You freed me from my cage of fear and made me bold enough to admit what I want from my life."

He took her gloved hand at the wrist and splayed her palm over his heart. "You are the missing piece of us, Rosalie. You are the fourth piece we always needed, but never knew how to find. You belong with me. You belong with *us*. Please, say you feel this too."

She pushed against his chest, needing to see into his depthless blue eyes. "Tom . . . I love you so much that I fear it might break me and leave me a devastated ruin."

He cupped her face gently, his forehead dropping to rest against hers as he breathed her in. "Keep going," he murmured.

"I'm no good at this," she replied, voice shaking. "I'm sure to say the words wrong."

"Just try, Rose."

She nodded. How did she even make this make sense? "I didn't think it was possible to love a person the way I love Burke. My love for him is something wild," she whispered, feeling the way her heart quickened. "With Burke, I feel so free. In loving him, I have set my soul free. It scares me. It thrills me. He makes love feel like a leap of faith, and every day I get a little braver, a little more ready to test my wings."

"I know well the passions he can inflame in another," Tom replied.

"It confused me because my love for you feels so completely different," she admitted. "You came into my life and burrowed into my very soul, bringing me comfort and friendship, two things I thought I could never earn. And you offered both wholly without conditions. You *give*, Tom. Men have only ever taken from me. Even Burke takes all my passion, he rips it from my chest. And I want to give it," she added. "I give it gladly. I'd give him anything. Any piece of me. But you are the first man I've ever met who gives first. You make me laugh. You make me dream. Tom, you are my hope for a happier future."

He sighed with relief, taking her gloved hand and pressing kisses to her fingers.

She stilled, letting the rest of her emotions cascade through her. For this perfect moment was marred by a storm cloud. "She called me a whore in front of a crowded room," she whispered.

Tom stiffened.

"She called me a three-penny upright. She said I was going to ruin you, Tom. I'm afraid she might be right—"

"Don't," he growled. "Do not listen to her poisonous words. God, I don't know what I ever saw in her. The Marianne I knew was kind. Time has changed her. Whoever I thought I knew, that person is gone . . . perhaps she never existed at all."

Rosalie let out a shaky breath. "I said not to speak her name. Tom, I can't bear it."

His eyes narrowed. "What can I do to ease your mind?" She closed her own, trying to center her breath. "Rosalie . . ."

"You were with her," she whispered. Silence. He shifted on his feet.

"Yes."

"You were intimate together . . ."

"Yes." She could feel his eyes on her. His hand grazed down her arm. "Please, Rose, just tell me what you want me to do, and I'll do it."

Rosalie opened her eyes, resolve burning like a flame in her chest. "I will not be intimidated by a ghost. She is your past and we cannot change it." Reaching out, she wrapped a gloved hand around his cravat. "But I am your future, Tom Renley. And it starts now. You are *mine*. Every piece of you. I mean to have them all for myself." She paused, brushing her gloved fingers over his mouth. "Show me a piece she's never had."

"What?"

She took in his uniform and felt a smile curve her lips. "Give me the sailor. You threatened me with him in the woods, do you remember?" She leaned in close, licking his mouth with a flick of her tongue.

"Do that again and I will lose control," he warned, his voice low.

Her smile fell as her resolve hardened. "Do it. Unleash yourself on me. Take me and use me and *fuck* me. Give me something you have never given to her."

With a growl he was on her, his mouth claiming hers in a fierce kiss. Their hands worked fast, Rosalie tugging desperately at her gloves, aching to feel his skin with no barrier between them. Tom ripped off his coat, throwing it aside. His hands went to his black cravat, tugging it loose as his tongue pressed into her mouth. He tasted like the pink punch Burke hated so much and Rosalie smiled.

Tom got himself free of his cravat, jerking on his shirt to loosen the buttons at his collar. The "V" opened wide enough to expose the top of his cross tattoo. Rosalie dropped her chin and licked it, making him groan. He grabbed her by the arms and jerked her back, his expression wild as he took her in.

"Hit me," he growled.

She blinked, sucking in a breath. "What?"

He gave her a grin so sinful it had her sex ready to weep. "You called me a friend again, and while I appreciate the sentiment when it comes to our love, you need to understand that when it comes to sex, I am not as kind nor as gentle as you seem to believe. You cannot hurt me, and I will *never* hurt you . . . but there can be worlds of pleasure found in a little pain. Now, take that sweet hand of yours, and hit me."

Her hand moved on its own, striking his face with a slap that left her gasping.

His pleasure was evident on his face as he smiled wider.

He snatched her other hand and pressed it against his hard cock. "Do it again."

This time she felt bolder. She slapped his jaw, feeling the sting of it across her palm . . . and the pleasure of it in her core. The slap left a little pink mark on his cheek, and she couldn't help herself from leaning forward, pressing her hand over it.

His entire body was coiled tight. Heavens, he was her masterpiece. Adonis in the flesh. He was the broadest of the three—wider in the hips and shoulders, with thick, strong legs, a well-muscled chest. She trailed her hand down the ridges of his stomach, cupping his cock. "Fair is fair," she whispered, her voice sounding much braver than she felt. "Hit me."

He captured her mouth with another kiss, bruising and harsh. His hands worked fast, bunching up her dress until his calloused palms could slide up the length of her silky drawers. He found the buttons on her hip and tugged at them with his large fingers until the drawers slipped down her legs.

"My dress," she panted between kisses. "Take it off."

"Not a chance," he growled, smoothing his hands over her bare bottom. "It stays on tonight. We're fucking with our clothes on. This is a claiming. You're all mine. My sweet, golden girl."

She gasped as he spun her around, pressing her towards the sofa.

"Kneel," he ordered. "Hands on the back, and lean forward."

She sank to her knees on the sofa, and her shaking hands reached out to grasp the curled wooden frame along the top. Tom was right behind her, pressing his weight against her. With one hand, he held her dress up, exposing her backside to the chill of the room. The other reached between her legs from behind, seeking out her aching sex.

"Are you ready for me?"

His fingers slid right through her wetness, and they both groaned as two fingers sank inside her. She gripped tighter to the sofa frame, feeling the sharp press of the scrolled vine detailing against her palms as she pushed back on his fingers.

"Yes," Tom growled. "Ride my fingers. In a moment you'll ride my face and come all over it. Then I'll bury myself in you until you scream."

She was ready to come now. At the first clench of her sex, he jerked his hand free and dropped to his knees. She barely had a moment to breathe before his strong hands curled up her thighs. He pressed his shoulders forward, his hot breath blazing against her sensitive skin before his tongue was teasing her.

"Oh, God!" At the first touch of his tongue against her sensitive bud, she wanted to scream.

His fingers joined his mouth, two fingers swirling in tight circles. She basked in the strange delight of being speared by his tongue. She widened her legs and pressed back against him, making him hum with pleasure. The vibration felt sinful. With their clothes on, it all felt dirty and dangerous. It was perfect. *He* was perfect.

There was no way to hold off her release. In moments, the coiling inside her burst outward and she was undone. Her breath left her in a rush and her legs shook. She sank forward, forehead resting in the curve of her elbow as she panted for breath.

Tom was on his feet in moments, leaning over her with both hands at his breeches. "You taste like heaven, Rose. Sweet as pineapple and sultry as sin. I've never been so hard in my goddamn life."

"Take me," she panted. "Please, take me—*ah*—"

Without ceremony, he gripped her hip with one hand and guided his cock to her entrance with the other, impaling her with a sharp stroke. They both cried out, Rosalie shaking with the thrill of being filled. Behind her, Tom's hands smoothed up her hips and over the round curves of her backside. Before she could beg him to move, his right hand gripped her tight enough to make her gasp. Then she felt a sharp sting as he gave her cheek a slap.

"*Oh*—" Her eyes went wide with surprise, even as she felt herself clench around his thick cock.

Tom's hand smoothed over the stinging cheek as he thrust out and back in, burying himself to the hilt. "That was one," he rasped in her ear.

Panting, she glanced over her shoulder to see the feral look on his face. "Do it again," she whispered.

His large hand came down on her with a slap, even as the other jerked her hips back against him, sheathing his cock.

"Oh God, Tom—" The sting of the slap brought tears to her eyes, but it wasn't painful. It was exhilarating. She felt ready to come again, squeezing him tighter. "Tom, please—*ah*—"

Another slap, this one to the other cheek. Then he was rutting into her with such force she let out a silent scream. Her hands gripped painfully tight to the sofa as she did everything to hold herself upright, pressing against him as he took his pleasure, making her own spiral sky high.

"From this moment, we start anew," he said in her ear. "I

was a fool for taking so long to see you for what you are. My love. My mate. My wife in my heart, if not on paper. You will not doubt my constancy again. Do you understand? You will *never* doubt me or our love again. Say it."

"*Ah*—never," she cried. "Tom, I love you. Please, don't ever leave me alone." The words slipped out unbidden. A plea. A prayer.

He stilled for a moment, panting behind her. Then his hands became impossibly gentle. He curled himself around her, his hands cupping her breasts over the fabric of her dress. His thrusts changed from claiming to loving. He pressed in, holding her tight, his cock as deep in as their bodies would allow. "Never," he murmured, kissing her neck. "You will never be alone again. I mean to make you my world. You, Burke, and James are my entire world now."

Her body ached for the release she still craved.

"I only ask one thing of you," he said, thrusting deep.

"Name it," she replied, losing herself in the exquisite ache building inside her.

"Make more of an effort with James."

She sucked in a breath. Of all the requests she thought Tom might make while buried deep inside her, that was nowhere on her list. "Tom—"

"We need him, Rosalie," he whispered, tucking her loose hair behind her ear as he thrust in again. "He is part of us." Thrust. "Only you can bring him in. Please, I know you love him. Try harder. For me, for Burke. Make us whole."

Make us whole.

She imagined a bright, perfect future where she could let herself chase James Corbin, and he would let himself be caught. The four of them together. Happy. Hearts whole. Untouchable in their love. It was a beautiful dream, one Rosalie doubted could truly be hers. Nothing in her life had ever been that kind. Perfect was a word that stayed as far away from her as possible. And yet, she wanted to try.

It all came down to choices. We choose who we love. We choose who we fight for, who we die for, who we burn the world to ash for. She chose Horatio Burke. It was perhaps the easiest decision of her life. He was her shadow and she his. They would not be parted for anything.

She chose Tom Renley, her sweet, passionate sailor who wore his heart on his sleeve. He would love her and protect her, make her laugh every day. And he would fiercely love her Burke. They deserved their own happiness together, aside from whatever they shared with her. She would protect their love with everything she had.

Rosalie now had a final choice to make. Was she going to sit back and let life pass her by, afraid to live for fear of getting hurt again? Or would she be brave and dare to believe her life could be more? Choosing James Corbin terrified her. Choosing James Corbin meant choosing to be more. Did she have the strength for it?

Feeling Tom curled around her, his cock buried deep, she felt fortified. She gave him a little nod. "I will try."

50

Rosalie

AN INCESSANT TAPPING woke Rosalie from her dream. She was grateful, for the dream had involved a feral Marianne, eyes red like a demon, chasing her through the dark halls of Corbin House.

She sat up with a gasp, Burke's arm curling tighter around her, ready to soothe her even in his sleep. By the light of the fire, she could just make out the face of the mantel clock. *Three in the morning.*

And someone had most assuredly just knocked on her door.

She shook Burke by the shoulder, rousing him with a finger to her lips. He blinked awake and she pointed silently at the door. At first, he was bleary eyed and befuddled, but another soft rap at the door had him more alert than a wolf on the hunt.

His entire body tensed as he slipped his bare legs off the side of the bed, reaching for his breeches. Someone was knocking on the door, and they both knew it wasn't Tom. The hospital charity bazaar was in the morning, and Tom had already traveled on to Greenwich to help Hartington with the setup.

Rosalie put a hand on Burke's arm. "You must go. Now."

He stared daggers at her. "Who is knocking on your door, Rosalie?"

"I don't know," she mouthed, slipping out the other side of her bed. The floor was freezing on her bare feet. Her chemise slipped off one shoulder as she flicked her long braid over the other, reaching for her robe.

Burke took a step towards her door, his hand outstretched.

She rushed forward, her robe still undone, and grabbed for his arm, giving him a desperate push towards his own room. Useless. The man was a tree.

He glared, curling his arm possessively around her, his intentions clear. No one would be opening that door but him. Before either of them could silently argue, a deep voice murmured through the solid wooden door. "Burke, open the door."

James.

They both breathed a sigh of relief and Burke crossed to the door. He turned the lock with a click, opening it a crack to let James slip in.

James stood in her room for the first time, his eye glancing to Burke, who was naked but for a pair of breeches slung low on his hips, still undone at the waist. James' eyes trailed over to Rosalie—her hair set in ribbon curlers, her robe open over a chemise all askew, down to her bare toes curling on the cold rug. James was dressed no more formally. He wore a shirt and breeches, velvet tasseled slippers on his feet. His shirt sleeves were rolled up to the elbows and the buttons were open at the neck.

Her mouth quirked into a smile as she remembered he was the first of the three men she'd seen completely naked.

That afternoon with Madeline by the water's edge, she saw every wet, glistening inch of him. It felt like a lifetime ago instead of only a few weeks.

"What happened?" Burke started buttoning up his breeches. "What's wrong?"

"Nothing," James replied, seeming suddenly unsure. "I . . . this was a mistake." His eyes darted to Rosalie.

Her smile fell as she really took him in—the dark circles under his eyes, the tension in his shoulders. After everything between them over the past few days, he was still hurting, confused and angry and alone with his lofty principles.

She stepped up to him, cupping his cheek with a gentle hand. He leaned into her touch, closing his eyes, his dark lashes brushing the tops of his cheeks.

"You look exhausted," she murmured.

He covered her hand with his own, opening his eyes. "I can't sleep," he admitted.

With a nod, she dropped her hand from his face and stepped back. She didn't need Tom's plea sounding in her ears to guide her next steps. She knew what she wanted, what he needed. "Come to bed."

James glanced from her to Burke, a brow raised in silent question.

Without hesitation, Burke began unfastening his breeches. "I sleep nude."

"I know." He followed behind Rosalie to the far side of the bed.

Rosalie slipped off her robe, flashing Burke a little smile as he climbed back into her bed.

He tugged back the coverlet, letting her slip in. "Stoke the fire," he directed at James. "And close the curtains on your side. It's colder than a witch's tit in here."

James moved silently over to the fireplace, adding a few logs and shifting them with a fire iron. With his back turned to them, Burke took the moment to tip her face towards him and ask his own silent question. She nodded, leaning over to kiss the corner of his mouth. Assuaged, he rolled over, tugging the curtains on his side of the bed closed.

James returned, the fire blazing behind him, casting long shadows down the walls. He shrugged off his breeches, leaving on his billowing white shirt. It was long enough to cover him as he sank down onto the bed.

Rosalie could sense his nerves warring with his desperate fatigue. Wasting no time, she pulled him down to her, letting him sink his face onto the pillow and curl around her, his chin tucked against the curve of her breast. His left arm wrapped around her middle and she tangled their bare legs together. With her free hand, she brushed his wavy curls off his brow with slow strokes.

Burke waited for them both to settle before scooting in behind Rosalie. He buried his face in the curve of her neck. She felt him sinking into sleep, totally at peace with James' presence.

"This pillow smells like Tom," said James, his breath warm against her shoulder.

"Aye, well that's Tom's side of the bed," Burke mumbled. "You'll have to fight him for it when he returns."

"Perhaps they can simply wrestle *you* to the floor, and their problem will be solved," Rosalie replied with a sleepy smile.

"Not a fucking chance." He slid his hand around her stomach to cup her sex, pressing her back against his hips. "You sleep nestled against my cock, or not at all."

"Learn to share, or I will sleep alone," she countered.

He grumbled, not loosening his hold on her as he grazed his teeth over her neck, giving her a little nip. He soothed the spot with a lave of his tongue, which sent a shiver down her arms. She was too tired to let herself become aroused. These men were wearing her out, body and soul. She was desperate for sleep.

And yet there was something she did want before she let sleep claim her. She brushed her fingers through James' hair again. "James . . ."

He hummed to let her know he was still awake.

"Any man who sleeps in my bed must always kiss me good night."

A sleepy smile tipped his lips as he obliged, lifting his chin to press his mouth to hers. She returned his kiss. Their mouths both opened slightly as she flicked his lips with her tongue. He echoed with his own lick before breaking away, settling himself back at the curve of her breast.

It was the most chaste kiss they'd ever shared, and yet something about it felt earth-shaking. There was a promise in it. That same promise of more that scared her half to death.

Burke was not James. Nor was Tom. They bent to her whims eagerly—joyfully, even. She set the rules, and they simply adjusted course. The bastard and the sailor, carefree second sons willing to follow her every lead. But this was James bending. If she forced him to bend much further, he would break. She knew the truth deep in her heart. She'd known it almost from the moment she met him. If Rosalie meant to keep James close, or bring him even closer, the only way would be for her to learn to bend too.

51

Burke

THE GREENWICH HOSPITAL Charity Bazaar proved to be too delightful a distraction for the house party to ignore. All the young people chose to skip church with the duchess in favor of attending. It took three carriages and nearly two hours to ferry them all across London. By midmorning, Burke found himself on the packed grounds of All Saints Church, Blanche Oswald on one arm, Mariah Swindon on the other. James walked behind with Rosalie.

The young ladies twittered at every little thing they saw, and there was quite a feast for the eyes. Rows and rows of tables were set up in the shaded space between the church and the vicarage. Locals were selling everything from homemade breads and jams, cheeses, and honey meads, to painted fans, jewelry, and hair pins and baubles.

"Oh, look at that pretty blue," Blanche cried, squeezing tight to his arm.

"Mr. Burke, can we go explore?" Mariah asked with a bat of her long, red lashes. "We promise not to go far."

"By all means." He had no interest in chaperoning them.

"We shall all meet back here at four o'clock," Elizabeth directed. "Mariah, spend all your pocket money, and Mama is sure to be cross."

But the younger Swindon wasn't listening. She dropped Burke's arm in favor of Blanche's, and the girls darted away in a flurry of giggles.

"Mariah!" Elizabeth shrieked, following after them.

"They seem happy to be here."

Burke turned to see Rosalie at his shoulder. She was a vision this morning in a pelisse of deepest sapphire blue. Black velvet framed her collar and wrists. Her bonnet was a fashionable thing of blue satin with yellow-gold ribbons.

"Burke! James!"

They all turned to see Tom striding towards them, weaving between the tables. He wore his white sailor's breeches with double buttons up the front. A red sash was tied at his waist. While he was still shirted, it was unbuttoned.

"There you are," he called. "I've been keeping a look out. The matches start at noon. I was worried you might be late."

"Are you to exhibit, then?" Burke asked.

"Aye, well, they wanted the matches sorted, and the only one without a pairing was Hart," he replied, his smile tipping into a frown. "Given your last interaction, I thought it better you not be put in a ring with free rein to pummel him."

"Your last interaction?" James muttered. "What is he talking about?"

"Nothing," the men replied together.

"Oh, Burke, what did you do?" Rosalie asked from his other side.

"Why am I the one suspected to have done something?" he said with a huff of indignation. "Why does no one question the conduct of the dashing sea captain? Perhaps he earned what he got."

"And did he?" James asked.

Burke glanced at Tom, letting his own frown tip into a smile. "He did. And Tom's right, if Hartington is my competition, there will be no competition. I'd flatten the lout in a single round. That would hardly provide the crowd with a good show."

"Well, I'm third up," Tom replied. "I was hoping you'd stand ringside," he added with a hopeful look.

Burke's smile widened. "A front-row seat to watch the captain eat your fists? I'd be delighted."

Not a stone's throw from All Saint's Church, the bazaar organizers had commandeered the use of an old warehouse. A makeshift boxing ring had been set up in the middle of the floor, with risers on three sides providing seating. The crowd was growing with each fight. They may not be professional boxers, but Hartington was right: Some of these wiry sailors really knew how to swing their fists.

Tom danced on the balls of his feet, shaking out his arms. He'd shed his shirt, his tattoos now on full display. Burke couldn't deny he found them sensual. It hadn't escaped his notice how Rosalie would trace them with her fingers, her tongue. Burke secretly ached to do the same.

Tearing his hungry eyes from Tom's chest, he looked at the ring just as the wiry sailor with a black mustache landed a facer on an opponent twice his size. Mustache danced away as the big man dropped to his knees, then flopped forward on his face, out cold. The crowd erupted in cheers as the bell rang, ending the match.

"I'm up next," Tom called over the roar.

Across the room, Hartington appeared to more cheers. Burke hated that scar on his face. Damn, but the man *did* look dashing. If Rosalie or Tom glanced at him just one more time with even the politest bit of interest in their eyes, he was going to tie them both to his bed and ravage them until they begged for mercy.

This isn't jealousy . . . it's territoriality.

"Have you seen him fight before?" he asked Tom as they pushed their way towards the ring.

"Aye, he's strong as an ox," Tom replied. "But he's slow. I'll use it." He slipped between the ropes, giving a nod to the referee: a burly man stripped down to his waistcoat with a thick yellow mustache and beady dark eyes. Then he turned back to face Burke, his eyes scanning the crowd. "Where are they?"

Burke glanced over his shoulder, letting his well-honed sense for finding James draw his eye to the end of the third row. "There." He pointed to where James sat on the crowded bench, wedged between Rosalie and Elizabeth. Olivia sat on Rosalie's other side.

"Christ, she looks gorgeous today," Tom muttered. "Blue is her color. I thought it was pink, but I am a man reformed—"

Burke snapped his fingers in his face. "Focus. For the next fifteen minutes, she doesn't exist."

Tom huffed. "You think Hart will last five rounds against me?"

"Never. You're going to flatten him in three."

Across the ring, Hartington slipped through the ropes.

Like Tom, he wore only a pair of white sailor's breeches. His waist was wrapped in a gold sash. And now he was shirtless, his broad chest glistening with oil as he swung his fists.

Burke's heart stopped as his eye landed on the anchor tattoo emblazoned on the captain's chest. It was a mirror to the one on Tom, carved over their hearts.

Mine.

The word flooded through him, drowning out all other thoughts. Fuck territoriality. This was jealousy. This was rage. Burke ached with it. He burned with the need to claim Tom in front of the captain. Hell, in front of this entire crowd.

"Easy, Burke," Tom muttered with a grin. Of course, he knew what had him upset.

Burke glared at him, eyes aflame. "Make him bleed . . . or I will."

52

Burke

THE FIRST TWO rounds were over in a blink. Tom and Hartington each landed a few good jabs. Hartington was broader in the shoulders and taller. But Tom had a better center and better control in his swing. If he could stay on his feet, Burke was sure he'd win.

The bell rang, ending the second round, and Tom and Hartington split apart. Burke waited with a towel, tossing it to Tom as he approached. Other than battered knuckles, a cut lip, and being out of breath, Tom was faring well against the behemoth. He tossed the towel back to Burke, sagging against the ropes. His sides were heaving, and his chest and arms glistened with sweat.

"Christ, I forgot how hard he hits. His fists are like bloody iron."

"You're doing well," Burke replied, handing over a cup of water.

Tom drained it in three gulps.

Across the way, Hartington leaned against the ropes. He

had a cut on his brow. A mate had a towel pressed over it, trying to staunch the bleeding.

"He drops his left shoulder when he's about to hit hard with the right," Burke muttered.

"Aye, I noticed," Tom replied through deep breaths. "I can take him down next round. God, I can't wait to humiliate him," he said with a chuckle. "He hates to lose." He bounced on the balls of his feet, taking a few practice punches in the air.

Burke stood there, dazed, as an idea fine as smoke drifted through his mind.

No . . . no, this can't be happening.

He glanced over his shoulder to where the others watched. Rosalie was on the edge of her seat, eyes wide. On one side of her sat James, arms crossed over his chest. He gave Burke a nod of approval. Tom was doing well. But on Rosalie's other side sat the gorgon. He followed her gaze across the ring to where Hartington stood, flexing his shoulders. She was trying to hide it, but the worry was there. Her fan was frozen as her eyes soaked in Hartington's muscled back.

"Goddamn it," he muttered. Was he really about to do this? Leaning over the ropes, he snagged Tom's shoulder, tugging him back to whisper in his ear, "Tom, you have to throw this fight."

Tom's neck twisted so fast he nearly gave himself a crick. "What? *Why*? Burke, I've got him—"

"Because sometimes you have to lose a battle to win the war."

"Battle? What the hell are you talking about?"

The crowd cheered as the referee moved back into the middle of the ring, ready to start the next round.

Tom flexed his shoulders, giving the air a few more jabs. "I can do this—"

"Look at me, you bloody fool."

Tom's eyes narrowed in annoyance. "What—"

"Olivia is here," he pressed. "She's watching, Tom. She's on the edge of her seat with worry for Hartington. You must throw the fight. You must let him win. Let her *see* him win. Do it for me—"

Tom shrugged him off. "I'm trying to *beat* him for you, you horse's arse. A win for me is a win for you. And I've got ten pounds on me to win."

"Forget the bloody money. James will pay you back!"

Tom snorted. "Unlikely. James put down fifty."

Hartington was moving out of his corner. The referee glanced over at them with a raised brow. Christ, he was out of time. Burke had to say something to get through to Tom. *Anything*.

Suddenly, he grinned and leaned over the ropes. "I'll let you call me Horatio."

Tom looked sharply at him, then barked a laugh. "Nice try. I told you how I want to earn that right." He turned away, ready to rejoin the fight.

Burke took a deep breath and called after him, "Then earn it!"

Tom turned back.

"Let's go, Lieutenant," the referee called. "Time's up!"

Tom ignored him. He ignored everything. Burke did too. In the span of a single moment, the crowded warehouse had narrowed to just the two of them. Burke watched Tom's shoulders tense, a question dancing in his blue eyes. These words needed to be said. They'd been choking him for days. "Everything you said that day in the alley . . . everything you offered . . . I want it. Throw the fight, and it's yours."

A faint smile quirked Tom's mouth as his gaze heated. He glanced over Burke's shoulder, no doubt seeking out Rosalie in the crowd. Then his eyes settled back on Burke. "It was always going to be mine," he said with a confident grin. "But I'm a patient man. I'll wait for you."

Burke's cock twitched, even as he forced himself to take a breath. "No more waiting. I'm all in. Are you?"

Before Tom could reply, the referee was in their corner, one hand on Tom's shoulder. "Let's go, Lieutenant. We finishing this fight or not?"

Tom turned away without a word, following the referee to the middle of the ring. Burke could do nothing but watch as Tom and Hartington took up their stances and the referee rang the bell. The crowd screamed and the third round began. Hartington came in swinging strong, just as determined as Tom to end their dance this round. Tom took one hit but ducked the next. His footwork was excellent; he could jab in and dart, perfectly balanced on his toes. Hartington relied more on twisting from his hips.

Tom slipped in under a swing and gave Hartington two sharp jabs to his ribs. The captain wheezed, stumbling back, his left arm clamping down against his side. Tom danced away with a grin.

"Goddamn it, Tom!" Burke barked. He wasn't going to throw the fight. He was going for the knockout. Burke seethed, feeling himself being torn apart. He wanted nothing more than to see the captain bleeding on the mats.

Well . . . almost nothing.

Even more than seeing Hartington humiliated, Burke wanted to see himself free of Olivia Rutledge. This sea captain had the power to free him. Olivia was a gorgon and a witch and an all-around terrible person who Burke loathed. But for some reason, Captain William Hartington liked her. Hell, the confounded idiot loved her. He'd even proposed to her once. If the lady would just get out of her own way, she could have him and Burke could be free.

His goal was clear. He had to persuade Olivia to admit to wanting the captain. But what lady would admit to wanting a man bloodied and bruised, defeated by a lower-ranking officer?

Fucking hell, Tom. Please, throw this fight. He sent out his selfish prayer, watching as Tom danced closer to the captain, ready to fake a low swing. He was going to plant a facer. It would be a knockout hit.

"No!" Burke's shout was lost in the chaos of the crowd.

Time slowed as he watched Tom dart in, right arm kept low for the fake as he readied his left. Hartington fell for it, twisting to protect his tender ribs. That opened Tom to swing up with his left, clocking the captain on the jaw.

Only Tom didn't take the swing. He followed through with his right hand, landing the useless punch that Hartington was ready to block. It was Hartington that got to come in swinging with his right hook, knocking Tom to the mats.

The crowd jumped to their feet, shaking the stands as Tom rolled to his stomach. The referee counted down as the crowd shouted for Tom to get on his feet. Tom let his body go slack and the referee slapped the mat.

It was over.

Behind them, the bell rang in finality.

In the flurry of activity, Burke narrowed his eyes on Tom. He waited with bated breath as Tom lifted his chin just enough to catch his eye across the mat. His mouth a bloody smile, he winked.

53

Rosalie

"OH TOM, ARE you alright?" Rosalie pushed her way through the excited crowd, throwing herself at Burke's side as he helped Tom climb out between the ropes.

Tom sank down on the ring's edge, his face a bloody mess. He was panting, each breath making him wince. She hated seeing him like this.

"You were doing so well," she cried, snatching the towel from Burke's hand to dab at Tom's bleeding brow. "James was sure you were going to win. He can't believe it."

"I'm fine." Tom wrapped his hand around her wrist.

The contact made her stifle a whimper. His knuckles were bloodied. Boxing was a terrible, worthless sport! Men pounding each other like sacks of meat, and for what?

"He's fine, love," Burke murmured at her side.

She felt ridiculous for being so emotional. "I saw you fall . . . the blood . . . you weren't moving. We were all so sure you'd win—"

"He was never going to win," Burke soothed.

"What?"

Tom took a sip of the water Burke offered, swirling it in his mouth and spitting it on the floor. The pink tint made Rosalie's stomach churn. Seeing one of her men hurt, even when they'd signed up for the pain, was apparently something she couldn't tolerate.

"Someone start talking," she hissed, lifting the towel away to check his bleeding brow.

"Burke made me an offer I couldn't refuse," Tom replied with a grin.

"An offer?" Her eyes darted to Burke. "What is he talking about?"

Burke ignored Tom, bandaging his knuckles with a practiced hand. "Hart needed the win more."

"What? Why?"

"Because the gorgon was watching," Burke replied. "And we needed to show our dashing Perseus in the best possible light. Losing to a lower-ranking officer in a charity boxing match was not the way to win her heart."

She glanced between the two of them, her frustration rising. "Oh, you two are ridiculous! You cannot scheme so willy-nilly, or you risk making things even worse. Do you both now require a chaperone? Tom could have been seriously injured!"

"When it works, I expect a truly heartfelt apology," Tom replied, dabbing at his cut lip.

"I guarantee you it will not work. Olivia will not have her head turned or her heart softened by a round of bloody fisticuffs."

Burke put a firm hand on her shoulder, his face lowering to her ear. "Then explain *that*."

She and Tom both turned to see Olivia standing before Hartington on the other side of the ring, holding a towel to his cut brow. Her blush was evident, even from this distance. As they watched, Hartington leaned in and whispered something that had her laughing, covering the proof with her yellow-gloved hand.

Rosalie's shoulders sagged. She couldn't bear to see the look of triumph on Burke or Tom's face. "I hate you both," she murmured.

"Well, let us see if we can't just win you back before the day is over," Tom teased.

She glanced from one to the other. "What am I missing? What else have you done?"

"It's not about what we've done," said Burke, his heated gaze locked on Tom. "It's about what we plan to do."

54

Rosalie

"IS SOMEONE GOING to tell me what's happening?" Rosalie murmured.

The whole group was back from the bazaar having a late dinner in the dining room at Corbin House. Rosalie was seated next to Tom at the end of the table. Burke and James were on opposite sides at the other end. Tom took his loss gallantly, letting the ladies coo over his injuries, which were thankfully minor.

He lifted his glass of red wine to his lips, taking a sip and wincing slightly from the sting of his cut lip.

"Tom . . ."

He smiled. "Burke and I have an outstanding debt that must be cleared. He'll need your help to clear it."

If the meaning in his words were lost on her, the look on his face certainly wasn't. He meant to devour her. Her cheeks flamed with warmth as she felt her stomach do a little flip. Heavens, whatever had these men discussed? What other plans were they hatching without her?

The dinner ended, and the whole group returned to the

drawing room for drinks and cards. Despite the late hour, no one seemed ready to retire. Even the duchess and the older ladies stayed for a round of whist.

Rosalie sat on a sofa in the far corner of the room with a book, letting the gentle hum of voices calm her as she read. James and George sat at a table with the Swindon sisters, while Prudence and Piety played against the duchess and Lady Oswald. The third table was made up of Blanche, Mariah, the countess, and Olivia. Sir Andrew and the marchioness were the only others not playing. Sir Andrew sat asleep on the opposite sofa, his paper hanging open in his lap. The marchioness sat alone by the fire, her needlework in hand.

Burke and Tom were missing.

Before Rosalie could question their absence, a footmen entered the room, silver tray in hand, and came right for her. She set her book aside as he offered her a letter.

"This arrived for you earlier, Miss," he muttered.

She took the letter off the tray, not recognizing the heavy handwriting. Using the paper knife, she loosened the seal and opened it. The footman backed away as she read the short message through twice.

If anyone asks, this is from your aunt. Pretend to read it slowly. Perhaps smile a bit. Do whatever ladies do when reading letters from their relations. Wait two minutes, then excuse yourself to write back. We're waiting for you.

-B

"Bad news?" said James, his eyes narrowed on her.

She swallowed, folding the note closed. She hated lying to him, but his question drew others' eyes. She put on a forced smile. "Not at all, my lord. It's from my aunt. She chastises me on the silence of my pen." She tucked the note into her pocket. "Your Grace . . . I think I will retire. I believe I have just enough energy left to write her a dutiful reply."

"Yes, fine," the duke said with a wave of his hand, not even turning around. "James, will you focus? Hearts are trump and you just played a spade."

Not waiting for him to change his mind, she bowed a curtsy to the room and darted away.

She returned to her room to find it empty. The maids had prepared it for the evening—covers pulled down and pillows fluffed, her fire blazing, candles lit on two tables, her robe laid out upon the end of the bed.

With a tired sigh, she kicked off her slippers and tugged off her evening gloves. The door connecting her room to Burke's was closed. As she took a step towards it, she heard the unmistakable sound of a man's low moan.

Her man.

After crossing to the door, she opened it. Her heart flipped. Burke and Tom were standing shirtless together in the middle of the room, wrapped in each other's arms as they kissed. Their hands moved feverishly, touching every inch of the other's skin. Tom ran both hands over Burke's arse and pulled him closer, making both men groan.

Rosalie was on fire, all thought of fatigue utterly forgotten. Their passion set her ablaze. She was trembling with it. She wanted to see more. She wanted to see them unleashed and undone.

Burke noticed her first, his lips glistening with Tom's kisses. The storms swirled in his eyes as he took her in. Then

Tom looked her way, his gaze just as heated. They relaxed their hold on each other but didn't pull away.

"We couldn't wait," Burke said, almost as if in apology.

"You shouldn't have to," she replied, feeling breathless. "You are so beautiful together." She'd never seen two men share intimacy before, but it was true. Burke and Tom looked perfect in each other's arms. "I want to see more," she admitted.

"Come kiss us first," said Tom, holding out his bandaged hand.

She went eagerly, feeling them each put a hand around her waist as she claimed Tom's lips in a kiss. She felt how they were slightly swollen, the bottom one split in the middle, but it didn't stop him from devouring her. She licked the cut and he winced.

"No more getting punched in the face for fun," she chastised, raising a hand to touch his tender brow. "This face means too much to me to let another man crack his fists against it."

Tom just chuckled. "I'm a fast healer."

She turned to Burke, running a hand up his arm. "So, do you want to taste my Tom? Is that the bargain you made? You think you need my permission to take your pleasure with him?"

Burke grinned, cupping the back of her neck as he pulled her close. "My sweet siren, I want to *fuck* your Tom . . . while he fucks you. We will claim him together and make him ours until he is moaning our names and coming between us. We will give him such pleasure that he is broken and remade by it. Would you like to help me with that?"

As Burke spoke, Tom groaned, his forehead falling to

Burke's bare shoulder. Burke wove his fingers possessively into Tom's curls. His eyes didn't leave Rosalie's face.

She was sure, if she were to lift her skirts and check, her thighs would already be wet with her desire. "Yes," she whispered. "I want that very much."

Burke leaned down, giving her a chaste kiss. "Good girl. Now, turn around."

She turned, heart pounding in her chest. "Tom, help her with her dress," he directed.

Tom's fingers were at her back, brushing over her skin as he undid the fastenings of her silvery evening gown. It was the work of moments before he slipped it off her shoulders and it fluttered to the floor. She turned back around, still wearing her stays and silk drawers.

Burke nodded his approval. "Get the rest of your clothes off and get on my bed, love. I need to tease Tom some more."

With a smile, she backed towards the bed, her hands going to the hooks of her stays. She didn't want to miss a thing. Both men watched her as she undid each fastening. The stays slipped from her shoulders, followed quickly by her silk drawers, leaving her standing in nothing but her stockings. She bent down to slip them off, but Tom's voice stopped her.

"Keep those on, sweet girl."

"Get on the bed," Burke repeated. "And don't touch your cunt. That belongs to Tom tonight."

She sat on the end of Burke's bed. She'd never actually been on his bed before. He always came to her. There was something about being in this space that excited her, further proof that she wasn't in control . . . nor was she the center of attention. It didn't discomfit her. In fact, it thrilled her. Her sex may be aching with the desire to be touched, but there was something so exhilarating about knowing she had to wait her turn. In the meantime, she got to watch.

Burke turned his attention back to Tom. He had one hand on Tom's shoulder, the other at his waist. They held each other's gaze as Tom's hands slid up Burke's torso, over his chest, and cupped his face. He pulled Burke to him in a kiss that had them both sighing again. In no time it went from fevered to desperate, with Burke taking charge, dropping his mouth to Tom's neck, his collarbone.

Tom tipped his head back, eyes shut in bliss, as Burke teased him with lips and tongue. Rosalie held in a whimper as she realized Burke was tracing his tattoos. How many times had Rosalie done the same thing? He worked his way over from the ship to the cross, his lips brushing against the anchor over Tom's heart. Wrapping his arms tightly around Tom, Burke's kiss turned into more, bending Tom back until he was barking out in pain.

The men broke apart, both panting. Tom raised a hand and brushed it over the anchor tattoo on his chest. Burke bit him hard enough to draw blood. Tom's eyes were wild as he looked at Burke.

Burke swiped a finger over the bite mark, looking down at the faint smear of blood on the tip. As Rosalie and Tom watched, he licked it clean. Then he wrapped that same hand in Tom's hair, jerking him close. "You're mine, Tom. You've waited fifteen years for me. Say the words, and you can have me in all the ways your heart desires."

"Oh, Christ. I'm yours," Tom murmured, kissing a line up Burke's neck, pressing himself against him. "I'm yours, I'm yours. I'm hers and I'm yours. God, please, take me and fill me, Burke. I'm dying with wanting you both. Need you so goddamn much." He plunged his hand inside Burke's breeches, wrapping it around his cock.

Rosalie whined with need, resisting the urge to touch herself. She was aching, weeping, begging to be filled. But she also wanted to keep watching.

The men heard her needy sound, and both turned. Tom held her gaze as he pumped Burke's cock, his eyes hooded with desire. Burke dropped his mouth back to Tom's chest, licking again at the bite mark. Tom shivered, his hand stilling.

"Our sweet siren needs attention now," Burke murmured, curling his hand around to cup Tom's backside. "I don't touch this perfect arse again until she comes on your face."

Tom pulled his hand loose from Burke's breeches and all but stumbled towards her. He undid the fall of his breeches as he walked, slipping them off before he climbed naked onto the end of the bed.

Rosalie sat back on her elbows, watching him kneel over her. The longing in his face had her heart overflowing. She opened her knees in invitation. Tom climbed between them and up her body to claim her lips in a heady kiss.

"I love you, Rose," he said against her lips. "I love you so goddamn much. I'll never get used to saying it. It's a gift to say it."

"I love you," she replied, trying to be gentle with his tender lips but feeling ravenous all the same.

He didn't kiss her for long before he was inching back, peppering her breasts and stomach with fevered kisses. He pressed her thighs apart, resting his forehead on her pubic bone and inhaling deep. She quivered with nervous excitement.

"God, this scent, it haunts me. And you're so wet, you're

dripping for us. Your cunt is what dreams are made of. Burke, come look before I claim it. Look at how beautiful she is for us."

She whined, fighting the urge to squirm as Burke came to the end of the bed, trailing his hand up her stocking-clad leg. He leaned over Tom, his eyes hungry as he looked at her spread open for them. "Let me taste her."

Tom reached out his unbandaged hand, sinking two fingers into her. She gasped as he gave them a little twist, dragging them along her inner wall. He pulled them out and held them up. They glistened in the candlelight.

Burke leaned over his shoulder and sucked them into his mouth. "Divine," he muttered. "The sweetest sacrament."

Not wasting a moment with chaste kisses or teasing licks, Tom dropped down onto his bruised and bitten chest and buried his face between her legs. She cried out, gripping the coverlet with both hands, curling forward as Tom ravaged her, spiraling her so high so fast she thought she might spark like a lit candle. Thinking of the two of them kissing tipped her over the edge and her first release shivered through her. Legs shaking, she pushed on Tom's forehead, begging for mercy.

He sank back, his hands smoothing up her thighs as he panted for breath.

"If he's touching me, you have to touch him," she directed at Burke.

"You don't want to come again first?" Burke said with a raised brow, his arms crossed as he leaned against the post of his bed. He stood there as casual as can be, as if he didn't just watch Tom feast on her.

"I want you with us," she replied. "Please, love. We need you."

"I'm dying," Tom muttered, brushing her inner thigh with kisses.

"Tell me what you want, Tom," Burke replied. "I've never—"

He stopped himself, but not quick enough. It was then that Rosalie realized the truth. Burke was nervous . . . or at least hesitant. He'd never been with a man before. He didn't want to get this wrong.

Tom heard it too because he was turning on his knees. He pulled Burke into his arms, kissing his neck. "It's no different than when you take Rosalie. You won't hurt me."

"It *is* different. This is different, Tom. You're not all interchangeable to me," Burke said, almost irritated.

Rosalie rolled to her knees and joined Tom at the end of the bed. "Burke, I love you. I know I don't say it as often as you'd like, but I do. I love you, and I love Tom, and I love what you've found in each other. *Be* with us. Claim us both. We are yours. We want to be yours."

With a pained expression, Burke uttered one word: "James."

Rosalie sank back as Burke wrapped an arm around Tom's neck. "I want this so badly, I can scarcely breathe. I want you, Tom . . . but I feel like I'm cheating on James. He and I are nothing, I know that. We've never—but he is my world—"

"You and James are *everything*," Rosalie replied, trying to control the tremble in her voice. "No one who has seen you together for two minutes can doubt the affection he holds for you."

"You are his world too," Tom added, cupping his face. "You are more than a brother to him, more than a friend or a partner or a lover. You are his soulmate, Burke. You are one spirit made two. I've always known that about you. I've been jealous more times than I can count."

Burke groaned. "Having him on the outside is killing me. I need him here with us. I need him to *want* to be here. Why can he not just come in from the cold?"

Tom was quiet, giving Burke's arm a soothing stroke.

Rosalie bit her lip, knowing how much she was to blame for this tension. "James' timing is his own," she replied. "I know I've made things difficult. He wants what I'm afraid to give. And without realizing it, he punishes us all. If I give in, perhaps . . ."

"No," Tom growled. "You shouldn't have to make such a sacrifice. Your freedom is valuable to you, so it is valuable to me. I'll not let him take it. Nothing is worth you losing yourself to gain his love."

She nodded. But she didn't want a cloud over this moment. She looked from Tom back to Burke. "In this moment, *this* feels right. We need you, Burke. Make us whole. Make three become one. And have no doubt that, when James is ready, he will be the center of our world."

Burke nodded, licking his lips as he glanced from Tom to Rosalie. "I want you both so badly. I need you in my arms."

"We are right here," she whispered, scooting back on the bed and lying down. "Tom, come. Make love to me again, and let Burke take care of us."

Tom followed her to the middle of the bed, rolling on top of her as he lost himself in the feel of her, kissing and roving with his hands, shifting between her legs until his cock was pressing at her entrance.

"Wait," Burke said, sinking onto the bed behind them. He pulled back on Tom's hips, taking hold of his cock. Tom groaned, and it only took Rosalie a moment to realize Burke was slipping on a French letter.

As soon as it was on, Tom lifted her hips and slid home, filling her with a thrust. He adjusted his position, curling his hand under her thigh to spread her wider, letting his cock sink deeper. She shivered, gripping his hips, as he touched a point deep inside.

"Yes," Tom rasped. "Feel you there, sweet girl." He pressed in again, and she clenched tighter. "Right there. God, your cunt is my heaven. Burke, please."

Burke shifted on the bed behind them. "Need to stretch you out," he muttered at Tom's shoulder. "I don't want my thick cock to damage this sweet arse."

Tom buried his face in Rosalie's shoulder, his whole body going still.

"Tell me what you're doing," she whispered. "Tell me how it feels."

"I have a finger inside him," Burke muttered.

"More," said Tom. "Feels so good—*ah*—"

"Two fingers," Burke said with a smirk. "Move, Tom. Fuck my hand and fuck our girl."

With a growl, Tom thrust into her once, twice.

She couldn't contain her smile, as turned on by Tom's cock inside her as she was by Burke taking him for the first time.

"Please, Burke," Tom whined. "Please, I'm ready. Stop teasing me and give me what I need."

Burke shifted into position, gripping tight to Tom's hip. Rosalie felt Tom's cock twitch when Burke penetrated him

"God, *yesss*," Tom said in a hiss, moving his hips in little thrusts.

"Not yet," Burke panted. "Not—almost—holy hell, you're so tight."

"It's been a while," Tom huffed, trying to control his breathing.

"Christ, I'm in." Burke folded over them.

"Move, Burke," he said. "You have to move. Own me."

"Own us both," Rosalie pleaded.

Wasting no time, Burke began thrusting. It was a wholly new sensation for Rosalie to be so weighed down by the press of her men, feeling one moving inside her as the result of the other moving inside *him*. She tipped her head back and closed her eyes, savoring the feeling of union she felt in their arms.

Shifting her leg let Tom sink in a little deeper. She cried out, feeling new glorious friction. "Harder," she panted. "Please, take us harder."

Burke grabbed hold of Tom's hips and began to rut, slamming into Tom hard enough to have Rosalie inching back on the bed.

"Yes," she cried, feeling every muscle in Tom's body go tense. "God, please—don't stop—"

Burke adjusted his position, taking one arm and wrapping it around Tom's throat, pulling him back until they were both nearly upright. It was all Tom could do to grab hold of her hips and tip them up to keep himself buried inside her. Something about the change in angle had her seeing stars. Her entire body coiled tight, and her mouth opened in a silent scream. Wave after wave of release crested through her, sending a ripple effect through her entire body. She gripped tight to Tom's cock as she leapt from the height of her ecstasy, willing to take them both crashing down with her.

Tom came first, all but collapsing on top of her, his arms and legs useless for holding his weight. A few more thrusts and Burke was gone, spilling his seed inside his friend.

Rosalie opened her eyes to see both her men euphoric on top of her.

"You're both mine now," Burke panted. "All mine."

"Yours," Rosalie echoed, smoothing the hair off Tom's sweaty brow.

"We've been yours," Tom replied.

Rosalie didn't miss the happy, sated smile that flashed across Burke's face.

"And what did this little endeavor earn you, Tom?" he teased, leaning over to kiss Tom's cheek.

It was Tom's turn to smile. "Horatio," he murmured, still resting his face on Rosalie's chest. "I get to call you Horatio."

55

Rosalie

THE MORNING AFTER the boxing match, Rosalie woke in the most glorious way. It was still early, the house was dark and quiet, and her men were teasing her nipples with their tongues, their naked bodies pressed against her. She squirmed beneath them, looping an arm around each of their necks as she stretched, feeling the wonderful ache between her thighs that told her she was claimed. Loved. Cherished.

Before long, lounging between them wasn't enough. In a stroke of genius, Burke flipped her around atop him so she could ride his face. Meanwhile, it put her in the perfect position to take his cock with her mouth. It was sure to be her new favorite position.

Never one for being left out, Tom joined her in pleasuring Burke with his mouth. The added gift of getting to tease him with her tongue just made it that much easier to chase her release. Curled as he was with his feet towards Burke's head, Rosalie and Burke used their hands together to stroke his thick cock.

No one rushed. Tongues worked slowly, and hands

cherished rather than possessed. The release that built inside her rolled in like a thunderstorm. A feeling of heavy clouds resting deep inside, building in intensity until, with a crack of lightning, the storm broke and she was coming on Burke's tongue.

Burke groaned, following her with his own release, which she shared with Tom. Desperate to have them both, she flicked Burke's hand away and sank her mouth down onto Tom, claiming his release too.

"Greedy thing," Burke teased, his mouth still warm between her quivering thighs.

She hummed her agreement, her lips around Tom's cock as she drank his release. Sated, she flopped off Burke, wedged between his side and Tom's legs.

"We should wake up like that every day," Tom panted.

Rosalie couldn't agree more. But she couldn't risk staying abed. She sat up, climbing over Tom's legs.

"Where are you going?" Burke muttered, his face pressed in the pillow.

"It's still early," Tom echoed.

"Not so early that I cannot start my day," she replied.

"Come back to bed so we can do that again," said Burke, blindly holding out his hand.

"You both have work to do too," she chastised. "We still have a wedding to plan for the duke, a wedding to make sure *never* gets planned for you, sir . . . and don't forget we all agreed we need a better plan for saving James from himself."

Burke dropped his hand. "Give a man a minute to recover from having his cock sucked to oblivion."

"If you two cannot keep up with me, I shall have to ration you," she warned, smiling to herself as they both scowled. "I propose that, at least for today, we play the opposite game. Tom, you work on getting Burke unengaged, and Burke, you work on getting James . . . unJames'd."

"And what will you do?" Tom muttered.

Rosalie sighed, picking up her discarded clothing. "I have to go see a duchess about a tiara."

"Oh, Piety, you must choose this one," Mariah cried. "Look at the sapphires, how they sparkle!"

The other young ladies rushed to Mariah's side to gaze at the delicate tiara glittering with diamonds that sat clustered around three square-cut sapphires, each as large as a quail's egg.

Rosalie stood in the corner of the morning room, watching the chaos unfold. It was time for Piety to pick the tiara she would wear for her wedding. The duchess had all the family pieces brought out and displayed. Just before breakfast, Rosalie had helped Mrs. Robbins set each piece in a semicircle around the room.

There were eight in total, each one beautiful in its own way, and three came with a matching set of earrings. Rosalie enjoyed helping Mrs. Robbins get them ready for viewing. The woman was highly knowledgeable about Corbin family affairs, and she told Rosalie stories about the different pieces as they set them up—who commissioned them, who wore them to what event, which paintings in the house feature a past duchess wearing it.

For these tiaras were so much more than jewelry. They were history. The history of this family, this house, the title and its legacy. The weight of it made plain Rosalie Harrow feel small and insignificant . . . wholly unworthy.

"I like the one with the teardrop pearls," said Elizabeth, ghosting her fingers over the matching earrings on the velvet cushion.

But Piety had eyes for only one tiara. It was the largest piece in the collection. A spray of diamonds was arranged in little sunburst patterns, the stones polished to shine like glittering starlight. "This one," she whispered, eyes hungry.

"Would you like to try it on?" said the duchess.

The ladies squealed again as Mrs. Robbins stepped forward and held up a hand mirror. Prudence picked up the tiara and turned to her sister. "Goodness, it's heavier than I imagined."

Piety did a little dip, lowering her head, and Prudence placed the tiara atop her golden curls. All the young ladies sighed as Piety looked at herself in the hand mirror.

"You look like a queen," Blanche whispered with awe.

"No one say that on the day," said the duchess. "Her Majesty will be quick to take offense."

The other girls twittered with laughter.

Rosalie blinked. "Is . . . will the Queen be coming to the wedding?"

"Of course," the duchess replied with a haughty sniff. "Miss Harrow, you do remember my son is a duke of the realm, do you not? The Queen will come and show her support for his union."

"Daddy says she will be the first one to call me 'Duchess,'" Piety added, still admiring herself in the mirror.

A footman knocked twice and entered. "Your Grace, Madame Lambert has arrived," he called. "I've put her in your parlor."

The girls squealed anew. "The modiste!"

"Your wedding clothes are ready!"

Piety turned as if to leave.

"Not so fast, Miss Nash," the duchess called. "You are not a duchess yet. The jewels stay here."

"Oh." Piety gave a soft little laugh. "Of course, Your Grace." She slipped the tiara off her curls and set it back on its stand before leading the way out of the room.

With all the ladies cleared out, Rosalie could glance across the room and see James standing there, his arms folded over his chest. Like her, he'd watched the proceedings with a careful eye.

Mrs. Robbins replaced the hand mirror and righted the sunburst tiara on its stand. "I'll go see they have everything they need with the modiste and then begin packing this away," she said to the duchess.

"I can help," said Rosalie.

"Don't you want to watch Miss Piety try on her wedding clothes?" the duchess said with a raised brow.

Rosalie smiled. "Not particularly. Quiet suits me this morning. Please, Mrs. Robbins, let me help."

"Of course, dear," said Mrs. Robbins. "I'll only be a moment, and we'll finish together." With a curtsy to the duchess, she took her leave.

James made to follow her out, but the duchess called to him.

"James, wait."

He stilled, halfway to the door.

The duchess turned to Rosalie. "Which would you choose, Miss Harrow?"

Rosalie glanced warily from James back to the duchess. "It

is not for me to choose, Your Grace. I am not marrying the duke."

"Humor me," she replied. "I want to see something."

Rosalie raised a brow. "This is a test, then? What happens if I fail?"

"Absolutely nothing," the duchess replied. "You are no longer my ward, remember? I have no say over what happens to you."

Rosalie glanced at James, and he gave a curt nod. She swallowed, surveying the jewels. Walking past the starburst crown and the one with the square-cut sapphires, she paused in the corner. There, on a green velvet cushion, sat a pretty tiara made of thin-spun gold. It was made to look like leafy vines, with clusters of amethysts for grapes. It had no matching earrings. A few diamonds added sparkle, but it was nowhere near as ostentatious as the starburst crown, nor as queenly as Elizabeth's choice with the dripping teardrop pearls.

"This one," she said, pointing to it.

The duchess pursed her lips. Had Rosalie passed the test? She couldn't tell. "And why this particular one?"

Rosalie glanced at it again. "It reminds me the most of Alcott, I suppose. There is something pastoral about it. This was not made for a queen or a duchess floating the halls of St. James's Palace. This was made for a lady who lives her life quietly in the country. This is a tiara she could wear in front of her tenants at Christmastime and not be seen as putting on airs. At least . . . that is how it makes me feel," she said with a shrug.

James and the duchess both watched her closely. "What do you know of this one?" said the duchess.

"Nothing at all," she replied. "I could be mistaken entirely. Perhaps this was only ever worn at St. James's."

The duchess stepped forward, eyeing the tiara with a confusing mix of reverence and disdain. "This tiara was bought by the third duke and presented to his wife upon the birth of their son and heir."

"How do you know?" asked James, stepping towards them.

"Because there is a letter in the lining of the box," she replied. "I found it when I was newly married. I'm sure it is still there, hiding behind the velvet. It's an obnoxious thing, full of the worst kinds of flowery sentiment. It's all dreams and promises and sighs of happiness." She sniffed, glancing down at the offending piece of jewelry.

Rosalie's heart was in her throat. "What did you do after you read the letter?"

"I returned it to the box and never looked at it again until this morning. I've never worn it," she added quietly.

Rosalie shared a glance with James. "Why not?" she whispered.

"Because I knew I did not deserve to wear such a symbol of goodness and kindness," the duchess replied. "The third duke's first wife represented everything I am not. She was loving where I am cold. She was graceful where I am calculating."

"His first wife?" Rosalie repeated.

"Oh yes, she died in childbirth with their fourth or fifth child. A girl, I think. I can't remember, and it doesn't matter," the duchess said with a wave of her hand. "She died, and he remarried, as all men do. Sentiment goes out the window when there are children to raise and a home to keep and a bed that needs warming."

Rosalie's heart broke for the duke, thinking of him all alone, their children without a mother, his dukedom without a duchess.

"Mother, where did you get the money?" James murmured.

The duchess and Rosalie both stilled. Rosalie closed her eyes, heart pounding. The duchess turned slowly to look at her, scorn in her eyes. "You told him?"

"No," she whispered.

"George told me," he added. "You paid off all her family's debts. Seventeen thousand pounds. Don't tell me why. At this point, I think I'm afraid to know your reason. But please, tell me *how*."

She sniffed. "Almost from the moment your father and I married, I set up a secret account and began moving money into it."

"Why?"

"Because all ladies ought to have a plan of exit," she replied, her eyes on Rosalie. "I lived quite frugally, taking most of my allowance and finding ways to secret it back into my own pockets. I would write bills of sale for jewelry and baubles, never delivered. Ornamental trees, never planted. I got bolder. I once commissioned a Grecian temple that was never built. Your father always thought I was spending the money. He never checked. He never cared. Over time, I stopped bothering with taking *his* money and I simply multiplied my own."

"How?" said James.

"I invested some in properties. I speculated a few times, but I don't enjoy the risk." She turned to her son. "I have not taken a farthing of the estate's money since he died. Yes, I made a show of being a spendthrift, and you rightly cut me off from the house accounts, but that was more a test of *you*. A test of your mettle. Would you protect the estate, even from me? It gratifies me greatly to know that you would."

James narrowed his eyes. "How much, Mother? How much of a fortune have you amassed in the shadows?"

She pursed her lips, her eyes revealing how much she was enjoying this moment. "I'd have to have my agent give me a full accounting, seeing as there are properties involved. But it's somewhere around two hundred thousand."

Rosalie gasped, raising a hand to her mouth.

"Bloody fucking hell." Wholly undone, James sank down onto the closest sofa. He pressed his hands to his temples. After a minute, he raised his head. "Two hundred? You have, in your name, a fortune worth two hundred thousand pounds?"

The duchess gave him a self-satisfied smirk. "Well, give or take seventeen thousand. Will you stop worrying now about my generosity to Miss Harrow? Can we all move on, James?"

"Move on?" he cried, launching to his feet. "Do you have any idea what even a *portion* of that money could do for the upkeep of this estate? Do you know how hard I've worked to keep it all together? The tireless hours I've spent considering selling off pieces of our land. The work I've done to innovate, to expand, to safeguard what we have, to fill our coffers!"

"You *needed* the experience, James," she countered. "You came into your role a young man, hopeful and naïve. You needed to learn to fight. You needed to learn to *win*. If I had just given in and paid your debts, offered you loans, you wouldn't be the brilliant lord you are now. You needed to stay hungry. You needed to work. *I* taught you how to work."

"And now? What do we do now?"

"Now you keep running your brother's estate as the silent Duke of Norland. You are more than capable, James. You don't need my money, nor my help. Should you ever find yourself in a position where you do . . . simply ask."

With a growl, he stormed out of the room, closing the door with a snap that made the pictures rattle and Rosalie flinch.

The duchess made to leave too. Pausing by the door, she turned, her eyes leveled on Rosalie. "Your mother would have made the perfect duchess," she murmured, tears in her eyes. "Patient and demure, lovely as a painting. She would have been worthy enough to wear that tiara on her wedding day."

Rosalie nodded, not bothering to wipe away the tear that slipped down her cheek.

The duchess gave her a soft smile. "If it is ever her daughter's wish to become a viscountess, I will not stand in the way."

56

Rosalie

A VISCOUNTESS. IN what world would Rosalie Harrow, the orphaned nobody without family, position, or connection, ever deserve to become a viscountess?

No. Not *a* viscountess. *The* viscountess. The Viscountess of Finchley.

It had been a day since the duchess let those words fall from her lips, and still Rosalie was in pieces over it. She knew what James wanted from her. His principles would not accept a life of living in the shadows, always being afraid to show his affection, even in the privacy of his own home.

But was inconvenience the right motive to *marry*? Certainly not.

Even if there was hope that marriage to James might be different, that he might one day confess his love and lead with her at his side rather than her following in his wake, now everything was far too complicated.

Doubly complicated.

Burke and Tom belonged to her and she to them. There would be no marrying James Corbin at their expense. And what man could marry knowing he was guaranteed to find his best friends in his wife's bed?

Now the word "viscountess" echoed in her ears like the pounding of a drum. In all her worrying, Rosalie had foolishly given no thought to James' title. He wouldn't be just some country gentleman living an eccentric life with his wife and her lovers. He was a viscount. If George and Piety failed to have children, he would be the next Duke of Norland. She could already imagine the headlines:

Honorable V— Finchley to wed the jezebel of C— House. Stones to be thrown at four o'clock.

It was laughable. Unsupportable.

Rosalie would never . . . *could* never put James in a position to be questioned or ridiculed by the vultures of the *ton*. She would leave first. As he so rightly predicted, she would disappear like a puff of smoke, and they would all eventually be better off without the misery and heartache she brought them.

It was with all these dark thoughts swirling that she sought out the one person who might give her some much-needed perspective. She found him in a lonely back corner on the third floor of the house. The footman standing sentinel outside the door didn't question her as she gave the door a soft knock, opening it a crack.

"Your Grace, I was hoping we could talk . . ."

"Cabbage?"

She pushed the door open a bit more.

His surprise was eclipsed by his panic as he squawked, "Don't come in! I'm—there's—naked!"

She paused, her hand on the doorknob. She could already see a bit into the room. If the piles of canvases stacked along the walls were not a giveaway, the pungent smell of oil paint was. Curiosity won out, and she pushed open the door, letting herself in.

"You're not naked," she chided.

The duke stood in the middle of the room behind an easel, which was turned towards the window to catch the best light. Narrowing his eyes, he clamped his mouth shut and stared daggers over her shoulder at the footman.

"Harris, you're fired," he snapped. "I told you not to let anyone bother me while I'm in here—*no*, don't touch that—"

Rosalie dropped her hand away from the canvas she was about to flip over. "What are you working on?"

"I'm not working on anything," he replied quickly.

"You are painting. May I see—"

"I'm not painting, I'm merely . . . cataloging. This is where we store art." He gestured around at the stacks of canvases.

She pursed her lips. "Your Grace . . . you still have a brush in your hand."

He glanced down. "Goddamn it." He rattled it on the tray beside him.

She fought the urge to laugh, instead using the distraction to move around the other side of his easel. "What do you paint so secretively?"

"No—I—it's not . . . well, it's not very good," he muttered, cheeks going pink as he watched her look at the canvas.

It was a portrait of two women with fiery red hair and freckled faces. The proportions of their faces were too narrow, but the resemblance was there. "Are . . . is this Elizabeth and Mariah?"

"Oh, well spotted," he sniped. "Apparently I am accomplished enough that the identity of my muses can be discerned."

The style of the work stirred something in her. With a gasp, she turned to face him. "They're yours, aren't they?"

"What?"

She brushed past him and moved for the other stacks. "No, those aren't done either—"

She ignored him, flicking through each one, looking for similarity in stroke and style. A still life of flowers, a naked woman in profile, a pastoral scene that looked very much like a view of Alcott. "The paintings," she murmured. "Here at Corbin House and Alcott. The gentleman on the stairs . . . the knight with the ugly horse by your bedroom. *You* painted them . . . but you don't tell people? I saw a bill of sale for the one with the knight. It is a fake?"

He narrowed his eyes at her. "Why would I tell them, hmm? So they can laugh at me? Mock my vision? Tell me how deficient I am even in this?" He stalked off to the corner and began washing his hands, muttering under his breath.

"George Corbin, are you a perfectionist?" Rosalie could hardly believe the words were coming out of her mouth.

"Me, a perfectionist?" He huffed a laugh. "Can you imagine?"

She glanced around the room again. "I can, actually. In fact, I believe you've never made more sense to me than you do in this moment."

"Don't pretend to know me," he warned.

"You're a perfectionist," she repeated. "Just like James. Only instead of being afraid to fail, you are afraid to even try . . . am I right?"

"You know nothing," he grumbled, pushing past her to shrug himself back into his coat.

"Is that why you refuse to lift a finger to help James manage the estate? Why you dare everyone to think the worst of you, parading around with your drinking and your fornicating in stairwells, jumping out of windows when you're bored, juggling—"

"I think you should leave," he snapped.

She held her ground. "Why do you let yourself be so wildly unhappy by pretending to be bad at everything?"

He spun around. "What makes you think I am unhappy? I am handsome, ridiculously rich, entitled within an inch of royalty. I have everything I could ever want. All I need do is snap my fingers and it is mine." He snapped them in her face to prove his point.

"And yet you are unhappy," she repeated. "It is plain enough for anyone to see."

He shrugged away. "Why did you come here? What do you want from me?"

She blinked, remembering her own unhappiness from moments before. "I wanted to ask your advice, actually."

His brows shot up. "You want my advice?"

"Yes."

"Mine, as in . . . *me*?"

She chuckled. "Yes, Your Grace. That is something friends do for each other," she added. "We are still friends, are we not?"

Slowly, he nodded. "Yes, Cabbage. We are friends. In fact, I think you might be my only friend."

She gave him another smile, knowing well the feeling of being alone in the world. She struggled to come up with the right way to ask her question. "I wanted to ask you about marriage. What are your thoughts?"

He slapped a hand over his chest. "Saints alive, is this a

proposal? I'll need to fetch my smelling salts . . . and a pistol. For James is sure to hunt me until I'm dead."

She laughed, stepping closer. "No, Your Grace. If you'll remember, you are already engaged."

"Oh, damn," he murmured. "I'd nearly forgot."

"You will marry Piety Nash in *two* days," she reminded him. "Surely, if one such as you is willing to place his neck in the noose, well, you must believe in marriage . . ."

He snorted. "It's a goddamn nightmare. Can you imagine *me* married to another person? Cabbage, do you know how many people I've slept with just since we announced our engagement? Can you even guess?"

She didn't want to guess. "So, this will be a performance for you, a ritual act for the sake of society. You will not hold to the vows you take, and that doesn't bother you?"

"I think you'd be hard-pressed to find a lord that has *not* broken his marriage vows on at least one occasion. And I'm not just talking about the 'forsaking all others' bit. That's a laugh." He waved his hand, dismissing the idea entirely. "But there's the bits in the middle about tending in sickness, honoring and cherishing, etcetera. What two people in today's modern society marry with those goals at the center? It's all about power, isn't it? Who has the power, who wants more power, and how two people can find power together."

She pursed her lips. "So you're marrying for power, then?"

"I am marrying so my mother leaves me the hell alone," he replied. "It seemed the easiest way to appease her. Piety is the power-seeking one in this match. I have no doubt she feels nothing for me. Oh, do not fret on my account," he added, stepping forward to pat her shoulder. "It is just the way of things for our set. She seeks the power my position can give her. In return, we'll fuck occasionally. I suppose the fucking will be more rigorous until she's with child. But once she has a son, I can leave off it. I'll deal with her living here, but it's a big house. I have others. And I like to travel. I can still enjoy my freedoms."

"And you would live that way, knowing you can do and be anything else your heart desires?"

He frowned. "What do you mean?"

She scoffed, hands on her hips. "I mean you are a man! You are a duke. As you say, you are practically royalty. There is no power you cannot wield, nothing you cannot have, and yet you're making the choice to live this small life. This—this half-life," she cried, gesturing around.

"Half?" he repeated, his mouth turned down in a frown.

"I don't know about you, but I want more," she whispered. "I *need* more. I want to live fully. I want to live out loud. Boldly. Freely. I want to . . . run naked through a forest, scream in a crowded room, leap from a cliffside and splash into the ocean below." She stepped closer, eyes glistening with tears as she reached for his hand, holding it in both of her own. "I see the same spirit in you, and it frightens me, George."

"Why?" he whispered, his lips barely moving.

"Because if you cannot be brave, you who has *everything* . . . how can I ever hope to be?"

57

Rosalie

ROSALIE RETURNED TO her room, humming with nerves after her talk with the duke. She knew what she wanted; she just didn't know how to get it. And it wasn't entirely up to her. Three other people had to be willing to go along with her plans.

The gong had just rung, and it was time to change for dinner. She wasn't going to bother with ringing for a maid. They were just eating at home, so she could change her own clothes.

As soon as she sat down at her vanity, there came a knock at her door.

Her *other* door. "Enter," she called.

Burke swung the door open, stepping through with a smile. "See how I improve?"

"Leaps and bounds," she murmured, tugging loose a few of the pins holding her hair in a simple braided bun. At the very least she would update her style to something more fitting for the evening.

"We've been looking for you," he said, coming around the end of the bed. "You need to get dressed or we'll be late."

"ThaswhatImdoin," she replied, her teeth full of pins.

"Not for dinner. We're taking you out on the town, love. It's all been arranged."

She turned, her hands dropping from her hair. She spit the pins into her hand. "We?"

"Well, everyone is going out. The Marchioness of Marlborough has invited us all to the opera tonight. With so many in attendance, we'll need to use the duke's box as well." There was a glint in his eye that told her she ought to be wearing her pearls already . . . so she could clutch them.

"Burke, what are you hiding in that mind of yours?"

He inched closer, dropping to one knee next to her stool. His hand wrapped around her waist as he leaned in, resting his forehead at the curve of her neck. She took a deep breath, filling her senses with his scent, his warmth, his presence that stirred her to life, even as it calmed her.

He lifted his head with a hazy smile, pecking her lips with a quick kiss. "I have something for you." He lifted his other hand and set a black velvet pouch on her knees.

She knew without any investigation it was a jewelry case. "Burke," she whispered, her fingers ghosting over the clasp.

"To be fair, it's not from me," he admitted. "James asked me to see that you get it for tonight."

She glanced up, meeting his stormy grey eyes. "Why—"

"Because unfortunately he cannot join us. He's already beholden to a night of dinner and political talk at Lord Talbot's. I weaseled my way out of it, thank God." He tucked a curl behind her ear, getting to his feet. "He'll join after, I'm sure. We're all invited to take a late supper at Marlborough House."

She looked back at the pouch on her lap. "And this is . . ."

"Consider it armor," he replied with a grin. "The Theatre Royal is little more than a social gladiatorial ring that masquerades as a place where operas are performed. Your fan shall be your sword. Let that be your shield." He gestured at the pouch. With a wink, he left, ringing her bell for her before he closed her door with a soft snap.

Taking a breath, she undid the clasp and flipped open the velvet pouch. She gasped, covering her hand with her mouth. Resting on the black velvet was a diamond choker that dripped with brilliance. The stones cascaded like water droplets, some as large as her thumbnail. A small paper sat folded beneath it. She slipped it out and read the note in James's slanted scrawl.

I know you will never accept a tiara from me, or anything that comes with it. So this will have to do. And before you give me a thorough tongue lashing, know this is fake. The stones are polished glass. You can wear it tonight without any awkwardness or feelings of obligation.

Yours, J.C.

She couldn't breathe. First the duchess' casual remark in the morning room. Now this. James Corbin wanted to marry her. He wanted to see her in a tiara, marked before all as his viscountess.

But he still believed she would never marry *him*. She'd said as much . . . more than once . . . to his face. In her heart, even a day ago, she'd believed it. But being with Burke and Tom changed everything. Seeing their love for each other, sensing their longing for James, it shifted her priorities. They were both doing everything to bend to meet her needs, giving her exactly what she wanted. If she loved them all, was she willing to do the same?

58

Burke

As Rosalie came floating down the stairs, it was all Burke could do not to drop to his knees and cry out for her to marry him on the spot. That, or he would throw her over his shoulder and drag her back up those stairs to his bed, never to leave. Tom and James could relieve him when he found himself in need of water or a nap.

She looked like a goddess. A queen. An enchanted fairy princess. Her dark curls were piled artfully high on her head, with one tendril draped over her shoulder. Her dress was a thing of shimmering white beads that sparkled in the candlelight. Each movement of her legs as she descended the stairs made it blink like so many stars.

And that necklace. Eros, have pity on a poor mortal soul.

Next to him, Tom stilled. "Oh shit," he muttered, his hands suddenly forgetting how to put on gloves.

Burke could easily sympathize. How he was going to survive this night with this aching cockstand, he had no idea. He cleared his throat, and Tom tugged his glove on.

"You still think this is a good idea?" Tom said under his breath.

Burke still had his eyes locked on Rosalie, who was now accepting a wrap from the waiting hands of her maid. "It's the best idea we've ever had."

The ride to the Theatre Royal didn't take long. Burke was wedged in a carriage with Tom and the Swindons. Tom did an admirable job of distracting the ladies, making them twitter and laugh. It seemed, now that all thought of marriage to any of them was firmly off the table, Tom could be himself again and flirt without appearing constipated or possessed.

As soon as they arrived, Burke took the arm of the countess and led the way into the receiving hall. It was crowded with guests. All the ladies glittered in their jewels, towers of feathers in their hair. Groups stood together, laughing and talking loudly, waving hands and clinking glasses.

The countess quickly slipped off his arm, called away by a friendly face.

"How do we do this?" Tom muttered, coming to stand at his back.

"Meet us in the box," he replied, his eyes scanning the crowd. "Make sure all is ready."

Rosalie entered the room a few moments later, arm in arm with Blanche. She caught his eye and smiled, her dark eyes sparkling. He slipped through the crowd to stand beside her, looping her arm in with his. "If you want to follow me, Miss Harrow, I can take you up to the duke's box."

"We're all the guests of the marchioness tonight, silly," Blanche said with a laugh.

"There is not enough room for us all in Lady Marlborough's box," he replied. "The duke is graciously opening his own box for a few of us stragglers. Do go on, though, Blanche. I believe Mariah is waiting at the stairs."

She glanced over her shoulder, giving Mariah an enthusiastic wave, before turning back around. "Oh, but I would hate for you to feel left out," she said to Rosalie.

"Don't worry about me," she replied. "I am such a fan of opera that I may prefer to sit wedged between Mr. Burke and the lieutenant. I can only imagine they will have little to say on the performance and will leave me to enjoy it in peace."

Mariah twittered a laugh. "Very well then. You're not to distract her, Mr. Burke," she said with a warning look.

"I wouldn't dream of it," he replied, letting Rosalie feel the slide of his hand along her arm. She stiffened, losing nothing of his meaning.

Mariah darted away and Burke crowed with victory, leading Rosalie in the opposite direction.

"Are you going to tell me what's going on?" Rosalie murmured. "Or will I have to guess?"

As they ascended the stairs, he placed a hand on her back and leaned in. "You are still owed a punishment for your behavior last week. You wouldn't let me take it out on James. That price has yet to be paid."

Her lips parted in surprise.

"Running off with James, sneaking out of windows, calling yourself the other woman . . . You have much to answer for, little siren."

She glanced around. "Burke, you cannot possibly mean to do something *here*."

"The punishment is mine to collect when and how I see fit," he growled in her ear. "Now, keep walking. The sooner I get you up the stairs, the sooner I can get you out of that drcss."

59

Rosalie

THEY ENTERED THE duke's private box and Rosalie spun around, raising a hand to Burke. "You cannot be serious. This is madness, even for you."

He locked the door, leaning against it. "Your dress. Take it off."

She sucked in a breath, turning away from him to take in the features of the box. It was tiny, with little more than a plush green settee and two chairs. A drink cart sat in one corner. A screen sat in the other to be used for privacy.

The thrum of the growing audience echoed all around. Nothing but a heavy curtain separated them from the front of the box where the opera could be watched. It was pulled closed, leaving them in a semi-darkness lit only by a candelabra on the table and two wall-mounted sconces set with silver reflecting plates.

She spun back around, heart in her throat. "Burke, someone will hear us."

"Nothing happens until the opera starts," he said with a wicked grin. "Then the audience will be so enraptured with the delightful overture of *Die Zauberflöte* that they will not hear your whimpers and moans. The dress. Take it off."

She swallowed, heat pooling inside her. "It fastens in the back," she whispered. "I cannot reach it."

His smile widened. "Then Tom will have to help you."

She glanced over her shoulder with a start to see Tom standing at the curtain's edge. He always looked so handsome in his naval uniform. It set off the narrow cut of his hips. He stepped forward, giving his black cravat a tug as he moved. "Did Burke tell you the plan?"

Tom came up behind her, pressing his front to her back. She could already feel the hardness of his cock on her hip. His fingers brushed down the line of her spine to the top of her dress. With a few deft pinches along the seam, he opened it.

She sighed with need as he grazed his lips over her exposed shoulders, tracing them up the curve of her neck. He flicked the sheer sleeves off her shoulders, letting the heavy beaded gown slink to the floor. She spun around in his arms, and he claimed her mouth with a hungry kiss. She melted into him, clutching the lapels of his uniform coat.

From the stage came the warning notes announcing that the opera was about to start.

"It's time to get into position," Burke said, leaving his sentry post by the door. Like Tom, he was quickly unraveling his cravat.

"The stays and those pretty silk drawers need to come off," Tom said, his gaze heated as he stroked her hip. "We want you undone, sweet girl. Ours for the taking."

Swallowing her nerves, she raised her hands to the buttons at her hip. After a moment, she let her drawers slip down her legs, exposing her naked bottom half to the room.

"Don't forget, this is a punishment," Burke said, edging closer. "Your pleasure will be secondary to ours tonight. In fact, it will give me the greatest pleasure to watch you squirm, begging us for release."

"Don't be cruel," she said on a breath.

"Don't run away from me," he countered.

"Don't call yourself the other woman where we can hear you," Tom added.

Burke stepped forward, gripping her chin tight as he tipped her face up. "And don't ever doubt our constancy again. You are my reason. Everyone has one. A reason to live, to fight, to bend the rules . . . or break them entirely. You three are mine."

"Burke—"

"Take off your stays," he growled, dropping his hand away from her.

Silently, she fumbled with the front of her stays, loosening the laces until she could drop them to the floor.

"Give me a glove," said Tom, holding out his hand. She slipped one off, wordlessly handing it to him. "Good girl. Now, sit on the settee."

She sat, trying to control the way her stomach flipped. Beyond their box, the crowd simmered to a hush. It sent a shock rippling through her. On the other side of that velvet curtain, several hundred people sat ready to watch an opera. They had no idea she was naked in front of two men, about to be ravaged. Her core was all but weeping with need as she leaned back.

Tom and Burke gave each other a nod. Then they dropped to one knee on either side of her, each taking a hand.

"What are you doing?" she whispered.

The first notes of the overture began, and the crowd clapped. The sound hummed through her as Burke and Tom exchanged a smile.

"We're going to tie you down," Tom replied.

She whimpered, squirming on the settee as they began wrapping their cravats around her wrists. Using the frame of the settee as anchor points, they looped their silk cravats through the wooden scroll work, securing her arms out to either side.

"Oh, God," she whispered, her breasts rising with each breath.

Burke ducked his head, sucking her nipple into his mouth, teasing it with his teeth.

Tom held up her long, white opera glove. "Have you ever seen *The Magic Flute*, Rose?"

She nodded, heart in her throat, as Burke kissed her other breast, his fingers trailing down her ribs.

"Good, then you won't mind missing the first half." Dropping back to his knee, Tom wrapped the glove around her eyes, blindfolding her.

With a gasp, she was immediately plunged into darkness. All her other senses were suddenly heightened as she tried to determine where they might move and what they might do. The sound of the opera meant it was harder to hear them.

Tom leaned in, brushing his lips over her collarbone. "Do you know how beautiful you look like this? Your flushed cheeks, your parted lips . . . the delicate points of these perfect breasts." He grazed the back of his hand over her nipple and she sighed, her body coiling tighter.

Then Burke was leaning in, his fingers brushing over her lips. "I can't wait to sink my cock into this needy mouth."

"Yes," she whispered, letting the thrum of the music fill her, driving her excitement higher.

"Patience, little siren. This is a punishment, remember? Feeding you my cock now, when you're aching for it, would be a treat. We can't have that. Not *yet.*"

She sank back against the velvet of the settee.

"I'm going to let Tom play with you for a while," he teased. "I want to watch him worship you. Maybe we'll take a break and leave you tied here while I fuck his mouth. You'll just have to imagine what it looks like."

"You're both devils—"

"We are *your* devils," he hissed in her ear, smoothing his fingers over her sex and dipping one finger inside. He groaned, dropping his head to her shoulder. "Fuck, she's so wet, Tom. Why are you always so wet for us? So needy, so desperate for our cocks."

She opened her legs wider, silently begging for more, but he pulled away. She sucked in a breath as he swiped his wet finger over her bottom lip. Then he claimed that lip with his mouth, sucking the taste of her onto his tongue.

It was sinful. These men had ruined her. There would be no love, no lust, no passion outside of the heights they carried her to.

Burke shifted away, leaving her with Tom.

"I wish you could feel how hard my cock is for you," Tom said in her ear. "Do you want me to untie you so you can put your hands on me?"

"Yes," she whispered, tugging on the silk ties.

He grabbed her jaw tight, turning her face towards him. "That was a test," he growled against her lips. "We've barely begun, and you want the pleasure to end? Can you not feel how your body is responding without the use of your eyes, your hands? Can you not sense your heightened emotions, your ability to taste, to smell, to feel every little brush against your skin?" He grazed his fingers featherlight down her sternum, around her navel, and down. "You really want this to end, you say the word."

"Don't stop. Please, Tom. More—"

He claimed her lips in a kiss. She let him lead, tipping her head back and opening her mouth as he teased with his tongue. He was the most playful kisser of the three. Burke was all passion and fire, wanton lust. James kissed with a hunger. An aching need. He was driven, determined.

James.

Her heart ached. He was missing this. Missing them. God, she needed them all. She needed to feel complete. Tom was right—they were all meant to be together.

Tom pulled her back to the present when he dropped to his knees, pushing her legs wider apart. His mouth latched onto her desperate sex as his hands slid up her sides, cupping her breasts and tweaking her nipples. Her back arched off the settee as she pulled on the binds that kept her hands tied. Tom wrapped his hands around her thighs, tugging her hips to the edge of the settee. She lost herself to the feel of him moving with her, panting for more.

If this is how her men punished her, she made a vow to misbehave more often

60

James

JAMES TWITCHED IN his chair, trying not to let his annoyance overtake him. Where the hell was everyone? He was told to meet the group at the opera house, yet here he sat, all alone, pretending to watch *The Magic Flute*. Tom had been here for exactly two minutes, but then he disappeared, saying he needed to use the necessities. He'd yet to return.

James waited for the others to show and was just about to leave when he looked across the hall to see half the house party piling into the Marquess of Marlborough's box. He didn't see Burke or Rosalie amongst them. Surely that meant the rest of the party would find their way to this box.

But they didn't.

The first act started, and James was stuck. It would be rude to leave now. People would notice. Curious faces from the crowd constantly glanced his way. He could practically feel the dozens of sets of eyes on him. Some were more deliberate, even giving him a little wave to catch his attention—gentlemen from the club, friends of his mother. Others used binoculars, measuring him as competition or a potential suitor for their daughters.

He was used to it. As the brother of a duke, everyone wanted to find a way to use him to get to George. That's why he so loathed coming to the opera. He hated this feeling of being on display, sitting at a great height where the rest of the *ton* could ogle him. And Burke knew this well. Why the hell had he suggested coming? And why wasn't he here? Something was wrong.

Before he could stew any longer, the edge of the curtain shifted back and the man himself appeared. The look on his face immediately had James on edge. He sank down in a chair next to James, picking up a program and pretending to read it.

"You're late," James muttered, trying not to move his lips.

"No, I'm not."

"You *are*—"

"I was on time, I assure you. I just didn't take my seat. I was otherwise occupied."

What the hell was he on about? Was he . . . did he forget to put on a cravat? James narrowed his eyes at his friend. "Where are the others?"

"They are occupied," Burke replied, the corner of his mouth curving into a grin.

"Speak sense," James growled, quickly losing his already limited patience.

Burke lifted his program higher, lowering his dark brows as he pretended to read it. "I need you to come with me, but I need you to stay silent. Not a word, do you understand?"

A sense of foreboding sank into James' gut. "Burke, what did you do?"

"It's not about what I *did*," he replied. "It's about what I'm *going* to do. Now, are you coming or not? Remember, not a word." Without waiting for his response, Burke slipped out of his chair and ducked back behind the curtain.

Steeling himself, James got to his feet and followed him. The moment he went behind the curtain, Burke was there, a finger to his lips and a warning in his eyes. But James didn't see him. All James saw was Rosalie . . . blindfolded, tied to the settee, her throat wrapped in his necklace, her perfect breasts arching forward as Renley devoured her cunt.

James' mouth opened in shock. Heat rushed through his body, zapping him in the crotch with such force he had to fight the urge to double over, panting for breath. Recovering his senses, he snapped his mouth shut and glared at Burke. The bastard had the audacity to grin.

While the music of the opera's first act trilled, James could make out the little pants and moans Rosalie was trying to stifle. If she bit her lip any harder, she'd make it bleed.

Burke pointed to one of the chairs, his intention clear. James was meant to sit and watch silently as his two best friends pleasured Rosalie right in front of him. Could he let this happen? This was wrong. She was blindfolded. She didn't know he was here. Or did she? Would she *want* to let this happen if she knew? Did she want him to watch?

He focused on her again, taking in every inch of her perfect body. The strength of her arms as she tugged at the restraints.

Holy shit.

They were cravats. One black, one white. And the blindfold was one of her own evening gloves. She was still wearing the other one on the arm tied with Burke's cravat. For a moment it almost seemed like she was looking at him. Her head lolled on her neck, arching in his direction. Oh Christ, could she somehow see through the glove?

But in moments, she was panting and turning the other way as Burke sat down next to her, claiming her lips in a fierce, open-mouthed kiss. They fought each other with their tongues, Rosalie pulling against her restraints as Burke dropped a hand to Renley's hair, weaving his fingers through his curls. He gave Renley a little tug and Renley lifted his head away from her wet cunt.

Renley flashed a look over his shoulder, giving James a wink before turning back to Rosalie, sinking two fingers inside her, his other hand on her hip holding her still.

"Have you come yet, sweet siren?" Burke murmured.

"No," she whined. "No, he won't let me."

"Good," he replied with a grin. "Remember, this is a punishment. The only way to be sure you learn your lesson is to make the memory of this night something you can't soon forget."

Entranced, James sank into the chair, eyes locked on the three of them.

Renley worked his fingers in her slowly, his pace almost bored. But James could see the effect it was having on her, coiling her tight. "And why are you being punished?" Renley murmured, kissing her stocking-clad knee.

"I . . . I left with James without telling you," she panted, trying to move her hips to get more friction.

His name on her lips had James stifling a groan with his fist.

"And?" Renley pressed, slipping his fingers out of her to rub gently on her sensitive bud. This had her toes curling, but he stopped as soon as he started. He peppered a few kisses on her bare thigh.

"And I left with George without telling any of you. I—*ah*—"

Her words were cut off when both men leaned forward together, each taking one of her exquisite breasts in his mouth. James had never felt so hard in his life. His cock could cut glass. And then Renley had to go and move. The bastard left his place between her legs and sat next to her on the settee. James knew exactly what he was doing. If there was any doubt, in the next moment Renley hooked her leg over his own, spreading her wide. Rosalie panted, straining against her binds as Renley sank his fingers back into her cunt and Burke dropped his hand to her bud, teasing her with little circles.

And James could see it all. Every movement. He'd never seen a woman shared by other men before. Group activities were simply not his forte. He'd always been a one-woman kind of man, and even then, it was mainly about scratching an itch. Rosalie was different. Rosalie was . . . *everything*. The very idea of another man touching her ought to send him into a rage. He should be committing murder at this very moment.

But these men . . . *his* men? To watch them touch her felt like a gift, something precious they were offering him. He didn't feel like an outsider or a voyeur. Renley and Burke kept glancing his way, heat in their eyes, drawing him in.

This was sensual. Hauntingly beautiful. He wanted to join. He wanted *more.*

"What was your last offense, sweet siren?" Burke murmured.

"I doubted you," she whimpered. "I doubted us. I was afraid to let you in."

"And are you afraid anymore?" asked Renley.

"No," she replied, biting that bottom lip again.

"Have you suffered enough, siren? Should we let you come?"

"*Please*—"

Burke flashed James another heated look before leaning in. "I'm not sure I'm ready to end your suffering. You look so beautiful like this." He nuzzled her face, lifting his wet fingers away from her cunt to swirl them around her peaked nipple.

James' cock twitched. If he didn't relieve this ache soon . . .

"Just imagine it," Burke teased. "Imagine if we had but one more set of hands here to please you. One more cock to claim you with. Would you like that?"

"Yes," she begged.

James was on the edge of his seat. He couldn't look away.

Burke glanced at him again, then back to her, kissing along her collarbone. "If James were here right now, would you let him touch you? Would you let him bury himself inside you and claim you in all the ways you should be claimed?"

"God—*yes*. You know I would. Burke, I *need* him. Need you all."

"Where would you want him if he was here?" Renley teased, taking his fingers from her cunt and bringing them to her lips.

When she arched forward, sucking his wet fingers into her mouth—wet with her own desire—James was ready to die. Renley dared to flash him another grin, his eye trailing down to where James' achingly hard cock was pressing against his pants. He winked before pulling his fingers from Rosalie's mouth, leaving her panting.

"Tom, it's too much. Please, love. Please, let me come."

Burke gave Tom a nod, and they both scooted away from her. As one, they stood, leaving her tied to the settee.

She tried to follow their moments. "Wait—where are you going?"

"Hmm . . . I think I'd like to watch the opera," said Tom, passing James with a squeeze to his shoulder.

"What—"

"You'll be fine in here for a few minutes," Burke teased. "Besides, you've already seen it, so it's not like you'll be missing anything."

She snarled, tugging on her binds. "Untie me!"

Burke held James' gaze. Stepping forward, he raised a hand and cupped his cheek. James' eyes went wide. With a look heavy with meaning, Burke brushed his thumb over James' parted lips. "Take care of our girl."

Rosalie stilled. "What's happening?"

Without a backwards glance, Burke followed Tom through the curtain into the front of the box.

James let his gaze fall on Rosalie. She sat on the settee, her tied arms stretched out to the sides, her legs falling closed as she panted, chest and cheeks pink. She licked her lips, the necklace glittering in the candlelight with each movement she made.

James revealed himself at last. "You sure know how to wear a necklace."

61

Rosalie

ROSALIE GASPED, HER heart racing out of her chest. So, it was true. James was in the room. She hadn't wanted to believe it at first. She hadn't wanted to hope. But he was here.

"James." She tried to put everything she felt into the name. "James, please."

She felt more than heard him moving closer. The music was reaching a crescendo as the singer belted an aria. He sank down on the settee next to her and she turned her face towards him. He dropped his brow against her temple, and they breathed each other in, taking comfort in the other's presence.

"You're missing the first act," he murmured, stroking her cheek.

"I've already seen it three times. James, please—"

"Why are you begging me, angel? What do you want?" His low voice was heavy with need. She could tell he was aching as badly as her.

"You know what I want," she replied, gritting her teeth.

She was done waiting. Done with games.

"Say it," he whispered, his breath hot in her ear, making her shiver with need.

"Put your hands on me, James."

He ghosted his lips over her skin. "And why would I do that?"

"Because I am desperate for you," she replied, her body trembling. "Because your every denial splinters my soul, while your every stolen look sets me on fire. I feel your eyes on me, James. I always feel you. I knew you were in the room by the feel of your eyes watching me. I am burning. James, *please*, just this once, catch fire with me—"

He silenced her with a desperate kiss. His hands raised to her face, gripping her tight as he poured himself into her mouth, opening her deep and claiming all her air. Heavens, to feel him so close, to feel him wanting her—it was everything. But without her hands, she was utterly at his mercy. The punishment game worked with Tom and Burke, but she was done playing games with James.

"Untie me," she panted, breaking their kiss. "Oh God, James, untie me. *Now.* Need to feel you, need you in my hands."

His hands went to the knots at her wrists, loosening one, then the other. In moments he had her free and she was throwing herself atop him. They sank to the floor, her straddling him naked. Neither of them bothered to remove her blindfold. She didn't need it off to share pleasure with him. If anything, keeping it on was helping to ground her in the moment. She could feel him, listen for his heartbeat, his labored breaths, taste the heat of his kisses.

She jerked off her remaining glove and tossed it aside before helping him shed his evening coat, his waistcoat. "Need to feel your skin against mine," she pleaded.

He unwound his cravat and opened the collar of his shirt, and then she was plunging both hands inside the "V," smoothing them over the warm skin of his chest as she sank her tongue into his mouth.

She broke the kiss, panting for breath. "You should be kissed like this all the time," she murmured, still cupping his face. "Every hour of the day. Worshipped. Loved. Pursued."

"You can't talk to me of worshipping, I'll go mad." He smoothed his hands up her sides, cupping her breasts before he took each one in his mouth.

She arched into him, desperate for more.

"The way I want to please you . . . worship you. I would set you as the axis on which my world spins."

She stilled, heart racing. With a swift movement, she tugged off her blindfold, letting herself look at him. His lips were parted. Those beautiful green eyes were blown black with desire. She brushed his auburn curls back behind his ears with shaking fingers, licking her lips as she steadied her breath.

"Why must you keep yourself from me? From everyone?" she whispered, tracing her fingers over his lips. "Can't you see how we all need you? You say I am the one with walls, but I am trying, James. I lower them again and again, begging you to meet me halfway." She sank against him, pressing her forehead to his, breathing him in. "You have called me a mere distraction, a passing infatuation—"

"Don't," he growled.

"Inferior, improper, reckless, loose—"

"Stop." His expression was pained as he held her gaze, his eyes giving his apology.

But she couldn't stop. "Is that truly how you feel? Am I an

itch you seek to scratch? Will you have me once and then set me aside?"

"No."

She gripped tight to his shoulders. "Then what am I to you, James?" She could practically hear his heart thundering in his chest, even over the sound of the opera thrumming around them. She waited, eyes wide, praying he would be bold and speak the truth they both so desperately needed to hear.

Suddenly, his eyes heated, his lips closing as he clamped his jaw tight. Warmth simmered off his skin as he pulled her face closer. He dug his fingers into her hair, tipping her head back to hold his gaze. "You are my viscountess."

Before she could respond, he was flipping her over, laying her down, his hips pressing between hers. She let her head fall back, her fingers digging into his hair as he lowered his mouth to her breasts, worshipping her with his lips, his tongue. One hand snaked between them, and he was sinking his fingers inside her. She bit her lip to silence her cry. His thumb rested on her sensitive bud, providing the most glorious pressure.

"Christ, I can already feel you squeezing my fingers," he said, his mouth on her breast. "They expect me to finish the job they started. You're going to come for me," he ordered, lifting his eyes to hers. "Only me. Choose how you want it, angel. My hands, my mouth, or my cock."

"All three," she replied, her double meaning clear. "I will have all three."

A feral glint in James' eye told her she should be careful what she wished for. He sank back, keeping his fingers buried inside her as he dropped his mouth to her sex. There was no gentleness, no easing in. He devoured her.

She tipped her head back on a silent scream, too far gone

to hold out for a slow-building release. She clenched her legs around his face as the release ravaged her, leaving her breathless.

James worked fast, unfastening the fall of his breeches. "Again," he growled, positioning himself between her hips. He lined himself up, sliding his hard cock between her legs, teasing her entrance. "Come again. I want you to come on my cock."

She whimpered, wrapping her legs around him as she silently begged him to enter her. The need was tearing her apart.

His hands softened. "Look at me," he murmured.

Her lips quivered as she did as he asked, taking in the tenderness of those green eyes that haunted her dreams. Reaching up, she cupped his cheek. "I can't bear to be apart from you anymore," she whispered. "I can't pretend I don't need you, watch for you, ache for you. No more stairwells. No more shutting me out. Please, James . . . it's so cold outside your walls. Let me in—"

With a groan he pressed at her entrance, his cock sliding through her wet heat as he sheathed himself to the hilt. "You're in," he panted, his hips grinding her into the floor as he leaned over her. "God help me, you're in, and I can't get you out."

"I love you," she cried, burying her face in his shoulder as he claimed her so beautifully. "James, I love you. I'll give you anything. You can have anything if you'll only let me stay inside your heart."

She was right on the edge, ready to come apart. She moved with him, chasing her release. She didn't even care if he came inside her. In fact, a secret part of her thrilled at the idea. She clung to him, ready to ride him out.

But he'd stopped moving. His hips were still. He panted

above her, body going tense. Before she could ask what was wrong, he pulled out, shifting back on his knees.

She lifted herself on her elbows. "James—"

"I have to go," he muttered, already shoving his hard length back inside his pants.

Anxiety gripped her. "What?"

He stood, snatching for his clothes.

She sat up, her arms reflexively covering her naked breasts as hot shame boiled through her. "I don't understand—"

"It is not for you to understand," he growled, shrugging on the waistcoat. His cheeks were pink. He couldn't look at her.

Even through her humiliation, her urge was still to comfort him. She scrambled to her feet as he turned away, heading for the door. She reached out, taking hold of his arm. It was hard as iron, his entire body like a suit of armor. Impenetrable. "James, *please*—" She was begging, and she didn't care. A tear slipped down her cheek. "Tell me what I've done wrong now."

He turned, his face a mask of misery and longing. Her James was still inside, hiding behind those shielded eyes, warring with himself. Over what, she didn't know. But he lifted a gentle hand, brushing her tear away with his thumb. "I will not be the man who breaks your spirit."

With that, he left.

62

Tom

IT WAS ALL Tom could do to sit still and wait for the opera's first act to finish. Judging by the way Burke kept drumming his fingers on his knee, he felt the same way. But they'd agreed James would have this time alone with her. They needed it. Burke and Tom could wait.

As soon as the last notes were sung and the crowd began to clap, Burke launched to his feet. "Finally." He slapped his program down on his chair.

With a chuckle, Tom got to his feet, stretching his arms just to be an arse.

Burke gave him a shove, impatient to get behind the curtain. Tom let himself be pushed, laughing as he stepped past it. His smile immediately fell.

James was gone, and Rosalie— "Oh, Christ." Tom darted forward.

Rosalie was curled in a ball on her side on the settee, her hands holding to the front of her dress, as she silently wept. Her face was wet with her tears.

She sat up as he approached. "I cou-couldn't get it back

on," she sobbed, holding it to her chest. The back of it was still open.

Tom scooped her into his arms and sat, cradling her across his lap. He brushed her hair back from her face, kissing her brow. "Oh, my sweet girl. What happened?"

"Where is he?" Burke muttered.

Tom glanced up to see his eyes, dark as two stormy seas. "He-he left," she cried. "And I couldn't get my dress back on—"

Tom shushed her, gently rubbing her open back. She'd replaced her stays, her gloves, she'd even tried to fix her hair. He gave Burke a pleading look. He knew Burke was at war with himself—comfort Rosalie . . . or thrash James.

"I ruined everything," Rosalie mumbled. "I can't do this. I ca-can't make him love me. And if he can't love me, if he won't have me, I can't have either of you."

His decision made, Burke swept forward and dropped down next to Tom on the settee, his hands immediately reaching for their girl. "What can you be saying?" he muttered, threading his fingers in with hers, pressing kisses to her exposed shoulder.

She looked between them. "I will not come between you," she declared. "I will not break what the three of you share. You were fine before you met me—"

"We were *nothing* before you," Tom pressed, cupping her face and turning it towards him. "Rose, my darling love, look at me."

She blinked up at him, her long, dark lashes wet with her tears.

"We were nothing at all," he repeated. "Three second sons, utterly adrift. God, I was so lost to my own selfish misery, I was seriously considering marriage to Blanche Oswald."

"Hell on earth," Burke grunted.

"I was utterly alone," he went on. "Sailing the far sides of the world, dreaming of a love I couldn't speak of with mere mortal words. Drowning in a sea of broken hopes, desperate for someone to see me and love me for all that I am."

She sniffled, raising a gloved hand to cup his face. "Tom . . ."

He tipped his chin to kiss her palm. "I won't lie to you and say it was our first look in the billiards room that sealed my fate."

"I know," she murmured. "Sometimes love takes time to take root and grow."

He shook his head with a smile. "It was the second. The next morning by the stairs. Do you remember?"

She nodded, eyes wide.

"You turned around, and the air was sucked from my lungs. That blue dress . . . your face framed in beautiful dark curls . . ." He brushed his finger along her jaw. "I'm pretty sure I would have carved out my heart then and there had you asked for it."

She sniffed, leaning forward to rest her brow against his jaw.

"For me it was watching you punch that lout in the alley," Burke murmured. "I watched you swing that left hook, and I was gone."

Rosalie made a strangled sound of laughter and sob.

"I have never felt hope like this before," Tom went on, placing his hand over their entwined fingers. "I will not let either of you despair. Whatever happened with James, we can fix it."

"I told him I loved him . . . and he left," she whispered. "He left me naked on the floor, my love unrequited."

Behind her, Burke tensed.

"James is lost and confused," Tom soothed. "He carries a weight none of us can truly understand. If he gives in to this . . . to us . . . he will feel responsible for all of us every day for the rest of his life. Our reputations, our futures, our very lives, they will be his burden to shoulder. It is a lot to ask of any man. What we seek to have together is . . ."

"Uncommon," Burke finished for him.

"It's more than that," Tom replied, glancing over Rosalie to meet Burke's eye. "To live together, the four of us in one house, sharing one woman. Not to mention what *we* share—"

"Don't even say it." Burke dropped Rosalie's hand to touch Tom's face. "This is not a sin."

Tom closed his eyes at the touch. "I know," he whispered, opening his eyes again. "It's so much more than a sin, Burke. It's *illegal.* We could be pilloried before all of Mayfair. Stripped of our titles and positions, our families ruined, our lives haunted by the shame evermore. Hell, Burke, we could be hanged for it."

"Please don't say such things," Rosalie cried, wrapping her arms around him. "I can't bear it. Why is this world so unspeakably cruel?"

"It needs to be said," Tom replied, still looking at Burke. "We all need to understand the risks as well as the rewards. James will be taking the greatest risk of all of us. He is the highest in rank; he has the furthest to fall."

"We would be discreet," Burke muttered. "No one need know."

Tom raised a brow. "Like kissing me in front of Hart was discreet?"

A muscle twitched in Burke's jaw. "He won't talk." He said it as a statement, but Tom heard the silent question.

"No, he won't," Tom admitted. "But slips like that cannot happen again, even in front of those we trust. This is not merely about protecting our own reputations. The *ton* will drag James down faster than we can blink if he is linked to us in any way other than friendship."

Burke gave a curt nod.

"None of this matters," Rosalie murmured. "If he will not have me . . . if I cannot win his trust . . . if I cannot earn his love—"

Burke cupped her face. "He loves you, Rosalie. Do not doubt that fact. He is lost in love with you; it eats at him night and day. He grows weak with loving you."

She placed her gloved hand over his. "You can't keep being the one who says it for him," she replied.

With a growl, Burke got to his feet. "Enough. This ends tonight." He stalked off towards the door.

Tom slipped Rosalie off his lap and stood. "Burke—"

Burke spun around, one hand on the door. "He is *ours*. It ends now. Tom, get her home."

"What will you do?" Rosalie called from the settee.

Burke flashed them both a furious scowl. "I warned him that the next time he runs, I'll break his goddamn legs."

Tom closed the space between them, grabbing for his arm. "Burke—"

Burke stiffened, eyes swirling with storms. "If you're about to spew your drivel about leading horses to water, I swear to Christ, I'll knock you out flat. The time for gentleness is over. I will have my way in this, or he will crawl away from me on broken legs."

Heart racing, Tom jerked Burke closer and kissed him. Burke only hesitated for a moment, lost in his anger, but then he was returning the kiss, his mouth opening to overpower Tom with his tongue. They broke apart, both of them panting. Senses swimming, Tom gave him a little nod. "Go get him."

63

Burke

BURKE STORMED UP to the third floor of Corbin House, heading straight for James' room. He didn't even bother knocking. He just shoved his way inside, emotions flooding his body in waves.

This ends tonight.

Burke was done. No more waiting. No more goddamned civility. A hunger for too many things left unsaid ate at him. He could scarcely breathe. Rosalie needed him. James needed him. The future they all wanted was right within reach. He couldn't fail them now.

He shut the door with a snap, leaning against it. He'd always hated this room. Like his own on the floor below, at one point it belonged to George. James never bothered with making a space his own unless it was an office. This room still screamed George Corbin—the furniture was too ornate, the patterns too loud, the style too French. James looked wholly out of place, like a blacksmith's hammer in a silver cabinet.

From the middle of the room, James spun to face the door, an angry retort dying on his lips as he took in Burke standing there. He'd clearly been pacing. He always paced when he was upset. The man was a mess. His coat was slung over a chair, waistcoat unbuttoned, no cravat. Unless Burke was very much mistaken, it was still lying on the floor of the opera box.

"You shouldn't be here," James muttered, turning away. "You should be with her."

"Tom is with her," he replied, still not trusting himself to leave the safety of the door. He smoothed his hands against the painted wood.

James spun around when he reached the fireplace. "She needs you, Burke. Please . . . just go. Leave me."

"I'm right where I'm meant to be." The words fell from his lips and soothed him like a balm. He let their truth sink down to his very bones. He was right where he was meant to be. *With James.*

It always came back to James.

James Corbin was the center of his world. Burke smiled. Nothing could ever be so bleak that they could not find the horizon together. No task too arduous. No problem unsolvable.

James dragged both hands through his hair. "Is she alright? Did she . . ." He pressed the heels of his palms against his eyes. "*God* . . . did she tell you what happened?"

Burke pushed off the door and moved to the middle of the room. "I'm sure there are a thousand better ways I could've done this, but we are quite literally at the end of our rope."

James stilled.

"If we don't correct course now, I'm afraid we may drift too far apart and this mooring between us will fray and snap. Such a severing will be a mortal wound to us both, and we will bleed inwardly until the pain leaves us worse than dead."

James narrowed his brows, lips parted in confusion. "I don't understand—"

"I love you," he declared, taking a step closer. "I've always loved you," he added with a helpless shrug. "From the time we were children, my love of you has been buried deep in my heart. Over the past two decades, that seed of fidelity has bloomed inside me. You've completely filled my heart. It beats for you. But that's not enough. Nothing is ever enough for you. You claimed my lungs too. So now I *breathe* for you. Every breath I take is yours."

"Burke—"

"Shut up, and let me finish," he growled, taking a step closer.

James set his mouth in a firm line.

"To admit that I love you goes against everything we've been taught," he went on. "Men are not meant to say those words to another man. It is an expression of sentimentality denied to us. Wrongfully so, in my opinion," he added. "Because the most resounding truth of my life is that I love you. I've stayed by your side all these years. I help run your estates—not because I care whether the Corbin name shines like silver—but because I fucking love you. I handle the tempers of George, a man I loathe, out of unyielding love for *you*."

He closed the distance between them. "I am standing here with you, not out of any lack of love or concern for Rosalie. I love that woman more than my own life. In fact, I know with a surety marrow-deep that she is the love of my life . . . but your love *gives* me life, James. Without it, my lungs will falter. Without it, my heart ceases to beat. So, I will not be with her now. I am going to stand here . . . with you. *This* is my place, James. By your side. Always."

James was utterly still. "Burke, I . . ."

The men stood feet apart, and for the first time, it felt like James was looking at him. James was *seeing* him. Words failed them both as James reached out with both hands, clinging to Burke's lapels as he pulled him closer. The men bowed their heads together, foreheads touching. Burke didn't move. He just stood with him, breathing his air, waiting for him to collect his thoughts and emotions. Burke could wait. He'd been waiting for twenty years. What was a few more minutes?

"That was a lot for me," James admitted at last.

"I know."

"You know I'm no good at this—"

"I know," Burke murmured, raising a hand to gently cuff James' neck. His fingers brushed the curls at his nape.

James lifted his head away, meeting Burke's gaze. "But you do know I love you too . . . right?"

Burke sucked in a breath as relief crashed through him. He dropped his forehead to James' shoulder. "You've never said the words. Not once."

Then James was hugging him. He held him close, his arms like bands of iron around his back. "I have failed Rosalie enough. I cannot possibly fail you too," he said, his breath warm on his cheek. "Horatio Burke, I love you. For everything you do, everything you are. I'm sorry if I've ever made you doubt it."

Burke turned his face towards James' neck. His lips brushed the exposed skin there as he let out a slow exhale, his entire body trembling. He pulled away, needing to see James' eyes. He had to know. "But are you *in love* with me? Could you ever learn to love me in that way?"

"I think I already do," he muttered. He glanced back up, eyes wary. "But I . . . Burke, I don't like men. Hell, I hardly even tolerate them."

Burke chuckled. "I don't either," he said with another shrug. "The thought of being intimate with one never crossed my mind until . . ." He paused, worried to admit too much too quickly. James was like a startled fawn at the edge of the forest. He had to be coaxed slowly. "George has always made jokes about us, and I always just ignored them."

"George is an arse," James muttered.

"He *is* an arse . . . with a level of intuition that runs almost occult," Burke corrected. "He saw what was between us all even before we did. He's been pulling the strings for weeks."

James scowled. "What do you mean?"

"The letters he gave you, dragging Rosalie out a window, inviting Marianne to the engagement party—"

James' brows shot sky high. "*He* did that?"

"Aye, I cornered him about it the next morning and threatened to burn all his ugly paintings until he confessed. And you already know he told her about our stupid game with the names in the hat."

"Why would he meddle to bring us all together? What does it gain him?"

Burke shrugged again. "Your happiness, perhaps? And we all know he's created an odd attachment to Rosalie. He takes being her benefactor surprisingly seriously."

James grew quiet, shifting away from him. "Is she alright? She must hate me."

Burke just rolled his eyes. God, how he loved them. But they were fools. "James, she is so completely in love with you that I think she might shatter beyond repair if you dare deny her again. Run from our girl again, run from your feelings, and I'll break both your legs like I promised."

James paced away. "Burke—I can't—I can't bear it. She

said she'd give me anything." He spun around. "She wants to give me everything. She said it without saying it, but I think she'll marry me."

Even a week ago, hearing those words might have broken Burke's heart. He wanted her so badly for himself. But this made sense. This way, they all got what they wanted. With Rosalie and James married, the *ton* would be appeased, and Burke and Tom could continue in their bachelor ways with everyone none the wiser. There might be gossip, but Rosalie and James could behave so much in love as to quiet any rumors.

Burke sighed with relief. "That's good—"

"It's the opposite of good! To her, marriage is a cage. Marriage is violence. It is losing oneself to the whims of a husband who will be like a master holding all the keys. You've heard her yourself, Burke."

"Perhaps her opinions have changed—"

"Or perhaps she is so desperate to have all three of us, she is willing to sacrifice herself on the altar of love for the sake of you and Tom. She will give in to my cruel demands. Everything or nothing. She will appease me. Well, I will not be the man who breaks her spirit. I will not be the man who chains her in a marriage she doesn't want all for the chance to love her. Marriage is *off* the table," he said with a swipe of his hand, pacing away again.

Burke took a deep breath. "James, we *need* you to marry her. Can't you see it? That's the only way this all works. You are taking the most risk, so you must reap the most reward. You are the only one who will get to call her 'wife.'" He laughed, dragging a hand through his hair. "God, I could kill you for it . . . if it didn't make me so happy I could weep."

James spun around, his face murderous. "Did you not

listen to a word I just said? She does not want to marry me!" He enunciated each word. "Not like this anyway. Not with such a power imbalance between us. If she wasn't so goddamn stubborn, I'd settle a dowry on her and make a legal contract blocking me from accessing it. But I can barely get her to accept a dress from me without a fight. Hell, I even told her the diamonds were fake!"

Burke frowned. "You what?"

"The diamonds!" James barked. "The necklace. The one she wore tonight. I told her they were fake." He gave a bitter laugh. "They're not fake; they're worth a fortune. She could sell it and pocket the money, use it as insurance to leave the moment she tires of us. Hell, between the jewels and all the clothes, she could live a comfortable life."

"Is that why you keep giving her things?" Burke pressed with a raised brow. "You're trying to pad her with feathers, so she sees a life with you as a nest and not a cage?"

James closed his eyes, taking a deep breath. "She is everything to me. I want to give her everything. She's lived such an ugly life, Burke. I know we can make it beautiful again. She deserves to be surrounded by such beautiful things."

"What she deserves is *you*," Burke murmured. "That is all she wants, James. You see her agreeing to marry you as her abandoning her principles, tearing herself asunder to be what *you* need. I don't see that at all. I see growth. I see a woman willing to meet you halfway and give you what you need, while resolutely refusing to yield her own wants and desires."

James paused in his pacing, turning to look at him.

"Christ, James. *Look* at us. Look at what we're arguing over! You want to marry a woman who wants to marry you. A woman who loathes marriage and all it stands for *wants* to be your wife. Her only condition will be that you accept not one, but *two* other lovers into the marriage. It's madness, but there we have it," he said with a laugh. "She will not marry you if you cast us out. To marry Rosalie Harrow is to marry Horatio Burke and Tom Renley. Can you accept her terms? Can you gain two husbands with your wife?"

James swallowed, eyes wide. "I—this is—"

"Before you keep blubbing like a fish, there is more you should know." He knew how he'd wanted this reveal to go, but James was not always predictable, especially when it came to being territorial about Burke. "While you've been chasing your lovesick tail, desperate to avoid us, we none of us have been idle."

"What does that mean?" James muttered, his body going tense.

Burke took a breath, placing his hands on James' shoulders. James stiffened. Not a good sign, but Burke had to charge ahead. No retreat. All cards on the table. No surrender. This ended tonight. "James . . . Tom and I are lovers. As much as I want you, I want Tom too. As much as I can't wait to have you, I already have Tom."

James hissed and shrugged away.

"We've kissed and we've fucked, with Rosalie between us, under us . . . and he sucks my cock like a goddamn dream—"

James rounded on him. "Why the hell are you telling me this?"

Burke smiled. "Because you need to face all your fears, James. We're not leaving this room until you do. I told the others this hesitancy you have ends tonight."

James scoffed and stomped off. "You think I'm afraid of Tom? Or, what . . . afraid to share Rosalie with another man?"

He paused by the fireplace, his lip curled into a sneer. "Or perhaps you think I'm afraid to share *you* with another man? You, who I've always kept on such a short leash. Is that it? You want me jealous of Tom? You want me to prove I can fuck you as well as he can?"

"Your words, not mine," Burke needled.

"You're *all* fucking mine," James growled, surging forward. In a rage, he wrapped a hand around the back of Burke's neck. "You know me better than any person living. You know my greatest weakness is also my greatest strength: I *covet* things," he whispered, his breath hot in Burke's ear.

God, Burke was so hard. If James inched any closer, he would feel it.

"So be careful how you push me, Horatio. If you unleash me, I will claim you so fully, so fiercely . . . you will *never* escape me. I will brand myself on every inch of your fucking soul. You say I am your air?" He shifted his hand on Burke's neck, wrapping it around the front, giving his throat a squeeze.

Burke couldn't contain the groan that escaped his parted lips.

"Then breathe for me," James rasped, inching closer until their mouths were almost touching. Burke slowly exhaled, his cock twitching as James sucked in a sharp breath, Burke's air filling his lungs. "Do you want me to covet you, Horatio?"

"I want you to see how we covet *you*," he replied, voice tight.

James gasped, leaning away.

Burke held his gaze. "You are the one who is coveted, James. You are the one who is wanted beyond all reason. You are the only one Rosalie chases. She made Tom and I scale her walls, content to sit back and watch us struggle every step of the way. *You* are the one she fights for even now."

James blinked, lips parted in surprise.

"As for Tom, every time he gets leave from his ship, it is to your side he runs as fast as his legs can carry him. Without fail, he returns home to *you*." He raised a hand at the first sign of protest. "And don't say he comes for me too, because four Christmases ago he had a choice between us, do you remember? You were in London, and I was in Devonshire with my brother. Whom did he run to then?"

"Me," James muttered, crossing his arms.

Burke smirked. "And as for me, we've already established that you are my everything. We are yours, James. Claim us like we want to be claimed. Love us and let us love you."

James raised his hand, letting his finger trace over Burke's parted lips. "How is this possible? I am the most undeserving of men . . ."

Burke leaned into his touch. "You are the light in our darkness. You are the safe harbor in the storm-swept seas of our lives. Without you, we wilt and die. Without you . . . God, help me—" Unable to hold back another second, he cupped James' face and kissed him. It started slow. A few soft pecks. A seeking press of the lips. An invitation as his mouth parted ever so slightly. A plea as he flicked James' bottom lip with his tongue.

And then they caught fire.

The flickering flame of their hesitant kisses blazed like an inferno. Strong hands groped shoulders and rasped over rough jaws. Fingers curled into hair in a claiming hold. Burke slanted his mouth over James', opening himself to him. They drank of each other like two men dying of thirst, moaning their shared need as their teeth clacked and their tongues danced. They broke apart, gasping for breath, chests heaving.

Burke smiled, biting his abused bottom lip, feeling that

tender ache of being well-kissed. He ran both hands down James' chest, smoothing over the fabric of his open shirt as he inched his fingers lower. James went utterly still.

"Let me show you how well I mean to love you." He flipped his hand over, brushing his knuckles over James' hard cock. He smirked when he felt it twitch against his hand. "I have never been on my knees for another man. Do you understand what I mean?"

James licked his lips. "Not even with Renley?"

Burke shook his head. "Not even him." He leaned in, his lips brushing the shell of James' ear as he whispered, "I would live on them for you."

The sound in James' throat was almost feral as Burke slid his hand inside the top of his breeches, seeking out his hard length. Burke wrapped his hand around James' cock and both men cursed. "You didn't get a release with Rosalie earlier, did you?"

James winced.

"You are aching," he murmured in his ear. "Put me on my knees and take what you need."

"Fucking hell," James panted.

But he made no complaint as Burke slipped his hand out and started undoing his breeches. Burke fisted James' hair with his free hand, giving it a tug. Their eyes met and Burke leaned in, stroking James from root to tip. "Tell me to get on my knees, and I will take your cock in my mouth. You will watch as I devour you."

James snapped. One moment, he was standing at Burke's mercy, his cock in Burke's hand, groaning like he was in pain. The next he was stripping off his shirt, tossing it aside as he shoved his open breeches halfway down his thighs. His hard cock sprang out, the tip glistening with desire. He put both hands on Burke's shoulders and pushed him down. "Get on your fucking knees."

A thrill rushed through Burke as he shrugged out of his evening coat and waistcoat. He couldn't shed himself of his cravat fast enough. He was about to drop to his knees when James shot out a hand, cupping his chin and tipping it up.

"Before you get too carried away, know this: Mine will be the first and *only* cock to touch these lips." He brushed his fingers over Burke's mouth. "Renley can have anything else he wants, anywhere he wants, but this mouth belongs to *my* cock."

Burke sucked in a breath, his heart racing as he eagerly stripped off his own shirt. "Yes," he groaned, crashing his lips against James's mouth, burrowing in with his tongue until James was clinging to him. Burke broke the kiss, taking a panting breath. "But fair is fair," he teased. "The only man who will ever put his mouth on you is me. This cock is *mine*."

James grinned. "Then get on your knees and claim it."

Burke dropped to his knees, gripping James roughly by the hips. He'd had his own cock sucked enough times to feel certain he could do an adequate job. He didn't bother with a few teasing licks. He just opened his mouth and sank onto his best friend, moaning as the first taste of salty come coated his tongue.

"God help me," James muttered, digging his fingers into Burke's hair.

Burke quickly figured out a rhythm, sucking and teasing as he worked James' hips. He took him as deep as he could, pressing him to the back of his throat.

"Don't stop—"

His hands slid around James' hips, cupping his arse as he pulled him closer. When James didn't move on his own, Burke popped off him and glanced up. "James . . ."

Panting, cheeks flushed, James looked down.

Burke squeezed his arse cheeks. "I told you to keep your eyes on me. Now, fuck my mouth."

"I don't want to hurt you."

Burke grinned, tightening his hold on him. "Fuck my mouth like you own it, or I'll fuck you in the arse." He laughed as he felt James clench and pull away. Opening his mouth, he sank back down on him. He grunted his approval as James started to move, taking control. They found their rhythm together, Burke secretly thrilling as James pushed his limits, making him swallow until he gagged.

"Oh God, I'm going to come."

Burke jerked James forward, sinking as deep as he could as he sucked.

"*Ahh*—Burke—" James came hard with a shudder, releasing in his mouth. As promised, Burke drank him down, savoring the sweet and salty taste.

When he was spent, James sank to his knees, pressing his forehead against Burke's once more. "You're mine," he murmured. "Mine to love. Mine to covet, to own."

Forever.

Burke nodded, hands still shaking as he smoothed them over James' bare shoulders. "I've always been yours . . . but now I need your help."

James lifted his head away. "What? Anything."

Burke held his gaze. "Tell Rosalie you love her. Propose to her. Make her ours."

64

James

James followed Burke back to his room. No one noticed them moving through the dark of the house, for it was late now, long after midnight.

He stepped into Burke's bedroom, looking around. He rarely ever came in here. It was simply furnished, with little touches of Burke everywhere. The only light came from the half-dying fire.

"Lock the door," Burke muttered, tossing his outer clothes on the back of a chair. Like James, he was dressed only in his white muslin shirt and black dress pants. Both men had their sleeves rolled up and their collars open.

James turned the latch, locking them both inside. He stilled, one hand on the door, as he heard it. A faint moan. He spun around, eyes narrowed on Burke, who flashed him a weak smile.

"Do you want to wait until they're finished?"

A mix of emotions surged through James all at once—jealousy, need, hunger, curiosity. They swirled like a hurricane, and he stood at the center. He took a steadying breath.

"Fuck waiting." He moved purposefully towards the other door and pushed it open without knocking.

With a soft chuckle, Burke followed.

Rosalie's fire was blazing strong, with candles lit for extra light. James stepped past the curtained bed post, his eyes searching, settling on his quarry. Rosalie was naked in bed with Renley, wrapped in his arms. They were both lying on their sides, her right leg slung over his hip. His hand framed her rounded arse, holding her hips tight against him as he fucked her with slow, easy strokes. With the sheets tangled around their legs, their bodies danced with golden firelight, the heavy shadows playing off their movements as they kissed, whispering lovers' words.

Rosalie's back was to them, and Renley barely noticed the opening door. Clearly, he was unfazed by the idea that Burke might enter. That fact alone had jealousy and want surging inside James, cresting like an angry wave. Christ, how practiced were they at this already? How much had he missed by being such an unyielding arse?

Renley met his gaze and cursed. "Fucking hell, James."

Rosalie glanced over her shoulder, gasping as she saw him standing next to Burke.

"Don't stop on my account," he muttered, his eyes hungrily taking them in. She was so beautiful. They were beautiful together. Rosalie looked at him warily. She was right to be confused. He'd behaved so abominably. If she never forgave him, he'd understand.

Burke stepped in close behind him, one hand curling around his waist. "You heard James. Our girl is needy, Tom. Finish her."

Rosalie whimpered as Renley kissed her neck. "Do you

want them to watch, Rose? Shall we drive them mad with longing for you?"

She whined again, her hips moving with his as she buried her face against his tattooed chest.

Renley glanced over her shoulder at them. "James can look, but he can't touch. He deserves to watch you come on another man's cock."

James stood at the side of the bed, his own cock growing harder by the second as he watched them together.

Suddenly, Renley pulled out of her. James spied his thick length wrapped in a French letter. James hadn't even thought of it in the opera box. Too lost to his lust. Rosalie protested, but Renley slung her leg off his hip. "Roll over, sweet girl," he murmured. "I want him to see all of you."

She moaned as Renley rolled her. She had nowhere to look but directly at him as Renley shifted her hips, lifting her leg slightly so he could sink back inside her from behind. At this angle, James watched Renley's cock slide into her sweet cunt. He wanted to die as the firelight danced, highlighting the glistening desire between her thighs. His heart hammered as he remembered the feel of her—the warmth, the wetness, the silky-smooth perfection of her sex. He wanted to taste it again, bury himself there and never leave.

She clung to Renley's hip with one hand as he thrust into her over and over. The movement arched her back, bouncing her perfect tits as he got rougher, chasing his release. "Oh God," she whined, her eyes locked on James.

Burke stepped close behind him. James could feel his hard cock pressing against his hip. "How does he feel, love?" Burke murmured, his breath fanning over James' ear.

"So good." She threw her head back against Renley's chest. "I feel him everywhere."

Burke smiled. "How close are you?"

"So close—*ah*—" She let out a little cry as Renley tweaked her nipple with his free hand.

He hummed with pleasure, his face pressed against the curve of her neck. "You're so tight, Rose. So beautiful. Look how they both want you. Three men desperate for you. Want to please you, make you come, worship you body and soul."

"I want them too—*ah*—" Her words were cut short as Renley snaked his hand between her legs, his fingers working her sensitive bud. Her response was immediate, her lips parting in a silent cry as she went rigid. She was right on the edge, coiling tighter. James could see it in her eyes.

Burke let out a low laugh. "Did you hear him, James? Tom says you can't touch her, but you're welcome to touch me. Perhaps that will be incentive enough for them both to come."

With a growl, James turned, tugging Burke to him as he pressed a kiss to his lips, teasing his mouth open with his tongue. Burke sank into the kiss, dropping a hand to cup James' painfully hard cock.

"Holy shit," Renley rasped.

Desperate for more, James jerked off Burke's shirt and tossed it aside. He slid his hands across the smooth plane of his chest, shivering with want as Burke pulled him closer. Burke hummed low in his throat, tracing a line with his finger up James' neck before licking it with his eager tongue. James groaned, his hands fisting in Burke's hair.

"Oh God, I can't—" Rosalie came, her body coiling forward in a series of spasms. Behind her Renley grunted, thrusting hard twice more before he spilled into his letter. They both trembled with their releases.

Burke smiled, nuzzling James' neck, teasing with a nip of his ear. "See what you've been missing, *my lord*?"

James growled, trying to shove him off, but Burke held fast to him.

"This is the only thing that matters," he pressed, his breath warm against his ear as he soothed a hand down James' arm. "This is the only truth we need, right here in this room."

James watched as Renley curled around Rosalie, smoothing back her hair from her face. She was trembling, her face pressed against the pillow. Her dark hair fanned out behind her. She nodded at whatever he said. It was too low for James to hear. Then Renley was sliding out of her, rolling away to discard the used letter. He sat up, his back turned to them, cleaning himself up.

"Tom, let's give them a minute," Burke said, his hand still on James' shoulder.

Rosalie lifted her head slightly, eyes blinking open as she glanced from Burke to James.

Renley stood from the bed, shrugging himself into his shirt. It was long enough to cover his bare arse. He turned back to Rosalie, sinking one knee on the bed as he leaned over her. "Do you want me to stay?"

She bit her bottom lip nervously but shook her head, her eyes still on James.

Renley kissed her temple, tugging the sheet up over her. James watched how she relaxed, holding the sheet to her naked breasts as she sat up. Tenderness bloomed in his heart for Renley, noting how he cared for her, anticipating her needs before she could voice them.

Renley stepped around the end of the bed, a question in his eyes as he looked from Burke to James.

"Come on, Tom," Burke said, stepping back.

Renley went to move around him, but James curled an arm around his arm. "Wait."

Renley met his gaze, his blue eyes calm and clear.

James lifted his chin. He had to know. It was one thing for Burke to say it, but it was quite another to hear it directly from Renley's lips. "Why are you here?"

Renley blinked, glancing from Burke back to James. "What do you mean?"

"I mean you were given leave from your commanding officer, and you came to Alcott Hall . . . why?"

The corner of Renley's mouth quirked into a smile. "Because I wanted to go home."

"Foxhill House is your home. A Renley has managed that estate for generations."

"The *first* Renley has managed Foxhill, you mean," he replied. "I am a second son, James. Same as you. Same as Burke. My home is where I say it is, and I say it is with you."

The two men held each other's gaze as a moment of truth settled between them. James broke it, reaching behind him for Burke. He wrapped an arm around his shoulder, pulling him close. Burke let himself be reeled in. James held Renley's gaze as he brushed his fingers along Burke's collarbone. "And what about our Burke? Do you want him for yourself?"

Renley glanced from Burke back to James. "Yes, I want him. I want him madly."

Feeling bold, James leaned in, pressing his lips against Burke's cheek in a lingering kiss. With his free hand, he traced a line down Burke's bare chest to the top of his high-waisted breeches. Burke stifled a groan, his hand fisting into James' shirt. James broke the kiss and turned back to Renley, noting how his eyes heated with desire. "Burke is *mine*," he growled. "If you want him for yourself, you will ask my permission."

Renley sucked in a breath, eyes wide. When Burke didn't contradict him, he nodded. "James, I want him. I want Burke in my bed and in my life. Please, don't keep him from me."

James turned to Burke. "And do you want our Renley?"

Burke nodded, his stormy eyes locked on the sailor. "I do. I want you all. Every minute of every day. I'm aching with it."

James leaned in, his forehead pressed to Burke's temple as he breathed him in. The spicy floral scent he sometimes smelled on Rosalie clung to Burke's skin. James wanted to taste it. Christ, he was going mad with this desire. How had he suppressed it for so long? He turned, looking at Rosalie for the first time since their exchange started. She was sitting up in the bed, the forgotten sheet pooled around her waist, her perfect tits on full display. Her dark eyes were wide as she watched them. He held out a hand to her. "Rosalie, come here."

Warily, she slipped out of the bed and moved around it to stand by Renley.

James reached for her, grateful when she didn't pull away. "I'm sorry," he murmured. "I've been an incomprehensible fool when it comes to you . . . all of you," he added, glancing from Burke to Renley. "I understand what you all want, what you'd be asking of me. As Burke said, the risk is high. There will not be a day where we will not have to be careful, even in our home. We'd have to pick staff carefully, relying on discretion and our own ability to control ourselves unless we're alone."

Rosalie glanced at the others. "What are you saying, James?"

"I'm saying I intend to build a life with you, all three of you," he added.

Rosalie broke, throwing her hands over her face to try and contain her sobs. James had her in his arms in moments, wrapping himself around her naked shoulders.

"I'm sorry," he muttered. "I'm so sorry. I was an arse. A scared fool. Rosalie, look at me." He pushed her shoulders back gently to cup her face. "My angel, please look at me."

Sniffling, she looked up, her eyes red and puffy.

"I am in love with you. We are *all* in love with you. If you will give me one last chance to prove myself, I will never make you doubt me again. You are the moon in our skies and we the tides, helpless to avoid your pull. There is no escaping you. I don't want to escape. I want to be lost in love with you forever."

She sucked in a breath that was half laugh, half cry. Her eyes shined with tears, but now her face looked different. She was smiling. It made his heart thrum in his chest to see it. "I love you, James," she murmured. "I am so in love with you."

He kissed her, tasting the salt of her tears on her lips and hating himself for it. He would make it up to her. Every day he would show her how much he loved her. How he meant to cherish and protect her. He pulled back, wiping beneath her eyes with his thumbs. "Tonight, you offered me a precious gift. You implied you would marry me. Did you mean it?" He searched her eyes.

She glanced from Burke to Renley. "I . . . you said you'd only be with me if I gave you everything. I assumed you meant marriage. I want to make you happy . . ."

"But would marriage make *you* happy?"

She swallowed, fresh tears springing to her eyes.

He smiled sadly, having his answer . . . at least for now. "Alright, angel, here's how it will be. First, you should know that if you and I ever do marry, I have every expectation that I will be cuckolded every day of my life."

She gasped as, behind her, Renley smirked.

"Don't think I will mind it, but fair is fair," he added. "For every morning I wake to find Burke in your bed, you can expect to wake and find him in mine."

Behind him, Burke chuckled, wrapping an arm around his shoulder. "We could avoid any morning unpleasantries by just sleeping in the same bed."

Rosalie glanced between them, hope and longing in her eyes.

James let his eye fall to Renley. "Renley, you recently told me you wanted a tree. I'm not quite sure if the analogy still fits, but I'm offering you a forest. Roots buried deep . . . entanglements . . . leaning branches. We can go at whatever pace you want, but—"

"Yes," Renley said, inching closer.

"If you want a captaincy, I'll sponsor it," he added. "Or you can retire and try your hand at farming life. Whatever you want. Your home will be with us regardless. From this day, you're mine."

Renley pressed forward, wrapping his arms around James in a hug. James swallowed his nerves, letting himself hug Renley back. It was chaste, but tension simmered between them. A promise of more.

Rosalie was crying again, and James desperately wanted that to stop. Her tears were a physical torture that had him aching with a need to fix it. He let Renley go, his eyes back on her. "Do you have any rules you need stated?"

She glanced around at all three men. "No other women. I

know how that looks," she added, cheeks blooming pink. "And I know I'm the worst kind of siren . . . but there can be only me."

Renley just chuckled, sharing a grin with Burke.

But James narrowed his eyes. "There will never be another woman for any of us," he said fiercely, taking a step closer. "But know this, angel. If you even think of seeking comfort in the arms of another man, I will walk away."

"I wholeheartedly second his threat," Burke muttered.

"Agreed," said Renley.

"We will share you, and cherish every moment as we do, but this harem ends with the three of us," he finished.

She reached for him. "You're all I want. No others. Ever. I swear it to you. Please, James—"

He held himself away from her. "Within the four of us, there will be no jealousy, no questions of fidelity . . . and no marriage," he added. "Not yet, at least. Not until we reach an equilibrium where we all agree it is for the best. For now, George's title will protect us. We can retire to Alcott as soon as the wedding is over. Our life in the country can go unremarked by the *ton*. Do we all agree to this plan?"

"Of course," Rosalie whispered. "I want us all to be together more than anything. I want—" She swallowed, tears in her eyes. "God, *please*, James, I want you." She held out her trembling hand. "Please, just take my hand. I need you. I need *us*. Take my hand and make us whole."

Instinct took over and James had her in his arms, claiming her mouth in a hungry kiss. Her body went limp with relief as she let herself kiss and be kissed. He smoothed his hands down her naked shoulders, her sides. Cupping her arse, he pulled her close, letting her feel his hardness. Too much was still in the way—his shirt, his breeches. With a groan, he released her.

"*No*—" Her plea died in her throat as she watched him tug his shirt off over his head, the hunger still burning in his eyes.

Next to him, Burke was trembling with need, but he still had the patience to lean in and mutter, "Do you still want us to leave—"

"Don't you fucking dare," James growled. "Get me a letter." He kicked off his shoes, holding out a hand to Rosalie. "Come here, angel." He cupped her cheek, sighing as her hands smoothed up the bare skin of his chest, wrapping around his shoulders. "I need to be inside you again," he muttered, pressing kisses to her chin, the corner of her mouth, anything he could manage as he worked himself out of his breeches. "Now."

"Take me," she panted, teasing his bottom lip with her teeth. "I'm yours. Take me, James."

"I will. I'm going to claim you. Bury myself in you. Own you. No beginning, no end."

"Yes," she begged.

He traced the arc of her neck with his tongue, sucking the taste of Renley off her skin, savoring it. Then he dropped his hand between her legs, loving the way she dripped with desire as he pressed two fingers inside her. She clung to his shoulders as he worked her sweet cunt. Renley had clearly treated her well. She was more than ready.

Burke appeared beside him again, sliding a French letter into his hand. "What do you want?"

"I want her wrapped around me," James directed, his eyes locked on Rosalie. "I want my cock in her cunt while you fuck her perfect arse."

Shifting to her side, Burke nuzzled her ear. "Do you want that, sweet siren? We'll take such good care of you. Let us share you, make you so full."

Beside them, Renley watched, a pleased smile on his face.

"Yes," she cried, kissing them both—first James, then Burke, then James again. "I'm yours. Please *God*, stop talking and make me yours."

65

Rosalie

JAMES WAS IN her room, naked in her arms, and Rosalie could scarcely draw breath. He was holding her close, his hands trembling as he touched and kissed her. Even as he said such heated words, his hands and lips were all tenderness. She melted for him, moved with him, opened herself to him in every way he wanted. All the pieces of her life felt like they were falling into place. These men were her world now. What had James said?

No beginning, no end.

James worked himself out of his clothes as Burke did the same. Then she was back in James' arms, their naked bodies molding together. Burke pressed to her back, kissing her neck, her shoulders, while James dropped his mouth to her breast, sucking on her nipple.

She reached out blindly, knowing what she needed. "Tom, please—"

When Tom claimed her lips, her heart burst open. The bars of its cage shattered like glass and the primal creature she kept buried deep inside spread her wings. Three beautiful, perfect men had their mouths on her. Kissing her, loving her, claiming her. It was too much. She sighed against Tom's lips, her legs quivering as James pressed his fingers inside her, driving her to the edge of bliss.

She broke her kiss with Tom, eyes only for James. This man would learn his place at last. She cupped his face. "You are *mine*, James Corbin. I'm done waiting. Do you hear me? I'm done watching you hide from this. From *us*. The Viscount Finchley stays in my bed now." She pressed closer until her lips brushed against his, until they shared breath. "Unleash yourself on me," she whispered. "Hold nothing back."

James groaned, fumbling to put on the French letter.

"Get yourself ready too," Tom directed at Burke. "I want you both in our girl as long as possible." He raised her hand to his lips, kissing her fingertips. "Are you ready to take two of us?"

She nodded, a wave of desire burning through her.

Tom grinned. "You'll be perfect. You're made for us, Rose. I'm going to watch you take my men. Watch them fill you. Watch them come inside you."

She whimpered as James spun her around, walking her back the five steps to press her up against the wall. The chill of the cool surface made her shiver, a gasp escaping her parted lips. James swallowed the sound as his strong hands slid down her sides. He cupped her bottom, lifting her off the floor. Then he braced her against the wall with his hips, his cock pressed at her entrance. She panted, loving the feel of him right where he should be.

"Look at me, angel."

The moment she met his gaze, he thrust into her, sheathing himself. She moaned, feeling herself stretch around him. They both took a shaky breath, adjusting to the feel of each other. Then he was moving, slamming into her so hard the painting on the wall rattled. She laughed with a relief that verged on euphoria, tipping her head back as James claimed her with all his passion. It was better than she dreamed. Nothing compared to feeling his body moving with hers, his panting breath, his desperate touches.

Behind him, Tom and Burke moved closer, their eyes hooded with desire as they watched their best friend take her. Burke was naked, his hand fisting his glistening cock. She knew it would be oiled and ready for her. She needed the fullness, the feeling of being so complete.

"Burke. I want you—"

"I'm here," he murmured, one hand on James' shoulder.

James slowed his thrusts as Burke wrapped a hand around his throat, pressing up behind him. Burke leaned in, his lips by James' ear. "Do you want to keep her for yourself—"

"No," James rasped. "Want you. Need to feel you both—"

"Please, love," Rosalie repeated. "Take me to the bed."

Burke chuckled. "Not a chance, you wanton siren. You look perfect just like this. Tom, help James hold her. We're fucking her right here."

Tom stepped in and helped James keep her still as they shifted off the wall. Burke stepped up behind her, his hands smoothing over her bottom. She trembled with anticipation, her greedy core fluttering around James' length.

"So perfect," Burke muttered, massaging her tight hole.

She clenched around James as Burke pressed a finger inside.

James groaned.

"Just wait," said Tom, leaning in to kiss her lips, teasing with his tongue. "You have no idea, James. She's a goddess. You'll never be the same."

Burke pumped his finger, pulling out to add a second.

"Relax, love." His free hand soothed her shoulder with gentle strokes. "Are you ready for me?"

"Yes," she whispered, her voice barely audible. Burke glanced at James.

"Do it," James muttered.

"Go slow," Tom added. "Rose, relax. Let him in."

She sighed with want as she felt the tip of his cock press against her. His hands joined those holding her thighs as he inched his way in.

"Holy God," said James. "I can't—"

"Don't you dare come," Tom challenged, pressing his lips to James' neck, sucking his pulse point until James moaned. "You haven't even started."

Seeing her men love each other unlocked something feral in Rosalie. It made her protective of them, fierce and wild. She wanted them to take every ounce of pleasure from each other and then unleash that same passion on her. One circle without end.

Please God, never let it end.

"She's so tight." Burke pushed the head of his cock fully inside her.

Rosalie panted. Suspended between them, James was already impossibly deep, pressed in all the way to the hilt. She could only imagine feeling the full thickness of both their cocks together. "Fill me," she cried. "Burke, please—"

Burke stepped forward, sinking himself fully inside her.

All three of them trembled as they adjusted.

"How does she feel?" Tom murmured, his arms still wrapped around James.

"I think I might die," James panted.

"Move," Tom directed. "Find your rhythm and fuck our sweet girl until she shatters. She'll strangle your cock so beautifully."

Rosalie could do nothing but hold on as her men began moving, taking turns thrusting with their hips. Their cocks slid against each other so deep inside her as they brought her right to the edge. She could feel every perfect inch. She leaned forward, claiming James' mouth in a hungry kiss. He broke it as he thrusted harder, pounding into her.

"Tom," she whined, sinking back against Burke's chest.

Tom stepped in, cupping her face with his calloused hand as he buried his tongue in her mouth. "You are our goddess," he muttered against her lips. "We worship only you. Our queen, our north star," he said between kisses. "We'll bury our cocks in you forever. Every perfect hole. Claim you. Brand your soul."

His words shored her up inside, building a new kind of cage around her heart. It was a cage of *their* making, rather than her own. With each kiss, each caress, each word of longing, they strengthened her. Her body may be powerless now, wholly at their mercy, but she was still in control. "Harder," she panted. "God, *please*. Fuck me harder. Own me. Ruin me for all other men."

James' grip tightened as he pressed all the way in and held still. "Take her, Burke. Christ, end us both."

Burke gripped her tight enough to bruise and began slamming into her. She and James cried out as Burke pounded them both with his relentless thrusts. She tipped her head back against Burke's shoulder, her whole body coiling tight as she let her release take over her.

When Tom snaked his hand between her and James, pressing on her sensitive bud with his thumb, she shattered. She clenched down hard, crying out in her ecstasy. Burke slammed into her, his hot release filling her. The sensation of his come spilling inside her had her clenching again. That was enough to have James coming too. She shook from head to toe as she came down from her high.

"Take her, Tom," Burke murmured after a minute, shifting his position.

Tom braced her thighs with his strong arms as Burke pulled out. "Rose, let go," Tom whispered in her ear. "I've got you, sweet girl. Let go of James."

She blinked, struggling to hold the pieces of herself together as James suddenly stepped back. To go from feeling so full to so empty . . . she fought to keep from crying. But Tom was there, cradling her in his arms as he took her to the bed. He tended to her, washing gently between her legs, murmuring soft words.

Once James cleaned himself up, he was crawling across from the other side of the bed, wrapping himself around her, tangling their legs together. He buried his face in the curve of her neck, breathing her in. "Did we hurt you?" he whispered, pressing his lips against her warm skin.

Hurt her? She blinked, not understanding his question. They took her and made her feel whole. Their shared closeness did the opposite of hurt her. To be in their arms was to feel complete. But she didn't know how to articulate all those feelings, so she just whispered a soft, "No."

Tom sank onto the bed, pressing himself against her back, his thick arm curled around her.

"This bed is too small for the four of us," Burke grumbled, dropping on the edge of the bed behind James. He slung his arm over James, reaching for Rosalie's hand. Weaving his fingers in with hers, he kept his arm draped over James' torso.

"The beds at Alcott are larger," James muttered, his voice muffled.

"I can sleep in my room tonight," said Tom, rubbing his calloused hand up and down the length of her naked thigh.

"No," she whined, wrapping her hand over his. "I need you to stay."

He huffed a laugh. "Always so greedy. Two men should be more than sufficient to hold you while you sleep, eh?"

They were all quiet for a moment, their breathing slowing.

"Do you really think this will work?" she whispered to the room.

"In two short days, George will be married," said Burke. "All we have to do is keep our heads down, keep the party entertained, and keep George on a short leash—"

"*And* get the gorgon engaged to someone else," added Tom. "Don't forget about that Sword of Damocles."

Burke groaned, pressing his face into his pillow.

"But your reputation must and will come first, Rosalie," James pressed. "We must all keep this quiet for your sake. Nothing can be amiss as the *ton* descends on us. We survive the wedding, the party, and then we are free."

"It's just two days," Tom said, curling his large frame tighter against her. "We can all behave ourselves, surely."

"Speak for yourself," Burke muttered. "Now that I know what sex with the three of you is like, I intend to ravage you separately and together every hour of the day until my cock falls off."

"Ignore him," said James, his warm breath fanning over her ear.

She fought a smile as Burke gave her hand another squeeze.

Behind her, Tom let out a yawn, his voice heavy with sleep. "I have a feeling it's all going to be fine."

66

Rosalie

THE MORNING OF the wedding arrived, and Rosalie awoke feeling like everything was just as it should be. She was curled up in James' arms, Burke at her back, Tom on his other side. Her men loved her. They loved each other. They were content. George would marry Piety and they would take off for adventures in Lisbon and Greece for the next four months. Meanwhile, Rosalie would go home . . . to Alcott. The dream of calling a place home had never been so tantalizingly close.

It was a beautiful, crisp morning, and Rosalie and several of the others opted to walk the few blocks to the church, rather than ride in the carriage processional following the duke and Piety. She paired her favorite green and pink morning dress, layered with a blue pelisse and the navy blue bonnet with golden satin ribbons. She strode out on Tom's arm, Burke following behind escorting Mariah.

As James hinted, that was another benefit to this wedding business finally coming to a close: All the house guests would leave. It was quite the boon to learn even the duchess was opting to stay in Town, citing her strong dislike of the bitter cold of long winter carriage rides. The only people returning to Alcott would be James, Rosalie, Burke, and Tom.

Rosalie couldn't hardly wait.

"Oh, look at all the ribbons," cooed Blanche.

The streets leading from Corbin House to St. George's at Hanover Square were draped with colorful ribbon garlands that fluttered in the breeze. Society weddings were quite the draw, and the mood was festive. Eager spectators were already milling about, ready to see the duke and Piety pass by in their carriages. Even more exciting than seeing a duke and his bride was the chance to see the Queen. Rosalie wasn't too shy to admit she was giddy with anticipation.

"Why do you smile?" Tom said in her ear.

"I'm happy," she replied.

"We have plans for you tonight," he teased, mirroring her smile. "Burke has put together something special."

"Oh, yes?" A flutter in her chest had her smiling wider. "Can you give me a hint?"

"Not a chance," he replied, placing a hand at the small of her back to guide her up the stairs and into the church. The noise of the crowd quieted once they were inside.

"Let's find our seats," said Burke, leading the way down the side aisle towards the front.

Within the hour, the church was fit to burst. Outside, the crowd squealed, announcing the arrival of someone important. A few minutes later, the duchess floated down the main aisle, a vision in burgundy and pearls. She nodded to various assembled guests before taking her place in the pew in front of Burke, Tom, and Rosalie.

"Stop fidgeting." Tom placed a hand over Rosalie's. She'd been twisting her program into a tight coil, ruining it and getting ink on her glove.

"I've never seen her before," she whispered. "Not up close, at least."

On her other side, Burke gave her hand a squeeze. She glanced over her shoulder and gasped.

"What is it?" said Tom, turning his head.

"Don't look," she hissed, facing back towards the front with a little smile.

"Rose, what—"

"Hartington just arrived," she whispered. "He just wedged himself onto the pew next to Olivia. I said *don't* look—" She groaned as both her men turned their heads.

Tom turned back with a chuckle, while Burke narrowed his eyes with interest. "She looks miserable."

"She always looks miserable," Tom replied, earning him a pinch from Rosalie.

"This will never work," Burke muttered.

"We must have faith," Rosalie whispered.

"I'll give them two more days to settle things, then I'm locking them in a closet and losing the key until they come out engaged," he warned, turning back around.

"I'm not certain that would be the outcome," Tom replied with a smirk. "Hart is stubborn as a mule. She's more than met her match."

Burke turned away. "Oh, here he is."

The three of them glanced towards the front of the church,

watching as George and James appeared from a side door, following the archbishop over to the altar space. As soon as George was in place, the crowds outside erupted in exuberant cheers.

Trumpets blasted and the whole church got to their feet. Rosalie bounced on her toes, trying to see through the thick sea of people towards the back of the church.

"Don't worry, you'll see her," Tom teased. "She'll sit beside the dowager, so you'll have the best seat in the church."

Rosalie smiled, ignoring the way they both smirked. She didn't care if she was being ridiculous. It wasn't every day one got to see—

"Her Majesty, The Queen!"

The trumpet sounds now filled the inside of the church, echoing off the high stone walls. As one, the crowd sank into bows and curtsies. Rosalie kept her head bowed but flicked her eyes up, smiling as the Queen swept past her row, taking up the end seat next to the duchess.

Rosalie gasped, overcome by her beauty. She wore an elaborate gown of teal and cream, embroidered top to bottom with glittering gold thread in a pattern of florals and swirls. She wore a powdered white wig of massive curls festooned with jeweled pendants. Waves of delicate white lace spilled over at her cuffs.

The Queen smiled at the duchess with closed lips, though Rosalie noted a sparkle in her eye. She and the duchess were friendly, then. She entered the duchess' pew and gave a nod to the archbishop. With a gesture of his hand, he signaled for the rest of the congregation to remain standing.

Outside the doors of the church, the crowd cheered again. Piety's carriage must have arrived at last. It wasn't long before

Prudence was walking down the aisle looking beautiful as ever in a butter yellow gown. She clutched a small bouquet in hand, all smiles and her eyes glistening with tears.

As the music crescendoed, the congregation inched closer. And then Piety Nash was walking down the aisle on her father's arm. Rosalie's eye focused on the Corbins' sunburst tiara perched atop her golden curls. A veil flowed behind her, catching the sunlight from the open doors beyond and making her glow like an angel.

While the rest of the congregation watched Piety make her long walk, Rosalie glanced towards the front. She let her eye fall to George, curious to know his feelings as he watched his bride draw nearer. He stood stoically, his chin held high. He was almost *too* still. The duke Rosalie knew was prone to fidgeting, slouching, and all manner of appearing visibly discomfited. But this was a solemn occasion. Perhaps, for once, he was doing his duty admirably.

Piety and her father paused at the Queen's pew, giving her a curtsy and a bow before they proceeded past. Mr. Nash deposited her at the altar at George's side, and the archbishop raised his hands for the congregation to sit.

Rosalie sank onto the hard wooden bench, feeling Burke and Tom press in at either side. She appreciated how close they sat, letting their shoulders and arms brush together. Even if she couldn't openly hold their hands, she could feel their touch. She smiled.

The archbishop cleared his throat and gave a nod to the Queen before he called out in a raspy orator's voice. "Dearly beloved, we are gathered here in the sight of God, and in the face of this congregation, to join together this man and this woman in Holy Matrimony; which is an honorable estate, instituted by God in the time of—"

"I object!"

Rosalie stilled, unsure if she heard the words spoken aloud.

A buzz hummed all around the church as the archbishop blinked, looking up from his notes.

Piety's saccharine smile fell.

James stepped in, leaning over George's shoulder. They whispered a few hushed words before George waved him away.

"No, *no.* I said I object!" George called in a strangled voice. He glanced around at the crowd before his eye settled back on Piety, whose bottom lip was quivering.

The archbishop cleared his throat. "Your Grace, if you require a moment to—"

"Yes," he squawked. "A moment. I need a moment. James!" Grabbing his brother by the collar, the Duke of Norland dashed away from the altar, leaving the archbishop, his blushing bride, the Queen of England, and all assembled behind as he dragged James down the side aisle and out the closest door.

The congregation erupted in gasps and whispers.

To either side of Rosalie, Burke and Tom were still as stone.

Burke slowly exhaled. "Well . . . shit."

67

James

GEORGE BURST THROUGH the side door of the church, dragging James behind him. He shouldered his way into the sacristy, pushing James ahead of him with both hands, and slammed the door shut, sagging his weight against it.

James righted himself with a scowl. "George, what on earth—"

"I can't do this," he panted, one hand over his chest. "I can't. Oh God—*oh*—I can't breathe—"

"Whoa, easy," James said, stepping forward to brace George by the elbow.

"James, I can't breathe," George gasped in a panic.

"Loosen your cravat," James soothed, holding tight to his brother's arm.

Both hands went to George's neck as he clawed at the cloth strangling him like a noose, desperate to untie the knot.

"Why don't you sit down." James eased his brother back towards a chair.

"I can't possibly sit at a time like this," George cried. Tugging away from James, he strode across the room, spinning when he reached the narrow window. "I can't do this," he repeated.

"Alright, so we cancel the wedding. Or we postpone. Whatever you need—"

"Not the wedding—*this*!" He gestured wildly around the room. "All of this! I can't be this person anymore. I cannot do this. It's killing me, James."

"What are you talking about?"

George made a sound somewhere between a choke and a shriek. "I'm talking about *you*! I'm talking about me! I'm talking about bloody all of it!"

James felt his stomach lurch. "Me? What the hell do I have to do with it?"

"You are the very middle of it!" George cried. "James, you are the worst second son to have ever lived! The position is utterly wasted on you." He strode forward, eyes wide. "Do you know how unfair it is for me to have to watch you squander your chance to be a useless spare to the heir? It's infuriating. This envy, it eats at me. It burrows inside me and makes me *hate* you."

"George—"

"*I* should have been the second son," George snarled, jabbing at his chest with his thumb. "Not you. *Me*! I would do it so much better than you!"

"Goddamn it, George—"

"And *you* should have been born the duke."

A sharp silence fell between the brothers. George stood before James in his wedding clothes, chest heaving. Taking a breath, James gave his waistcoat an irritated tug. "Unfortunately for both of us, those are not the cards we were dealt."

George huffed, flapping his arms. "Well, who says we have to keep playing cards, then?"

"What?"

George took a step closer. "James, you and I are two of the most powerful men in England. Why do we let the rest of the rabble make us play a game we both loathe so very much? What if I don't want to play cards anymore? What if I want to play hazard or chess or—or backgammon!"

"Speak English, George," James growled.

"I want you to trade lives with me!"

James just blinked. "Trade lives? What, like I start calling myself George and you will go by James, and we'll just hope that by some miracle no one notices? Am I expected to waltz out there and marry Piety?"

"No," George said with a laugh. "That would be ridiculous. You're in love with Rosalie—"

"Oh yes, that's what is ridiculous about it," James muttered.

"But in theory the idea should work—"

"Look around you," James barked. "That's not how *any* of this works! *You* are the duke. *I* am your brother. That is the way it is."

"If a king can abdicate, why can't a duke?" George challenged.

James fell silent, utterly at a loss for words. George had often complained before, but he'd never taken his dissatisfaction so far. James raised a wary brow. "You would disclaim your title?"

"Disclaim!" he cried with a snap of his fingers. "See, you even know the proper word for it."

"George, this is serious. Do you really want to disclaim your title?"

"Of course, I want to disclaim it," he replied with an exasperated laugh. "I should have done it years ago. I'm wasted as a duke, and everyone knows it."

Before James could respond, a sharp fist rapped on the door.

"In a minute," James barked.

The knob rattled as someone tried to force their way in. "James, you let me in this instant!"

It was their mother.

"Don't let her in," George whispered. "I'm not ready. She'll make me change my mind."

"Well, if you can be talked out of this decision so easily, then perhaps it's not the right decision—"

"It *is* the right decision!" George cried. "You know it too."

The door swung open, nearly hitting James in the shoulder. He spun around as their mother pressed her way in, Burke and Rosalie on her heels. The archbishop stood in the doorway, sheepishly holding a key.

"Is someone going to tell me what is going on? George, get back out there at once," their mother demanded. "The Queen is waiting!"

But George took one look at Rosalie, then puffed out his chest. "Mother, I have something very important to tell you. All of you." He paused for dramatic effect. "I intend to disclaim my title in favor of James. We're going to switch our roles. He will be the first son, and I the second."

Their mother spluttered. "You—*what*?"

But James couldn't think about her. He had eyes only for Burke and Rosalie. He held their gazes, glancing between them, desperate to glean their thoughts with a look. They were both shocked.

"George, you speak nonsense," their mother cried. "You are the duke. You were born to be the duke."

"But I don't *want* to be the duke," he replied. "It makes me miserable; it always has. Am I to have no say in my own life?"

"This is madness! You're overtired. We will delay this wedding while you rest and—"

"We will *cancel* this wedding because I do not wish to marry Piety Nash!"

"George . . ." Burke's voice cut through their bickering. All eyes turned to him. "Just help us understand what brought you to this pass."

George shrugged. "I suppose I've always resented my lot in life and wished mine and James' roles were reversed. He makes a perfect duke. I have never tried to compete with him because . . . well, I can't. And I suppose I tend to not try at all, rather than risk trying only to prove myself a failure."

James didn't miss the way George's eye kept darting to Rosalie as he delivered that speech.

"But something must have changed," their mother pressed. "What happened that you are now so willing to abandon your birthright, your family?"

"There will be no abandoning my family," George murmured. "I am still a Corbin. If there is to be abandonment, it will come from you. As to how or why I now find myself at this pass, the answer is simple. It was all down to her." He pointed his finger, and the group collectively followed the line with their eyes, landing on Rosalie.

Her eyes went wide, her mouth opening in surprise.

"What?" James muttered, feeling his jealousy and protective instincts rise.

"What?" shrieked the duchess, ready to drag Rosalie by the curls.

"*WHAT*?"

The group spun around, all eyes on the doorway as Piety Nash pushed her way in.

68

Rosalie

ROSALIE GASPED, FEELING Burke's arm go around her as he dragged her out of the way of Piety's wrath.

The woman stormed into the sacristy, eyes murderous. "You swore!" she shrieked. "You swore to me you had no designs on the duke! You gave me your word, you wretched, unfeeling snake!"

"And I did not break my word," Rosalie replied, eyes wild with confusion as she glanced from Piety to the duke.

"You have dashed all my hopes," Piety sobbed.

"Whatever I did or said, I swear to you, it was wholly without intention," Rosalie countered, looking desperately at the duke, willing him to intervene.

"George, please just explain yourself," said James, inching closer to Rosalie.

The duke shrugged. "I just wanted to be brave for once. I wanted to believe I could have a say in my own life." He glanced around at each of the faces in the room. "I've spent my entire life failing you. All of you. Over and over again. I fail you because I cannot bear to see those hopeful looks on your faces, daring me to rise to the occasion, rise to the great and noble task set for me as a duke of the realm."

He turned to face the duchess. "Mama, I entered the world a disappointment to you. I was weak and mewling. My nursemaid told me how you could hardly stand to hold me. How I cried and squirmed like the devil's own imp. Apparently, I was born to be your torment."

"George . . ." she whispered, tears in her eyes.

He turned to his brother. "James, to count the ways I have failed you would take more time than we have left in our lives. I have been the worst possible example to you of what an elder brother should be. I have been selfish and insolent, dismissive, uncaring, unhelpful. I don't deserve your fidelity."

James crossed his arms. Rosalie saw how he struggled. His desire to placate his brother warred with his well-earned feelings of resentment and frustration.

The duke smiled weakly at Burke. "I've even failed you. I've never given you your due as an unspoken member of this family. I didn't even ask if you wanted to be a 'Corbin,' I just thrust the name on you without a second thought. Do you?"

Next to Rosalie, Burke stiffened. "Do I want to be called 'Corbin'?" He glanced from James to George and shook his head. "No, I will never be a Corbin. I am a Burke through and through."

"The Burke name will get you nowhere in life," the duchess retorted.

Burke had the audacity to smirk. "Good, then I shall be exactly where I want to be."

"Oh, how can you be so aimless? So-so irrational? To take our name and marry Olivia Rutledge would secure you for life—"

"I am already secure," he replied. "James provides me with all the living I need. I seek nothing else. If any of you had bothered to ask me, I would have told you how I felt."

She raised an indignant brow. "So, you are content to just live in his shadow?"

He glanced at James and smiled. "Yes."

The duke gave a curt nod. "Then it's settled. My last act as duke will be to rescind the offer I made to you at the Michaelmas ball. You are no longer Horatio Corbin. And unless I am very much mistaken, you have no interest in being Baron Margate either . . . am I correct?"

Burke huffed a laugh. "George, I would rather chew off my own arm and throw it at the lady than take her hand in marriage."

The duke smiled. "Then consider yourself free of her."

The duchess swept forward. "George, you cannot do this. The agreement is already struck—"

"The way I see it, the only thing keeping their sham of an engagement in place is you, Mama. I tell you now, it is done. You are to leave Burke *and* the lady alone."

Rosalie could scarcely breathe. Was this all really happening? Was George Corbin finally standing up for himself? Standing up for his family? He'd apologized to James, freed Burke from his engagement. And now—

"Wait. Your Grace, you cannot do this," Piety cried. "You cannot where does that leave me?"

The duke turned to his teary-eyed bride. "My dear Piety, I would have hurt you worst of all. I am not fit to be any lady's husband. You should walk out that door right now and thank your lucky stars for your escape."

Her beautiful eyes were wide, her cheeks pink with emotion.

She glanced from George to his brother to the duchess. "Well, don't think I will go quietly, Your Grace!" she shrieked. "My father will be expecting a remittance for this. You cannot so greatly embarrass me and my family!"

"You're not seeing the bigger picture," he said with a sigh. "This will be wonderful for your social climbing career. As I fall from grace, my life burning all around me, you, my sugared date, may rise from my ashes as the one who got away. You'll have to bat the men of the *ton* away with a stick."

Before Piety could reply, a handsome woman appeared in the doorway. She held her chin high, her fashionable dress and powdered wig denoting her as someone of high rank. She cleared her throat with a little cough, eyes leveled on the duke. "Her Majesty asks to speak with you, Your Grace. Now."

69

James

JAMES FOLLOWED HIS brother behind the Queen's lady-in-waiting as she led them down the narrow hall to a large receiving room at the back of the church. Both brothers paused at the doorway, bowing as they spied the Queen seated in the center of the room, flanked on all sides by more ladies-in-waiting.

"Enter, my lords," she directed with a wave of her hand.

James stayed a step behind George, bowing again as they came to stand before her.

She pursed her lips at them, eyes darting from one to the other. "I came here today because I received an invitation to attend a wedding. But now the air out there is as festive as a wake. Tell your Queen what is happening."

When George remained quiet, James took a deep breath, ready to step around him and try to smooth this all over.

But then George stepped forward. "Your Majesty, this is my fault. I . . . well, I am just the worst duke to have ever lived." He gave a shrug. "I know who and what I am, and I hate being a duke. I hate the responsibility. I hate having people rely on me for anything. *Ever.* I have no head for figures. I cannot stand the monotony of farming. I would rather die than be expected to raise children, and if you make me marry today, I can tell you I will break all the vows I make before God and man."

With each word of his speech, the Queen's posture hardened. The ladies-in-waiting flanking her shared confused looks, shifting on their feet. "What am I supposed to do with that information, Norland?" the Queen replied with a raised brow.

"Yes, well . . . I was—well, that is to say *we*"—he jabbed his thumb over his shoulder at James—"My brother and I were very much hoping we might just . . . switch places? If it's alright with you, that is . . ."

The Queen frowned. "Let me make sure I am understanding this correctly . . . one of my dukes is so highly dissatisfied in his role of dedicating his life as a servant to the Crown that he wishes to upend centuries of tradition and foist his title and all the responsibility therein over to his younger brother. Did I miss anything, Norland?"

George cleared his throat with a nervous cough. "I am highly satisfied with both the Crown and the head that wears it," he hedged.

James let out a breath, thankful George was showing such decorum.

"My dissatisfaction is all to do with my own personal deficiencies," George went on. "I defy you, Your Majesty, to find yourself a worse peer than myself. I drink far more than is good for me, I gamble my estate's hard-earned money away, I fornicate with anything that moves. And I don't actually think I'm a Christian. It's not so much that I get a feeling of being underwhelmed with the nature of God . . . it's more that I simply don't care. The stories are boring on the whole, the Almighty seems like a vindictive twat most of the time, and I cannot stand all the rules and regulations of the middle bits and—ow—*ouch*, James. Stop elbowing me." George glared at him, inching away.

James growled, dropping his arm back to his side. Christ, this was a disaster.

"Viscount Finchley?" The Queen settled her eye on him. "You wish to speak?"

He cleared his throat. "No, Your Majesty. I only wish my brother to stop speaking."

A few of the ladies-in-waiting hid smiles behind their hands.

The Queen sighed. "I believe I have heard enough. Norland, step forward."

Casting a wary glance at James, George took two steps forward.

James took a deep breath, readying himself for the worst.

The Queen squared her shoulders. "It hurts us more than we can say that a duke of our realm is so dissatisfied in his position," she began. "To serve the Crown is a great honor, one that far too many take for granted. Still more assume that this position is a right, not a privilege. Our system is a good one on the whole. But there are moments . . . there are people, who test it. Norland, I have known you all your life. I knew your father before you. The Corbin family is well-respected as being dutiful servants to the Crown. Should we allow for one weak link to break the Corbin chain?"

George swallowed, hands balled into fists at his side. "Your Majesty could simply remove the weak link and remake the chain anew. I am happy to be removed. I've never wanted anything more, in fact."

She sighed, dismissing George with a wave. Then she narrowed her eyes at James. "Viscount, step forward. Let me look at you."

James inched around George until they were standing shoulder-to-shoulder.

"Do you know what it is Norland asks of us?"

James gave a curt nod. "Yes, Your Majesty."

"He wants to disclaim his titles and pass them to you."

"Yes, Your Majesty," he muttered.

She raised a curious brow. "It is the dream of all second sons, is it not? To inherit all while an elder brother still lives? To rise to the top and become the rooster that crows."

"Not all, Your Majesty," he replied. "Second sons are not all cut from the same cloth. I am pragmatic by nature, and a rule follower to a fault, so I never allowed myself to think such a thing would be possible. It is not done," he said with a shrug. "And I am no such schemer that I would wish my brother's demise. No matter what else he is, George is family. That means something to me. It means everything to me."

She nodded slowly, lips pursed in contemplation. "And what would you do differently . . . *if* such an honor were bestowed upon you?"

James took a deep breath, deciding his next words carefully. He would not lie to his Queen. "Nothing, Your Majesty," he replied. "I would continue on my present course. Rents have never been higher, my granaries are full, the sheep are sheared. We've recently struck a lode of copper, which is promising. And I am in negotiations to expand my land holdings. I will change nothing about how I currently run the dukedom."

The corner of the Queen's mouth curled slightly. "You should know I do not take kindly to the idea of stirring scandal amongst the peerage. The *ton* is ravenous enough without such bold provocations from me. But what you are asking of me now is to willfully pick up the spoon. What guarantee can you give me that one lord will succeed where the other has admittedly failed? For I will not be made a fool of a second time."

It surprised James when George relaxed his shoulders and smiled. "Your Majesty, allow me to tell you a bit about my dear baby brother."

70

Rosalie

IT TOOK EVERYTHING in Rosalie not to pace. She was back in the sanctuary with Burke and Tom and all the rest of the anxiously waiting guests. Practically no one had left, even when it became clear the wedding would not be continuing. Rosalie knew why they all stayed. They were hungry for gossip. They were hoping to see or hear something juicy—a dramatic reveal, a tearful admission, a happy renewal of sentiments that might lead George and Piety back down the aisle.

Vultures, the lot of them.

"It's been a while," Burke muttered, eyes narrowed on the side door. He didn't seem able to look away from it, still waiting for James to reappear.

"James is not verbose, but George certainly is," Tom replied, trying to keep calm for their sakes. "And so is the Queen. We must wait."

"What does this mean?" she whispered for the third time.

She couldn't wrap her mind around it. This was politics played at a level so far above her station. George wanted to willingly pass his title to James. It was unheard of. Titles were passed at the moment of death, and not before . . . unless the bearer of the title was somehow incapacitated. Or they so greatly offended the Crown as to have the honor stripped away. But in those cases, the entire family was typically dishonored. Might the Queen, in her annoyance, remove all titles from the Corbin family? Where would that leave James? Where would that leave the four of them?

"I doubt she'll touch his titles," Tom muttered. "James should still be a viscount, even if she takes the dukedom away."

"This changes nothing between us," Burke added firmly, sensing her unease.

But he knew that to be a lie as well as she. This would change everything. If James was now the duke, it placed him on a pedestal even higher than his previous post. His power would increase exponentially, yes. But so would the attention placed on him, and by extension all of them. Their risk of exposure would become that much greater.

If the Queen stripped the Corbins of all titles, would she leave their family estates intact? The land and the wealth was still theirs, right? Without his wealth, James would have nothing. Rosalie couldn't bear the thought of watching him lose everything. And she was to blame. She told George to be bold. She told him to live his life on his own terms. But she *never* expected him to interpret her words in such a way.

This was her fault. Either way, James would blame her for this. His rise or his fall would be due to her unintentional meddling. She sniffed back tears, refusing to feel sorry for herself. She didn't deserve tears.

"Oh, here we go." Burke stepped forward as the side door opened. He immediately fell back, hands out to his sides to drag Rosalie and Tom back with him as the Queen swept into the room, a flurry of ladies-in-waiting fluttering behind her.

Rosalie gasped, feeling Burke's arm band around her middle. She held to him with both of her own, eyes wide as the Queen walked past close enough for Rosalie to smell the cloud of her heavy floral perfume.

The tail of the Queen's handsome teal and cream gown whispered across the stone floor as she walked. She stopped before the altar and turned to face the assemblage. "There will be no wedding here today," she announced to the room.

In the hush that followed, you could have heard a pin drop. Rosalie's heart was in her throat. She couldn't help herself when she slipped her hands in with Burke's and Tom's, giving them each a desperate squeeze.

"But just because there is no wedding," the Queen called, "does not mean we have nothing to celebrate this day. For there is nothing more worthy of celebration than a life of loyalty, duty, and sacrifice . . . to one's family, one's people, and one's Crown. These are gifts that must be cherished above all else. Let it be known that your Queen always rewards loyalty. Thus, it is my privilege to present to you all the Seventh Duke of Norland . . . His Grace, James Corbin."

Rosalie watched, hands clutched tight by Burke and Tom, as James stepped through the open doorway. He walked right past them, offering the smallest of reassuring nods, before he came to stand before the Queen. A rush of excited whispers waved over the assembly.

The Queen raised an imperious brow. "Well, duke? Make your oath before all those assembled."

James dropped to one knee and spoke in a loud and clear voice. "I, James Richard Eustace Corbin, do swear that I will be faithful and bear true allegiance to His Majesty King George the Third, and all his heirs and successors, upholding my role as Duke of Norland. So help me God."

The Queen nodded. "Then rise, Duke, and do your duty to the Crown."

James got to his feet.

Rosalie squeezed tighter to Burke's and Tom's hands as he faced the crowd. Squaring his shoulders, he called out in a deep voice, "Long live the King!"

"Long live the King!"

"Long live the King!"

"Long live the King!"

"And long live the Duke of Norland," called a deep voice from the back.

The crowd erupted in cheers.

71

Rosalie

ROSALIE CLUNG TO Burke and Tom as the crowd surged out the doors of the church. By the time they made it outside, James and the Queen were gone, whisked away in carriages. The crowd outside had more than doubled, filling the streets. They were jubilant at the sight of their Queen. Word spread like wildfire about James, leaving all to gossip and exclaim.

"Hurry," Burke muttered, shouldering his way forward, holding tight to Rosalie's arm. Tom boxed her in from behind as they pushed their way towards one of the waiting carriages. The footmen wearing the Corbin livery stood back and Burke helped her in.

From inside the carriage, eager hands reached for her. "Oh, Miss Harrow, it is pandemonium out there," cried Mariah, pulling her safely inside. She was soon wedged on the bench seat next to the Swindons, their mother already seated across from them, Blanche at her side.

Rosalie spun for the door, still holding to Burke's hand. "Wait—"

"We'll meet you at the house," he said, letting her go as the footman shut the door with a snap.

"Drive on!" Tom barked, rapping the side of the carriage with his fist.

The coachman called to the horses and the carriage lurched forward, wheels creaking on the cobblestones. Rosalie quickly lost view of her men in the sea of faces.

All the ladies exclaimed about the sudden change of events as Rosalie's mind spun faster than the carriage wheels. James had looked at her. He held her gaze and nodded. What did it mean? Was he pleased? Was he angry with her? Did he resent her?

They arrived back in no time, all the ladies spilling out of the carriage. Inside, the house was in uproar as servants darted about, whispering excitedly.

"Mrs. Robbins, what's happening?" Rosalie called, catching the lady by the arm as she rushed past.

"Oh, Miss Harrow, we just heard the news. It's so wonderful—we've been told to prepare for a larger party, and we have no time. Even now they are on our doorstep!" she cried, hurrying away, calling out orders to maids and footmen as she went.

Already, guests were arriving, eager to celebrate the investiture of the new duke (and gossip about the fate of the old one). Rosalie didn't miss how the subtle touches of a wedding ceremony were quickly being altered. Before her eyes, three men swept past and snatched up the large wedding cake, shuffling away with it balanced between them. She spun on her heel, trying to look everywhere at once.

Where was James? Had he already returned? Was he somewhere in the house? And where was poor George? She wove through the crowd, looking for a familiar face. Each moment, more guests seemed to appear. A footman passed with a tray, and she snagged a glass of champagne. Before she could get it to her lips, it was snatched from her hand.

"Give me that," Olivia panted, draining the flute in three gulps. She looked flushed, anxious.

"Olivia, are you—"

"This is *your* fault," she hissed, shoving the empty glass back at her.

Rosalie's heart stilled. "My fault?" To own the truth, at that moment Olivia could have been referencing any number of things and be correct. The name Burke gave her all those weeks ago seemed fitting at last. She was the siren who sat upon the jagged rocks, luring all men to their demise.

"Oh, he is insufferable," Olivia said on a soft breath. "Why can he not just leave well enough alone?"

Rosalie followed the direction of her gaze across the crowded room. It was impossible to miss the towering form of Captain Hartington standing by the punch bowl. Like Tom, he looked devastatingly handsome in his uniform—not that she'd ever admit it aloud, especially where Burke might hear. "Has something happened?" she murmured, depositing the empty champagne glass on an obliging side table.

Olivia scowled at her. "As if you don't know. As if you haven't been egging him on all this time."

"I have done nothing—"

"Then your men have been hard at work," Olivia countered.

Rosalie furiously fought her blush as she took a steadying breath. "My men?"

Olivia gave a very unladylike roll of her eyes. "Don't play stupid with me, Miss Harrow. Blanche and Mariah may be twittering fools, but I am not. And neither is Elizabeth, you should know," she added with a level look. "Mr. Burke and Lieutenant Renley are in your pockets. How deep, I will not speculate, but I do know they've been whispering in William's ear, spinning him up."

Rosalie held Olivia's gaze. In a daring move, she chose not to deny her claim. The time for games and half measures was over. They were quite literally out of time. "Olivia, Captain Hartington still loves you."

Olivia stilled, tears springing to her eyes. "Did he tell you that?" she whispered.

Rosalie shook her head. "No. He would hardly admit such a thing to me. But he told Lieutenant Renley *and* Mr. Burke." She reached out a hand, curling it around the fine satin of Olivia's sleeve. "I say he is in love with you. A handsome, rich sea captain with a bright future who claims as his relation one of the most illustrious peers in the land. You would be the wife of a captain. Goodness knows he will advance, perhaps all the way to the admiralty. A sister to a duke. Why do you hesitate?"

Olivia blinked back tears, turning her gaze from the captain. "Why does *he*?"

Rosalie's heart was fit to gallop out of her chest. Burke's freedom was inches away, she could feel it. "What can you mean?"

"Why hasn't he asked me to marry him? Is he afraid I'll say no again?" She turned to Rosalie, clinging to her hand, hope blooming in her eyes. "I wouldn't."

Rosalie heaved a sigh of relief. "Then for goodness' sake, *tell* him that. Tell him to ask you again, Olivia. Tell him your answer before he asks—"

"I couldn't possibly," she cried. "It's not right—not proper—a lady does not—"

"Fuck what a lady does," Rosalie hissed, losing all patience. Her men were clearly rubbing off on her. She'd never said that word in her life before.

Olivia blinked in surprise, eyes wide.

Rosalie took her by both hands. "You have a chance here, Olivia. A *real* chance at happiness. Do you know how rare that is? Forget about all these people and their rules. The only thing that matters is that you love him, and he loves you. So, leave your horrible pride behind you, and choose to be happy."

"You make it sound so easy," Olivia said, her voice so small and unsure.

"Nothing is ever easy for us," Rosalie replied solemnly. "The life of a woman is a life of making choices that follow us for forever and a day. You made a choice regarding him once. Life has given you the rarest of gifts: a second chance. It is time to make your choice again."

Olivia sniffed, glancing down at their joined hands. "You know, I think I might be learning to like you . . . despite the fact that you stole my fiancé away."

Rosalie smirked. "He was never yours to steal. And I don't know that I'll ever be able to do more than merely tolerate you," she added.

Olivia revealed her feelings with a soft smile.

Rosalie gave her hands a squeeze. "Now, I don't mean to hurry this along, but your Captain Hartington is headed this way."

Olivia gasped, dropping her hands. "Oh heavens, he's insufferable. He can't mean to approach me here!"

Rosalie grinned, pointing over the lady's shoulder. "If you follow that hallway, there's a painting of hounds on the hunt.

The next door is a servant's stair. Lead him that way. At least it is some privacy," she finished with a wink.

"Heaven, help me," Olivia breathed. Snatching a second glass of champagne off a passing tray, she turned and darted away. Within moments, Captain Hartington adjusted his course, ever so like a hound on the hunt.

Rosalie stood alone in the crowded room, taking a few deep breaths. This day was already so overwhelming, and it was barely halfway over. She didn't know how many more surprises she could take. Centering her thoughts back on James, she glanced around, determined to find him. They needed to talk. She had to know. Their stairwell was taken, so she'd have to improvise.

"We're to have dancing!" Blanche cried, coming up behind her and looping their arms together. "They're opening the courtyard for dancing, come and look! It's a bit cool, but how can we mind the chill when there is such excitement to be had?"

Rosalie gave a weak laugh. "Surely this event ought to have an air of solemnity—"

"Oh, tosh," Blanche cried. "How can you not be excited, Miss Harrow? Lord James—excuse me—*His Grace*," she twittered, "is now the most exciting, the most handsome, the most eligible peer in the land!"

Rosalie stilled, heart beating wildly. "Eligible?"

"Of course, silly," Mariah laughed, suddenly appearing at her other side. "When he was just a viscount, he was eligible enough, but now that the title is really his, every unmarried lady in the *ton* will be throwing themselves at him left, right, and center."

"And *we* have the advantage," Blanche said, her voice suddenly conspiratorial. "For we already share such intimacy with him." She paused, giving Rosalie's arm a little pat. "Well, perhaps not you, Miss Harrow. He's never really shown you much interest."

Rosalie sucked in a breath. The thought of another woman sharing intimacy with James was enough to make her want to scream, cry, tear apart this house stone by stone.

"Blanche, don't be cruel," said Mariah. "He danced with her at Michaelmas, remember?"

"Well, he'll not be dancing with her tonight," Blanche replied. "Not if the rabid ladies of the *ton* have anything to say about it."

This was all too much. Rosalie needed to see him. Needed to talk to him. Had this changed things for him? Had she ruined everything?

"Good morning, Miss Harrow," came a quiet voice behind her.

She spun around, sighing with relief to see the wide eyes and soft smile of Lady Madeline Blaire. "Madeline," she said, reaching out for her.

The ladies embraced, Madeline taking a step back and pulling Rosalie with her.

The other young ladies darted away, too excited to go and inspect the new dance floor.

"You looked like you needed rescuing," Madeline murmured, letting Rosalie go.

"Thank you," she replied, blinking back tears. "I—heavens, I know I'm just being silly."

"Much is changing." Madeline gave her a knowing look. "Has he made you any promises already?"

Rosalie's eyes darted up as she stilled, searching Madeline's face. She was such a sweet thing, so young and innocent, with her wide doe eyes and freckled cheeks. And yet, Rosalie got to know her over the weeks they spent at Alcott. She saw the quiet strength in her, the cleverness, the resolve. Madeline was smart enough to see what the others apparently did not.

Slowly, Rosalie nodded.

Madeline pat her arm reassuringly. "He will hold to them. He is too proud to falter once his path is chosen. If he made you a promise, he will keep it."

"It's complicated," Rosalie whispered. "He would risk too much for my sake. Even if he wanted to keep his promise, dare I let him?"

Madeline considered for a moment. "I think . . . if you expect him to respect your choices, you must respect his in turn. If he chooses you, accept it. If this changes things too much for him, then you can move on."

Rosalie closed her eyes, willing her heart not to break. Nothing could be known until she talked to James. Until they all spoke together. Her senses hummed as she felt eyes on her and she turned. There, at the far end of the hall, stood James. Apparently, he'd been taken upstairs and changed out of his wedding attire. He now wore fashionable evening clothes, the sash of his new title draped across his chest.

Swallowing her fears, she took a step forward. As she did, Burke and Tom came into view, standing to either side of James. They put their heads together, speaking low, before the other two turned, watching as she crossed the room towards them. James looked stoic, Burke resolved . . . but then Tom smiled.

Breathing a sigh of relief, she moved faster, desperate to be by their sides, to hear James say this changed nothing. He still wanted her, wanted all of them. Together.

A face in the crowd caught her eye, and Rosalie felt all her senses hiss with alarm. She glanced from her men back to the intruder, following their path with her eyes. Possessive anger flooded her chest as she veered off course, weaving through the growing throng of excited guests.

"You should not be here," she declared, turning her back on her men to block Marianne's path.

"Out of my way," Marianne hissed. "This does not concern you anymore, *whore*."

The woman looked mad. She wore her finest clothes—a perfectly tailored morning dress and pelisse, a fashionable bonnet trimmed with bright ribbons, feathers, and bows—but her eyes were red-rimmed and glassy. Her hair looked unkempt, and she quivered with a nervous energy that set Rosalie's teeth on edge. She'd had dreams of this madwoman, but the reality was somehow so much worse.

Rosalie raised her hands, alarm ringing loud as church bells in her ears. "Your quarrel is with me. Marianne, *please*, leave Tom out of it."

The lady snarled. "You don't understand! No one ever understands. Tom is *mine*." She panted, chest heaving as she narrowed her eyes with resolve. "And if I can't have him, no one can."

Rosalie gasped, doom flooding her very bones. The room suddenly seemed to spin, the crowd a swirl of smiling faces. Colors and music and laughing couples. But Rosalie saw nothing except the large pistol Marianne raised in her shaky hand. She felt nothing but the arm the lady shoved against her chest, tipping her off balance. She heard nothing but the shot, ringing in her ears. And she smelled the smoke of the powder, stinging her nostrils.

The crowd erupted into chaos all around as Rosalie tumbled to the floor. In all the madness, one voice echoed over all others. It was a haunting, desperate wail. James' voice pierced her soul.

"No! Burke, *noooo*!"

72

Burke

BURKE WATCHED ROSALIE cross the room towards them, fierce love burning in his chest. He wanted to drag her upstairs right here and now. All three of them. Leave the guests to their quiches and cakes. They'd consummate this new union in the duke's bed all night. Every night until kingdom come.

Well, perhaps not *his* bed. No, George's bed would have to be burned. There was no other option. Here and at Alcott. And the furniture too. Burke could only imagine the ways in which all George's chairs had been used and abused over the years. And the carpets too.

Suffice it to say Burke would be overseeing a total renovation of the duke's chambers. Then and only then would he claim his lovers in those rooms. They'd have to improvise for now. He was about to turn and mutter something to that effect to the others when Rosalie stilled, her dark eyes going wide with panic. Before he could blink, she was darting away from them.

Tom frowned. "What the—"

"Where the hell is she going?" James muttered.

Burke was the tallest of the three, if only by a few inches.

He tried to see what drew Rosalie away, but the room was filling with people.

The crowd parted slightly, and Burke saw her near the wall, squarely in front of Marianne. Christ, the woman looked possessed. Rosalie was inching back as the ladies spoke. "Fucking hell. It's Marianne."

Next to him, James tensed. "How did she get in here? I'll get the footmen to throw her out—"

"No," said Tom. "This ends now." He stepped forward, hands balled into fists, ready to throw Marianne out himself.

Suddenly, a fear like Burke had never known filled him. One moment, he was watching Tom stride away. The next, he saw Rosalie forced back. Then Marianne raised the pistol.

All conscious thought left him. He felt only fear. Possessive, desperate, fear. One word filled his senses.

Tom.

Lunging forward, Burke grabbed Tom by the shoulders, shoving him out of the way. He cried out as a lancing pain stabbed him through the chest. He stumbled against Tom, dragging him down. As his shoulder hit the floor, his entire body spasmed, pain radiating through him as if he were on fire.

He groaned, rolling to his back and lifting his left hand to gingerly touch his shoulder. Panting for breath, he pulled his hand away, seeing bright red blood coating his fingertips.

"Damn," he muttered.

He was shot. How the hell did he go from perfect happiness one moment, to being shot on the floor the next?

Chaos.

Screaming.

Panicked faces.

Hands on him. Touching him. More lancing pain that had him crying out.

One face.

James.

His heartbeat slowed as he reached for him.

James is here.

His hand fluttered uselessly at his side. Why couldn't he reach him? Darkness closed in at the corners of his vision. He blinked, trying to stay awake.

James was still floating above him, barking out orders. "Tom, *go*!" He pointed with his free hand, for the other was pressing against Burke's wound. Then he had his eyes back on Burke. "Stay with me, Burke. Stay awake. There's a doctor here. He's coming now. Stay with me."

The darkness was growing. He panted, trying to swallow his fear. He didn't want James to see it. "I love you," he muttered, needing whatever words he spoke now to matter. "I-I love you. James . . ."

Darkness took him.

73

Tom

TOM HAD HIS eyes narrowed on Marianne. She was snarling at Rosalie, her mask of gentility utterly abandoned. For the first time in his life, Tom felt like he *saw* her, the real Marianne. The poor woman was undone with grief or madness. Both.

Then he saw the pistol. His first thought was that Marianne meant to shoot Rosalie. At point-blank range, she'd kill her for certain. Rage and panic erupted from his chest in the form of a guttural cry as he lunged forward. But then a force slammed into him from behind, twisting him as the weight dragged him to the ground. At the same time, the shot rang out, echoing around the great hall.

All around, people screamed as Tom scrambled out from under the weight of whoever had shoved him aside.

Burke's body went limp as he slid to the floor. "No," Tom panted. "Oh God—Burke—*no*!"

Behind them, James let out a feral cry, shoving his way forward. He dropped to his knees, helping Tom turn him over. "Where is it?" he barked, his hands searching frantically against the black of Burke's coat. "We need a doctor! *Now*!"

Burke groaned as they jostled him. His eyes were open, but his gaze was unfixed as he panted through his pain.

"Shoulder," Tom grunted, sighing with relief even as he blinked back tears of rage. Right shoulder. Away from the neck. Through and through. If they could staunch the bleeding. If the bullet had broken no bones. If no fragments remained to poison the blood. If—

"Rosalie," James growled, placing both hands over Burke's wound, red blood seeping through his fingers. "Renley—"

Burke's blood.

Tom was going to be sick. "Tom!" James barked. "Rosalie!"

Tom gasped as a wave of new terror flooded him. "Wha—where is she?"

"I don't fucking know," he snapped. "Go fucking get her! We can't lose them both!"

Stumbling to his feet, Tom took off. He barreled through the crowded hall, shoving people aside. "Out of the way!" he bellowed. "*Move*!"

He couldn't think about Burke bleeding on the floor. He couldn't think about James and the terror in his eyes. Rosalie was all that mattered now. Finding Rosalie. Keeping her safe. He blinked as he spied a familiar face in the crowd. Little Madeline Blair.

"They ran off," she cried, tears wet on her cheeks. "The lady with the pistol ran, and Rosalie followed."

"Which way did they go?"

"That way." She pointed with a shaking finger.

He took off, slamming through the side door into the

music room. This room connected on either side to a long set of en suite rooms. He ran to the middle of the room, glancing sharply left, then right. Both doors were open. They could have gone either way.

Damn.

He paused, taking a deep breath and holding it, quieting all sounds but the echo of his beating heart. He closed his eyes tight and waited.

A shriek.

A slamming door.

Right.

He took off again, sprinting through the right-side door, into the ladies' sitting room, though to the morning room. He came skidding into a back hallway. At the end of the hall, he spied the tail of Rosalie's blue pelisse disappearing around the corner. Desperation filled him. She was chasing after Marianne. She was going to get herself hurt or worse.

At the end of the hall, he darted left, nearly crashing into an ornate pair of glass double doors. The left one was partially open, and he shoved it, spilling into the conservatory. The heat of the room and the thick smell of exotic flora filled his nostrils.

"No!"

"Getoffme!"

"Give me the gun!"

With a growl, he sprang forward, darting down the row of fruiting trees. His heart dropped from his chest as he cleared them. There in the corner, near the wall of glass, Rosalie and Marianne were tangled together on the ground, scrambling for control of the pistol that shot Burke.

"Marianne, enough!" Tom barked, stepping forward.

Both women stilled at his voice. The distraction was all

Marianne needed to tug a knife free from her leather half-boot. Tom watched in horror as she brought it up to Rosalie's neck.

"I say when it's enough," she shrieked, pressing in with the knife point at Rosalie's throat.

Rosalie gasped, going still.

Terror filled Tom as the knife pricked Rosalie's skin. A bead of dark red blood streaked down the silver.

"Get up," Marianne grunted. "Up, get up."

Together, she and Rosalie shuffled to their feet, all while she kept the knife at Rosalie's throat. The pistol lay forgotten. It was madness to fight over it anyway. It only had one shot. Marianne would've had to reload to use it again.

"Burke," Rosalie whimpered, tears falling.

"Alive," he replied.

"Don't speak!" Marianne cried. "Don't even look at her." She pressed in with the knife and Rosalie strained her neck, trying to shift away from its sharp point.

Tom took a slow exhale, raising his hands in surrender. They were both stained with Burke's blood. He saw the look of horror on Rosalie's face, but he ignored it. He had to. "Okay, it's alright. We'll do this your way. I'm not looking at her. Marianne," he coaxed, his voice soft. "Mari . . . look at me." Marianne blinked back her tears, pulling Rosalie back a few steps. In a panic, Rosalie put her hands around the arm holding the knife to her throat, but Marianne stiffened, pressing in again with the point until Rosalie stilled.

"Mari, just look at me," he pleaded. "*Talk* to me. I'm right here. You wonder why there's such confusion between us, but you don't talk to me anymore. You only talk to her. But she doesn't matter," he soothed. "She is nothing compared to the history we share, you said it yourself—"

"Don't placate me," she cried, tears falling. "And don't you dare pity me!"

"I don't pity you," he replied. "Only, help me understand. What is it you want from me?"

"Why-why won't you just love me?" she cried. "I've done everything I can to make you love me. I wanted you to fight for me, but you didn't. I had to marry Thackeray. And then in the spring, when I heard you'd come back, I knew this was our chance. But you're spoiling it with her!"

Confusion swirled with suspicion in his gut. "Oh, God," he whispered. "Mari, when did you learn I had returned to England?"

She shook her head, her lips a thin line.

His suspicions turned to a deep sense of knowing. "Mari, what did you do?"

"I did nothing!" she spat. "Nothing except fight for the future I've always wanted. The future we are meant to have together! I will not let one more person stand in our way!"

Rosalie let out another whine that threatened to tear Tom apart.

"Mari, tell me what happened to Thackeray."

Suddenly Rosalie stilled, putting the pieces together. Her eyes went wide, and he knew she shared his suspicions.

"It was a carriage accident," Marianne replied, her tone emotionless. "A foggy day. The coachman was going too fast, and Thackeray was clipped crossing the street."

"Did you arrange it?" Tom whispered. "Did you push him?"

Marianne hissed. "How *dare* you suggest such a thing?"

Tom shook his head, putting the pieces together. "I arrived back in England . . . then your husband suffers an accident that claims his life. You wait barely three months, hardly even a proper mourning period, before writing to me, seeking to renew our friendship."

"I did only what I had to do! I would do anything for you, Tom. Shall I prove it yet again?" She pressed in with the knife and the blade sliced Rosalie's skin, red blood dripping onto the white lace at her collar.

"Tom, please—"

"Don't speak to him!" Marianne shrieked.

"Mari, *look at me*," Tom barked. "Look at me right now."

Her red rimmed eyes focused on him, and he took a breath. "She does not exist. Just let her go. She is nothing. A penniless ward. The only one in this house who truly cared for her is George, and he just let his title be stripped away. She has no one left. There is no one left to care for her. You've won. You've already won."

He couldn't bear to look Rosalie in the eye and say the words. It was all he could do to inch closer, ignoring her panting breaths, her blood dripping from her neck.

"Mari, let her go now," he soothed. "You don't want to hurt her. She's harmless. Just let her go and come to me. I didn't understand before how much you loved me. I see it now. You don't have to keep fighting so hard to win me. I just want your love. Come." He took a step closer, holding out his hands. "There is only us."

Her bottom lip quivered. Slowly, her grip on Rosalie loosened. In moments, she was shoving Rosalie away.

Rosalie dropped to her knees, gasping for breath through her sobs, her hand at her throat.

Tom rushed forward, wrapping Marianne in his arms. Marianne sobbed, clinging to him as the knife clattered to the flagstones. He held her tight, trying to soothe her, even as his pulse raced out of control.

"I just wanted you," she cried into his chest. "I've only ever wanted you."

"You have me," he replied, banding one arm around her waist and one around her shoulders. "I'm right here, Mari."

Giving Rosalie a nod, he held tight to Marianne.

With a feral shriek, Rosalie raised a potted plant and slammed it down on the back of Marianne's head. Tom felt her go limp in his arms. He sagged to his knees, letting her fall with him, and laid her down. Putting two fingers to her neck, he checked for a pulse. It was faint, but there.

"She'll live," he muttered.

Shaking with emotion, Rosalie dropped to her knees on Marianne's other side. He reached for her, but she slapped his hand away, tears falling thick and heavy.

"If you meant any of what you just said—"

"I didn't," he growled. "You know I didn't."

She sniffed, wiping her nose with the back of her hand. "I think she killed her husband," she whispered, looking down at Marianne's prone form.

Tom nodded. "I think she did too." They were quiet for a moment.

"We need to go," she said at last, getting to her feet. "Come." She held out her hand. "Burke needs us."

"You go," he replied, ignoring her hand. "And send Mrs. Robbins or Wilson as soon as you can. I'll wait here with her. We need them to call the constables."

Rosalie stood over him. He could feel her eyes taking apart each one of his threads. "You are not to blame for this," she declared. "Marianne is unwell. She has been for a long time. None of this is your fault."

Tom just nodded. He knew it was the truth, but he wasn't ready to hear it. "Go, Rosalie. Burke needs you. If he wakes and you're not there, the doctor may have to do the same to him," he said, gesturing to the shards of broken flowerpot.

She put her hands on her hips, her gaze boring into him. "I love you, Tom Renley. Find us later, or there will be hell to pay. You think she's possessive? You clearly haven't considered what it means to belong to James Corbin."

74

Burke

PAIN SEARED THROUGH Burke's shoulder. He winced, blinking awake. His entire body felt wrong. His limbs were heavy, his vision groggy, and his mouth felt full of cotton. He tried to take in the features of the room. Corbin House. His bedroom. Daytime. The curtains were open halfway, letting light pool into the room by the fireplace.

"Oh, he's awake."

That voice. He needed to see the face that made the sounds. He turned his head, wincing as even that much movement jostled his shoulder. He blinked again, taking in Rosalie's face. She smiled down at him, dabbing his brow with a wet cloth.

"Burke? Are you awake?"

He grunted. "Yes."

She sighed with relief, her lips pressing to his brow in a hurried kiss.

"James," he muttered. "Tom."

"Here." James stepped forward, sitting on the side of the bed and taking his left hand in his. "I'm right here."

He took another breath. "How long have I been out?"

"Three days," James replied. "The doctor gave you laudanum each time you came to. We needed you not to move. You couldn't agitate your shoulder any more than . . ."

"Any more than being shot already agitated it?"

Rosalie worried her bottom lip. "We weren't sure how much you'd remember."

The details were fuzzy, but the picture was complete. "I remember everything," he mumbled. "How bad is it?"

"The bullet went through your back and out your shoulder," James explained. "The doctor says you're very lucky. You nearly bled to death."

At those words, Rosalie sank forward, pressing her face next to his, kissing him on the cheek. "It was so awful." She brushed his hair back from his brow. "We were so frightened. Doctor Evans saved your life."

"I'm alright," he said, wincing in pain as Rosalie jostled him. He didn't have the heart to tell her. He didn't want her to move away. "I can't . . ." He took a breath, afraid to say the words out loud. "James, I feel like I can't move my arm."

James nodded. "Evans said that might be possible . . . and it might be permanent."

Burke closed his eyes, letting the words sink in.

"You'll have pain, certainly," James went on. "Stiffness, perhaps some numbness, even down to your fingers. Evans says you may have trouble with the whole hand. He'll be here in a few hours to check on you again."

Burke nodded, then glanced around. "Where's Tom?"

They both looked over their shoulders towards the corner of the room.

With a heavy sigh, he heard Tom call from the corner. "I'm here."

"Well, I can't really sit up at the moment, so I'm going to need you to come over here where I can see you," Burke replied.

He heard Tom get out of the chair and stomp across the room, sitting on the other side of the bed.

Burke let himself look at Tom—his golden curls, his strong jaw, his deep blue eyes . . . deep blue eyes full of hurt, wariness . . . regret. "What happened?" Burke reached for him with his injured arm, but then hissed, wincing in pain.

"Christ, man, don't move it," Tom muttered.

Burke sank back with a tired sigh. "Look at you. I'm the one who gets shot, yet you intend to carry the pain of it."

Tom just shook his head, still not looking at him.

"Shall we have Rosalie fetch the paper knife from my desk? Want me to stab it in your shoulder so we're even?"

"Stop," Rosalie begged. "That's not funny—"

"I'm not trying to make him laugh," Burke replied. "Tom, look at me." Tom tensed, biting his bottom lip. "Look at me," he said more gently. Tom lifted his eyes, meeting his gaze. "I am alive, and this was not your fault." Tom groaned, trying to move away.

"Goddamn it, Tom, don't you dare turn away from me! I took a bullet for you. So, you are going to sit here at my bedside, and you're going to tell me why."

Tom stilled, his face a mask of deepest misery. "Why, what?"

"Why did I do it? Why did I take a bullet for you?"

Tom crossed his arms. "Because you're a good person and you saw a chance to save a life."

Burke chuckled, the sound dying in his throat as it jostled his shoulder. "Wrong. I am a terrible person. I'm selfish and lazy. I live off the hard work of others, and I am more than content to lie, cheat, and steal to get what I want. And I have no warrior's heart. I can't even bear to be in the stall when they put an injured horse down. So, try again. Why?"

Tom's eyes flashed over to him, even if he quickly looked away. "Because we are friends—"

"Don't even finish that sentence," he snarled. "What happened to Rosalie the last time she tried to use that word?" *Ah, progress.* That raised some color in Tom's cheeks.

"That was a condition for Rosalie," he muttered.

"It applies to you too," Burke replied. "Call me that again, and see what happens."

Tom pursed his lips, looking at him at last. "You've just been shot. I'd like to see you try it."

"Oh, I won't have to lift a finger," he countered. "I'll make you do all the work. Or you could just tell me what I want to hear. Why did I take a bullet for you?"

Tom glanced across him at James and Rosalie, who sat still, watching their contest of wills unfold. He closed his eyes and shook his head.

"Say it."

Tom licked his lips, eyes still closed. "Because you love me," he whispered.

"And?"

"And I'm yours." Slowly, Tom opened his eyes again, his hand dropping to cover Burke's resting atop the coverlet.

A warmth that had nothing to do with the fire in his shoulder spread through Burke's body. Fierce love and protectiveness rose inside him like a fire-breathing dragon. "And what does that mean, Tom? Look at me and say it."

Tom swallowed, lifting his eyes to Burke's face. "No one touches what is yours."

"Damn right," he replied. "Is she dead?" Tom shook his head.

"Well, if I ever see her again, she will be. Mark me," he intoned, feeling the heat of his oath warm his chest. If he ever saw Marianne Young again, it would be she who took a bullet. He didn't care if the woman was mad. No one was going to threaten his family.

He glanced back at Tom, wiggling the fingers of his weak arm. "I love you, Tom Renley, and you are mine. You're all mine," he added, glancing over at James and Rosalie. "I take what I want, and I protect what I take. Let's not make it a habit of testing my will again, but now you all know. There is no limit to what I would do for you. Any of you."

Tom fell forward on top of Burke, his face pressed to his stomach as he gripped his hips. "I thought you were dead. Oh *God*, Burke. You were so still and covered in blood. I thought I lost you right when I'd finally found you, and it was my fault—"

James dropped Burke's good hand to let Burke brush his fingers through Tom's curls. "It wasn't your fault. You didn't make her pull the trigger. Tom, kiss me and put it behind you."

Tom lifted off Burke's hips and leaned over to kiss him once, twice. Chaste pecks, but Burke would take what he could get.

James put his hand on Tom's shoulder. "Tom, you were brilliant. You saved Rosalie, which is what was more important in the moment. If something had happened to her, to any of you . . ." He glanced at each of them, swallowing his words as fierce love overcame him.

Rosalie scooted closer to Burke, brushing her fingers against his brow.

"In the moment, my focus was on Burke," James went on, looking again at Tom. "I needed you to be there for her, and you were. We're all here for each other. We are trees." His lips quirked into a reluctant grin.

Tom's brows lifted. "You really mean it, J?"

James smiled. "If Burke is a tree, and Rosalie is a tree, then I must be a tree as well, eh? Roots entangled, we will *always* support each other. Yes?"

Tom nodded as Rosalie glanced curiously from one to the other. "That's the second time you've mentioned this tree business. What on earth are you talking of?"

Burke let his eyes close, settling back against the pillows with a contented smile as his three loves spoke softly atop him. He didn't care what they called each other—lovers, partners, trees, umbrellas. So long as they were together, he'd let them call him whatever the hell they wanted. He sank back into sleep, one hand in Tom's, one hand in James', with Rosalie's fingers smoothing the hair off his brow.

75

Rosalie

JAMES MADE THEM all wait at Corbin House for nearly a fortnight while Burke recovered his strength well enough to withstand the bouncing carriage ride back to Alcott Hall. Rosalie was beside herself with joy to see how quickly Burke was recovering. He'd regained most of his feeling down his arm and across each finger of his hand. He had mild complaints about numbness, but that was expected to fade as he continued to heal. Three doctors had seen him, and each said all they could prescribe for him now was time.

The gossip maelstrom swirling about the *ton* meant that no one left the house unless absolutely necessary. Even the servants were being accosted on the streets, the hungry vultures desperate for more details of what the papers were calling the Corbin Affair.

It didn't help that the house was embroiled in yet more gossip the day after the wedding-turned-investiture-turned-shooting. But the nature of this gossip filled Rosalie with so much happiness, she could hardly stop herself from smiling.

The house woke that Saturday morning to the shrill shrieking of the marchioness.

"She's gone!"

Rosalie emerged from her wing of the second floor, Tom and James on her heels, to find the marchioness standing in the middle of the ladies' wing still in her nightgown and ribbon curls. The other ladies were spilling out of their doors, eyes wide with confusion.

"Lady Deal, are you hurt?" James called, springing into action.

"She-she left!" the marchioness wailed. "My baby. My darling girl!" She sank to her knees right there in the middle of the carpet, a letter clutched in her hand.

Rosalie and Elizabeth rushed forward, putting comforting arms around her shoulders. "Where is Olivia?" said Rosalie.

"Gone," the marchioness sobbed. "She's ruined herself on that man at last."

A few of the other ladies gasped.

Rosalie's eyes shot up to James and Tom, her heart pounding in her chest. In all the horror of the previous day, she may have forgotten to mention her bit of meddling. She glanced down at the trembling marchioness. "Can I read the note?"

The marchioness shoved the piece of parchment into her hand and Rosalie read:

My Dearest Mama,

If you have found this, then you know that I am gone. Please don't hate me for claiming my own happiness. I have decided to marry Captain William Hartington, whom I have loved these long years, and who loves me. Love, Mama; it is a gift we all must cherish.

We are on our way to Gretna Green. Once we are married, we intend to return to his family estate in Derbyshire before he is recalled to his ship in the new year. If you can find it in your heart to join us for Christmas, I would dearly love to see you and Papa before we take up his new position in Jamaica.

All my love,

Your Livy

A swell of relief filled Rosalie, warming her from head to toe. Burke would live. James and Tom were safe. George was happy. Olivia would be married. All was well. All was as it should be.

When it was clear Burke was not only well enough to leave London, but desperate to do so, James finally relented. The morning of their departure, Rosalie was surprised to find George waiting for them in the entry hall.

"Are you sure you won't return with us?" James said, taking his hat and gloves from the footman.

"You know how I hate country life," George replied. "Oh, I almost forgot." He slipped the signet ring off the smallest finger of his left hand and held it out to James. "Here, this is yours now, I suppose. In all the drama, I quite forgot to give it to you."

Rosalie couldn't help the tears that filled her eyes as she watched James swallow down his own emotions and reach out to take the ring from his brother's hand.

"Thank you, George," he muttered, slipping it on his finger. He quickly put on his glove, curling his hand into a fist.

Rosalie smiled up at George. "What will you do now?"

George tucked his hands in his pockets. "I don't know. Town feels too confining while all the gossip swirls about. I was thinking I might go on my honeymoon."

Burke snorted. "All alone?"

Rosalie cast him a warning look. It was one of the great

mysteries of her life that she found herself feeling so protective of George Corbin. But she still remembered the moment they shared in his studio where he admitted to her being his only friend. It was an odd sort of friendship. He was an odd sort of person. But she intended to cherish it all the same.

"I think that's a lovely idea," she told him. "The world is a big place. It would be a delight to see some of it."

"Do you have a mind to travel, Rose?" Tom called, crossing the entry hall towards them, hat in hand. "I could always help with that. I'm rather good at sailing, you know."

"Perhaps you should take me on your ship," George said.

Tom donned his hat. "Perhaps I'll teach you to swab decks."

George crinkled his nose. "Not a chance."

"We must be off," called James from the doorway. "If we're doing this in one go, I want to keep the light."

"Mama still won't join you, then?" called George.

"She says she wants to be in Town for all the Christmas parties," James replied. "She'll return to us sometime in the new year."

"And that is agreeable to everyone?" George flashed Rosalie a knowing smile.

"Alcott is her home," James replied. "If it is her wish to return, I welcome it."

George crossed his arms. "Yes, but does your duchess feel the same?"

Rosalie stilled, her fingers on the buttons of her pelisse.

"I have no duchess," James replied, cuffing George on the shoulder.

"Yet," George added with a wink.

James sighed, dropping his hand away. "Well, until she is in being, I will make all the decisions about where our mother lives on my own."

"You are never on your own. Not when you have such faithful shadows to the left and right," George replied, giving a nod to Burke and Tom.

"We promise to keep him out of trouble," said Burke, offering George his good hand.

George looked at it, almost surprised by the gesture. Slowly, he reached out and shook it. Tom shook his hand next, following Burke out the front doors.

"We really do need to go," James said at Rosalie.

She nodded. "I will be right there."

With a final nod to his brother, he followed Burke and Tom.

"Well, Cabbage, I suppose this is farewell then," George said, looking oddly vulnerable.

She paused, glancing at the door to make sure the others were truly gone. "I must know . . . did I ruin your life? Did my words cause you to make a decision that you now regret? Will you come to hate me for it?"

George smiled, reaching out to wrap his arms around her. It felt odd to be in his embrace. He pulled away, holding her by the arms. "Cabbage, I meant what I said before. You are the only person who has ever liked me for me, saw me for me, listened to me as me. You are my one success. If I have only one, it is a good one. For however brief a time, you were my ward. I was your benefactor, and I was good at it, I think," he finished with a shrug.

She smiled, wiping the tears from her eyes. "You were . . . you are. Even if I am not your ward, I can still be your friend."

"I'd like that," he replied.

"Make me a promise?"

He raised a curious brow. "I've never been very good at those."

"Come home occasionally?" An idea struck her, and she smiled, knowing it was right. "The Michaelmas ball. You should come home for it. It is a celebration of the Corbin family. You are a Corbin. You should be there. James would like it if you were there."

He smirked, stuffing his hands back in his pockets. "Fine. A promise for a promise."

She gave him a wary look. "What can you possibly ask of me, sir?"

His smirk widened, flashing his white teeth. "If I return to Alcott for the next Michaelmas ball, and you are yet unmarried, you will marry *me*."

She gasped. "Sir, that is madness. We are the worst possible match on God's green Earth."

"And yet I shall be unmoved in my determination. Marry . . . or marry me."

"Are you threatening me with matrimony, sir? Daring to cage me in?"

"I am freeing you, Cabbage." he said with a laugh. "Get out of your own damn way and marry my brother already, or I will return on swift wings and woo you and together we shall beat our wings against our matrimonial cage until we are weary and broken things. Now, doesn't a life of bliss with my brother and his lovers sound infinitely more enjoyable?"

She crossed her arms. "I'm sure I don't know what you're talking about."

"Of course, you don't," he replied, giving her shoulder a pat. But then he leaned in, a wicked grin on his face. "But know this: If you expect me to keep my silence, you'll name your first child George. Now go, Cabbage. You can't keep your men waiting forever."

76

Rosalie

AFTER AN ARDUOUS day of travel, they arrived at Alcott Hall with the fading light. Rosalie begged them to stop at the last turn so she could admire the house for a moment, nestled so beautifully by gardens, hills, and trees. Love for the place swelled inside her.

Home. A family to love her.

It still felt too good to be true.

"What are you thinking?" said Burke from her side.

"I am thinking about how happy I am to be home," she replied, placing a hand over his knee.

"When we get inside, there is something we must discuss," James muttered. "All of us."

Rosalie glanced from him to the others. "Can we not get a hint of it now?"

"Best save it for when we're inside," he replied, rapping his fist on the carriage roof.

The coachman gave a call and the carriage rattled on. James left the unloading of the luggage with Mrs. Davies.

He only asked for one small travel case to be brought to

his study. He led the way, Rosalie, Burke, and Tom following. Rosalie knew it would be pointless to get him to say a word before he was ready, so she just helped herself to a place on the sofa and waited. Tom made them all drinks, passing the glasses around, while James stood behind his desk shuffling papers in the travel case.

"The suspense is killing us," Burke said at last.

"I just need to make sure I have it all in order," James replied, stepping around his desk with a thick file in hand. He took the glass Tom offered and sat down in the chair opposite Rosalie. "We haven't really had a moment in all the . . ."

"Chaos?" Rosalie offered.

"Aye," he replied. "I have something I need to show you. I think it's best we all know about it. I only received the report the day after Burke woke up, and since then it's been—"

"Chaos, yes, we've established," said Burke. "James, for the love of God, just show us the file."

"It's for Rosalie," he replied, giving Burke a pointed look.

"Oh, shit," Burke whispered. "James, if this—"

"Wait, what is for Rosalie?" She sat forward. "James, what have you done?"

James sighed, giving her a guilty look that set her heart to racing. "I knew you would never agree to marry any of us so long as your independence was at stake. You needed assurances that you would not be confined nor controlled. For a lady, freedom in a marriage means financial freedom. I knew I couldn't possibly give you money and have you accept it, even if it freed you to marry Burke, which was my original plan."

"Oh, God," she gasped, glancing from James to Burke. "You were going to *pay* me to marry Burke?"

"I was going to settle a dowry on you," he corrected. "I was going to settle a sum on you both so that money would be no impediment to your happiness."

She blinked back tears, knowing that was exactly the kind of heavy-handed gesture James Corbin might perform. "But something clearly changed your mind."

"You changed my mind," he replied. "All your talk of marriage as a cage, your outspoken loathing of the institution. And then there was the way you panicked and groused every time I spent so much as a shilling on you in any way you deemed frivolous. I knew you'd never take a settlement you hadn't earned. But what if there was money you *had* earned?"

"I don't understand."

He nodded, drumming his fingers on the folder. "You mentioned your father had a brother, a John Harrow? He emigrated to India some thirty years ago, and the family never heard from him again."

"You found him," she whispered.

"I tracked him down, yes. I hope it does not pain you to learn that he died four years ago."

"Oh, well that is . . . I never knew him." She glanced at the others. "Is it wrong to say I feel nothing for his passing?"

"I knew my father well, and I felt very little at his passing," Burke replied with a shrug.

"What did you learn about him?" said Tom. "You must have learned something."

"Aye, he died without wife or child," James explained. "Since his younger brother is also dead, you are his sole heir. Having tracked him down, I next had to track his assets. I found he has a business partner still living, a Mr. Occum. He provided a full accounting of your uncle's business affairs. He's willing to keep you on as a silent partner. Otherwise, he will buy you out of your share. I have his offer here, and I can set you up an appointment with my lawyer and an accountant so you can understand all the particulars before you decide."

Rosalie's head was spinning. "James, please—"

Tom leaned forward, eyes wide with interest. "How much is it?"

"His savings total about forty thousand pounds, and his half of the business is easily worth another eighty, less if you choose to liquidate your share," he added for her. "The point is that it is yours. Sign the top paper in this folder, and we can make it official. Perhaps, when my mother joins us in the spring, she can give you lessons on how to double it. You're tenacious and clever, I have no doubt you could manage it."

This was all too much. "James, when?"

He raised a confused brow. "When, what?"

"When did you do all this?" she cried. "This is investigating assets and meeting business partners and reports and . . . *when*?"

"The moment we arrived in London."

She sat back, heart pounding in her ears. The moment they arrived, when he sent her alone into his house wearing his evening coat, his rejection of her still ringing in her ears. That was the moment he began finding her a fortune so his best friend could marry her. "James . . ."

"We need to talk about our situation," he went on. "We need to come to a decision. The chaos with George changes everything. We cannot go on as planned."

"Why not?"

"Because with George as the duke, and with his marriage to Piety, Alcott would have been a safe space for you. You would have had my mother, the new duchess, her sister, their friends, quickly there would have been children. All these feminine touches would excuse all whispers of impropriety."

Her heart sank. "And now?"

"And now Alcott is home to a bachelor duke. I believe my mother refused to join us on purpose. She wants to create as untenable a situation as possible. You cannot stay here as my ward. It would be scandalous."

"If I cannot stay, then I wonder why you dragged me along at all," she said, rising to her feet. "You should have left me in London!"

"Rosalie, you're not listening to him," Burke soothed. "Did you not just hear him say I cannot stay—"

"As his *ward*," Tom pressed. "Sweet girl, he's right. Everything is changed. We said we'd not push the marriage issue unless we all thought it right. Protecting you is paramount, but to protect you, we must *also* protect James. Marry James, and you can stay at Alcott as his wife, not his ward. There will not be a hint of impropriety then."

"This is the best course," Burke agreed. "Marry James, and we all get what we want."

"And what is that?" she said, glancing from one to the other.

"To love and cherish you for the rest of our days," Burke replied. "Between the three of us, we will give you a life so full of happiness. There will be children, a family. Adventure if you want it. Tom can sail a boat, James is rich as Croesus, and I promise to make you laugh every hour of the day."

"You'd never be alone again, Rose," Tom added with a smile. "Never worry. Never struggle. No bars and no limits. Just . . . freedom."

Her heart was racing out of control. "This is madness. This

cannot be happening. You talk of children?" She spun to face James. "You cannot possibly be willing to accept this."

He frowned, setting aside the folder. "What makes you think I wouldn't want children?"

Did she really have to spell it out for him? "Well, what if the first child I carry is Tom's? What if it is a boy? Would it be your heir, Your Grace? Would the next Duke of Norland be Tom Renley's bastard?"

James had the audacity to shrug. "I would claim it. I would claim any children you have as my own. They will be Corbins. That's all that matters in society's eyes." He glanced from Burke to Tom. "Risk comes with reward. All the children are mine. Agreed?"

Tom nodded, while Burke just said, "Of course."

All the children? She pressed a hand to her fluttering heart. "You can't be serious. You would knowingly deceive everyone? Deceive the Crown? Defy your Corbin blood?"

"Corbin blood got us George," he replied. "And we all know how well that turned out. Renleys are upstanding people. I'd be proud to think of a Renley inheriting my title."

"Hmm . . . and what is the opposite of upstanding?" Burke teased. "For surely that explains a Burke. And if children are indeed on the table, you can be sure I intend to devour you, sweet siren. And every black-haired beauty you birth will be named after me."

"Rose has dark hair too, so that's hardly fair," Tom replied.

"I'm going mad," she murmured, pressing both hands to her chest. "This is madness."

Tom narrowed his eyes at her. "Rose, why do you hesitate? Is this not everything you want too?"

She turned to James, tears in her eyes. "You did all of this.

From the moment we arrived in London, you've been planning this out, moving the pieces in your chess game. You were going to watch me marry another man . . . why?"

He sighed, holding her gaze. "Because I wanted you both to be happy, even if it could never be with me."

A tear slipped down her cheek. "And now?"

"And now I want you to marry me. I want you all to stay here with me. I am your Atlas, Rosalie. It all falls on my shoulders. For us all to be together, I must be your husband. Only my title can protect us all. The only way it protects you is if we're married. But it must be your choice. Your money frees you to choose."

She turned to Burke. "What about you? This money could free you. We could split it—"

"I am exactly where I'm meant to be." He glanced over at Tom. "Tom, are you in?"

Tom smiled at Rosalie, a look so full of love and confidence. "Over the cliff, and over again."

She spun back to face James. "And you, Your Grace?"

He frowned. "Are my intentions not already clear?"

Burke sighed. "Yes, but we're speaking them aloud just now, trying to have a moment. Join us, won't you?"

James held her gaze. "I want to marry you, Rosalie Harrow. I want you to be my duchess and my wife. I want to wake with you in my arms every morning. But most of all, I want you to want me . . . want *us*. Enough to stay, enough to try this, enough to trust us with your heart and earn the right to love you. And I want this painful moment to be over, and I want you to answer me, because if I'm left wondering if you'll ever say yes much longer, the ulcer I've named after you will burst, and I'll die, and this will have all been for nothing."

She couldn't help the laugh that escaped her. Was it possible for a heart to feel so much happiness? She glanced from Tom to a smiling Burke, back to James. "Yes, Your Grace."

James blinked, lips parting in surprise. "Wait . . . yes?"

"Yes, I will marry you."

Before she could even take a breath, James was on his feet and crossing to her side. She readied for a kiss or a tender embrace. But no, he grabbed her around the middle and threw her over his shoulder.

"James," she shrieked. "What are you doing? Put me down—"

He held tighter to her, moving towards the door. "I'm marrying you."

77

Rosalie

ROSALIE WAS BOUNCED and jostled on James' shoulder as he took the stairs two at a time. She gripped to his coat, squirming as she feared he might tip her right off his shoulder and send her tumbling down the stairs. "James, put me down!"

"Never again," he growled, giving her bottom a slap that had her squealing.

Tom and Burke came around the corner, climbing the stairs after them, wide grins on their faces.

James turned right at the top of the stairs, sweeping down the hall and stopping at a pair of double doors. Rosalie glanced around, looking for George's portrait of the ugly knight with the uglier horse. But the painting on the opposite wall was one of forest nymphs.

"This isn't the duke's room," she cried as he shoved open the door and carried her inside.

"No, those rooms are off limits until Burke can have them exorcised," James replied, slinging her off his shoulder and setting her back on her feet.

She took in her new surroundings. It was a beautiful room

with arching ceilings and lovely floral-patterned walls. A large bed sat along the longest wall, with a fireplace on the wall opposite. A happy fire blazed in the grate. A wall of curtained windows took up the narrow end of the room. "What room is this?"

"The duchess' room," he replied, shedding off his coat, his waistcoat, his cravat.

"But your mother—"

"Has not lived in here since long before my father was even dead," he replied, stepping forward to claim her with a kiss. She melted into him, needing the support of his arm around her waist to keep her on her feet. "This is your room now," he said, breaking their kiss. "My duchess, my wife, my redeeming angel."

She was already on edge from all the wonderful things they'd said downstairs. James' every touch was fanning the flames. It was all she could do to unbutton her pelisse before James was tearing it from her shoulders and casting it aside.

He spun her around with strong hands, working the back of her dress. As soon as he got it open, that joined her pelisse on the floor. She turned in his arms, desperate for his kiss. Leaning up on her toes, she pressed her lips to his. Together, their hands fumbled on the laces of her stays, shedding her of the garment. She tugged down her chemise as he pulled off his shirt, leaving him in his breeches and her naked. He dropped his mouth to her breast, teasing her nipple until she was arching into him, her hands holding tight to his hair.

The door opened and Burke and Tom entered.

As James let his hands drift down her sides, inching closer to her aching core, she reached out a hand. "Come," she panted. "Come here."

Burke and Tom stepped forward, taking their time as they shed themselves of their coats and waistcoats. She didn't miss the way Burke winced. Tom joined them first, his calloused hand smoothing up her bare back as he did the same thing to James, dropping his mouth to claim her other breast, teasing and flicking her nipple, humming against her warm flesh when he got a response he liked. Then James' fingers were pressing against her sex, opening her lips to slide through her wetness.

"Oh, God," she moaned, tightening her grip on them both. Tom's hand curled around to cup her bottom as James pressed in, claiming her with two fingers. Tom swallowed her cry with a kiss, owning her mouth as James pumped with his fingers, his thumb finding her aching bud.

With the two of them pleasuring her together, she let her first release crash through her. She clenched James' fingers as she arched her back. Her knees quivered, losing the will to stay standing. They both wrapped an arm around her, holding her still as James finished her.

Panting, eyes wild with need, James pulled his fingers out of her and held them up to Tom. "Taste," he growled. "Taste my wife."

She sighed, her body already trembling again at the words. Then Tom was sucking James' fingers into his mouth, and she was sure one touch would send her over the edge again. "Please. Oh, please . . ."

"Please what, angel?" James replied, dragging his fingers from Tom's mouth to circle them around her pert nipple. "Tell us what you want."

"I want more. Everything. All three of you. Now."

James wrapped an arm around her, holding her tight

against his front, his hard cock pressing against her bottom. He turned her to face Burke and Tom, who were both stripping down.

"Look at your men," James said in her ear. "Look at how they want you. I mean to let them devour you. But first, you're going to marry me. Right here, right now."

She leaned against him, laying her head on his shoulder. "You're going to marry me because I only feel alive in your arms," he declared, grazing his lips up the curve of her neck. "Because your voice is my favorite sound. Because I breathe easier when you're in the room. You'll marry me because I love you. I've loved you almost from the first, I was just too stubborn to say it."

"James . . ." She wrapped her hands around his arm at her waist.

"Say yes. Make me the happiest man alive and be my wife."

"Yes," she breathed. "Yes, I'll marry you. James, I marry you. We're married. I'm yours."

He turned her face, smashing his lips against hers, his right hand sliding back down between her legs. He broke their kiss, taking a deep breath. "Burke, come here."

Burke stepped forward, now completely naked, his gorgeous body gleaming in the firelight. She let her eyes trail up from his hard cock, up the dusting of black hair over his abdomen, to his handsomely defined chest. Her stomach fluttered as she took in the angry red welt on his shoulder, proof of his still-healing gunshot wound.

"Come here," James said again, holding out his hand.

Burke took it with his good one, letting himself be reeled in. James claimed his first kiss and Rosalie watched, pressed between them. They teased and tasted, their deep groans fanning the flames of her passion even higher. She pressed her lips to Burke's chest, savoring the warmth of his skin.

James broke the kiss, his eye falling to Burke's shoulder wound. With the gentlest of touches, James kissed around the spot. Even when he winced, Burke didn't pull away. James cupped his cheek, taking his weaker hand and sliding his fingers through Rosalie's wetness. Their fingers teased her together until she was wiggling between them, panting for breath. She watched as James took Burke's wet fingers and sucked them into his mouth. He lifted his own hand and did the same for Burke. Both men tasted her wetness at the same time. It was enough to have her burst into flames.

James pulled his fingers away, leaving Burke panting, his eyes stormy with need. "I know it can never be official," James said, his eyes still on Burke. "But here in this room, I marry you."

Burke sucked in a breath, tears in his eyes. "James . . ."

"What about you, angel?" James whispered, tucking her hair behind her ear. "Do you want to marry my Burke?"

"Yes," she said, cupping Burke's face and pressing her lips to his. "I love you. My Burke, My Horatio, I love you, I love you." The words jumbled together as she kissed him, drowning in her need for him.

"I love you," he echoed, returning each kiss with equal passion. "I love you both so goddamn much. I'll never leave. Never stray. Yours forever. God, I'm yours." He was kissing them both, his arms around them.

"Tom, come," James said, holding them both.

Tom stepped forward, eyes hooded with desire. He tried to reach for all of them at once, his hand cupping Rosalie's face, then James', his other hand sliding up Burke's back.

"Tom, it's your choice," said James. "Do you want to marry us?" He brushed a hand over Rosalie's curls again, and she tipped her face into his touch with a smile.

Tom pressed his forehead against hers, his hand on James' shoulder. "More than anything."

"And what about my Burke?" James teased. "Will you love him as he should be loved?"

Tom turned, his eye falling to Burke's shoulder. "I'm so sorry," he murmured, wrapping his arms around Burke's naked waist.

Burke soothed him, kissing his temple, but then he pulled away. "And that's the last time any of you get to mention or look at my shoulder again while we're naked. The next person to apologize for a madwoman shooting me gets fucked in the arse. Agreed?"

Tom mumbled something unintelligible, his lips pressed against Burke's chest. Rosalie turned in James' arms, kissing his neck. He dug his fingers into her hair, jerking her back only to claim her mouth in a heady kiss. Next to them, Burke and Tom kissed too, their hands stoking each other's need as they teased with their tongues, healing all remaining emotional wounds with tender touches.

At Tom's groan, Rosalie glanced down to see Burke's hand fisting both their hard cocks, working them together. She whimpered, her own desire shooting sky high. She didn't know what it was about seeing her men take pleasure with each other that made her feel so ravenous.

James noticed too and growled, pulling on Tom's shoulder to separate them. "This is Rosalie's wedding night, and she will have us all." He turned to her. "Tell us what you want, duchess."

She couldn't believe any of this was real. She was standing

in a duchess' bedroom, a duke all but naked before her, calling her his wife. Her lovers—*their* lovers—flanked him to either side. No going back. Over the cliff, and over again. "I want all of you at once. I want to feel so full. I want to take all your come inside me. I want it dripping down my thighs. My husbands, my loves, I want to be claimed."

Burke and Tom let out hungry sounds as James nodded. "Get on the bed."

Turning away from them, she went over to the bed, climbing atop it. She slid to the middle and laid back against the soft pillows. Her heart felt fit to burst. She was sitting naked in this beautiful room, and it was hers. This was the view she would fall asleep to every night: her men naked before her, a happy fire in her hearth, curtains on her window, pillows on her bed. She'd never felt such a sense of peace.

She swallowed her nerves of excitement as they came towards her, all three having shed the last of their clothes away. It was almost too much beauty to take in.

Tom stepped forward first, climbing on the bed beside her, stretching his long body out as he curled around her, claiming her lips with playful kisses. "We had to coordinate ourselves," he murmured against her lips, his hands sliding down to curl around her bottom. "Will you let me take you here?" he asked, letting his fingers graze over her soft skin.

She shivered thinking of that thick length inside her. All her men were well endowed, but Tom was the thickest. She nodded, eager to feel such an exquisite stretch. "Yes. Please, Tom—"

"Good girl," he replied, smiling against her lips. "Then James is going to take your sweet cunt. We all agreed, as rank is rank, that he should get to have you first."

"It *is* his house," Burke teased. "And he's being so good as to let us share his wife."

Rosalie cast him an annoyed look. "In our marriage bed, there are no husbands or wives. There is only love and pleasure."

"Then we shall never leave it ever," Burke replied, leaning over the bed to kiss her, then Tom, then her again.

James returned to the bedside, a vial in hand. "Face Tom, angel."

She rolled eagerly to face Tom, letting him kiss her senseless while James slid onto the bed and poured oil in his hand. Tom swung one of her legs over his hip, opening her wider for James' fingers. She gasped as the first one pressed in.

James groaned. "She's so tight."

"Tighter than her cunt," Burke replied. "She's perfection. Where would we be if she'd never stumbled into our lives?"

"Don't even think it," said James, pressing in with two fingers, working her open.

"Tom," she panted. "I need—please—"

Tom chuckled, dropping his hand between her legs to tease her bud while James stretched her.

"She's ready," James muttered after another minute, slipping his fingers out of her.

She whined, feeling his loss, but the eager look in Tom's eye had her quivering with excitement.

"Letter," said Burke, slapping one into Tom's hand.

Rosalie's eye went wide. "Wait, no—"

"Trust us," Tom replied, nipping her lips as he slid the letter over his cock. "We have a plan." He scooted back on the bed until he could sink back against the pillows. "Come here, Rose. Get on my cock."

She glanced from him to James. "I . . ."

"You're going to ride me facing them," Tom instructed, grabbing her by the hips and helping her turn around.

Heart in her throat, she let Tom position her, feeling the press of his thick cock at her entrance. "This feels strange," she admitted.

Tom worked himself inside her. "Easy, sweet girl. Slide down. That's it."

She shook as she braced on his hands. He helped her take him to the hilt. The angle was so deep, she felt like she was being split in two. When Tom lifted his hips, she wanted to die.

"Good?" Burke murmured.

"I feel him everywhere," she panted. "So deep."

Tom thrusted again, and she was shaking, a new release coiling tight. She braced against him, her legs open wide, exposing her to the room. James crawled up the bed between her legs, but instead of meeting her mouth with a kiss, he dropped his head and kissed her wet sex, dragging his tongue over her until she was crying out. He teased her bud with sharp flicks until she was ready to come apart.

Only when she was shaking with need did he straddle Tom's legs, push her thighs apart, and slide his cock deep inside her in a single thrust.

Tom and Rosalie let out a strangled cry. She quivered with a feeling of such fullness, but it wasn't enough. "Burke," she whined, reaching out a hand. "I need you."

Burke climbed on the bed beside them, ducking his head between her and James to suck on her breast, flicking her nipple with his tongue, teasing with his teeth. She dropped her hand to his cock. At the first contact, she sighed with happiness. She was touching them all at once, pleasuring them all. Her men, her lovers. *Hers.*

"Lie back against Tom," James directed. "Tom, hold her."

She let herself lean backwards, knowing Tom would catch her. He cradled her against his chest. The change in angle had them both groaning. Her eyes went wide as she realized what James was doing. At this angle she could—

"Burke, fuck her mouth," said James. At the same time, he inched out and slammed in, making both her and Tom gasp.

Burke moved to the top of the bed, holding onto the frame with his good arm as he tapped Rosalie's lips with his cock. She opened, letting him slide inside. She teased with her tongue, sucking a salty bead of come from the tip.

"So beautiful." James flicked her bud with his thumb as he pounded into her. Tom could only hold on, keeping them both still as James had his way. Meanwhile, she choked on Burke's cock, trying to take him deeper, suck him harder. Then James was falling forward, his mouth finding the base of Burke's cock as Rosalie sucked the tip.

"Oh God—bloody hell—I can't," Burke panted, jerking his cock from their mouths and sinking back.

Rosalie protested, wanting his fullness, but then James was plunging his tongue into her mouth instead, claiming all her air as he rutted into her. "I'm going to—*ah*—" James cried out his release, his cock twitching inside her as he muttered her name. "I love you. My wife. My duchess." He kissed down her chest as he pulled out of her.

Then Tom's arms were around her, lifting her off him too. James' release dripped out of her as Tom put her on all fours, slipping out from under her. Burke took his place behind her. He dragged his fingers through the combination of James' and her release, licking his fingers before he plunged into her, sheathing himself to the hilt.

Rosalie's arms shook as Burke began to move inside her, his hands gripping to her hips. James sat back, one leg off the bed as he watched. Then Tom was there, the letter gone, his cock still hard and proud, the tip glistening. "Do you want this cock, Rose? Do you want two at once?"

"Yes," she panted, arching her neck as she reached for him, lips parted.

"She's insatiable," James murmured, smoothing a hand up Tom's side.

"She's our siren," Burke grunted, pounding into her. His hand curled around her hip, slipping between her legs to rub sweet circles on her bud.

The moment Tom sank his cock between her lips, a release tore through her, making her moan around his length. She clenched tight to Burke's cock and he was crying out, his release spilling into her as he curled himself around her, kissing her shoulder, her nape, whispering sweet words about her soft perfection.

Tom pulled out of her mouth as Burke pulled out too. Then she was being eased onto the bed, gently laid on her back. She breathed deep, her legs falling open as she reached for Tom. "Please, my love. Need you."

Tom folded himself over her, lifting one leg up, his hand curling under her hip, as he slid home. She felt the wetness seeping out of her, but it wasn't enough. She wasn't complete. Tom's cock stroked her inside, the angle of her leg letting him hit everything just right. She was going to come again, she could feel it. He would make sure of it.

He kissed her, matching the strokes of his tongue to those of his cock. He only broke the kiss when hands on his shoulders pulled him off her. James and Burke each took one of her hands, stretching them over her head, pinning them down. Her breasts bounced with each hard thrust as Tom owned her. She curled her other leg around his hip, trying to keep him closer.

On either side of her, James and Burke lowered their mouths to her breasts. As soon as they each took a nipple between their teeth, she shattered. She clenched Tom so tight he cried out, his hips jerking still as he poured his release into her, filling her.

She came down from her high, floating like a leaf on a gentle breeze. Peaceful. Carefree. Happy.

Tom slid out of her, flopping on the bed at her feet. Burke and James curled up to her on either side, their arms around her waist. Rosalie thrilled knowing they were all touching.

"What do we do now?" she murmured.

"Now, we sleep," James replied, kissing her shoulder. "And in the morning, we'll have breakfast and walk to the church in Finchley. I'll marry you with Burke and Tom to witness. Then we'll all come back here and do this again."

"Every day," Burke replied.

"Forever," Tom added.

Rosalie smiled. She couldn't help it. Forever sounded good.

EPILOGUE

Rosalie

Two Months Later

"Stop fidgeting," James muttered.

Rosalie's hand immediately stilled on the fur trim of her pelisse. "I'm not fidgeting," she replied.

Yes, she was.

James just smirked, curling his fingers protectively over the hand she had draped on his arm. He gave it a soft squeeze. "There's no reason to be nervous."

She frowned. James had been repeating that sentiment nearly every hour for the last week. It wasn't helping her anxiety. In fact, if anything, his own lack of concern was only making things worse. If he said it again, she was going to find a stick and whack him about the knees. She was about to say as much when Burke let out a soft laugh.

"Careful, James. The duchess is not above salting people's tea when they irritate her."

Rosalie shot him a knowing look, the corner of her mouth quirking into a little smile.

He returned it, his grey eyes as stormy as ever against the December sky.

Between them, James just sighed, checking his pocket watch for the fourth time. He glanced over his shoulder at Lawson, the butler. "She did say two o'clock, yes?"

"Yes, Your Grace," Lawson replied with a nod.

"She will come," said Rosalie, her smile falling. "I doubt very much she will miss this first chance to excoriate us both. What a fine Christmas present for herself."

"If she dares try it, she will sleep in the stable with Magellan," James replied.

"Perhaps a Christmas miracle might occur, and we will find the dowager on her best behavior, merely happy to be home amongst family for the holiday," offered Burke.

James cast him an incredulous look. "You've met my mother, right?"

Burke just chuckled again.

Rosalie tuned them out, her eyes locked on the sweeping curve of the drive as it disappeared into the stretch of woods separating Alcott's northernmost grounds from the little village of Finchley. The trees were a tangled mess of leafless brown branches, dotted by the dark green of an occasional pine. Everything held a silvery glaze, dusted by the frost. Rosalie smelled snow in the air. She exhaled again, her breath coming out in a little puff of smoke. She inched closer to James, feeling the chill down to her toes.

"This is ridiculous." He jabbed his watch back in his pocket for the fifth time. "Rosalie, go wait inside where it's warm."

"She will come, James," she replied, soothing his arm with a stroke of her gloved hand.

They stood on the front steps of Alcott Hall, flanked to

either side by a set of servants, waiting to receive the Dowager Duchess of Norland, who was now late by over half an hour.

Exactly one week ago, Rosalie was sitting alone in the morning room, enjoying a good book and a cup of oolong, when a footman entered with a letter on a tray addressed to Her Grace, the Duchess of Norland. Rosalie flipped the letter over to see the dowager's seal in red wax. She opened it in a rush and read the contents:

December 15, 1812

Dear Duchess,

I have at last tired of the London air and wish to return home. Expect my coming one week hence. I shall send a man ahead to inform you of the hour.

Yours etc.,

Harriet Wakefield Corbin, Dowager Duchess of Norland

Two months. Rosalie had enjoyed two whole months of wedded bliss alone in her new home with her husband . . . well, *husbands*. For that is what Burke and Tom were to her. For two perfect months, she'd been able to live as if the outside world did not exist. There was only their love. The deepening of it, the exploring, the delicious testing of limits . . . and occasionally tempers.

True to his word, James woke her the morning after their return to Alcott Hall, his lips and hands rousing her from sleep. He'd claimed her so sweetly, Burke and Tom watching to either side, and said once more those two perfect words, words that had for so long terrified her.

"Marry me."

"Yes," she replied, with no feeling of hesitation or doubt.

The four of them shared each other in bed before sharing a breakfast. Then they walked to the church in Finchley and

James and Rosalie were married. Just like that, she became a duchess.

Now here she stood, in the freezing December air. Her serene bubble was about to be popped, and the one to hold the pin was none other than her scheming mother-in-law, the lady who set this all in motion by inviting Rosalie to Alcott in the first place.

"She comes," said James.

Rosalie tensed, seeing for herself a team of four black horses trotting down the lane pulling a carriage. Her hand tightened on his arm. "Umm, James . . ."

"What the . . ." Burke muttered from James' other side.

As Rosalie watched, one carriage became two, became four, became four and a luggage wagon, with two more carriages trailing behind. It was a caravan. The dowager duchess may have tired of the London air, but she had apparently not tired of her London set, for she had apparently brought half the *ton* with her.

"Bloody fucking hell," James muttered.

"James," Rosalie whispered, heart fluttering. This could not be happening. She hardly felt ready to entertain the dowager, let alone all her high-society friends.

James turned to stare daggers at Lawson and their housekeeper, Mrs. Davies. "What is the meaning of this? Did you two know?"

Mrs. Davies had the good sense to look a little sheepish. "I'm sorry, Your Grace. She made us promise. It was to be a surprise. A Christmas present, she called it."

"Are we really all that surprised?" Burke said with a shrug.

James turned to Rosalie, cupping her cheek with a gloved hand. "I'll send her straight home. She and all her friends will not even alight from their carriages. Just say the word—"

"No," she said quickly, placing her hand over his. "James, I'm fine. No reason to be nervous, eh?"

His frown deepened.

Determined to soothe him, she tipped up on her toes and kissed him. His lips felt like marble in the icy air. "Do you now doubt your duchess? Shall I disappoint you, Your Grace?"

His arm curled around her waist as he pulled her closer, kissing her again. "Never."

She broke their kiss with a smile. "Then let her come and be dashed upon our rocks, for she will not break us."

He smiled too. She could sense the want in his look, his touch. "You are fierce, wife."

"This is my house now," she replied, keeping her arm around his waist as she turned to watch the caravan approach. "You wanted a duchess, and you have one. It's your own fault you picked one who prefers to solve her problems by hurling fists rather than whispering gossip."

"I think James has excellent taste," Burke said from his other side. "I could not have picked a more perfect duchess for you."

"You claim credit for this?" James said with a raised brow.

"Of course, I do," he replied. "I was the one who discovered her in that back-alley brawl. I practically served her to you on a silver platter. You should be on your knees in gratitude to me every day of the week." He flashed James a sly smile that had James rolling his eyes.

Rosalie ignored them. The front carriage rattled past, the wheels crunching on the pea gravel. In moments, the doors of the front two carriages were open, and the footmen were fishing out the passengers. The dowager duchess was the first down the steps of the first carriage.

James let go of Rosalie and descended the steps, offering his mother his arm. "Mother, you're late."

"A horse went lame and had to be changed out at Newbridge," she replied, her bright blue eyes settling on Rosalie.

Rosalie felt that look pierce straight through her very bones. The dowager duchess had a sense about her, a knowing. It had unsettled Rosalie from the moment of their first meeting. She *saw* people. She saw through disguises and artifice. She saw Rosalie. In fact, Rosalie may as well have been waiting naked on the stairs, for no amount of fine fur-trimmed coats or feathered hats could disguise what she was: a nobody, unworthy, wholly undesired for this lofty role. Rosalie swallowed back the negative thoughts as the dowager had her gaze pulled away by James.

"What is the meaning of all this, Mother?" he declared with a wave of his hand.

She lifted her chin most haughtily. "George denied me the joy of one wedding. I'll not let you deny me a second time, James. I am here to see that I get what I want."

Rosalie's eyes went wide, glancing from James back to his mother.

"And what is it you want?" James replied, leading her up the stairs. "Rosalie and I are already married. We'll not be repeating the act just for your benefit."

She paused, turning on the stair to look up at her son. "I want an apology. A heartfelt one."

He stiffened. "An apology?"

"For not inviting me," she replied. "I am your mother, James. With Rosalie's mother gone, I am all she has too, or did you forget this? It may be too late for me to see you both married, but you will not deny me this chance to see you celebrated. A new duke and his duchess, and thus, a new era of the Corbins begins."

James glanced back over his shoulder at the pooling guests. "So, you brought half the *ton* with you to what? Offer us their congratulations and drop off a few belated wedding gifts?"

"No, I am hosting a ball," she replied. "Tomorrow night, we shall celebrate Christmas, as well as the new Duke and Duchess of Norland." She let her eye settle on Rosalie. "Does that suit you, Your Grace?"

But Rosalie was distracted, watching as the passengers from all the carriages were escorted out. One lady had just exited the last carriage. Her shockingly pink pelisse instantly drew Rosalie's eye. "Is that . . . Madame Lambert?"

"Of course," the dowager replied with a dismissive flick of her wrist. "Madame Lambert is the best modiste in town, and I wanted the Duchess of Norland dressed by the best. We have a reputation that must be maintained."

"Of course," Rosalie replied with a growing smile.

"I'll go welcome her," Burke said, trotting down the stairs towards the modiste.

The dowager huffed. "Well, is someone going to show me inside, or shall I expect my feet to freeze here on this stair?"

Recovering himself, James offered out his arm again, leading his mother past Rosalie and into the house.

Rosalie watched as the rest of her house guests began climbing the stairs. There was the Viscount and Viscountess Raleigh, with Madeline smiling between them. The Marchioness of Marlborough and her two young children. The Duchess of Somerset, a close friend of the dowager, was instructing two footmen on the care of her pair of corgis. The Countess of Waverley stepped past her, flanked by a giddy

Elizabeth and Mariah, who came bounding up the stairs to give Rosalie hugs. Rosalie greeted them warmly, shooing them inside with promises of hot chocolate and dancing after dinner.

George had arrived back from his travels a week prior and promptly hid himself away in one of the attics, surrounded by his paintings. Rosalie would have to send a footman after him and drag him out in time for the night's dancing. Her attention caught on Burke.

"Rosalie, you remember Paulette Lambert," he said, climbing the stairs towards her.

"Of course," she replied, offering out her hand.

The modiste took it, dipping into a slight curtsy. "A pleasure to see you again, Your Grace." The one and only time they met, the lady had been so sure James meant to court Rosalie with his extravagant wardrobe purchase. Now here Rosalie stood, his duchess.

Burke patted the lady's gloved hand. "Let's go inside where it's warm."

"I shall find you in an hour, ma chérie," said Paulette over her shoulder. "I 'ave a new gown for you and we must get you fitted. I call it *Les Trois Diamants*," she added with a wink, letting Burke lead her into the house.

With a warm feeling settling deep in her chest, Rosalie followed them all inside.

Just as she promised, an hour later Paulette was ordering Rosalie to her bedroom so a new ball gown could be tried on and properly fitted. They left the rest of the boisterous house guests below. Mrs. Davies led the way as Rosalie, Paulette, and the dowager made their way towards her room.

Paulette wasted no time directing the maids. They soon set up a trifold mirror in the corner. A set of boxes were arranged on the end of the bed, their lids already removed. "I 'ave three for you to try, Your Grace," Paulette explained.

"Tell me my James at least offered you a nosegay on the day," the dowager said with a sigh, sinking into a chair.

Rosalie stilled, her hands on the clasps of her dress. "Umm . . . no, he didn't."

"Did you have a veil? The barest trim of lace? Anything that might denote you were a bride on her wedding day?"

"No," Rosalie replied. "It was all a bit rushed," she admitted, focusing her attention on her clasps rather than the sternness of her mother-in-law's eyes. "We had breakfast together and walked to the village. Burke and Tom joined us as witnesses. It was quiet. Perfect, actually," she finished with a smile.

"It sounds like a dream," said Paulette distractedly. "Aha, zis is ze first choice." She lifted a beautiful cream silk gown out of its box. "Simple but elegant, non?"

"No," the dowager replied with a frown. "She is not a debutante at her first ball. She is a duchess. What else did you bring?"

Paulette was unfazed by her rudeness, handing the dress off to a waiting maid as she reached for the next one. "Zis one is a new design," she said, holding it up. It was a lovely thing of soft pink satin with a lace overlay. "I call it *La Rose Rose*," she said with a chuckle.

"Your thoughts, Duchess?" the dowager asked with a raised brow.

"It's beautiful," Rosalie replied.

Paulette narrowed her eyes at her. "Hmm . . . and back in ze box she goes," she said, stuffing it unceremoniously away. "But now we come to ma précieux trésor. Zis one you cannot deny." She folded back the paper of the last box and lifted out a stunning ball gown. It was ivory silk, gathered at the bodice. A geometric diamond pattern in shades of blue and silver beads circled the waistline. The diamonds grew in size as the eye fell to the floor. The bottom hem was scalloped, ending with a lovely little train.

"It's beautiful," Rosalie sighed. "The diamonds are like snowflakes."

"Try it on," the dowager directed.

In minutes, Rosalie stood on the stand before her trifold mirror, marveling at the cut and style of the gown. The sleeves were sheer and capped. The beading made the bottom of the dress heavy, swaying a bit as she moved.

"This is the one," the dowager declared.

"Absolument," chimed the modiste. "I always know ze right gown for ze right lady. I shall take ze others and burn zem."

"Don't you dare," Rosalie cried. "Please, would you go to Elizabeth and Mariah and offer them the other dresses as my gift? Could you alter three dresses in a night? Oh no, that is too much," she said more to herself.

Paulette just laughed. "As long as your belle-mère is content paying a hefty bill, I shall sew until my fingers bleed, ma chérie. I 'ave your measurements from before, so zis gown is almost parfaite."

Rosalie smiled at her reflection in the mirror. She caught the dowager's eye and her smile fell. "Could you, umm . . . would you mind giving us a moment?"

"Of course," Paulette cooed. "I shall go find my Horatio and feed him too much cake."

The two maids followed her out, softly shutting the door behind them.

Rosalie stood still, her eyes on her own reflection in the mirror. "Why did you really come?" she murmured.

"I told you why," the dowager replied, tapping the edge of her teacup with her sugar spoon.

"And that's it, then?" she pressed with a raised brow. "You came to throw us a ball to celebrate our marriage and you have no harsh words for me? No admonishments? Shall I walk through the doors of my dining room only to have a piano fall on my head?"

The dowager snorted. "Do you want harsh words from me, Rosalie?" She lifted her gaze to Rosalie's reflection in the mirror. "Do you want me to hate you, child?"

"No," Rosalie replied. "But I wouldn't blame you if you did," she added softly.

"And why would I hate you?"

Rosalie balled her hands into nervous fists at her sides. "Because I did the one thing you asked me not to do. You asked me to keep my distance from the gentlemen in this house. From James and from Burke . . . even George. I did not. George is my friend. In the end, he took my advice over yours. Burke is . . . well Burke," she added, eyes darting away. "And James is my husband."

"Burke was never mine to keep," the dowager replied, taking a sip of her tea. "I knew that first morning when he brought you to me that he was lost. He has always been obstinate and passionate. I tried to rein him in, but the man is wild," she added with a sigh. "He's yours now to make or break. I wash my hands of him."

Rosalie's breath caught in her throat. "And James? You don't resent my marrying him?"

The dowager caught her eye's reflection in the mirror again. "Having arranged the thing myself, I'm not sure why I would now resent it?"

Rosalie blinked. "What can you mean?"

The dowager laughed. "Who do you think had the special license issued?"

"The—what?"

"Come, Rosalie, don't be a fool," she said, setting her tea aside. "James is a peer. He cannot simply marry on a whim. Either the banns must be read, or he must apply for a special license directly from the Archbishop of Canterbury. The day James was invested as duke, I had the archbishop issue the license. I knew it was only a matter of time until you set aside your confounded pride and married him. In truth, I was already planning for a Christmas wedding," she added. "But it is easy enough to change one's plans from a wedding to a ball. I doubt I lost more than fifty pounds in the exchange."

The air left Rosalie completely. "The license was your doing?"

"Of course," the dowager replied. "Almost from the moment you arrived in my house, I saw the change in James. He was always so focused, so driven. In the span of days, you began unraveling him. You broke him down, piece by piece, remaking him into something new. Something better, stronger."

Rosalie could hardly believe the words she was hearing.

"I always knew something was missing from my James, some piece of him that would take him from excellent to extraordinary. Of course, it had to be a woman," she muttered, almost to herself. "How can I deny you what you've rightfully won, when it will clearly bring only benefit to my family? You were most unexpected, Miss Harrow. You vex me, it's true. For you are willful and proud and too often indiscreet. The fact that you forced my son to accept your lovers into your marriage is obviously a chief concern, but I imagine if I try to wedge Burke or Renley away from you now, I'll only get my hand bit for my trouble. Am I right?"

Rosalie stepped off the dress stand and sank onto the nearest chair. The dowager knew. Of course, she knew everything. How long had she known? Did everyone know? Rosalie had kept her eye on the papers and read nothing except recycled stories from the day of the investiture—the failed wedding, the shooting, Olivia's midnight escape. The Corbins were mentioned just last month when the news of Piety Nash's wedding was announced. Apparently, she'd bagged herself a wealthy earl. But there was nothing about Rosalie being a jezebel in the house of Corbin.

"Am I right?" the dowager pressed.

Rosalie raised her chin, meeting her mother-in-law's gaze. "I see there is to be a truth between us. I know your secret, and you wish to know mine. But can I trust you with it?"

The dowager pursed her lips. "I am a woman of the world, Rosalie. I imagine I already know your secret." She leaned forward, those eyes holding Rosalie captive in their gaze. "What I care about is that the center holds. James would hardly be the first peer in England to have an unconventional marriage. And he's made it clear he cares nothing for my ideas, nor my advice. If I give it, he will be sure to run in the opposite direction as quickly as his legs will carry him. I am thus resolved, at last, to stay out of his affairs."

Rosalie raised a brow in wry disbelief.

"Well, for the most part I mean to stay out of things. I am still a Corbin, and I have my own opinions," the dowager added with a sniff. "But my paramount concern is that the public face of House Corbin shines without a blemish. Whatever happens behind closed doors shall be your own affair. But what society sees. What the *ton* sees. This matters, Rosalie. It matters immensely."

"I know," Rosalie replied. "And we would never dare act in a way as to bring any undue suspicion to the family or the title. No one will ever doubt we are happy and in love because we *are*. I love your son madly, wildly, utterly and completely."

"But what of Burke and Renley?" she said with a raised brow of her own.

Rosalie took a steadying breath. When the day began, she hadn't been sure how much she was willing to reveal to her mother-in-law. But the thought of sharing a life with her—sharing a *house* with her—and hiding how she felt about Burke and Tom felt intolerable. It would be miserable for everyone involved.

The last thing she wanted was for his mother to be forced out of Alcott—her home for the last forty years—all in the name of making them more comfortable in her absence. But a life of hiding her feelings for Burke and Tom in every moment not shared in private felt like a kind of torture the likes of which would cause so much pain as to leave her a broken and bleeding thing.

"Burke has accepted a position as James' steward," she replied. "Tom stays with the navy for now. He is returning from Town as we speak. He had a meeting with his captain. We believe he may soon be called out."

"So, they intend to stay here at Alcott . . . with the two of you."

Rosalie focused her attention on her own cup of tea. "Yes."

"And if there is gossip—"

She glanced up sharply. "Horatio Burke and Tom Renley have been dear childhood friends of the Duke of Norland for nigh on twenty years," she replied, her speech already well-practiced in her dressing mirror. "Long before he met me, James had a well-established record of housing them here. Nothing has changed now that we are married. James sees them as family, and so do I. They will always find a home with us."

The dowager held her gaze. "An answer without answering."

"You seek my frankness, and I have given it," she replied. "Enough for you to understand our feelings on the subject, at least. If there ever comes a time where I believe I can trust you with more of my frankness, I will most agreeably oblige. For now, I have said enough."

The dowager pursed her lips. "All I really need to know is that you love my son, and you are committed to being his duchess. That is the only thing that matters. The public face of things must hold. Alcott *must* hold."

Rosalie rose from her chair, taking the dowager's hand in both of hers as she sank into the empty chair beside her. "I will love your son until my last breath. I will be a duchess, a wife, a mother, a proud lioness. We Richmond ladies are strong, are we not? I didn't know my own strength at first, but James helped me to see it. He is so good and kind, so strong, so loving. I will not fail him. Not ever. And I love Alcott. It is safe in my hands . . . besides, you're not dead yet," she added with a soft grin. "I imagine you may continue to be useful to me, at least for a little while. I should like to have your mentorship as I learn to run this grand estate."

The dowager gave Rosalie's hand a pat. "Good. Love my son as he should be loved, manage this estate as it should be managed, and you'll hear no complaints from me. I think . . . is it wrong of me to say that I think Elinor would be proud of you?" She raised her hand and tucked one of Rosalie's dark curls behind her ear.

Rosalie's eyes bloomed with tears at the touch. "I am not my mother," she whispered.

"No," the dowager replied. "You are something . . . more. You are wiser and stronger than ever we were. You will be the duchess I could have been, the duchess I *should* have been . . . the duchess worthy of wearing a tiara born out of love and self-sacrifice. A kind duchess. A loving one. You will do well here."

A tear slipped down Rosalie's cheek.

"And I brought it, you know," the dowager added, rising to her feet.

Rosalie rose too. "Brought it?"

"The Duchess Mary tiara. Spun silver vining with diamond and amethyst grape clusters. You'll need to wear something for the ball tomorrow night. A duchess must always be properly dressed," she counseled with a frown. "You should wear it."

Rosalie nodded, her voice still thick with emotion. "Thank you for your kindness to me. I-I don't know where I'd be had you never written . . . had you never invited me to Alcott—"

"Do not dwell in the past, dear. Look forward. That's what I do. Everything we do now is for our future, yes?"

Rosalie nodded again. "Yes."

"Thank you, Sarah." Rosalie smiled at her maid's reflection in the mirror.

Sarah smiled back, stepping back from her handiwork. Rosalie's hair was expertly styled in a column of curls. The dress was on, as were Rosalie's long, white gloves. The finishing touch was to add her jewels. Rosalie glanced sidelong at the box on the edge of her dressing table.

It was the tiara. The one the third duke bought for his wife. The tiara that symbolized love and fidelity and the hope of a happy, growing family. This would be Rosalie's first occasion to wear one. It felt significant. She wanted to remember the moment. Glancing back at Sarah's reflection, she nodded.

With a giddy sigh, Sarah opened the handsome wooden box and lifted out the tiara. "It's beautiful," she murmured, letting her fingers trace over the vine design. The purple amethysts that made up the grape clusters looked almost black as Sarah nestled the tiara atop Rosalie's dark hair. "Earrings, Your Grace? Or a necklace?"

Rosalie shook her head, her eyes locked on her own reflection and the glitter of silver and diamonds atop her head. "No, nothing else."

"Make a statement," Sarah said with a knowing smile.

Rosalie caught her eye. "Thank you, Sarah."

"Do you need anything else from me, Your Grace?"

"Nothing," Rosalie replied, rising to her feet. "You may go. And do be sure to join us," she called after Sarah's retreating form. "It's Christmas, and I want all the staff to enjoy at least one glass of punch. And all you young ladies are welcome to seek out a dance partner. You'll remind everyone?"

Sarah paused at the door and dipped into a curtsy. "Yes, Your Grace." She closed the door quietly behind her, leaving Rosalie alone in the room.

Far below her, the sounds of the growing house party echoed. The quartet was practicing, playing a merry jig. She could only imagine Elizabeth and Mariah were already below, leading a few others in a private dance. Rosalie checked the time on her mantel clock.

Six o'clock.

The ball was set to begin in one hour. Carriages were already lining up outside, delivering guests who were too excited to stay away a moment longer.

Nodding to her reflection in the mirror, she moved towards the door that connected her bedroom with an en suite sitting room, bathing chamber, and a dressing room she shared with James. The en suite rooms connected on the far side to his bedroom.

In two months, she'd already made many pleasant memories in all these rooms. Her men hardly ever slept separate from her. If they did, it was only one or two of them at a time. They were all careful to give her time alone with each of them. And she loved when they took their own time together too. Nothing pleased her more than to catch them together, entangled and in love, holding nothing back.

She stepped through her door into the sitting room, half expecting to find them waiting. But the room was empty. A door off to the left led to the bathing chamber, but the other door directly across was wide open, leading through to the dressing room. She crossed that room too, seeing the door to James' room open.

She heard them before she saw them.

"Don't tell her," came James' curt voice. "Not yet. At least, not tonight."

"I agree," said Burke.

Heart fluttering, she stepped through the door to see all three of her men standing together in James' bedroom. Burke and James were already changed for the ball, their crisply cut black evening coats framing their broad shoulders. But Tom was clearly only just back. He was still in his travel clothes.

"Tell me what?" she said, pausing in the doorway, her hands on her hips.

Her men turned as one to face her.

"Bloody hell," Tom muttered, his blue eyes wide as they trailed from her head down to her slippered feet and back up.

Burke's mouth curled into a devilish smile, while next to him James went still as stone.

"Don't tell me what?" She leveled her stare at Tom. His pained look gave everything away. Her heart sank through her chest. "You've been called out."

He nodded.

It was then she noticed the thickly folded piece of parchment in his hand. No doubt they were his new orders. She glanced from Burke to James, fighting to keep her tone casual and her tears at bay. They'd all known this was coming, but it still felt too soon. She wasn't ready for everything to change. "How long do we have?" she murmured.

"Two weeks," Tom replied.

She swallowed, doing her best to find him a smile. "And how long will you be gone?"

"Six months."

She breathed a sigh of . . . what was this feeling? Relief? Loss? Acceptance? It wasn't as bad as it could have been. Tom had spent the last two weeks preparing her for a reality where he was gone for a whole twelve-month, or relocated altogether, like Hartington who was leaving for a new posting in Jamaica just after the new year.

"This changes nothing," Tom said, stepping closer.

"I know," she replied.

"Six months will hardly be noticeable," said Burke with a false smile. "It's barely enough time to even start missing you.

Before we know it, you'll be back, eating all the chicken and hogging half the bed."

Neither Rosalie nor Tom shared his hollow laugh. James stood still and silent as the grave. Slowly, Tom turned to face him. "Christ, J. Say something."

"I told you I would buy you out if that's what you wanted," James replied, his tone flat. "You said no, and now you must leave us."

"I'm not *leaving* you." Tom tossed his orders on the end of the bed and crossed over to him, placing both hands on his shoulders.

James stiffened.

"Over the cliff, and over again. That was the vow I made, and I intend to keep it. Work calls me away, but I will return in six months," he said, letting his gaze drift from James to Burke to Rosalie.

"That work being fighting for King and country in the middle of *two* wars," James replied. "They could send you to the Americas—"

"They won't," Tom replied. "It's to be the Mediterranean. Italy and Greece, Malta, perhaps Constantinople, but then back again. Six short months. Please, J." He cupped his face with one hand, and James stiffened further.

Rosalie understood his anxiety. James was always slowest to accept change. He wasn't angry or resentful about Tom keeping his job in the navy, he was just afraid. His fear was urging him to pull back, retreat, fortify the walls of his emotions. He needed someone to drag him back from the ledge before he tipped into darkness.

Burke stepped in before she could, clapping a hand on both Tom's and James' shoulders. "Right, well we have a fortnight to accept Tom's news, but for now we have over a hundred guests filling the rooms downstairs. We cannot possibly go down there looking as if we are attending our own funerals." He cast Rosalie a reassuring smile, adding, "Besides, it's Christmas, remember? We must appear jolly and joyous. Surely, we can focus on that for tonight instead of Tom's leaving."

James was still too quiet. Tom dropped his hands away from his shoulders, looking defeated.

"At the very least," Burke tried again, "can we not all acknowledge the way our goddess floated into our midst? For the first time in her life, she is bedecked with a tiara denoting her proper station. James, for the love of God, do you of all people have no comment?"

James let his eyes settle on her. She saw the heat there, the need. He was aching with it. Between the dowager's sudden reappearance and Tom's upsetting news, he was feeling out of control. Her Atlas hated nothing more than a loss of control.

She lifted her chin and smiled. "Well, Your Grace? Do I pass muster?"

He gave a curt nod, the darkness receding somewhat from his eyes. "Yes."

Tom had turned too, crossing over to her with a smile. "How much time do we have? I want to get lost in your cunt before I'm forced to go mingle." His thumb brushed over her bottom lip. "My sweet girl. My life, my love." He made to grab for her dress, but she instinctively thrust out a hand, pressing it flat against his chest.

"Hold on," she said with a laugh. "Do you have any idea how long it took Sarah to get me looking like this?" She gestured to her perfectly set curls and powdered nose. "And if even one bead of this dress is out of place, Paulette will murder me."

Burke came up behind Tom, one hand on his shoulder. "And how are we to pleasure you, if we cannot touch the dress?"

Her smile wavered as a thought sparked in her mind. It was weak, like the flame of a candle lit on a blustery winter's night, but growing warmer, heating her from the inside out. They needed this. Her men were on edge, unsettled, ravenous. She needed this too. She dropped her hand from Tom's chest and took a step back. "Pleasure can take many forms, can it not? You know how much I love watching you together."

Burke's devious smile spread. "Say what you want, little siren."

She held his gaze. "I want you to please me."

She stepped around them, crossing over to James. His eyes traced up her body, lifting to note the sparkle of the tiara in her hair. She saw the ache in him, twisting and fighting as he tried desperately to lock it away. She cupped his cheek with a gloved hand, and he closed his eyes. "Look at me, my love," she murmured.

He opened his eyes, the green slowly being swallowed by black.

"Tom needs you."

He stilled under her hand, eyes darting over her shoulder to where she knew Tom stood.

"He doesn't need you to protect him, or fight for him, or make his decisions for him," she went on, drawing his eyes back to her. "He just needs *you*. Not the Duke of Norland. He needs James. We *all* need James. I am your duchess and your wife, and I'm telling you to comfort him. Nothing will give me more pleasure in this moment than to watch you please him."

He swallowed, dropping his gaze to her lips. "I can't protect him outside of this house, outside of my reach," he admitted softly.

She smiled in understanding. "And thank God for that, for your hands are already more than full." She brushed her gloved fingers over his brow, sweeping an auburn curl back into place. "Tom has always been a free spirit. He was made to sail away, but he always sails back again. Shall we be his safe harbor?"

James nodded.

Relieved, she tipped up on her toes, placing a soft kiss on his cheek. "Then show him."

James let out a deep breath and nodded again, holding out his hand. "Tom, come."

Tom came without hesitation, wrapping himself in James' arms, burying his face in his neck and breathing him in. James held tight to his shoulders. "I love you," Tom murmured, the words muffled by James' cravat. "I love you so goddamn much. Push me away, and I will die."

"Never," James replied, digging his fingers into Tom's curls. He pulled Tom's head back, holding his gaze. "You are mine. Christ, I would give you the Corbin name if I could," he said, kissing Tom's cheek. "Shower you with my love for all to see." A kiss to his brow. "Call you 'husband' in a crowded room—"

Their lips met, Tom fighting James for dominance as they began feverishly shedding their clothes. Rosalie stood back and watched, love blooming inside her, matched by her white-hot, aching need. But she could wait. She was more than happy to wait and to watch. Tom and James needed this. "They're beautiful," Burke murmured, coming to stand at her side. "How did we ever get so lucky?"

Before Rosalie could respond, James was breaking his kiss with Tom, glancing over his shoulder. "Burke—I need—" His words died on his lips as a shirtless Tom latched his mouth onto James' neck, sucking on his flushed skin. Tom's hands roved, stripping James of his waistcoat. He broke his fevered kisses long enough to drag James' shirt off over his head. "Burke," James groaned again.

Next to Rosalie, Burke chuckled. "You have to actually ask me, James. I'm not a mind reader."

"Yes, you are," James panted.

Tom shoved his hand inside James' high-waisted dress pants. Both men groaned as Tom wrapped his hand around James' hard length.

"Please, Burke," James tried again. "Let me have him. Let me—*God*—" Tom squeezed him, silencing his request.

Burke laughed, and Rosalie let out a relieved sigh.

"Does this mean I win?" Tom muttered, his lips and tongue still hungrily teasing James' flushed skin.

James went still in his arms, his eyes losing some of their haze. "Wait—what?" He looked from Rosalie to Burke.

"Oh, we wagered on how long your stupid rule would last," Burke explained. "You know, the one where Tom cannot take you with his mouth?"

Tom chuckled, not minding when James tried to shove him off.

"What?" James growled.

"Rosalie's been out for ages," Burke added. "She didn't think you'd last three weeks."

She had the good sense to blush, using Burke as a shield when James glared at her.

"But I know your stubborn streak," Burke went on. "And I know how much you love my mouth, so I rather assumed it would take you half a year to bend or break. Tom, the sly devil, bet he could break you by Christmas. I'll put on a brave face and pretend this doesn't wound my pride. The only balm will be to see you give in to him now."

James blinked, glancing around at all of them, his eye landing on Tom. His surprise hardened into resolve as he reached out a hand and grabbed Tom by the hair, jerking him forward. "How much money did you bet?" His voice was low, hungry.

"Ten pounds," Tom replied, his hands on James' hips, a smile tipping his lips.

"Is that all I'm worth to you?" James growled. "Perhaps I'll make a bet of my own, then. I wager one hundred pounds I can go without this sweet mouth for a whole year."

"Don't you fucking dare," Tom snarled, dropping his hand back down to stroke the hard length still concealed in James' pants. "Admit it, *Your Grace*. You want me so badly you can hardly breathe. I feel your heart racing." He leaned his face closer, licking James' throat, his face dropping to James' shoulder. "I taste your need, James. I want to taste more. And I have been more than patient. All I've ever wanted is to be yours. How much longer must I wait?"

James pushed him back, smoothing his hands over Tom's tattooed chest and down his arms. He leaned in close and murmured loud enough for the others to hear, "I was ready to break the first night we were all together. The moment I saw your cock sliding inside my wife's cunt, I wanted it in my mouth. I wanted to taste you both together."

Tom whimpered. Rosalie did too. It was too much. She was shaking with need. Beside her, Burke was barely holding himself back.

"You will walk around my house tonight feeling me inside you," James went on, wrapping his hand around Tom's throat, brushing his thumb against his pulse. "You'll laugh and charm my guests, you'll dance with my duchess, and you'll think of me all the while. Agreed?"

Tom wordlessly nodded.

"Good. Now, get on your knees, and show me what ten pounds is worth to you."

Tom groaned, dropping like a stone to his knees. "Yes. Please, *God*. Own me, James. Ruin me." He worked the fall of James' pants, sliding them down his hips until James' hard length was out and in Tom's hand. Tom wasted no time, sinking his mouth onto James, swallowing him to the hilt.

"I can hardly bear it," Burke murmured, his eyes locked on the thrusting of James' hips against Tom's face.

Rosalie understood his pain. They were heartachingly beautiful to watch. The trust, the longing. It engulfed them, daring to set Rosalie and Burke aflame too. Her men made her so happy.

"God, enough," James panted, jerking himself out of Tom's mouth. "Get on my fucking bed."

Tom stumbled to his feet, working himself out of his boots and riding breeches. James stepped around him, striding purposefully straight for Rosalie, fire burning in his eyes.

Her own eyes went wide. "I'm sorry about the bet—"

He silenced her with a kiss, nearly tipping her off her feet with his need to dominate. She returned his kiss, her gloved hands smoothing over his bare shoulders. He broke first, gripping her by the hips to keep her standing. He captured her gaze, his own so intent it made her quiver. "I want to fuck Tom. Do you consent, wife?"

She nodded, her hands still on his shoulders. "Of course," she whispered, finding her voice. "James, I love you and I love

Tom. There is nothing you could do together that I would not desire. He has waited for you for so long. Go to him. Burke and I will be here."

Next to her, Burke groaned.

James turned to look at him. "You want to join us."

"Of course, I bloody well want to join you. My cock is hard as stone. I'll frighten off your guests if I must go downstairs without relief."

As if thinking it over, slowly, James nodded. "Give me a moment with him, then join."

Burke sucked in a breath, glancing from Rosalie back to James. "Join you? What would you have me do?"

Surprising them both, James flashed him a smile. "If you really need instruction, perhaps its better if you just watch." Not waiting for Burke to respond, he turned away, crossing the room back towards their waiting Tom.

James kicked off his shoes and dropped his pants to the floor, stepping out of them. Tom was waiting on the bed. With a dizzy smile, he sank backwards, rolling onto his stomach. Then James was behind him, his firm hands sliding over Tom's naked hips. James dipped down, running his tongue over the curve of Tom's arse. Beneath him, Tom quivered and groaned. James repeated his exploration on the other side.

"Turn over," he muttered.

Tom glanced at him over his shoulder. "Are you sure?"

"Turn the fuck over, Tom," James repeated, tugging at his hips.

Tom let himself be turned, his proud cock pointing in the air as he settled on his back, James standing between his spread legs. James slid his hands up Tom's strong thighs, smoothing them over his hips, as he dropped to one knee.

Rosalie's heart hammered in her chest as she watched James take Tom in his mouth. Tom groaned, arching up to meet him, his fists gripping tight to the coverlet.

"Fucking hell," Burke muttered.

James popped his mouth off Tom's cock and leaned forward, placing two fingers against Tom's lips. "Suck."

Tom dragged James' fingers inside his mouth, hollowing his cheeks as he sucked them. After a moment, James pulled them out, wet and glistening. With his left hand, he dragged Tom's thigh up, opening him wider. Then his wet fingers trailed between Tom's legs. In the shadows of the room, Rosalie couldn't see, but she knew the moment James pressed them inside. Tom groaned, letting his leg open wider as he dropped his head back against the bed, eyes closed. Her own body reacted too, knowing well that aching sense of fullness.

Losing his patience, Burke left her side, crossing the room towards them. He stepped behind where James stood and fished in the drawer of the bedside table. Uncorking a little vial, he oiled his hands. Then he stepped behind James, wrapping both hands around him and fisting his cock. James groaned, dropping his head back against Burke's shoulder, even as his fingers continued to stretch Tom.

"He likes to be dominated," Burke muttered in James' ear.

"I know."

"Don't be gentle with him—"

"I bloody well know." James pulled his fingers out of Tom's arse and curled his hands under his thighs. Tom lay there, panting on the bed, his tattooed chest glistening with a sheen of sweat. "Do you want this, Tom?" James said, all his attention narrowed on Rosalie's beautiful sailor. "Do you want my cock?"

"Yes," Tom panted, fisting his own cock with one hand

while the other reached blindly for James. "If you make me wait any longer, I'll go mad. I'm yours, and I'm aching to be filled. Put your cock in me, James. Tear me apart."

James grabbed Tom's hips with both hands, dragging him to the edge of the bed. With one hand on Tom's hip, the other on his own cock, James pressed in. Rosalie watched as he claimed Tom for the first time, sinking his length in to the hilt as Tom trembled.

"How does he feel?" said Burke, standing at James' side.

"Like home," Tom replied, a look of pure bliss on his face. "James, you have to move. Don't hold back."

James gave a few teasing thrusts, both hands holding tight to Tom's hips.

Rosalie stepped to the side, reaching blindly for the closest chair as she watched her men together. Slowly, she sank down onto it, feeling the heat and need burning through her. They were magnificent, strong and confident. They were more aggressive with each other than they ever were with her—holding tighter, driving deeper, seeking a gasp of pain with their pleasure. Part of her envied them all. They shared a history together so much richer than anything she yet had with them. Friendships nurtured for twenty years. Trust, yearning, peace.

Looking at them together, she saw her future. Or she saw what she *wanted* for her future. She wanted to need and be needed. She wanted to be the center of their world. She wanted to know them better than she knew herself.

Please, God, if you have any mercy in you, spare a little for me. Let me keep them. Let me earn their love. She whispered the prayer in her mind, locking it away deep in her heart.

"Seven," Tom said on a breathless laugh, pulling her back

to the present. He stretched his arms languidly above his head.

"What?" James panted.

"This is seven pounds worth of bliss, and I am owed ten." The playful glint in Tom's eye made Rosalie's stomach flip. James did not like to be teased.

A feral sound escaped James as he lunged forward. Keeping himself buried to the hilt, he wrapped a hand around Tom's throat and jerked him closer, crashing their lips together in a bruising kiss. Tom did a half curl, grabbing hold of James' arms as James pounded into him.

Tom gasped, nearly falling back when James wrapped both arms around Tom's thighs, pressing them back against Tom's chest, opening him even deeper. "Yes," Tom panted. "Fucking Christ, you feel so good. Burke, *please*. Take him."

Burke stepped in behind James, wrapping his own hand around James' throat. He pressed his whole weight against him, bending James over Tom. Rosalie held completely still, eyes wide. In all their times together, James had only given of himself; he'd never received.

"Tom asks me to take you," Burke breathed in his ear. "He wants me to drive you into him. He wants his duke worshipped and claimed. Shall we give him what he wants, Your Grace? Shall you yield yourself to me while our wife watches?"

James gasped between them, his eyes locked on Tom. "Is this what you want?"

Tom licked his lips and nodded. "No beginning, no end, James. You promised us."

Rosalie could hardly believe it when James returned his nod. Then he said three words that had her ready to shatter without a single touch. "Do it, Burke."

Burke wasted no time. He didn't even shed his clothes. He just opened the fall of his pants, oiled himself, and began pressing in. James choked on a groan as Tom arched up to kiss him, greedily swallowing each sound.

"Relax, and take it, Your Grace," said Burke, easing himself in with careful strokes.

"Holy God," James groaned, dropping down to his hands, framing either side of Tom.

Tom held him by the hips, keeping him in place. "Burke, move. Take us," he demanded.

Burke didn't hesitate. Wrapping his own hands firmly around James' hips, he pounded into him, making James let out a hoarse cry, all but falling atop Tom.

"Yes," Tom cried, gripping James by the shoulders.

"I can't," James panted, eyes shut tight. "Oh, God—"

"Kiss me." Tom pulled him closer. "James, kiss me."

James sank atop him, meeting Tom in a hungry, open-mouthed kiss. He broke it with a strangled groan as Burke dared to smack his arse.

"Stroke Tom's cock," Burke demanded between thrusts. "Make him come."

James pushed his weight off Tom with one hand, reaching for him with the other. Tom sighed with relief when James wrapped his hand around his hard length and stroked him from root to tip. Tom arched his hips, meeting his every touch with eager sounds while Burke chased his own release. James' hand stilled on Tom's cock as he gasped, his body going rigid.

"Come, Your Grace," Burke growled. "*Now*."

James gave a guttural groan, soon matched by Tom. Rosalie watched it all, completely enraptured, as James and Tom at last found their joy together. Two more thrusts and

Burke broke, spilling himself inside James. All three men panted, breathing as one into the sacred silence that followed.

James moved first, slipping his hand off Tom and collapsing atop him, his cheek on Tom's sweaty anchor tattoo, his legs still pressed between Tom's open thighs. Tom curled his arms around him, stroking his hair with one hand as he closed his eyes, utterly at peace. Burke gave James' hip a soothing stroke before he pulled out and flopped down onto the bed next to them. It was odd to see him still fully clothed next to their naked forms. It was a stark reminder of where they were . . . or where they were all *supposed* to be.

Rosalie glanced up at the mantel clock.

Five minutes to seven.

She got up from her chair and crossed over to them, smoothing her gloved hand over James' bare back, up to his shoulder. "That was beautiful, my loves. You know, you all make me very happy."

Burke and James each gave a response somewhere between a grunt and a sigh. Tom just gave her a sleepy, satisfied smile, his fingers still brushing James' hair back from his brow.

"We're going to be late," James said, his words muffled against Tom's chest.

"Of course," Rosalie replied. "But I can think of no better reason to be late to a party we did not ask for nor plan."

"Don't worry, love. We will make sure His Grace is presentable," Burke muttered, curling back up into a sitting position with a reluctant grunt. "Up, James," he said, giving James' arse another smack.

James groaned, seemingly unable to lift his weight off Tom. It was all he could do to roll himself to the side.

Rosalie just smiled, joy and contentment bubbling inside

her. "The sooner you three ready yourselves, the sooner you can come celebrate with me as you ought."

"Christ, are we expected to sing carols?" James muttered.

"Hell on earth," Burke echoed.

Rosalie's smile widened. "I'm sure we'll do that too. But I'm thinking of another reason we have to celebrate tonight." She'd been keeping this secret to herself for nearly a fortnight, and it was eating her alive. She'd meant to wait until actual Christmas day, but this moment seemed as good as any other. In fact, given the nature of their unique relationship, the timing felt perfect.

Burke glanced sharply at her, his eyes narrowing. The man's ability to read her ran positively occult. "Rosalie . . ."

James and Tom sensed his tone and turned towards her as well.

Fighting the laugh that bubbled up inside her, she backed away from them, her smile spreading from ear to ear. "Make yourself presentable, husband. Then come downstairs and tell all your guests our happy news."

She had their full attention now. All fatigue forgotten, James and Tom both sat up. Burke stood, his body coiled tight like a fox on the hunt. "Rosalie," he repeated, a warning and a plea.

Backing away another step, she placed a gloved hand over her stomach. "Your duchess is with child." Soaking in the shared looks of surprise and delight on their faces, she turned and darted away through the open door. Laughing out loud, her smile filling her face, she glanced back to see all three of them stumbling off the bed, eagerly chasing after her.

BONUS EPILOGUE

Five Years Later

"YOU'RE DOING WELL, Your Grace. Keep breathing. One more push."

Rosalie took a deep breath, squeezing tighter to James' hand. With his other hand at her back, she leaned forward and bore down, pushing with all her might. She let out a garbled cry as she felt an exquisite release. After so many long hours, so many months, she was free. She sank back against the pillows, sucking in air, as the doctor tended to her red-faced, mewling, precious new baby.

Doctor Rivers glanced up, a wide smile on his face as he held the baby up for them to see. "Congratulations, Your Grace. Your wife has delivered you a healthy son."

James relaxed against the headboard. "Well done, angel," he murmured, leaning down to kiss her sweaty brow.

Rosalie held back her tears, reaching for her baby with a tired hand. "Let me hold him."

The nurse came around the side of the bed, beaming at

them as she handed the baby down to Rosalie. "A son and heir at last. The Corbin line has a bright future."

"Third time's a charm," said James, wrapping an arm around Rosalie's shoulder, letting her melt against him.

Rosalie shifted her chemise, opening it to let the baby suckle. He quieted in moments, rooting around until he latched. As soon as he did, she took another grateful breath. "He has a full head of hair," she murmured, brushing her fingers over the dark locks.

"He'll be as beautiful as his mother," said the nurse.

James looked to the doctor. "Is she well?"

"So far, I see no signs of bleeding," Doctor Rivers replied. "Nothing to cause any alarm. I will, of course, stay the night to monitor her and the babe, if that is your wish, Your Grace."

"It is," James replied.

Rosalie expected him to be anxious, especially given what happened the last time. Part of her wanted to tease him now and call him overprotective, but it was still a raw wound he carried. They all did. So she said nothing, focusing all her attention on the babe in her arms.

"We'd like a moment alone," James told those assembled.

"Of course, Your Grace," Doctor Rivers replied.

"Mrs. Davies will see to it you have everything you need. Food, fresh baths—name it and it is yours. We will call if you're needed again." James showed the doctor and the nurse out, shutting the door behind them.

As soon as she was sure they were alone, Rosalie relaxed against the pillows, her smile falling. "Tom missed it," she murmured, holding back her tears.

"He would be here if he could," James replied. "Shall I go

get Burke? I'm sure he's climbing the walls. He was furious about being kept out."

"Well, given how he behaved the last time, I needed a reprieve."

"You can't fault him for going a little mad."

She nodded, knowing James was right. She couldn't imagine if the situation was ever reversed and it was one of her men dying in the name of giving life. Seeing Burke get shot was all the pain she ever wanted any of them to experience. "Go get him."

James left the room, leaving her alone with her son. *Their* son. Their heir, born with the weight of such expectation and promise on his little shoulders.

"What shall we name you, little boy?" She brushed a finger over his soft pink cheek. He was falling asleep. His hands were curled into little fists, pressed against her breast.

The door opened and Burke swept in, crossing the room in a few strides. If he was angry at being kept out, he didn't show it. "Oh, my love. My perfect, brave love. Are you well? No complications?"

"None," she replied. "It was a smooth delivery. Look."

He folded himself against her, kissing her neck, her shoulder. She felt the shudders of relief ripple through him as he sucked in an exhausted breath. How long had he been up pacing? But then his hand was brushing over the baby's dark hair, a look of such love shining in his grey eyes. "We have a son," he whispered, his tone reverent. "Look how beautiful he is. You make the most beautiful babies."

She smiled, willing to indulge him in this overly affectionate state. She always preferred her sultry, teasing Burke to this worried, new father variety. He'd be back to normal in a few weeks.

They both glanced up as the door opened again.

"Mama, Mama!" A four-year-old girl with bright green eyes and bouncing golden ringlets raced across the room.

"Come here, Little G," said Burke, all smiles for the daughter he spoiled incessantly. He held out both hands. "Come see your new baby brother."

Georgina bounced into his arms, and Burke held her still so she didn't jostle Rosalie or the sleeping baby. "Mama, he's so pretty."

"Like a little doll, eh? One more for your collection," Burke teased.

James came through the open doorway, holding their other daughter in his arms. Only three years old, Madeline had a sleepy, just-woke-up-from-a-nap pout on her face. Her pink lips were puckered, and her dark hair was mussed on one side. She curled her face against James' chest, not quite old enough to grasp the enormity of the occasion.

James sat on the other side of the bed, tipping Madeline forward so Rosalie could place a kiss on her round, pink cheek. "Our new little fellow needs a name," he said.

Rosalie swallowed, giving a nod. "I just wish—"

The door slammed open, and Tom came stumbling into the room, clutching at his chest as if he'd just run a marathon. "Did I miss it? Did it already happen?" He was still in his traveling clothes, a fine powder of dust on his boots and his hair slicked with sweat. He tossed his top hat aside, stripping off his leather gloves and shedding his great coat.

Seeing him in the doorway, Rosalie burst into tears. She never imagined he'd arrive home in time. His ship only put in to Portsmouth on the prior Saturday. In her panic, she jostled the baby, and he started to cry too. Seeing her mama crying made Little G whimper in confusion, clinging to Burke's neck. Not knowing what was happening or why, poor Madeline let out her own wail.

Tom's mouth opened in surprise, eyes wide with horror as his family fell to pieces. He quickly recovered, racing across the room to scoop Little G up in his arms. "Is this the kind of welcome I deserve?" He blew kisses on her neck, tickling her to make her laugh before passing her quickly back over to Burke.

Burke got off the bed, jostling Little G on his hip to keep her laughing. Tom took his place, kissing Rosalie. He tasted like salt and smelled like a sweaty horse, but she didn't care. He was here, and that was all that mattered.

"I only got your note two days ago. I came as soon as I could," Tom said through his kisses. Then he gazed down at the new baby. "They said it's a boy?"

Rosalie nodded.

"He's perfect." He kissed the baby's brow.

"I couldn't bear to name him without all of us here," she said, glancing over at James.

He'd managed to soothe Madeline, rocking her as he paced. She was almost asleep again in his arms. "We know, angel. You don't have to explain. We're all here now, so let's name the little chap."

"Is George still blackmailing us?" Burke asked, tickling Georgina's ears. Her laugh was infectious as she slapped her hands over her curls. "Shall we have a Georgina and a George?"

Rosalie laughed too. "No, he only demanded a firstborn tribute."

"Well, you know my vote is for Claudius," said Burke.

Her smile fell as she rolled her eyes. "We are not naming our son after Hamlet's cruel uncle. No Claudius, no Hamlet, certainly no Romeo or Lear."

"I don't think any of you appreciated my idea for combining all our names," said Tom, moving to the ewer in the corner to splash some fresh water on his dusty face. "'James Horatio Thomas' or 'Horatio Thomas James' . . . though my name is actually just Tom."

"I just don't think it's very discreet," Rosalie replied with a patient smile.

"And if we're not using your names, we're not using mine," James added firmly.

"Well, then we can take G's idea and call him Carrot," Burke offered, tousling her hair. "Isn't that right, darling? Why did you want to name the new baby Carrot?"

"Because I want a pony," she cried, tugging on his lapels as he laughed.

James sat back down at Rosalie's side, both arms curled protectively around sleepy Madeline. "What name do you like?"

Rosalie smiled down at the babe in her arms. "I think I like Michael . . . for was it not the lure of the Michaelmas ball that first brought us all together?"

James frowned. "Why have you never mentioned that name before?"

She shrugged, petting the baby's feather-soft hair. She hadn't thought of it until the previous night.

"It's perfect," said Burke, his tone more serious now as he looked at the baby in her arms.

"Michael James Corbin," said Tom, testing it out.

"If we're not using your names, we're not using mine," James repeated.

"No, I like it too," Burke replied.

Tom glanced at her. "Rose, what do you think?"

She smiled down at her new baby, heart overflowing with happiness. "Is that your name, my little love? Michael James Corbin, His Grace, the Duke of Norland . . . hopefully not for a good long while yet," she added, resting her hand on James' thigh.

"He'll be Viscount Finchley until I meet my demise," James muttered.

"Don't even joke about that," Tom said with a scowl.

The baby squirmed in her arms, and she sighed. "Michael James Corbin," she repeated. "Yes, I like it." She brushed his soft cheek again. "Welcome to the world, my little love. It is strange and wonderful and full of so many beautiful things."

THE END

PLAYLIST

Meant | Elizaveta
I Wanna Be Yours | Arctic Monkeys
Stressed Out | Midnite String Quartet
The Swan from Carnival of the Animals | Camille Saint-Saëns (feat. Yo-Yo Ma)
There's Nothing Holdin' Me Back | Shawn Mendes
Don't Blame Me |Taylor Swift
Hollow (Acoustic) | Belle Mt.
Nocturne for Piano No. 5 in B-Flat, H 37: Andantino | John Field (John O'Conor, piano)
Hiding (Bonus Track) | Florence + the Machine
Dancing On My Own | Vitamin String Quartet
Dead in the Water | James Gillespie
Water Music Suite No. 1 in F Major, HW 348: V. Air | George Frideric Handel
Be Your Love | Bishop Briggs
Can't Feel Anything | World's First Cinema
Cello Concerto No. 1 in C Major, Hob. VIIb:1: II. Adagio | Franz Joseph Haydn
Secrets and Lies | Ruelle
False Alarms | Noah Reid
How Deep is Your Love | Kiris Houston
Adore You | Harry Styles
I Did Something Bad | Taylor Swift

ACKNOWLEDGMENTS

IF YOU READ the acknowledgment section in *Beautiful Things*, you'll know I pulled a selfish and thanked only myself, haha! *Beautiful Things* was the first book I ever self-published. Rosalie, James, Burke, and Tom launched my author career. It was a huge leap of faith, but so incredibly worth it.

Now, here I am, three years later, living out my wildest author dreams. And I didn't get to this point alone. No author ever does. So let's actually thank some other people this time!

First, to my intrepid alpha reader, Ashley. Your joy and infectious positivity make drafting each new project such a fun adventure.

To my beta team on this project: Katie, Rachel 1, Michelle, Rachel 2, Amanda, and Alex—I'll never forgot your support for an unknown author just following a spark of joy.

To my ARC team for HGTD, and all the early readers who shared their love of this story, thank you. To my amazing Emilyverse community, and especially to my Patreon members, you are so loved and valued by me.

To my PAs, Sam, Rachel, and Jess—thank you for keeping me organized and somewhat sane. And thank you for always seeming to know exactly when I need to see another silly raccoon meme.

It was shortly after finishing HGTD that I signed with my agent, Susan Velazquez Colmant. Susan, you took a chance on me and helped me launch my traditional publishing career. I'm so eternally grateful for your hard work and support.

Thank you also to my team at Kensington for taking on this series and giving the paperbacks a gorgeous overhaul. Here's hoping more readers will get to meet Rosalie and her gentlemen, and they'll have beautiful trophies for their shelves.

Lastly, I want to thank my muse, my goddess, and my queen, Jane Austen. You've brought so much immeasurable joy to my life and inspired me in so many ways. May both sides of your heavenly pillow always be cool.